Moving On, the eagerly awaited sequel to *Hester's Choice*, is Audrey Weigh's twelfth book.

She made an early start as a writer, selling her first story when she was only 11 years old.

A keen traveller, she has worked in several countries and her experiences have provided interesting material for numerous articles and short stories.

MOVING ON

Hester Carleton's husband died soon after the tragic death of her baby. Now she has to find a new home and some means of providing for herself and her two young children. The problems are daunting. Relatives help her to move to St Kilda and are ready to give practical advice, but where is Bruce? At the time of the tragedy Bruce had been attentive, so why does he seem to be avoiding her now? Times are changing. The threat of war looms over Europe and thousands of young Australians are rushing to enlist. Soon Hester's whole family becomes deeply involved in ways she could never have imagined.

Books by Audrey Weigh
Published by The House of Ulverscroft:

SOMEONE TO CARE
A FUTURE WITH YOU
BALLET FOR TWO
TO BE WITH YOU
HESTER'S CHOICE

AUDREY WEIGH

MOVING ON

Complete and Unabridged

ULVERSCROFT
Leicester

First published in Australia in 2003

First Large Print Edition
published 2004

The moral right of the author has been asserted

British Library CIP Data

Weigh, Audrey
   Moving on.—Large print ed.—
   Ulverscroft large print series: family saga
   1. Domestic fiction
   2. Large type books
   I. Title
   823.9'14 [F]

   ISBN 1–84395–409–5

Published by
F. A. Thorpe (Publishing)
Anstey, Leicestershire

Set by Words & Graphics Ltd.
Anstey, Leicestershire
Printed and bound in Great Britain by
T. J. International Ltd., Padstow, Cornwall

This book is printed on acid-free paper

For
Gwen Jones
A friend for many years
who has always shown
great interest in my writing

1912

1

Hester Carleton paused to muster her courage before rounding the corner of the narrow street she used to know so well. Thank goodness her brother-in-law had acceded to her wishes and let her dismount some distance away. He had understood well enough that the sight of a motor car in such a place would have drawn a crowd and she wanted to avoid being noticed, especially by anyone who would remember her. This meeting with Father was going to be difficult; emotional, no doubt, and more than a little embarrassing.

How was she to begin? Or would he speak first? She had not seen Father for six years at least, and she had never met his second wife. She had written to them every two or three months, feeling duty bound to keep in touch, but Father always had been a poor correspondent and Cora had never sent a letter. The invitation to come today had been just as stilted as all the other messages that Father had sent. Now that she had returned to Melbourne she must call on them. She must come on Sunday, when he would be free from business, and eat dinner with them.

She had removed the scarf that had held her hat in place during the drive, but her clothes attracted the attention of two passers-by and they dawdled to stare at her. She was obviously not a local resident. Although not conspicuously stylish, her outfit looked smarter and more up to date than any that were usually seen in that area. The black skirt was gathered at the waist, but was not so full as in previous fashion. It was topped by a plain white blouse and a black coat of a neat conservative cut, and the black hat was smaller than might have been expected.

The frank stares gave Hester the impetus to move on and enter the dusty narrow street. It did not seem to have changed at all. It was still a dreary thoroughfare, lined with identical terraced houses and littered with horse manure and scraps of rubbish. Some residents swept the roadway outside their own homes and cleaned their windows regularly, but their efforts were spoiled by more careless neighbours.

Cora was obviously one of the house-proud women. Hester stopped for a moment outside, glad to see that her old home still looked as though its tenants cared for it, then she took a deep breath and knocked on the door. Her father answered quickly, stretching

4

out a hand towards her and drawing her in as if he wanted to escape prying eyes. He pushed the door shut and they stood just inside the small front room staring at each other, both at a loss for words. Moments later she was in his arms, her head nestling against his chest, fighting back the tears.

'Hester! You're here at last,' he said huskily. 'It's been so long.'

Hester made no answer, content to linger in the warmth of his embrace. She should have known better — known she need have no qualms about her reception here. Father might have been mortified by those reports in the newspapers, but he would never reject her. If only she could have come home in happier times when he could have been proud of her.

At last Edmund Wellerby grasped her shoulders and stepped back a pace. 'Let me look at you properly. My goodness, Hester, you're so *tiny*.'

'I always have been small,' she reminded him.

'But not so thin! I've never seen you as thin as this. I never realised you were so ill. I should have come.'

'There was no danger,' said Hester, striving to sound light-hearted. 'I must admit I had no appetite, but there was no need for you to come.'

'Even so . . . ' Edmund could not throw off a feeling of guilt. 'You should have had family with you.' He gave a small nervous cough, seeking a change of subject. He was reluctant to broach the matter that was uppermost in his mind and Hester had no wish to mention it.

'Cora is looking forward to meeting you,' he said. 'I'll see if she can leave the cooking for a moment.'

He went to the inner door to call his wife and she came at once, as if she had been awaiting his summons. She was a tall woman with a trim figure and a ready smile. Hester knew she must be at least fifty years old by now, but she looked younger. She was wearing a royal blue dress designed for a less mature person, and Hester guessed that she enhanced the deep black of her hair with some solution from a bottle.

'Hester!' she exclaimed, coming forward with her arms outstretched. 'So we meet at last!'

She was adept at meeting strangers, having worked in a public bar for so many years in the past. She took Hester's hat and coat and invited her to sit down and make herself comfortable, announcing that dinner would

6

be ready before long.

'Your hair is really beautiful, Hester. Edmund told me about it. He said you could lose a gold sovereign in it, but I could never really picture it.'

Hester was about to reply that she took after her mother, her automatic response to such comments, but she stopped herself in time. Cora might not like to be reminded of her predecessor. However, Cora was not so sensitive.

'I believe your mother had hair exactly like yours. Such luck! I wish I had the same. However, I must go back to the kitchen and look after the dinner.'

There was an uneasy silence after she left them, then Edmund filled in time by giving news about their neighbours. Hester looked about during the pauses. It seemed that Father's financial situation had improved. The curtains were new and so was the square of carpet in this area which acted as a parlour. Cora had added some decorative touches of her own, such as floral wallpaper and a few small ornaments, but even so the room felt familiar. They moved to the dining table when Cora carried in the meal and Hester found they were using the dinner service that she remembered from childhood, the best one that was only brought out for special occasions.

It was Cora who kept conversation alive during the meal, again avoiding personal matters, but when the table was cleared and they had all settled in upholstered chairs Edmund could restrain himself no longer.

'Hester, how could you go to *his* family?'

'They have been very helpful and kind,' replied Hester.

'But to go *there*! After what happened! You should have come here.'

'Well . . . '

'This is still your home. You must have known that. We would have managed. I know this is a small house, but your mother and I brought up three children here.'

'Yes, but . . . ' Hester held back a sigh. This was the start of a discussion she had been dreading all day. 'Harold has been a really great help. He dealt with all the business affairs.'

'And so he should. It was his brother that caused all the trouble and harm. But for you to go there — and take the children — to the brother of a murderer!'

'Father!' Hester pushed herself to the edge of her chair, her cheeks flaming with indignation. 'Gerald was no murderer. It was an accident! He didn't intend to cause any harm.'

'He was a drunk!' retorted Edmund. 'A

bad-tempered drunk.' His voice softened slightly as he went on: 'How could you marry him, Hester, a man like that?'

'We were in love.'

'You were impetuous. Far too impetuous. You should have waited, got to know him better.'

Hester knew well enough that she had married in haste, ignoring advice to learn more about Gerald before committing herself. She would never admit to anyone how he had lied to her. Even the little he had told her had proved to be mainly false. She looked down at the carpet, unable to meet her father's eyes. She had married with such high hopes, and there had been good times. If their first child had been a boy, would that have made a difference? Gerald had so longed for a son. She bit her lip and managed to restrain a sigh. Boy or girl, how long would the peace have lasted? Gerald had no patience with children. He used to frighten her when he shouted at the young boys who came for private tuition, slamming that heavy ruler on the desk if they made an error.

Edmund jumped up suddenly, unable to stand the uneasy atmosphere.

'I'm going out for a newspaper,' he announced.

He strode to the front door and left

without a backward glance, closing the door with a sharp slam.

Cora immediately found some task that was awaiting her attention in the kitchen, but she only left Hester alone for a minute or two. When she returned she perched herself on the arm of Hester's chair.

'Don't take your father's words to heart,' she said softly. 'It's just that he wants the best for you. But he doesn't know what he can do to help.'

'I know he means well,' murmured Hester. 'But there isn't anything he can do really.'

'What's it like, staying at that house?'

'They're very helpful and kind,' said Hester for the second time.

'But . . . ?'

Hester gave a slight shrug. 'It's a rather noisy house. They have four children and they seem to rush about all the time and make a lot of noise. We are used to a much quieter life, so Dorothy and Susan are rather bewildered by it all.'

She could not say that her own children had learned to be as quiet as possible whenever their father was at home, but she suspected that Cora guessed as much.

'How long do you think you will stay there with that family?'

'I don't know.' Hester's voice began to

waver. 'No longer than absolutely necessary, but I just don't know where we will go from there.'

'Have you got much money?' Cora's forthright manner cut through customary etiquette. 'Money solves most practical problems.' Obviously she could see no sense in skating delicately around such issues.

'There must be a fair amount, but I don't really know yet.' Gerald had never discussed financial matters with her, but there had been a time when she knew he had a substantial sum set aside. He had obliged her to manage on a meagre budget, while saving hard for his own ambitious projects. How truthful had he been that last day, when he said there wasn't any money? There must surely be a certain amount left.

She looked up to find Cora watching her with compassion and her cheeks immediately reddened with the customary ready blush.

'The final details haven't come through yet,' she said. 'But I can apply for some money in emergencies.' She briefly explained about her uncle's Will, which paid for clothing and medical bills for herself and her children, and also allowed her to draw cash in emergencies. 'I don't know just how much I can claim, and I don't want to do that unless it's absolutely necessary.'

'It's there to be used, and this is the right time to call on it,' said Cora firmly. 'What are you planning to do? Will you go back to Mountcliffe or Thorn Bay?'

'Oh, no!' Hester could not repress a shudder. 'I couldn't possibly go back there! After all those reports in the newspapers . . . No, I couldn't go back. It would not be fair on the children to take them back there. Just imagine all the gossip!'

'So what are you going to do?'

'I don't know yet,' admitted Hester. She stared down at the carpet again, trying once more to face up to her dilemma. She must not use all the available money for rent alone, and what would she do when that money ran out? She obviously needed a job, but she had never been trained for any kind of work. A live-in situation would solve both the accommodation and financial problems, but who would offer such a job to her? She not only had no experience in working for others, she had two young children.

'I'll have to find some kind of work,' she said at last.

'It's not going to be easy.'

'No, I realise that. I suppose I will have to find somewhere to live first. Then perhaps I could take in washing or ironing.'

Cora patted her shoulder. 'Don't do

anything in a rush. Promise me you'll take your time and think about it carefully before you do anything at all.'

Hester nodded. 'Yes. I'll be careful.'

Edmund returned at that point, without a newspaper but determined to be cheerful. He smiled at the two women and acted from then on as though the previous unpleasant scene had never occurred.

'We must have a pot of tea before you leave, Hester. What time do you have to go? And when are you going to bring little Dorothy and Susan here to see us? Do you realise I've never met any of my grandchildren?' He threw his arms up in exasperation. 'Three in America. What chance do I have of ever seeing them? And your children always so far away until now.'

Hester smiled, glad that he was not going to subject her to any more criticism or complaints about the past.

'I'll bring them on my next visit if you like. They are rather shy, especially Dorothy, but I'm sure they'll soon get to know you.'

'Next Sunday.' Edmund turned quickly to his wife. 'Is that all right, Cora?'

'Of course. Yes, bring them next Sunday, Hester. We'll have dinner together again and all get to know each other properly.'

She served afternoon tea soon afterwards,

then Hester prepared to leave. She was to meet her brother-in-law in the main street at half past four and motor back to his large house in the foothills. Cora went to retrieve Hester's outdoor clothing and caught hold of her arm as she handed the hat to her.

'Don't do anything rash,' she cautioned softly. 'Even if you do find it tiresome, living with that family, put up with it for the time being. You don't want to do anything you'll regret later.'

★   ★   ★

Dorothy and Susan greeted their mother with heartfelt relief, clutching at her so ardently she felt a rush of concern. She turned to their aunt who was watching with a tolerant smile.

'Have you had a difficult day?'

'No, we've had a lovely day together,' Muriel answered jovially. 'They played with the other children outdoors, they've been down to the creek and they've helped me to make biscuits.'

The two girls still clung to Hester as she went to the large room they were sharing, and she had to tell them to move aside while she took off her outdoor clothes. They watched silently as she placed her hat on a shelf in the wardrobe and inserted a hanger into her coat.

'We thought you weren't ever coming back,' said Dorothy at last.

'I did tell you I would be a long time,' replied Hester. 'I had to go a long way, but I told you I would be back before your bed-time.'

'Papa never came back,' said Dorothy.

Hester swallowed hard and sank down onto the side of her bed. 'No dear. Papa won't be coming back.'

'Mama, is William coming back?' asked Susan.

Hester took a deep breath and struggled against tears. A sob was rising in her throat and she could not speak immediately. 'No, Susan. I told you — William won't be coming back.'

'Where is William?'

'He's in Heaven, darling.'

'Why? Why isn't he here with us?'

Hester held out her arms and the girls climbed onto the bed, nestling against her at either side.

'Why did William go away?' demanded Susan.

'Jesus took him to Heaven. He was very — ill. You must remember that he was always ill. He couldn't talk, or run and play with you, so Jesus took him back to Heaven.'

'And he's never going to bring him back?' asked Dorothy.

'No, dear. William was never strong enough to live in this world.'

A thoughtful silence followed, but in typical childhood fashion the girls' minds soon switched to more pleasant topics. Aunt Muriel had taken them all to the creek. She had told them to take their shoes and socks off and walk in the water with their cousins. She did not seem to care if anybody got mud on their legs, or even on their clothes. John had sat down in the mud and instead of scolding him Aunt Muriel had laughed.

Hester lay awake after she had retired to bed that night. She thought she knew now why she had felt so unsettled in the Carleton household. Until she returned to her children this afternoon, nobody in this house had ever mentioned William. Harold had said weeks ago that she must come for a holiday, and that was how he and Muriel were treating her stay. They had obviously made up their minds to be cheerful every minute of the day. Hester and the girls were on holiday and nobody was to spoil things by speaking of the tragedy. It was as though poor little William had never existed. Even when Father had let fly with his harsh words about Gerald he had avoided saying the baby's name.

Hester covered her head with the bed-clothes to muffle any sounds and allowed the tears to fall. The past weeks had been so terrible and sad. She recalled the final moments before she left that house in Thorn Bay for ever. It had seemed bigger without the carpet, the heavy armchairs and all the other things that had been sent away to be stored. When she entered the dining-room for the last time her eyes had gone immediately to the corner where William used to lie on his mattress. Perhaps . . . had he not started to cry at that vital moment . . . She had turned away and hurried to the back door for a last glimpse of the garden. It would have been impossible for her to stay. She could not bear to spend any more time there, reliving that terrible scene every time she looked towards that corner in the dining-room. No, she had to make a fresh start. She had told the man in charge of the wagon to sell the desk. It had been left to her by Uncle Jeremy, but it reminded her too much of Gerald's ill temper with his pupils. She never wanted to see that desk again; but Harold had advised her to put everything else in store until her future was more settled.

Her future . . . The tears started afresh as Hester tried to imagine what lay ahead. She felt so helpless and inadequate. Where could she go, and how could she provide for Susan and Dorothy?

2

There was little sleep to be had that night. Hester found herself turning from side to side, fretting over her present difficulties and the recent past, sighing over what might have been. If only events had lived up to her expectations. She even missed the beach. How nice it would be to walk freely on the beach again, away from all distractions, able to think clearly. She could not walk in the countryside around this house — it was so different from the tamed land she had experienced when she used to visit the farm. It had taken courage to go as far as the bank of the nearby creek with Muriel and the children, and the idea of venturing further was dreadful. Who knew what kind of creatures might be lurking in those bushes and tangled grass? Snakes, of course, spiders . . .

Hester shuddered and rolled over again, drawing her knees up towards her chest. As soon as daylight showed in the chink at the edge of the curtains she would get up. It was useless to lie in bed any longer than necessary, unable to stop herself from squirming restlessly.

She had already made a pot of tea and settled at the kitchen table when Muriel came in.

'My, you're up and about early this morning!' exclaimed Muriel.

'Yes. I didn't expect to see you so soon, either.'

'Ah.' Muriel weighed the teapot in her hand to judge how much it held then poured a cup for herself. 'Harold's got a long drive ahead of him today. He wants to get away early.'

'I see.'

'Have you got an appetite yet, or will you wait and have breakfast with the children?'

'I'll wait. I'm not hungry.'

'Mm. We'll have to do something about that appetite of yours. You've got to eat well if you want to be strong.'

Harold made a noisy entrance and greeted them with a cheerful 'Good morning.' He ate his usual hearty meal, and was enjoying a second cup of tea when the telephone rang. He strode away to answer it and came back with a look of resignation.

'The agent is not well today so he won't be there. We could have stayed in bed another hour.'

'Oh dear.' Muriel looked up from the pile

of sandwiches she was about to slice across. 'What are you going to do now?'

'Don't worry, Lass, those won't be wasted. I'll go down to the warehouse instead.' Harold gave a sudden chuckle. 'That'll give the workers something to think about, won't it? Me dropping in all of a sudden when I'm supposed to be twenty miles away. Keep them on their toes, eh?'

The sound of the telephone bell had aroused the children and they soon came filing in. Hester busied herself handing out plates and washing dishes, trying to make herself useful. Living with people who were almost complete strangers, despite being related by marriage, was no easy matter. They seemed to be regarding her as an invalid, someone to be cared for and protected. What she really needed was to be kept occupied, allowed to mop and sweep and help with the cooking. It would be interesting to learn how to use some of the modern equipment, too. Every job in the household appeared to be easier here, but she would gladly forego the privilege of new facilities if only she could have her own home. She wanted to look after things in her own way and make sure that Dorothy and Susan kept their good manners. She would hate them to become as rowdy as their cousins. Even so, she wished Dorothy would relax more, especially when Harold was present. He could make her smile now, but she was still wary of him.

When the children had finished breakfast they all went out to play and shrieks of merriment soon came from the back garden. Hester paused in her task of drying cups. That was surely Dorothy's voice, that softer tone. Dorothy must be losing her inhibitions at last, no longer afraid of being scolded for laughing or behaving like the child she was.

Harold strode back into the kitchen while Hester was still enjoying the sound of her daughter at play.

'Would you like to go into Melbourne today?' he asked. 'You might as well, seeing as I'll be going there today after all.'

'Yes, do go,' urged Muriel. 'The change would do you good.' She jerked her head towards the window as a cluster of children raced by. 'Dorothy and Susan will be quite safe and happy here. You could look at the shops or go visiting again.'

Hester hesitated. Here was a chance to buy a newspaper and check the advertisements. She needed employment and a place to live and she must not delay her search any longer.

'No, thank you,' she replied. 'I don't want to go to Melbourne. But I would like to go as far as the Post Office with you, Harold. I could walk back easily from there.'

'That would take you more than half an hour,' protested Muriel. 'It's a long way. If you've got anything to send, Harold will post it for you.'

'I'm used to walking, and I need the exercise.'

Harold shrugged. 'If that's what the lady wants to do, that's what she will do. I just have to wrap a package, Hester, then we'll be off.'

'Leave those dishes,' ordered Muriel. 'Go and get yourself ready and enjoy the ride. Although why you would want to walk all that way back, I can't imagine.'

Hester went to the bedroom and hastily made the beds, then donned her outdoor clothes and tied a scarf over her hat. Harold came into the hall carrying a parcel, and he nodded in appreciation when he saw her waiting there.

'Glad to see you can get yourself ready so quick. Not like some women — never knowing what to wear, or changing their mind from one minute to the next.'

Hester gave a brief smile. She was still wearing black so there were few decisions to make. 'I didn't have any chores to finish,' she murmured.

'Hm. Come on then, let's go.'

Harold was proud of his vehicle, which was a new Rolls Royce. He spent hours polishing the bodywork and the brass fittings, and frequently boasted about the time he participated in the Reliability Trial when he drove all the way from Sydney to Melbourne. Riding in a motor car was still an enjoyable experience for Hester, too, despite the long journey they had made to reach this place. As they bowled along the dusty road her thoughts returned to that day when they had left Thorn Bay. The one bright episode had been their visit to see the old seaman, Barnaby. The children had been delighted to see the cockatoo again and the strange curios that Barnaby had collected, while the old man had been visibly moved by her decision to call and say farewell. Hester sighed inwardly. There had been so many farewells; not to people so much, but to places and her way of life. Who knew how things would turn out now?

Harold broke into her thoughts. 'Are you sure you don't want to go anywhere else besides the Post Office?'

'Quite sure, thank you.'

'Expecting a letter, are you?'

'Hoping, rather than expecting.' Hester gripped her hands tightly together. Why hadn't she heard from Bruce? He had been so helpful at the time of the tragedy, travelling to Thorn Bay so often and keeping watch over her. He had taken them all out for drives, for walks and to cafés for afternoon tea. The children had warmed towards him, taking to him far more readily than to any other man. He had even looked upon her with signs of affection; but since that last visit, some weeks after Gerald's death, there had been silence. Harold seemed to have taken over from there, organising the removal and the storage of their belongings and providing hospitality in his own home.

The motor car came to a halt in the space alongside the building that served as a Post Office and general store.

'You can collect the letters, if you like,' said Harold as he helped her down. 'I have to pay a bill and fill in some forms first, and there's no point in you being kept in suspense. If you do get a letter, I hope it's the one you've been looking for.'

There were several items waiting to be collected, but they all looked like business envelopes. Hester flicked through them with sinking spirits, then suddenly stopped and stared. This one was addressed to her and it was marked PERSONAL. It was certainly not from Bruce. The name of the sender was written on the outside: OWEN, JAMES and THOMPSON, SOLICITORS.

Solicitors! Hester felt a quake of unease. It was not the firm that handled Uncle Jeremy's Trust Fund. Why would solicitors be writing to her? It could only be in relation to Gerald's case, but what was remaining to be done over that? Oh! It would have to be about his savings. Perhaps she could gain access to the bank account now. It would help so much if she could draw out some actual cash and not feel that she was dependent on charity.

She went outside and laid Harold's mail on the driver's seat of the motor car, then opened her own letter.

Dear Mr Carleton,
Re: The Estate of the Late Gerald Carleton
We acknowledge receipt of your cheque in the amount of One Hundred and Twelve Pounds, in settlement of the account sent to you on 21st ult.

What was all this about? What cheque? Hester read on, dismay creeping like a cold chill through her body.

As requested, we hereby list all the remaining claims against the estate of the deceased . . .

The bank account was not merely empty — it had been overdrawn to quite a large extent. Apparently Gerald had written cheques which amounted to more than the available funds, and worse still it seemed that he had borrowed from other sources.

Harold came out of the store to find her leaning against the vehicle, one hand clutching the letter, the other clasped over her mouth to hold back her sobs.

'What's the matter?' he demanded. 'What's happened?'

'Oh, Harold!'

'Let me see.' He took the creased page from her and scanned it quickly. 'Good God!' He looked around for the envelope and found it lying on the ground. 'This shouldn't have been addressed to you!' he exclaimed angrily. 'This was supposed to have come direct to me.'

'Oh, Harold. You sent money. I never realised. I never . . . '

Hester could say no more. Harold looked briefly at her then took a deep breath to control his rage and gently took her arm.

'Let's get into the motor car, Hester. You'd be better sitting down.'

The time it took to settle her in the passenger seat and then for him to clamber in at the other side provided a pause in which to compose herself.

'I don't understand,' she said. 'How could there be no money? Gerald was saving hard. He wanted to start his own school. Every spare penny went towards the new school.'

Harold shook his head. 'He'd obviously given up on that idea, Hester.'

'But where did all that money go?' She remembered all too well how she had to scrimp to make the household allowance last a full week.

Harold heaved a sigh and turned sideways in his seat so as to watch her reactions.

'Would you like some water? Or anything at all?'

'No, thank you.' Hester drew herself up resolutely. 'Tell me the truth about all this. I'm not going to faint or anything.'

'All right then.' Harold took a deep breath. 'You knew that Gerald was drinking.'

'Yes. It was the drink that caused that terrible thing to happen. Gerald would never have done that if he'd been sober.'

'He'd obviously been drinking heavily for a long time, Hester. It cost him his job. In fact, he lost his job several weeks before you knew anything about it. And drinking to that extent takes money. I had hoped that paying a few bills and overdue rent would be the end of the problem.'

Hester sat in silence for several moments.

Her situation was worse than she had imagined — far worse. How was she going to escape from this never-ending dilemma? And how could she ever repay Harold?

'To be in such debt,' she murmured at last. 'I never knew. And you have paid all that money, Harold. Why didn't you tell me?'

'You were not supposed to know. I'll have strong words to say to the clerk in that solicitors' office. Look, even the heading on the letter has my name on it!'

'I didn't see . . . '

'It's sheer incompetence. He doesn't deserve to keep his job. Imagine sending a letter like that to you. You've had enough to contend with, my dear.'

'But you can't be held responsible for my debts. They are my debts now.'

Harold took her hand in his and rubbed it gently. 'You can't be held legally responsible for most of this. But that's not the point. Gerald was my brother, Hester. This is a family matter, and you are part of my family.'

'You're very kind. But I can't let you take on such a responsibility. Who knows how many other claims might come yet? Perhaps my uncle's Trust Fund will allow me to pay off the debts. I am entitled to claim in times of emergency.'

'No, Hester. We will settle this matter

ourselves.' Harold suddenly sounded remarkably like his brother and she stiffened with the shock.

'Nobody outside the family need know any of this business,' he went on. 'Too much has been made public already and we don't want that state of affairs to continue.'

Hester made no response and he rubbed her hand again. 'Besides that, I feel responsible in a way,' he said. 'I knew Gerald — knew what he could be like if he didn't get his own way. I should have kept an eye on him, made sure he treated you right.'

'He told you never to come again.'

'That shouldn't have stopped me. I could have knocked him down if we ever came to blows. No Hester, I neglected you, got too engrossed in business.'

A lengthy silence followed, then Hester stirred guiltily. 'I must go. I must not delay you any longer.'

'I'll drive you home.'

'No! No, thank you. I'd rather walk.' Her need for a newspaper was greater than ever now, but she could not mention that to Harold. If he knew she was searching through advertisements he would only repeat what he and his wife had said so often before — that she was welcome to stay and there was no need to worry about the future.

Harold looked at her determined expression and after a moment of indecision he nodded slowly.

'You want to be alone for a bit. I can understand that. Are you sure you'll be all right?'

'Absolutely sure, thank you.'

'Well, here.' He fumbled in his trouser pocket and handed two shillings to her. 'While you're here by the shop, buy a little treat for Susan and Dorothy. And get something for yourself, too.'

Hester felt the tears welling up again and could only express her thanks by a quick press of his hand. He jumped down and came around the vehicle to help her down.

'I know it's easy enough to say — but try not to worry,' he said gruffly. 'Everything will be sorted out in time. We all have to take the rough with the smooth.'

Hester stepped away to make space for him to turn the motor car around, and gave an answering wave as he drove back onto the road. Once she was alone she went into the store again and bought a newspaper, then chose two halfpenny sticks of toffee. The woman behind the counter was eager to chat, but Hester made hasty excuses and left as soon as she received her change. She could think of nothing else for the present except her need to search through the newspaper.

She walked for more than half a mile to be sure of privacy before she stopped in a warm patch of sunlight and sank down onto the grass. She riffled through pages until she found the list of houses for rent and then moaned aloud. Prices were so high in Melbourne! Obviously she could not afford a whole house. She had already known that, she told herself firmly. It was silly to look at houses for rent when she already knew she would have to be content with shared accommodation. There seemed to be plenty of furnished rooms available. The first task was to find work, and then look for rooms in a convenient place.

Her spirits plummeted as she scanned the columns of Positions Vacant. There was so little she was able to do by way of employment. She could clean, she could cook, she could do any household jobs; she could surely learn how to serve in a shop. But look at the wages they offered for work like that! On those wages she could not possibly manage. She would have to pay for someone to care for the children while she was out working. She could not afford to pay rent as well as all the other costs on such a small amount. And what about the debts?

The sound of a motor car made her look

up, and she hastily wiped the tears away. Moments later the vehicle drew up nearby and the driver raised his goggles.

'Good morning. Can I offer you a ride?'

Hester recognised him as one of Harold's neighbours. 'No, thank you,' she answered, carefully shading her eyes with one hand to conceal the fact that she had been weeping. 'I am just taking some quiet minutes alone.'

'Having some time away from children for a while, eh? Sensible. Well, if you're sure . . . '

He gave a jaunty wave and opened the throttle, then bounced noisily away in a cloud of dust. Hester sighed and began to fold the newspaper. She would have to accept the hospitality of her in-laws for some time yet. As Cora had warned, it would not be easy to find either work or accommodation. It would be difficult enough as a single person, but the fact that she had two children posed even more of a problem.

3

During the week Hester began to prepare Dorothy and Susan for their first visit to their grandfather. They were excited at the thought of riding on an electric tramcar, but they were puzzled and doubtful about meeting strangers.

'We are going to see your Grandpapa,' said Hester again.

'Papa?' Susan shrieked. 'And William, too?'

'No, darling, not Papa. Your *Grand*papa. He is *my* father.'

'Mama used to be a little girl,' said Dorothy, pleased to be able to display her superior knowledge. 'When Mama was a little girl she had a Papa.'

'That's right,' agreed Hester. 'I always called him Father. You can call him Grandfather, or Grandpapa.'

'Grandfather,' declared Dorothy at once.

Hester nodded. The name Papa obviously had bad associations in Dorothy's mind and she had no wish to stir unpleasant memories.

'Yes, we are going to see Grandfather,' she said. 'Uncle Harold will take us in the motor car most of the way, and then we will go on a tramcar. That will be fun, won't it?'

Hester was almost as eager as the children to go away for the day. She felt guilty about staying so long with her in-laws, although Muriel had taken her aside only two days ago and tried to allay her concern.

'Don't be in such a rush to get settled, Hester. You've been here less than three weeks. Take a holiday. You were very ill after all that nasty business, you know.'

'Yes. That's another reason why I want to get the children settled. Other people have been looking after them for too long. I hate to be a burden to anybody, and we must make a new future together as a family.'

'You're not a burden, Hester. Never think that. But I can understand you wanting to make your own way. What about your aunt? The one who lives in Mountcliffe? What does she have to say?'

'Oh!' Hester recoiled from the suggestion that she might discuss her affairs with that member of her family. 'Aunt Amelia has no wish to be involved.'

'Cut you off, has she?'

'Not exactly.' Hester managed a smile. 'But she must have been relieved to hear that I was leaving the area. She is so frightened of scandal.'

'Huh! She'll contact you when she wants something.'

Hester's smile widened. Muriel had never met her aunt, but she seemed to have judged her character well enough. It had taken several years for Hester to admit to herself that Aunt Amelia only called on her when she wanted some kind of assistance.

'I don't think she will want anything more from me,' she said. 'I'm too far away now, and she has family members on hand.'

Harold was free and easy in many respects, but he was a keen businessman and when anything had to be done on a particular date he made detailed plans in advance. On Friday afternoon he came upon Hester working on her embroidery in the drawing-room.

'Right, now let's think about Sunday,' he said. 'Are you sure you don't want me to drive you all the way to the house?'

'Quite sure, thank you. The girls are looking forward to their first ride on a tramcar.'

'Well, I don't want you to feel pressed for time. We won't make a definite arrangement for your return trip.' Harold grinned at her startled reaction. 'That's what telephones are for. Just before you get on the tram to come back, you can telephone me and I'll set off to meet you.'

'Oh!' Hester blushed and bit her lip nervously. 'I don't think — er — that is — '

'Don't tell me you've never used a telephone!'

Hester shook her head. 'Never. I would not know how to do it.'

'Good Lord. And you lived with that rich aunt of yours all that time. Do you mean to say she hasn't got a telephone?'

'No. At least, she never used to have one. Aunt Amelia always preferred to write a note. Or she would send a messenger if something were urgent. She said it was more polite.'

'Frightened of telephones, more like.' Harold spread his hands in a gesture of exasperation. 'Look Hester, I'm going out. When that telephone rings, pick up the receiver. All right?'

He strode away before she had time to respond and almost immediately afterwards she heard the sound of an engine starting. Hester went to the hall and stared at the black instrument standing on a small polished table. It suddenly looked menacing. Why had Harold rushed away if he were expecting someone to contact him? Surely he would return in time to take the call himself.

She hovered near the window in the drawing-room, willing him to hurry back, but only a few minutes later the strident bell rang out. Hester approached warily, then picked up the receiver and held it to her ear as she had seen others do.

'Hello,' she said.

'Hello, Hester. It's me. Either pick that other part up, or bend down closer. Then talk to me.'

The voice was thin and distant, but unmistakably that of Harold. Hester lifted the mouthpiece and spoke. 'Hello, Harold.'

'That's good. Now, it's not difficult, is it?'

'Er, no. I'm still a little nervous, but no, it's not difficult.'

He kept her talking for two more minutes, then told her to replace the receiver.

'Something else you've learned how to do,' he boomed on his return. 'You never know when you might need to call someone, Hester, so you must start practising. On Sunday I'll show you how to use a public telephone.'

Sunday was a warm clear day and the two children chatted excitedly as they prepared for the journey. They proudly dressed in their best clothes and Harold grinned when they strutted outside to show off their dresses.

'My word, what pretty young ladies,' he said.

'You look lovely,' said Muriel. 'Now have a good day, won't you?'

'Yes,' they chorused. 'Good-bye, Aunt Muriel.' They climbed up and settled on the back seat, spreading their skirts carefully, and Harold helped Hester up into the front.

'We'll stop by the store and you can experiment with the public telephone,' he said.

The girls watched with awe as Hester learned how to insert coins and ask the operator for the number she wanted. It was the first new experience of a day that promised to be full of excitement and they could not keep still.

'Settle down,' said Hester worriedly. She was anxious for them to make a good impression when they were introduced to her father.

Beth's voice came in her ear and she turned her attention to the task in hand, nervously answering all the questions that followed.

'Did you ask for the number yourself? Has Harold written it down for you?'

She dabbed her face with her handkerchief when she had replaced the receiver, glad that the store was closed for the Sabbath. If any other people had been in the vicinity they would surely have been amused by the fact that she did not know how to operate an instrument that was coming into common use.

'Well done,' said Harold. 'Now we'll really get started.'

The drive calmed Hester and she enjoyed the children's excitement when they boarded the tramcar. They were interested in everything they passed along the way and the other passengers looked on with amusement, listening to their chatter and watching them turn their heads eagerly to look at all the new sights.

Hester looked for landmarks she remembered from years ago, and when she saw that it was nearly time to descend she told the girls to ready themselves.

'Hold hands,' she instructed when they climbed down. 'We have to walk from here, and there is a lot of traffic so we have to be very careful crossing the roads.'

When they eventually turned into a narrow, grimy street the girls were astonished to hear that this was the place where their mother had lived until she was a grown woman.

'What a funny little road,' said Dorothy.

'Where are the gardens?' asked Susan.

'There aren't any here, dear. Not all children have a garden to play in. You have been very lucky up to now.' That was probably one of the changes the children would have to face, thought Hester sadly. Accommodation in any of the more pleasant areas would be far beyond her means.

The girls grew silent as they neared their

destination, edging back to stand behind their mother when she knocked on the door. Edmund opened it briskly.

'So here you are! Come in!'

Hester ushered the children inside and they watched him close the door and greet Hester with a light kiss.

'Well, well,' he said, turning his attention to them. 'My little grandchildren. At long last I have met you.'

He was unsure whether to kiss them, pat them or merely offer his hand and they were too shy to either speak or move. The awkward moment dispersed when Cora bustled in, exuding goodwill. She was wearing pink today, a bright colour that accentuated the dark shade of her hair, and her dress was decorated with numerous frills and buttons.

'My little darlings!' she exclaimed, holding her arms wide in a gesture of welcome. 'How lovely to see you. I'm your Aunt Cora.'

Hester smiled with relief. She had been unsure how to introduce her stepmother, but the other had obviously decided that she did not want to be called Grandmother. She introduced the girls and they accepted warm hugs with quiet dignity.

'Let me have your hats, then you can sit down — any chair you like.'

Once the ice was broken the visit

proceeded in a more relaxed fashion. Edmund soon brought out two boxes of buttons and he invited the girls to play with them at the dining table.

'Set them out on the paper,' he instructed. 'Your Mama used to play with buttons for hours when she was your age. Some of the same ones must still be in there.'

Cora sat with them a little longer, chatting about the trivia of everyday life, then she went back to the kitchen to prepare dinner and Edmund turned to Hester with a more serious air.

'How are you getting along?' he asked.

'Quite well, thank you, Father. Harold and Muriel are both very kind and the children feel more at ease there now.'

'No plans for moving on, I suppose?'

'Not yet. I will have to start making plans soon, though.'

'There's always room here for you. Remember that.'

'Yes. Thank you.' Hester looked around uneasily. The parlour was clean and bright, but was tiny in comparison with rooms she had experienced since leaving here. No doubt Father's offer was genuine, but how long would the goodwill last if they had to live here for a lengthy period? Father was at an age where children could easily become a nuisance, and they would all find their lives constricted if they had to live in such close proximity for long.

'Have you had any news from Angela?' he asked, changing the subject abruptly.

'No, not for a long time.' Hester brought her mind back to the present. 'It takes a long time for letters to travel from America, so a letter could be on its way.'

'I should write more often myself.'

Hester made no effort to dispute that, knowing all too well that Father was reluctant to write letters, always too conscious of his weakness at spelling and grammar.

'I wrote to Angela a little while ago,' she said. 'I told her that baby William had died. And that Gerald had died also. I didn't go into details.'

Edmund nodded. 'Just as well. No point in upsetting anyone unnecessarily.'

Another awkward pause followed then he shifted in his chair. 'What about Timothy? Do you ever hear from him?'

Hester sighed. 'I've never had a letter. He called to see me soon after Uncle Jeremy died, but I haven't seen him since.'

They had parted on bad terms, a fact that had disturbed Hester a great deal over ensuing years, but she had been unable to control her rage at the time. Her brother had clearly visited her for one purpose only — to wheedle out of her as much as he could. He had been so certain that Uncle Jeremy would remember her in his Will.

'No doubt he would have stayed in touch if you had married money instead of a mere schoolteacher,' said Edmund disparagingly. 'Money was the only thing that ever interested him. I wonder if he will ever have any of his own? Honest money, that is.'

Another silence fell and again it was Cora who broke the tension. She came in carrying two trays.

'We have to clear the table for dinner,' she said to the children. 'What lovely patterns you're making. If I'm careful I'll be able to move them onto these trays without upsetting them, and then you can work on them again later if you like.'

In the middle of the afternoon Edmund glanced at Cora then rose to his feet.

'I would wager that these little grandchildren of mine like ice cream,' he said. 'Is that right, Dorothy? Do you like ice cream?'

'Yes, Grandfather.'

'And you, too, Susan?' The little girl nodded enthusiastically and he grinned. 'We will go together to the corner shop and buy some. Don't you think that's a good idea?'

The two children looked at their mother

for support and she smiled.

'Yes, that will be nice. You'll be quite safe with Grandfather. Be good, now, and hold hands if you cross any roads.'

Cora brought their hats and the two women watched from the doorstep as the little group set off along the road.

'Lovely children,' said Cora. She invited Hester to sit on the small sofa, then settled beside her with a confiding manner. She and Father must have planned this little strategy beforehand, decided Hester; but she was thankful for the opportunity to chat in private. Cora was a friendly person and she was keen to know her better.

'Time for some straight talk,' said Cora frankly. 'Have you made any plans yet?'

'Not yet,' admitted Hester. That sounded weak, as if she had done nothing to help herself, and she hastily added: 'I have been looking in the newspaper, to see what jobs are available.'

'And what have you found?'

'Nothing, as yet.'

'The best jobs are not always advertised.'

'No.' Hester looked away as she strove to hide her anxiety, and former vague ideas suddenly seemed to gather strength in her mind. 'I shall have to come into Melbourne during the week and go into different

44

establishments to ask what work is available.'

'And just where are you thinking of going?'

'Hotels might offer the best prospects,' said Hester, improvising rapidly. 'I need accommodation as well as work, and there must be lots of jobs that need to be done in hotels. If there's nothing else I could learn to become a barmaid. I know that barmaids are needed.'

'No, Hester! Definitely not.'

Hester looked at her in surprise. 'But you were a barmaid yourself.'

'Yes, and that's why I know it is definitely not right for you.' Cora reached out for Hester's hand. 'Look, Hester, people look down on anyone who works in a bar. You must know that. Think about your aunt. What would she say if she heard that you were working in a bar?'

'I can't let her opinions influence me,' Hester retorted. 'Besides, she has no say in the matter.' She felt a sudden rush of confidence and shifted her position so as to meet Cora's gaze squarely.

'You can help me, Cora. You will, won't you? You can teach me the things I need to know so that I can get work in a bar.'

45

4

Cora held Hester's gaze for several moments, her expression giving no inkling of her feelings, then she slowly shook her head.

'No, Hester. I can't do that.'

'Of course you can! You were very good at your job. Father told me. He didn't tell me a lot about you, but that's one thing he did say.'

Cora smiled. 'I won't deny it — I was good at my job. And that's why I know it is definitely not for you.'

'I don't care what other people might say.'

Cora shook her head again. 'It's not that. You're not cut out for working in a bar, Hester.' She raised her hand quickly to dismiss any protest. 'Have you ever been in a public bar? I thought not. You couldn't possibly imagine what it might be like.'

Hester drew herself up. 'If you could learn, I'm sure I could, too. You wouldn't have stayed if it had been as disreputable as some people say.'

Cora sighed with a mixture of exasperation and concern. 'Some of the people who drink in bars certainly are disreputable. For goodness' sake, Hester. You, of all people, know what drink can do. You've experienced some of the problems for yourself.' She sighed again. 'Think what it must be like to face more than one man who's had too much to drink. You'd never be able to keep control, to let them know who's boss.'

'You could teach me,' said Hester defiantly.

Cora gave a raucous laugh. 'You can't change your nature. I'm telling you, Hester, it's not for you. For a start you blush at the slightest thing. Look at you now! The men would lay bets on who could make you blush first, or who'd make you blush for longer. Believe me, you'd never last an hour.'

Hester stared down at her hands, fighting back the tears. 'I have to get work of some kind,' she mumbled at last.

Cora studied her for a moment, then moved closer and put an arm around her shoulders.

'What's happened, Hester? Why is it so urgent? Are they going to throw you out from where you are now?'

Hester shook her head despondently. How was she to care for her children, to give them everything they needed? And how could she explain her feelings, make anyone understand how uncertain her prospects seemed to be and how deeply she yearned to be independent? It seemed that other people had always

47

controlled her life. That state of affairs had gone on far too long already, yet now it seemed even more unlikely that she would ever be free to make her own way in the world.

Neither spoke for some time, and gradually Hester felt the urge to unburden herself. Cora seemed to have a natural warmth and empathy; she understood the ways of the world, and she would surely help with any problem rather than seek to blame or criticise.

'I need money,' she said at last. 'I thought there would be sufficient funds to tide us over for a few months at least, but there isn't any money at all. In fact, I'm in debt. Terrible debt.'

Cora gently drew the story from her and another pause followed while she considered the consequences. She was the type for whom practicality was far more important than pride.

'What does Harold do for a living?'

'He owns a business, buying and selling things. I don't think he deals in any one particular product.'

'And he's rich?'

Hester thought about Harold's house. It was comfortable and equipped with all kinds of modern accessories, but it was not ostentatious like those of her aunt's circle of friends.

'I would not say rich, but definitely on the prosperous side.'

'Quite able to stand the cost of those bills, which he has already offered to do. So we don't need to concern ourselves over the debt,' said Cora firmly. 'We have to deal with priorities, Hester. To start with, leave the debt to one side. That takes care of quite a lot of the problem, doesn't it?'

Hester forced a smile. 'If only it were so easy. What else do you suggest?'

She felt more inept than ever when Cora asked her to list her accomplishments. All she knew how to do were the tasks of any wife and mother.

'Think again,' said Cora briskly. 'Have you ever kept accounts?'

'Oh, yes. Gerald was very particular about the accounts.' Hester bit her lip, remembering the strain she felt all too frequently when trying to make the figures balance. Buying small treats for the children had often meant entering a false amount against one or more items on the list.

'So you can keep accounts. And we know you can read and write well. Perhaps we could consider a clerical situation. Can you use a telephone?'

49

'Oh, yes! Harold taught me, this very week. I am going to telephone this afternoon so that he can meet us with the motor car.'

'Well, then.' Cora clapped her hands together with satisfaction. 'We will achieve something worthwhile. I'm telling you, Hester, we will find something suitable. The first thing to do is tell yourself you're not going to panic. You are not going to rush into a job that is not suitable.'

When Edmund returned with the children, having brought them back by a lengthy route, Hester was feeling more cheerful and confident. Cora had met a great many people during her years as a barmaid, and she still saw some of her former customers occasionally. They might know of vacancies that were not publicly advertised, and Cora could speak on her behalf.

★   ★   ★

It was difficult to maintain patience during the days that followed. Cora had promised to telephone as soon as she had any hopeful news, but no message came. Hester filled the empty hours by sharing the housework, but she had to insist on being allowed to do so.

'I need to do something, Muriel. I like to be kept busy.'

Muriel regarded her thoughtfully. 'I'm pleased to hear you're feeling strong enough. You certainly sound as if you have more energy. Why don't we go into the kitchen and plan something special for dinner this evening? You can give me a new recipe or two, and I'll show you how to use some of my new gadgets.'

Hester agreed with alacrity. Anything that she learned now could come in useful when the chance of paid work came her way.

'Harold is always bringing something new home,' said Muriel, opening a cupboard to display a range of shiny utensils. 'I don't use them all, of course. Sometimes it takes longer to wash the machine than to do a job by hand, but Harold can't resist anything new. Sometimes he buys a heap of them to sell, especially if I say I like them.'

Hester trusted Cora and knew she would do all she could to help, but she could not bear to wait and do nothing herself. At the next opportunity she bought another newspaper, and this time she resolved to search through the advertisements quite openly at the house. Perhaps Harold would aid her if he knew she really was determined to obtain work.

He found her engrossed in the Situations Vacant column and gave a little cough to announce his presence.

'Planning ahead, eh?' he remarked. 'You don't need to waste money buying papers, Hester. I'll bring mine back every day and you can read that.'

'Thank you.' Hester glanced down at the page then looked up at him again. 'You know a lot of people in business, Harold. Would you please ask if there is any suitable work for me?'

Harold nodded. 'You're really keen to make your own way, aren't you? Well, as I said before, there's no rush — but if I hear of any vacancies I'll certainly put in a good word for you.'

Whenever the telephone rang Hester rushed to answer, and she had lost all fear of using the instrument before she finally heard the voice for which she had been waiting so impatiently.

'Hello, Cora, how are you? Have you heard any good news?'

'I know it's been a long time, Hester, but you can't produce things like this out of a hat.'

'Does that mean . . . ?' Hester's spirits sagged again.

'It means there's a possibility. Can you get to St Kilda tomorrow morning?'

'Oh, yes. Yes, I'm sure I can.' If Harold

were not driving to the city the next day she would ask him to take her to the nearest railway station. What time?'

'I'll meet you and go with you,' said Cora. 'Once I introduce you it will be up to you, of course. If you like the situation, I'll help as much as I can.'

'I'm sure it will suit, if you recommend it.'

'We'll see. I'll tell you all about it when we meet. Wear the outfit you were wearing when you came here to visit us.'

'But that's my Sunday b — '

'Wear it,' Cora interrupted. 'You have to make a good impression. Wear that same outfit and that hat.'

She hurried to give instructions about the place and time of their meeting then ended the call, leaving Hester with a host of unanswered questions.

Another restless night ensued, but this time it was excitement rather than concern that was keeping her awake. Cora had sounded hopeful, but why had she kept all the details to herself? She had not even given any hint as to the type of work involved. Hester finally fell asleep, but she was up again early, ready to go well before Harold had prepared himself for a drive to the city.

'I'll take you right to the spot,' he announced as they set off along the unpaved road.

'I don't want to make you late, Harold. The tram track will be perfectly . . . '

'Nonsense. What's the good of having a fine motor car if I can't drive members of my own family to wherever they want to go? Now, you have my office number, haven't you? It doesn't matter what time you call. I'll leave instructions for you if I have to go out.'

He stopped close to the corner where the two women had arranged to meet and helped her to alight.

'Good luck, Hester,' he said. 'I know this is important to you. But don't be too eager and don't take anything that's not worthwhile. You don't have to accept the first offer that comes along.'

'Thank you, Harold. Thank you for everything.' She could not afford to be too choosy, she told herself as she watched him pull away from the footpath. He had probably not even realised the extra difficulties that she faced. It must be so much easier for a man.

When he had gone from sight she began to wonder again about the kind of situation Cora had discovered. She might have given some inkling as to what was in store for her today. Was there any particular reason for being so mysterious, or had she merely been worried about the telephone call being cut short before she had made arrangements for them to meet? Perhaps they were going to take a tram to some other suburb.

Hester began to look about with growing interest, remembering that St Kilda always had been a popular and progressive city. She could recall making only one visit as a child, when the whole family had spent an afternoon on the beach, but that special event had lived in her mind ever since. Aunt Amelia tended to look down on the place because it attracted 'common' visitors, always boasting that Mountcliffe was far more genteel. The long distance from Melbourne had certainly prevented most ordinary people from reaching Mountcliffe, and that fact, together with the small local population, had undoubtedly helped Aunt Amelia to rise on the social scale. Hester shrugged and set off along Fitzroy Street to look at shop windows. She need not concern herself with Aunt Amelia's wishes or opinions. That part of her life was well and truly over.

Six minutes before the appointed hour Hester saw the conspicuous figure of Cora in the distance. She was wearing the same blue dress she had worn for their first meeting, topped now by a wide hat decorated with blue ostrich feathers and numerous silk flowers. Hester quickened her pace and Cora did the same when she caught sight of her.

'Hester, my dear!' Cora flung her arms around her in a rapturous welcome, oblivious to the stares of passers-by. 'How nice to see you. Let's take a pot of tea in that corner café and I'll tell you all about this proposal.'

She greeted members of the café staff effusively, and they responded as if they knew her well.

'A pot of tea for two, please,' she called, ushering Hester into a seat near the window. She sat down facing her and smiled as she removed her gloves.

'Now then, Hester, there's a situation vacant right here in St Kilda. I've been to the place myself and I think it would be suitable; but I have to warn you — it will be hard work.'

'I don't mind that,' said Hester at once.

'No. You must be used to hard work, looking after little William all that time.' Cora noticed the flicker of pain in Hester's eyes and hurried on. 'For a start, there will be cooking for ten men.'

'Cooking?' echoed Hester.

Cora nodded. 'That's right. The owner says he wants a Manageress, but what he really wants is someone more like a housekeeper.'

She went on to describe a large house, where the new employee would have to cook breakfast and dinner for ten permanent residents. Two young women also worked there, serving meals and helping with the cleaning.

'He calls it a private hotel, but it's a boarding-house, nothing more. There's no bar, no passing trade. You'd be in charge, Hester. In charge of the staff, collecting the rents, buying the food, planning the menus and everything like that. What do you think?'

Hester flushed and then paled. 'It sounds like a big responsibility.'

Cora waved one hand nonchalantly. 'Think about your own home. You had to organise all the cooking and shopping there. Just multiply the amounts, and hey presto. You could do it, Hester.'

Hester remained silent while she struggled to muster her courage. Any job was going to be a challenge at first and Cora seemed confident that she could cope. She cast about for something to say and finally asked, 'What about wages?'

'Very low. But there's an apartment on the premises, so you won't have to pay rent. And all the food would come out of household expenses, of course. The money won't sound much, but it will all be yours to spend as you like.'

Hester felt her excitement rising. The job sounded as if it would take care of all her problems at once; it was surely too good to be true.

'Did you tell the owner that I have two young children?'

'Of course. I assured him that little girls don't eat much. I also told him that raising a family gives anybody much better experience than simply working for somebody else. He's quite looking forward to meeting you. Now, drink your tea.'

Cora added more encouraging words as they walked together to keep the appointment.

'The job will be yours if you want it. If you decide to accept you'll be living near the sea. You like the sea, don't you?'

'Yes, I have been missing the beach lately.'

Two businessmen stared blatantly as they approached from the opposite direction, comparing the small woman in smart black with the much taller woman in blue. Hester noticed their interest and looked down at herself with sudden apprehension.

'Don't you think I'm a little over-dressed for this particular occasion?'

'Nonsense!' Cora gripped her arm and gave a friendly squeeze. 'This man says he wants a refined lady, and that's exactly what you look like. You sound right, too, so you don't need to have any worries on that score.

I tell you, this job is yours if you want it.'

They stopped outside a wrought iron gate and Hester stared at the huge two-storied building beyond. A well-kept garden separated the house from the street, and a balcony decorated with wrought iron lace and supported by ornate pillars ran across its entire front. The name BELLA CASA was engraved in the curved stone lintel above the front door, but there was no sign to indicate that this was a boarding establishment.

'It looks very smart,' she said, aware that Cora was waiting for some comment.

'Imagine how it looked when it was first built! It's come down in the world since then.'

They walked along the path and up three steps to the front door, where Cora pulled the bell. Moments later a uniformed maid opened the door and invited them inside.

'I'll tell Mr Hetherington you're here,' she said, and hastened away along a passage to the left, leaving them standing in the large hallway.

A man appeared almost at once and came towards them, nodding and smiling. 'Good morning, Cora.'

'Good morning. Let me introduce Mrs Carleton, the lady I told you about yesterday.'

He looked at Hester with obvious surprise. 'You're too small,' he said abruptly.

Hester instantly blushed, but her rigid posture gave the appearance of rage rather than embarrassment. Before she could speak or move, Cora had taken her arm.

'Come, Hester. This is no place for you. If size is more important than ability . . . '

Hester felt herself being drawn towards the front door. What a miserable failure I am, she thought desperately. To be refused so quickly and scornfully, when Cora had been so sure she would be accepted.

'Wait!' called the man. Cora paid no attention to that, but she halted by the door and made a small gesture with her hand as if directing him to open it for them, and he hurried forward. 'Don't go. Look, I'm sorry if I offended you, but — ' He spread his arms apologetically. 'I was expecting someone more, er — I don't know if you could — '

'I have never found my size to be a hindrance,' said Hester stiffly.

'Hester is strong enough to do whatever might be needed in a place like this,' Cora interposed. 'She was a nurse to a crippled child for two years. If she could manage to do that she could certainly lift your pots and pans.'

'I'm sorry. I didn't mean — look, we seem to have got off to a bad start. Can we begin again? I'm Roger Hetherington.'

He offered his hand and Hester accepted a brief handshake.

'I'm afraid I imagined someone more — er — someone sturdier,' he mumbled.

'I might have said we were related, but I didn't say she looked like me,' declared Cora.

'No, my mistake.'

He quickly recovered his self-assurance and surveyed Hester with keen interest, noting her neat figure, her bright hair and her well-tailored dress. His stature, his smart suit, slicked down hair and thin moustache reminded Hester of her cousin's husband, but she hastily thrust that thought away. She had never liked Cecil and she must not allow that fact to affect her demeanour now.

'Back to business,' he said. 'I understand you have had experience?'

'You cooked at Beach House, didn't you?' said Cora quickly.

Hester swallowed nervously. Cora had obviously exaggerated her expertise.

'Yes, I did cook there regularly,' she agreed.

'And you have references, of course?'

'Mr Harold Carleton will speak for me. He owns a business in Melbourne.'

'Yes, Cora said something about him. Quite a substantial businessman, apparently, but I've never had the pleasure . . . Is there anybody else, not a relative?'

'Dr Hutchinson has known me for many years. I could ask him to write, or perhaps telephone to you.' Bruce would surely support her, and writing to ask for a reference would give her the perfect excuse to contact him, rather than wait for him to make the first move.

'No need for that.' Mr Hetherington made a dismissive gesture. 'Perhaps I could show you the kitchen, Mrs Carleton?'

Cora suddenly stepped forward. 'Better to start with the accommodation. If Hester doesn't like it there's no point in wasting any more time.'

Hester saw an unladylike wink from beyond his shoulder and restrained a smile. Cora was taking control, giving the appearance of interviewing Mr Hetherington, rather than the other way around.

'Yes, I would like to see the accommodation,' Hester agreed.

He shrugged and gave a brief nod, then wafted one hand airily towards the staircase as if to prove he was still in charge of the situation.

'We can start upstairs and make our way down. There are two floors. Allow me to lead the way.'

As they followed him up the flight of red carpeted stairs he drew their attention to points of interest.

'As you can see by this beautiful banister and the designs on the ceilings, this was a luxurious home. It was erected during the prosperous days of the Eighties, when many of the big mansions were built. The original owner lost his fortune in the Nineties, and since then the house has gone through more than one set of hands. When I acquired it I was determined to restore both the house and its residents to a high standard, which is why I have been so particular about the quality of staff. I demand excellence from my employees.'

They turned into a passage leading off the landing and he gestured towards the first door.

'One of the bathrooms for residents. There are four altogether. We can look at them later. Now there is the entrance to the private apartment.'

He led them to a sturdy white painted door, opened it and invited them to enter. Hester found herself in another part of the same passage, with rooms opening off at either side.

'At one time this would have been the section set aside for the household staff,' he announced. 'The nanny, the housekeeper and so forth.'

Hester almost gasped aloud at the space as they went from room to room. They were all bare of furnishings, but she could picture

63

them in use. The two rooms at the front would make ideal bedrooms and the larger one at the rear would give plenty of scope for all their daytime activities. There was a kitchen with running water, and even a bathroom that had not only running water but a water closet in one corner.

Cora gave a mischievous grin from behind Mr Hetherington's back. 'Well, what do you think? Would this be suitable, Hester?'

Hester could not reply at first, but when she found her voice instinct warned her not to sound over-enthusiastic.

'I think it would do very well. Let me look out of the windows.'

The front rooms overlooked the garden and the road along which they had walked. The back rooms overlooked a much larger garden and beyond that another road. Hester gripped her hands tightly together, scarcely able to contain her glee. She had worried that she might have to take her children to poky rooms in a grim district with no gardens at all, but here they would not only have big rooms and a garden, but a balcony as well.

Surely there must be some drawback, she told herself. Perhaps something quite drastic. If this position were so easy to obtain, why hadn't other, more experienced, people rushed to take it?

5

'I'm glad this meets with your satisfaction,' said Mr Hetherington, breaking a rather lengthy pause. 'May I show you the rest of the house?'

They inspected one of the communal bathrooms, which he assured them was exactly the same as the other three, peeped into two bedrooms which had already been tidied by the maids, then went downstairs where he showed them a writing-room, a sitting-room and a dining-room.

The kitchen was at the rear, next to the dining-room. Hester moved in ahead of the others and looked around warily. She was still dubious about the reason for the generous offer and guessed that any faults or problems would prove to be here, but all seemed well. The floor was covered with clean linoleum in a plain deep red, the kitchen table was large and well-scrubbed, and the pots and cooking utensils on view appeared to be in good condition.

'This room is lighted by gas, of course,' said Mr Hetherington. 'Same as all the others. There is hot water, and you will find a good array of equipment.'

Hester nodded, carefully taking stock of the facilities. A huge cooking range stretched along the end wall, and she was surprised to see a gas cooking stove alongside it. Not many houses of this vintage would have gas for cooking, she thought. She opened the oven door and found it to be both clean and roomy.

'Well, what do you think?' asked Mr Hetherington, beginning to show signs of impatience. 'Have you any questions?'

Hester tried to think of the sort of queries a more experienced person would make.

'Is there a laundry?'

'Yes, of course. I should have shown you that. It's just outside. The bed linen and table linen goes out to a professional laundry.'

Cora made signs to represent money and Hester turned to face him again.

'We have not discussed payment,' she said with quiet dignity. 'What are you offering?'

'Ten shillings per week, plus board and accommodation.' He glanced at Cora and hastily amended the amount. 'That is, ten shillings and sixpence.'

'I see.' Hester's expression did not change, but she was thinking rapidly. She could not have expected to do so well. 10/6 per week, and no bills coming in. She could start paying off her debts almost at once. But the ease with which this offer had come still caused suspicion.

'When could you start?' he prodded. 'I would like you to come as soon as possible.'

Hester took a deep breath. 'I would like to walk awhile and think it over.'

She had caught him off-guard, but he quickly recovered. 'Ah, sensible. Yes, a very sensible course of action.' He gave an ingratiating smile and hastened to open the back door. 'Perhaps you would like to walk in our garden. There is a seat in the arbour and the day is warm enough if you would care to sit for a time.'

'Thank you.'

Hester went out to the large garden, closely followed by Cora. They walked side by side for two or three minutes without speaking, then Hester leaned closer to confide in her companion.

'I've got a feeling that he's upstairs now, watching us from a window.'

'Very likely,' responded Cora. 'Don't look. We'll go down to the far end and keep our backs to him.'

She took Hester's arm and they strolled towards the flower bed which ran along the inside of the rear boundary wall, stopping there to admire the roses.

'That was a wonderful idea, making him wait for an answer,' said Cora. You'll have him eating out of your hand now. Don't you think this is the ideal place for you?'

'It seems perfect, but just *too* perfect, and too easy. Cora, why didn't you tell me what kind of job this was? Why did you keep it all so secret?'

Cora chuckled. 'I didn't want you lying awake all night thinking up reasons why it would be difficult. You can do it, Hester. You'll be perfect, and he knows it.'

'Why were you so sure he would offer the job to me?'

'I happen to know that he's absolutely desperate. He's already lost one of his long-standing clients, and two more have given notice.'

'Oh dear. What's the matter with the place?'

'It's not the place itself. As you can see, the house is in good condition.' Cora tugged at Hester's arm and they began to stroll again. 'Roger's claiming all the credit for the quality of the accommodation and the service, but actually that's all due to the previous owner. He had a heart attack, or a stroke or something, so he had to sell in a hurry and Roger got a bargain. Unfortunately for him, the housekeeper didn't stay. She left to look after the old owner and his family.'

'Couldn't he replace her?'

'Oh, he did, which is where the trouble started.' Cora chuckled again. 'He had a married couple first, but the husband upset the paying guests. He offended just about everybody.'

'Why would he do that?'

Cora grimaced. 'Jealous, probably. Didn't like his wife spending all that time and effort on other men.'

'What happened after that?'

'He employed a single woman. But she had a problem with drink — or sedatives — doesn't matter which, same effect, she couldn't get up in the mornings.' Cora looked sharply at Hester. 'Look, I don't want to be rude, but are you taking anything? You went through a lot and you were very ill. Medicine can be as bad as drink if you take it too long.'

Hester shook her head. 'No, you don't need to worry about me. The doctor did give me something to make me sleep, but only for the first week or so. It was the thought of my children that helped me to get better, rather than medicine.'

'I'm glad to hear it. You'll do well here, Hester, I just know it. The residents will like you. Even those who've said they're leaving will change their minds and stay. They'll know you're a lady as soon as they set eyes on you.'

'It still seems too easy somehow.'

'I told you, Roger's desperate. He has to send his own housekeeper here every day just to keep his clients, and that's costing him money; extra pay for the extra work, cab fares to and from his house. And on top of that his own home is in chaos. He'll be stalking up and down now, just praying that you'll accept the job.'

'It sounds as if I have been very lucky.'

'Yes. But you can be luckier still. We'll ask for eleven shillings a week.'

'Cora!'

'He'll pay it, believe me. Come on, let's go in now. The first thing for you to do is tell him you want eleven shillings a week, then ask to see the books. You'll have to order all the food and everything, so you need to know exactly how much money is available each week.'

As predicted, Mr Hetherington agreed to the increase in wages without argument. He was plainly anxious to acquire Hester's services, and his efforts to please gave her all the confidence she needed. They sat at the kitchen table and he opened the account books for her, explaining how the residents' fees were calculated and which of the local traders she should pay by cash.

'Would I have to use the same traders, or would I be able to choose the shops where I do business?' she asked.

'You may choose, of course. But quality is more important than cost. I think you will find our usual suppliers will give you the best quality.'

Shortly afterwards they shook hands on the deal and Hester felt she was bouncing with exhilaration as she and Cora walked back towards Fitzroy Street. She was to move into the apartment as soon as she could arrange for her goods to be delivered. In the meantime Mr Hetherington's housekeeper would continue to provide breakfast, while Cora would take over the rest of Hester's duties until she was on hand to do everything herself. Hester silently vowed that she would find some means of travelling to the house each day, even if Harold were not available to drive her.

'I can't believe all this is happening,' she exclaimed.

'You're a marvel,' said Cora with genuine admiration. 'You behaved in there as if you had a lifetime of experience behind you. You've got backbone, I'll say that for you.'

'I owe it all to you,' replied Hester. 'I couldn't have done it without you.'

'I wasn't the one who taught you to act like Lady of the Manor. That aunt of yours obviously did some good for you. Anyway, now's the time to celebrate. We'll go to a restaurant for lunch and I'll pay.'

Hester was still bubbling with high spirits when Harold came to meet her. He listened with a tolerant smile as she described her good fortune, aware that Cora must have laid excellent groundwork before introducing her protégé.

'That Cora seems to be quite a woman,' he said.

'She certainly is,' agreed Hester. 'She has done a lot for Father, too. He was very depressed for a long time after Mother died and he started to let himself go. Cora changed all that. He was really lucky to meet her.'

'So it seems. Well, I'll be driving into Melbourne every day this week, so you won't have any problem getting there and back. It will be good to find out how everything is done before you actually move into the place.'

Muriel listened eagerly to the news and afterwards Hester tried to prepare her children for another change in their lives. Neither of them had enjoyed their first few days with their boisterous cousins, but now they had become used to the hurly-burly of a large family and had no desire to leave.

'You will have your own bed again and all your own toys,' said Hester. 'And there is a lovely garden.'

'I don't care,' said Dorothy rebelliously. 'I'd rather stay here. Why do we have to keep moving?'

'We all knew we wouldn't be here for long.' Hester decided this was not a time to insist on obedience and good manners. 'You will have a few more days here yet. We will be near the beach at St Kilda. I expect Uncle Harold will bring the children to visit sometimes and you can all play together on the beach.'

The next morning Harold drove Hester to St Kilda and asked her to direct him to Bella Casa. He pulled up on the opposite side of the road and stared thoughtfully at the house.

'Mm. A big place,' he commented. 'You'll have a lot of work on your hands there.'

'I won't be doing it all by myself,' replied Hester.

'No, well make sure that everybody does their full share.'

Hester smiled. 'Cora will make sure they do everything properly, and I'll follow her example.'

'Yeah. Just let them know right from the start who's the boss. Don't let them walk all over you.'

Cora had arrived only twenty minutes before, but she had already settled in as if she had been working there for weeks. Her dark green dress was hidden behind a copious white apron and she had covered her sleeves with protective armlets.

'Good morning, Hester.' She greeted her with a kiss and led her towards the kitchen. 'All your residents have gone off to work and we've done the washing up. I'm just putting things away.'

'You arranged all this before Mr Hetherington even met me, didn't you?' said Hester.

'Don't let a little thing like that worry you. You wouldn't believe how relieved he is, now you've agreed to do it. You've added years to his life.' Cora indicated a peg where Hester could leave her hat and coat. 'I've told the two maids they can meet you later. They're making beds and cleaning rooms just now and we don't want to upset the routine. In the meantime you and I can find out where everything is kept.'

They investigated cupboards and shelves in the kitchen and larder, then made their way to other regions and looked at neatly folded towels and linen, cleaning utensils and other essential items.

'It all looks very orderly,' said Hester with relief.

'Yes, if you leave things the way they are everything should go smoothly. But when you meet the maids you've got to make it plain that you're in charge. I'm only here as your assistant, remember that. Let's plan a few meals now. The delivery carts will be coming around soon and we'll have to know what to buy for today.'

They sat together in a small room known as the office, and Hester started to write out a list of main courses that they might cook during the week. Thank goodness Cora was there to help, she thought fervently. Left to her own resources she could have succumbed to panic, but Cora was calm and methodical and her manner gave comfort. If the worst came to the worst, she could always repeat the same meals in exactly the same order when she was left to cope alone.

She was introduced to the two maids when they came to the kitchen for a cup of tea at ten-thirty. They stared at her, judging her appearance and comparing her small stature with the taller woman who had given out instructions that morning. Hester studied them in turn, wondering if they would follow her orders without question. Edith, the older of the two, looked confident and robust, while Kathy was pale and seemingly far more timid.

'How long have you been working here?' she asked.

'Four years,' said Edith.

'About one year, Ma'am,' said Kathy.

'I see.' Hester gestured towards two chairs as an invitation for them to be seated and began to pour the tea. 'I am not planning to make any changes at present,' she said. 'Both of you have been here long enough to know the routine, so I want you to continue as usual for the time being. If I want to make any changes later, I will let you know.'

The two murmured inaudible replies and Hester handed a cup to each. Correct or not, this was the protocol she would follow. The kitchen was her domain and she was going to make sure it was seen to be so. This end of the table must be recognised as the head, and she would rule over the teapot at times such as this.

'As you know, Mrs Wellerby is acting as my assistant until I have moved in. Please follow any instructions she gives as if they come from me.' Hester paused to think what else she ought to say. Nothing came to mind and a rather tense silence followed.

'Do you live close by?' she asked Edith.

'Two streets back,' came the answer.

'That's convenient for you. How about you, Kathy?'

'No, Ma'am. I have to come on the tram.'

'I see. Thank goodness the trams start early.'

The two maids did not linger over their tea. They escaped as soon as good manners would allow, as if they were eager to resume work, but they returned to the kitchen at twelve-thirty exactly. Edith already had her coat on and was starting to fasten the buttons.

'We have lunch now,' she declared belligerently. 'I always go home.'

This could be the first test of wills, thought Hester. She must tread carefully here and be firm if necessary.

'At what time do you return?' she asked mildly.

'We are entitled to a full hour.'

Hester glanced at the clock on the wall. 'Very well. I shall expect you to be punctual. What about you, Kathy, do you go home too?'

'No, Ma'am. I haven't got time to go all that way.' Kathy watched with regret as the other woman departed.

'You'll eat here in the kitchen, I suppose,' suggested Cora.

'Yes, Ma'am. Er — that is — not always.'

'We can share the table today. Mrs Carleton will probably take her lunch upstairs when she has the family here, but she can't do that yet — the place is empty.'

Kathy's pale face coloured with consternation. 'Er — no — no, thank you — er — Ma'am. I'll go out. I sometimes go to the Esplanade. I quite like eating my lunch outside.'

She went quickly to a nearby storeroom to retrieve her hat and coat and a small bag, then hurried in again and went out by the back door, giving a self-conscious nod to the others as she passed.

'She's a nervous little thing,' said Cora. 'You'll have to keep your eye on Edith, though. If she gets up to any tricks she'll have a bad influence on Kathy.'

By the time Harold called for Hester that afternoon she was feeling exceptionally tired. How could Cora face the stress of serving the evening meal with such good nature? she wondered. The older woman guessed her thoughts and rested a comforting hand on her shoulder.

'Of course you're tired,' she said. 'I'd've been surprised if you weren't. You've been trying to take in too much in too short a time. Besides that, you're out of practice. You haven't been running a household for weeks. You'll be fine once you get into a routine.'

★ ★ ★

The next day Hester started to clean the empty apartment. Her furniture would be delivered on Saturday, which gave her two days in which to prepare. They had chosen Saturday for the move because four of the residents went home to their families every weekend, which reduced the work load by a vast amount.

'Only six breakfasts and dinners,' Cora had declared breezily. 'Just like a normal family. By the time those other men come back on Monday you'll be going well.'

Hester fervently hoped so. She had not even met any of the residents yet, but Cora assured her they were all perfect gentlemen.

'They'll take to you, Hester. They fancy themselves to be a bit above the average, just because they earn good money, but they're all right. They'll appreciate your style. Apart from that, all they're interested in is good food served on time. That's what you have to concentrate on, punctuality. They want to know that breakfast will be ready so they can get to the office without rushing, and they don't want to sit about waiting for the evening meal when they come back.'

Hester gazed at the floor she had just scrubbed and rinsed. Routine was essential to keep the house running smoothly. She had written copious notes to remind herself how

Cora had timed her preparations yesterday, but she would need to add extra minutes to do the same tasks herself. She could not imagine herself dicing so many vegetables so quickly, despite Cora's coaching. Apart from that, there were so many other jobs being carried out by the maids that she had not yet witnessed. She would have to learn more about their doings once she could handle her own affairs efficiently.

She looked at the fob watch that was pinned to the bib of her apron and hastily emptied the bucket of dirty water. It was time for morning tea, and if she were to expect everybody else to be punctual she would have to hurry down.

Cora had already boiled the kettle and she poured the water into the teapot when Hester entered the kitchen.

'I was hoping you wouldn't forget the time,' she said. 'The girls will be here in half a minute. How are you getting on up there?'

'Quite well, thank you. It's much easier to clean when there's absolutely nothing in a room.'

'Yes, well mind you don't overdo it. You'll have time enough to do things later.'

The atmosphere seemed a little less tense at the table during the short break and Hester breathed an inward sigh of relief.

'I will be moving into the apartment on Saturday morning,' she said conversationally.

Edith immediately bristled. 'Saturday is my day off!'

Cora raised her eyebrows, while Kathy bowed her head and seemed to shrink in stature.

Hester looked at the defiant woman in surprise. 'I don't think the removal will make any difference,' she said. 'Breakfast will be prepared exactly the same way as this morning, and Mrs Wellerby will be here to look after the evening meal. You usually manage quite well on a Saturday, don't you, Kathy?'

'Yes, Ma'am,' came the whispered response.

'What about Sunday?' demanded Edith.

'I shall take over then. I'm sure you will offer advice if I have any problems. I believe Kathy has a day off on Sunday.'

'That's right.' Edith seemed mollified by the response and it was she who carried the cups and saucers to the sink when they all rose from the table. Cora raised her eyebrows again but she refrained from speaking and work continued peacefully.

Hester felt a stab of guilt when she went down to make herself ready for Harold's arrival.

'It seems terrible to leave you here to do all

this,' she said, watching Cora baste the meat and push the dish back into the oven. 'I should have found some way to — '

'Think nothing of it,' interrupted Cora. 'Look, this is nothing to me. I used to be rushed off my feet most of the time when I was working in the bar. There's no crowd racing in here, all demanding to be served at once.'

'But it's a long time since you had to do anything like that,' Hester demurred. 'It must be six years, no — seven.'

'Just over one year, that's all. I haven't lost my touch.' Cora turned to find Hester staring at her in bewilderment. 'It's not long since I gave my job up.'

'But surely — I mean, I never — '

Cora shrugged. 'We needed the money. But it paid off, didn't it? Look how well off we are now. But never let your father know I told you,' she hastened to add. 'He thought the situation was rather shameful and it always grieved him a great deal. He thought he should be the sole breadwinner.'

'I can imagine.' Hester knew well enough that pride had played a great role in her father's life. Cora must be a strong character to have overruled his objections and continued to work for so long after their marriage.

'Anyway,' said Cora complacently. 'We have everything we could possibly need now, and no debts anywhere. If Edmund could bring himself to admit it, he'd have to agree it was all for the best.'

When Hester returned to the Carleton household Muriel repeated Cora's advice about not overdoing it, and Hester assured her that she was feeling perfectly fit, not even as tired as she had been the previous day when she had not exerted herself so much.

'I think everything is working out beautifully,' she said.

Dorothy immediately spoke up. 'I don't want to go. I like it here.'

Harold gave a good-natured grunt. 'You'll like it when you see it,' he declared. 'It's a nice place. Besides, every holiday has to come to an end, so you'll have to go *somewhere*.' He turned to Hester. 'Which reminds me — you remember that funny old place on the cliffs, where we visited the old man on the way here?'

'Barnaby?' asked Hester. 'Yes, of course I remember.' A tremor of alarm surged through her. 'What's happened to him?'

'He's all right, but he's had to leave that old shack. There was a massive storm a few days ago and apparently more of the cliff fell down.' Harold wagged his finger at Dorothy. 'You see, even that nice old man had to move. He didn't want to either, but it was too dangerous for him to stay any longer.'

'I'm glad he left in time.' Hester gave a regretful sigh. 'Poor Barnaby. He loved that old place, but he always said it wouldn't last. I always hoped it would stay safe until after he had gone.'

'What about Percy?' asked Dorothy. 'What happened to the big bird?'

'He would have taken him to the new place. He wouldn't have left Percy,' replied Hester. Another thought struck her and she turned to Harold with surprise. 'How did you hear about that?'

'I get the Mountcliffe newspapers sent to me quite often, and it was on the front page. I have some business interests there, so I need to keep in touch.'

'I see.'

'I've got that copy in my briefcase,' added Harold. 'You can read all about it after dinner. Would you like to see all the papers I get from Mountcliffe?'

Hester shook her head. 'No, thank you. I've left there. I'd like to read about Barnaby, he's a dear old man, but I don't have any desire to know about anything else there.'

She went to her room to tidy herself for the evening meal, thinking sadly that her old life no longer had any connection with the present. Her visits to the rickety cabin on the cliffs had always been a delight. Thank goodness she had been able to persuade Harold to call there when he was driving them away on removal day. She had known it would be the last time she would go there to see Barnaby, and he had known it too.

Later she read that Barnaby had suffered a chest infection several days before the storm had struck, and the illness had helped to persuade him that it was time to move to a place where help was more readily available. He now resided at the Retired Seamen's Home at Mountcliffe and he had donated his entire collection of curios and souvenirs to a new museum that was due to open in the near future.

So Barnaby was no longer surrounded by his strange artifacts, and he would no longer be so close to his beloved sea. His lifestyle would be vastly different now. Hester folded the newspaper and drew herself up with renewed determination. The past was over and done with. She also had a new future — a bright new future. For the first time in her life she was in control of her own destiny and she would make a success of it. She could not have imagined such a rosy outlook. From Saturday onwards she would have both a secure home and a secure income. She would not have a care in the world.

6

The bustle on Saturday morning proved to be so exciting that even Dorothy forgot her former objections. She had started the day in a rebellious mood, but that had soon waned and she hurried outside to board the motor car as soon as Harold tooted the horn.

'Move along, you girls,' Muriel instructed when Susan had clambered in beside her sister. 'You'll have to sit very close together to make space for me.'

'Oh! Are you coming too, Aunt Muriel?'

'I most certainly am. We can't let your mother do everything by herself. You saw Mrs Barrett come, didn't you? She's going to look after everything here while I'm away.'

'I'll sit in the back with the girls,' said Hester. 'I'm smaller than you.'

'Well, I can't deny that.' Muriel turned to wave to her neighbour and her own children, then she climbed up into the front seat and Harold tooted again before he released the brake and they set off on the drive to St Kilda.

Breakfast had been served and cleared away by the time they reached Bella Casa.

Kathy opened the front door for them, blushing with nervousness at the sight of so many new faces.

'Good morning, Kathy,' said Hester. She made hasty introductions, which made Kathy blush more deeply than ever.

She bobbed a curtsey and managed a faint: 'Good morning.'

'I am going to show everybody the downstairs rooms,' said Hester. 'Then we will go upstairs. You continue just as you always do, Kathy. We won't interfere with your duties. The furniture van will be here fairly soon, but you won't have to do anything about that.'

'Thank you, Ma'am.' Kathy bobbed another curtsy and darted away.

'She's a scared little thing,' said Harold.

'Yes, she is shy, but she does her work well,' replied Hester. 'Let's go to see Cora first. She'll be in the kitchen.'

The two children had felt at ease with Cora since their first meeting and they greeted her with delight, but they were soon drawn to exploring their surroundings more closely. They had never been in such a large house before, or in such a spacious kitchen, and when they saw the dining-room and the other public rooms on the ground floor they stared in awe.

'This house is even better than Aunt Amelia's!' exclaimed Dorothy.

'It must certainly be a lot bigger,' said Muriel.

They went upstairs and the children gasped at their first glimpse of their new home. They ran from room to room, looking out of each window in turn, and Muriel nodded with approval.

'You should be very comfortable here, Hester. It is a lovely apartment. But there must be a lot of work involved, catering for so many people. Are you sure you're going to be able to cope with it all?'

'Perfectly sure,' replied Hester. 'I'm not an invalid, you know. I am perfectly fit now.'

'It's a big responsibility.'

'I know, but that doesn't worry me at all.' Hester had been kept awake for more than an hour last night by a niggling little fear that she might have taken on a greater task than she could handle, but she would not admit to that. Cora had faith in her and she must cling to that thought, should her courage falter.

'You're a tough little thing,' said Harold. 'Don't worry about her, Muriel. She'll cope all right.'

Minutes later a large wagon turned into the street and the removal began in earnest. The children were happy to see their own possessions again and they took a delight in helping to unpack the crates and unwrap some of the contents. Muriel undertook to wash the glasses and china before Hester put them away, while Harold busied himself supervising the two removal men, occasionally adding his muscles to ease heavier pieces into place. When everything had been carried upstairs and into the correct rooms the two workers drove away and Cora came up to see the results.

'Lunch,' she announced. 'I must say you're getting on very well, but you have to stop now for a while.' She turned to the children. 'My goodness, young ladies! Just look at your black hands. What have you been doing?'

'It's come off the newspapers, Aunt Cora.'

'Well, the first thing you have to do is get that washed off. Come with me, and mind where you're putting your hands in the meantime.'

During the afternoon the children went outside to play in the back garden and Harold left to deal with some of his own affairs. When he returned the beds had been made up and nearly all Hester's possessions had been put tidily away.

'My, my! You've done well.'

'I couldn't have done all this without you two,' said Hester gratefully. 'Thank you,

Muriel. And thank you, Harold. I don't know what I would have done without you.'

'You would have got it all done — just a bit slower, that's all,' responded Muriel. 'Now, is there anything else that needs to be done before we leave?'

'Not a thing. Thank you again.'

They went downstairs together and Harold asked to see the telephone. Hester took him into the small office and he noted the number of the telephone there before propping a business card up against the base of the instrument.

'Both my numbers are on there,' he declared. 'The number on the front is my office. You can always leave a message there with my secretary. I've written our home number on the back, just in case you've forgotten it.'

'Thank you.'

'Call me. Any time you need any help, call me.'

Both he and Muriel seemed reluctant to leave when they reached the front steps.

'I do hope you'll be all right,' said Muriel.

'Don't worry. Everything will be perfect.'

Harold took her hand and patted it in a fatherly fashion. 'Don't forget,' he said. 'If there's anything at all that we can do, call us on the telephone.'

'Don't wait for anything to go wrong,' added Muriel. 'I shall want to know how you are all getting along. So telephone.'

'Yes, I will. Thank you again.'

At last they departed. Hester closed the heavy front door and leaned against it with a sense of relief. It was good to know that at least a few people cared for her, but their concern had begun to feel somewhat overwhelming.

Cora came into the hall and chuckled with amusement. 'Finally left you to stand on your own two feet, have they? I've just poured water into the tea pot. I thought you might need another cup of tea by now.'

'Thank you, Cora. That is just what I do need. Are the children behaving themselves?'

'Like proper little angels. Come and sit down for a few minutes.'

It seemed no time at all before Cora suggested that Hester change her clothes.

'You'll want to feel your best when you meet the residents.'

The residents! Hester felt some of her confidence ebbing away, but that sensation was immediately followed by a tingle of excitement.

'Only five of them this evening,' said Cora comfortingly. 'And you won't have to say much. Put on a good dress so as to make a good impression. I'm not going to let you do any work in the kitchen today.' She tilted her head to one side and studied Hester's face for a moment. 'What are you thinking?'

Hester smiled. 'I was just thinking about Aunt Amelia. Thank goodness she took me under her wing. Nothing could be as bad as the first At Home I had to go through at Beach House.'

'Well, I'm glad she proved to be useful.'

The training at Beach House had also ensured that Hester had already learned the names of the residents. The first to arrive was a very young fair-haired man who stopped short at the sight of the stranger waiting in the hall. He stared in astonishment for a few seconds, then thrust out his hand.

'You must be Mrs Carleton. How do you do. I'm Adam Frost.'

'How do you do, Mr Frost.'

'It's a pleasure to meet you, it really is.' He eyed her up and down with obvious approval. 'I'm sure we'll get on very well. You're a much better choice than I dared hope.'

'I hope you will continue to think so,' replied Hester with dignity. 'Mrs Wellerby is still in charge of the kitchen today. Dinner will be served at the usual time.'

She watched him stride buoyantly along the hall and up the stairs. He must have come from a wealthy background, to be wearing such an expensive suit and to be in possession of such massive self-confidence at such a young age. She doubted that he had turned twenty as yet.

Francis Pulham and David Mitchell came together, middle-aged men who greeted her in a polite, but reserved, manner. They were the two who had given notice of leaving, but Hester gave them no special attention. If they changed their minds it would be a triumph for her, but she would make no open attempt to persuade them unless they raised the subject themselves.

Graham Best was a rather tubby well-groomed man with a full head of greying hair. He greeted Hester with courteous enthusiasm.

'I am very pleased to meet you, Mrs Carleton. I understand that you moved in today and that you will be in charge from now on.'

'I will be in charge as from tomorrow, Mr Best. But if there is anything I can do for you in the meantime, please let me know.'

'I don't need a thing, thank you, Mrs Carleton. I'm pleased to know that the changeover has been accomplished, and I'm sure that everything will go smoothly.'

The last to come was Stanley Jamieson, an

elderly man who reminded Hester of her Uncle Jeremy. He was a slight man with white hair and a gentle manner.

'It doesn't seem appropriate for me, as a mere tenant, to welcome you to Bella Casa,' he said. 'But on behalf of the residents I would like to say that I hope you will be comfortable here, Mrs Carleton. I also hope that you will find all the residents to be pleasant and co-operative.'

'Thank you, Mr Jamieson. I'm sure everything will go smoothly.'

'Yes, well we have had a lot of changes here lately, so I hope this will see the end of all that and we can all settle down again properly.' He started to move away then turned back as another thought occurred to him. 'By the way, I never take breakfast on a Sunday. I don't know if anyone has told you that, but the girls know. They won't set the table for tomorrow.'

'I see. Thank you for telling me, Mr Jamieson.'

When the five residents had taken their places in the dining-room and Kathy had carried in a large tray with bowls of soup, Hester took the children up to the apartment and tried to settle them for the night. Despite their tiredness they were still excited by the events of the day and Hester had to sit by their beds for longer than usual.

'I'm going to read a story to you now,' she said at last. 'When I have finished the story I'm going to my own room and there is to be no more talking tonight.'

She felt so weary when she finally retired to her bedroom that she sank onto the edge of the bed, wondering how she would find the energy to undress herself. There would be no difficulty in falling asleep tonight, she decided. She must make just one more effort; she must stand up again, hang her dress properly in the wardrobe and make sure that her clock would ring early in the morning. It would not do to be late.

★   ★   ★

The next day Hester went down to start work in the kitchen, leaving the children asleep. She hoped they would not panic when they awoke to find themselves alone in their new surroundings. Dorothy in particular always seemed nervous of change, but Susan was more happy-go-lucky and they had their own toys and possessions about them.

Cora had left oatmeal in a pan to soak overnight, and had written a cheerful note wishing Hester well. She smiled at the hasty sketch at the bottom of the paper, turning it over as instructed to find a list of jobs written on the back. If she forgot to do something, or did things in the wrong order, she had only herself to blame. She must find a good way of expressing thanks to Cora. She had done far more for her than anyone could have expected.

Preparations for breakfast were well in hand by the time Edith arrived, exactly two minutes before she was due.

'Good morning,' she said.

'Good morning, Edith. I think everything is organised, but if you notice anything I have missed, please tell me.'

'All right. There's only four for breakfast today. Usually there's five on Sundays. Did you know?'

'Yes, thank you. Mr Jamieson told me last night. Doesn't he *ever* have breakfast on a Sunday?'

'No.' Edith gave a disparaging sniff. 'He goes to church. Says he can't eat before Communion. He'll be back for dinner, though.'

When she was preparing to wash dishes later, Edith came across the note that Cora had left.

'Is this important?' she asked, picking it up by one corner and holding it towards Hester.

'No, not important, but I want to keep it.

You can read it if you like. It's from Mrs Wellerby.'

'Oh.' Not even glancing at the list, Edith placed the paper further away from the sink where it would be safe from splashes. Hester thought she might lighten the stilted atmosphere by showing her the drawing on the other side, but decided against it. Edith had shown little sense of humour so far, and she might even think the unflattering picture of a harassed woman was a caricature of herself.

The morning passed quickly and uneventfully, the only awkward moment occurring when Edith came to the kitchen for her morning break and found the children sitting at the table.

'Are they going to be in here a lot?' she asked.

'I will be here to keep watch over them,' answered Hester. 'You knew I had two daughters, didn't you?'

'Yes, but . . . ' Edith looked warily at the girls. 'We've never had children here before. I hope it doesn't mean — '

'You won't be expected to take responsibility for them,' said Hester, hoping this was not going to grow into another issue that would rankle with the other woman. Edith seemed to regard anything that happened as a reason to complain.

The children responded to introductions as

they had been taught, showing respect to an adult, but as soon as Edith left the room again Dorothy wrinkled her nose.

'I don't like her.'

'Neither do I,' said Susan immediately.

Hester held back a sigh. 'Edith is just not used to children, that's all. It will be all right when you get to know each other better.'

Dinner was served promptly at twelve-thirty. Hester put two small portions on a tray and took Dorothy and Susan upstairs just beforehand.

'I want you to eat your dinner up here today,' she told them. 'We'll have it together tomorrow.'

'How long are we supposed to stay up here by ourselves?' asked Dorothy plaintively.

'Come down when you've finished, but leave the plates here. We'll go out this afternoon and explore. Perhaps we'll go to the beach.'

The two women ate their meal in the kitchen when Edith had cleared the dining-room. Edith then set about washing the used dishes and utensils, and it was not long before she announced, 'I've done everything now. Dining-room's set for the morning. I always go home when that's done.'

'Very well. I will see you in the morning then, Edith.'

Hester watched her hurry from the kitchen, thinking that of the two servants, Edith had the easier life. It seemed unfair that Kathy should have to stay all day on a Saturday because the main meal was served in the evening, but then perhaps seniority should bring some kind of reward. Hester shrugged and took one last look around to make sure that everything was tidy and safe. Now she had time to herself. At nine o'clock she would place the supper tray in the sitting-room, but until then she was free to do whatever she liked. She could now devote herself to the children and she would take them out to enjoy the good weather.

★   ★   ★

Kathy arrived before Edith the next morning, even though she lived so much further away, and she immediately began to make herself useful.

'Only five of them have porridge on a Monday,' she said, placing bowls handy to the pot. 'Usually, that is.'

'Does everybody have a cooked breakfast every day?' asked Hester.

Kathy flushed and hesitated. 'Er — yes. Mr Jamieson often has his eggs boiled, but he always seems to like them fried on a Monday.

The others like fried eggs most days, but they don't always want sausages. Mr Adams always has meat *and* sausages with his.'

Making breakfast for eight caused far more bustle than before and Hester was relieved that two of the residents had not yet returned from their weekend away. The baker's cart arrived in time to provide fresh bread for breakfast, and Edith came in soon afterwards, having left just enough time to don her apron and wash her hands before sounding the gong. She and Kathy went about their duties briskly and Hester began to relax. Tomorrow she would have to cater for all ten residents, but she would be well practised by then.

All the main dishes had been served when the two children came in.

'We've just seen lots and lots of men,' cried Susan excitedly.

'Only three,' Dorothy corrected.

'They were all in a big hurry.'

'Yes, but one of them stopped,' said Dorothy. 'He said we were very pretty little girls.'

'I hope you didn't get in anybody's way,' said Hester.

'No, we stood right back against the wall.'

'Good. They will be rushing off to work whenever you see them in the mornings,' said Hester. 'So you must keep out of their way.'

'Does that mean we can't come down the stairs when they're there?' asked Susan.

'No, this is your home now, so you can go up and down the stairs. But this is their home, too, and they don't want to be bothered with little girls, especially when they're in a hurry, so you must never be a nuisance to anybody.' Hester hugged them to take the sting out of her words. 'Now then, would you like a nice boiled egg for breakfast this morning?'

Edith came in with a loaded tray, took everything off it and went out again without speaking. Moments later Kathy came in and she smiled at the children with genuine pleasure. As soon as she had put her tray down she turned to the girls and stretched out her hands.

'Hello, my dears! I've been waiting to meet you properly.'

They each grasped a hand, warming to her instantly.

'You must be Dorothy,' she said. 'And you must be Susan. Mrs Wellerby told me all about you.'

'Aunt Cora,' prompted Hester as the girls gazed up with mystified expressions. 'Girls, this is Kathy.'

'Your Aunt Cora told me a lot about you,' said Kathy.

'Aunt Cora is nice, too,' announced Susan. 'Yes, she is. Very nice.'

Edith came in again and Kathy gave a guilty start. 'I must get on with my work now, darlings.'

The girls moved away as she started to empty the tray, but they continued to watch her. Susan's eyes widened and her hand went up to her mouth.

'Oh, Kathy, you've got a big dirty mark right on the front of your nice white apron.'

Kathy looked down at the large greasy stain and her face flooded with colour. 'Oh, Ma'am!' she exclaimed. 'I'm sorry.'

'First time on, too,' said Edith disparagingly.

Hester spoke quickly before Kathy could become more flustered. 'Accidents will happen. You'd better take that apron off straight away and we'll do something about that stain before it sets.'

'No! Er — that is — I'll just finish in the dining-room first. I'm sorry, Ma'am.' Kathy fled and Edith gave an expressive shrug.

'She can be a very silly girl sometimes.'

Hester went across to soothe the children.

'Kathy's embarrassed, that's all,' she murmured. 'Don't worry about her. She didn't do it on purpose and we can soon get it clean again.'

Kathy still looked upset when she returned to the kitchen. 'I'm sorry, Ma'am,' she said again. 'I'll take it home. I can wash it at home.'

'There's no need for that,' said Hester. 'Just take it off.'

Kathy obeyed with trembling hands and Hester took a closer look. 'Yes, it's grease. Bicarbonate of soda will soak up the worst of that, then it can go into the laundry basket. Go and get a clean apron out of the storeroom. The laundryman calls today, doesn't he?'

She whisked a pan off the stove and scooped two eggs into eggcups. They had boiled longer than she had planned so they would be harder than the girls liked. What a lot of fuss about a simple mishap! Poor Kathy had looked so fearful. Perhaps she had suffered a great deal from Edith's caustic tongue over the past year.

The butcher and the vegetable man came only fifteen minutes apart in the middle of the morning. Hester felt a glow of accomplishment when she had dealt with them, and decided that while she was in that mood she would talk to Edith about the daily cleaning duties. She waited until the morning break was over then asked her to wait behind.

'Edith, you must have started work when

the original owners were here,' she began. 'I understand that things have not been running so smoothly since then.'

'Smoothly!' retorted Edith. 'It's been a madhouse. A lot of men left. I'd have left meself if I didn't live so close.'

'Well, we must make sure we restore the original standards,' said Hester. 'Would you please take time to start writing a list of the duties that have to be carried out?'

Edith flushed. 'That's not part of my duties,' she protested.

'I realise that, but — ' Hester noticed that for once Edith was avoiding her gaze. When she had stated that she was going home and was entitled to a full hour for lunch she had stared directly into her eyes as if defying her to question that fact. It had been the same when she left early on Sunday. Now she looked distinctly uncomfortable and was staring at the carpet as if she were timid Kathy rather than her own emphatic self.

'I haven't finished my rooms,' she mumbled.

There was more to her response than mere rebellion, decided Hester, but this was not the time to pursue the matter.

'We'll leave it for now,' she said quietly. 'There's no rush. But please think about it during the day. Try to remember how things used to be done.'

Hester's thoughts returned to the problem several times as the hours passed and she finally decided on a little test. They were all in the kitchen and the two servants were setting out dishes for dinner when she spoke over her shoulder.

'Bring the vegetable list over for me please, Edith. It's on the side table. I want to add something.'

Edith took one step towards the table, where two sheets of paper lay side by side, then seemed to change her mind. She moved back and nudged Kathy with her elbow, giving a significant jerk of her head, and it was Kathy who brought the list. Hester added one more item and decided on her strategy for the next day.

Again she waited until the morning break had ended. 'Just a moment, Edith,' she said. 'Let's go into the office, just for a minute or two. You can tell me how things used to be, and I'll write it down.'

The relief that crossed Edith's face confirmed Hester's suspicions. She was sure by now that Edith could barely read, and her writing would be poor and slow — if she could write at all.

They went into the office and Hester seated herself at the desk where she had already placed a blank sheet of paper.

'What's the most important thing you remember about the original system?' she asked, picking up a pencil and writing a heading.

Edith's confidence returned as she began to recall the routine that had produced such good results in the past, and Hester thankfully jotted a series of notes.

'Thank you, Edith. If you think of anything else later, I'd be very glad if you would tell me.'

The other looked at her with greater friendliness than before. 'Are you really going to do all that, like it used to be?'

Hester smiled. 'Yes, with your help, of course. If we find better ways of doing anything we can make changes later, but there's no point in changing a routine that's working well.'

'You're not like those last women,' said Edith with a sudden rush of openness. 'They wouldn't have cleaned their own place like you've done up there. They'd have got us to do it — never mind all the work that was left undone down here.'

'I see.' It would never have occurred to Hester to order the staff to clean her private section of the house. It really must have been convenience that had persuaded Edith to stay.

'We are all working toward the same

purpose,' she said at last. 'Mr Hetherington is hoping that the residents who gave notice will change their minds. We'll have to try and make sure they do.'

'Yes, Ma'am.' For the first time Edith used the title and Hester felt an inner glow of satisfaction. It sounded as though the woman took pride in her work and she would do her best to please if the house were run methodically and fairly.

'The food is better for a start,' Edith suddenly declared. 'That last woman never did anything properly. She never even made a proper pudding. She'd buy a sponge cake and pour white sauce over it.'

'I see.'

Now that she had started to unburden herself Edith was eager to continue. 'She'd come in late and she was always in a rush to get away again. Said she had work to do somewhere else.'

'Ah. That would be the temporary housekeeper,' said Hester, remembering that Mr Hetherington had sent his own servant to keep this house running.

'She was better than the one before, though. That one lived in, but often enough she never even got down in time for breakfast. And we had to leave things undone to make sure the men got fed at all. You should have seen the stove! Black-leading? When was that ever done?'

'You must have all worked very hard to make the kitchen look so nice when I came to see it.'

'Yes, well I must say that was one thing in her favour, that last one, I mean. She did like a clean place, even if she didn't do a lot of real cooking.'

Hester set about her next task with increased vigour. This was going to be an enormous success. It was good to have had the air cleared so quickly. Now Edith would be working with her rather than against her and everything would go with a swing. Why had she been so nervous at the start? She was going to make a real success of this. Nothing could hold her back now.

7

The first changes began the next day, when Edith produced the caps and aprons that used to be worn for serving meals. The two servants obviously liked the different uniform and would be proud to wear it. Hester came to a quick decision.

'Very nice,' she said. 'Yes, I agree, I think you should use those when you're waiting on tables. They look very smart. You can start whenever you like.'

'I'll iron them,' said Edith. 'They haven't been used for ages.'

Hester nodded, pleased that the older woman had volunteered to do something outside the range of her usual daily tasks.

'Thank you. I'm sure the residents will appreciate it. They will notice the difference immediately.'

A few minutes before Edith was likely to rush away for her midday break Hester called both women down to the kitchen.

'I haven't seen you preparing anything for lunch,' she said. 'You are entitled to have lunch here. Did you know that?'

Kathy immediately flushed and looked

down at the floor, while Edith tilted her chin.

'I have more important things to do,' she declared. 'I don't want to waste time cutting bread and clearing up and all that kind of thing.'

'Very well, Edith. It's your choice. There's nothing to keep you here if you prefer to go out. But you can always change your mind, you know, if you want to eat here any day.'

'It's not likely. But thank you.'

'You can leave now if you like. It's almost time.'

Edith hastened away at once and Hester turned to Kathy.

'I think you must have been bringing your own food with you, haven't you?'

The girl coloured again, apparently too embarrassed to make any response.

'If you work a full day you are entitled to have lunch here, Kathy. It's part of your wages, you know.'

Kathy's blush seemed to deepen, but her eyes lit up and Hester thought she detected a deep relief.

'Thank you, Ma'am.'

'I'm going up to my apartment now. If you want anything for lunch today, help yourself. You can eat here, or take it outside, whichever you like.'

Thank you, Ma'am. Thank you very much.'

'You know where everything is, probably better than I do. So I'll leave you to get on with it.'

Hester left Kathy standing there and went up to her own quarters. She was fairly certain that the young girl had been eating only a skimpy lunch each day. Perhaps that was why she always looked so pale and thin. She was a shy girl, and no doubt she had always been too timid to claim her entitlements, had she even known about them. Edith would have enlightened her, would have made sure she received all due benefits, had she been there at the right time to notice that Kathy was missing the meal, but Edith always seemed so anxious to get away. What was it that was so important? Perhaps she had a sick relative at home. Hester shrugged. She would not pry, but perhaps Edith would talk more about herself when they knew each other better.

*   *   *

Friday brought the first day to collect rent. Hester sat in her office waiting for the residents to arrive and hoping that none of them would try to avoid paying on time. Until today young Adam Frost had hurried back from wherever he went to work and come in before any of the other men. He was already more than half an hour later than usual and she hoped that was not a bad sign.

Francis Pulham was the second person to come. He stood beside the desk, a folded newspaper in his left hand. He always seemed to have a newspaper with him and he spent most of his evenings in the sitting-room, eager to discuss the news with whoever else came in.

'Good evening, Mrs Carleton.'

'Good evening, Mr Pulham.'

He handed her the money and accepted the receipt with a nod, but did not leave immediately.

'Is there anything else I can do for you, Mr Pulham?'

'Yes. I gave notice that I intended to leave at the end of this week.'

'Yes, I did know that, Mr Pulham.'

'Has anybody else reserved my room?'

'Not yet, Mr Pulham.'

'I see. I have been reconsidering my plans.' He looked searchingly at her expression then continued: 'Would it be in order for me to withdraw that notice?'

'You mean you would like to stay, Mr Pulham? Yes, that can be arranged. I'm pleased to hear that you would like to remain here.'

'For a little time at least.' Mr Pulham

112

seemed unwilling to commit himself to a more permanent arrangement.

'Thank you, Mr Pulham. I will inform Mr Hetherington.'

He nodded again and departed, to be quickly replaced by Mr Jamieson. The elderly man gave a slight bow and handed Hester a sealed envelope.

'I'm sure you'll find that to be correct, Mrs Carleton.'

'Thank you, Mr Jamieson. Would you like to wait for your receipt?'

'No, no. Just leave it with my mail on the table in the hall. Thank you, Mrs Carleton.' He turned to leave and caught sight of the two children hovering just beyond the door. 'Good evening, young ladies.'

'Good evening, Sir,' they chimed in unison. They had become more accustomed to meeting residents as they moved about the house, but they did not know their names yet. They waited for him to go then scurried into the office.

'Can we stay in here?' asked Susan.

'Yes, if you can be quiet when the gentlemen come in.'

When Mr Mitchell arrived he also announced that he wanted to withdraw his notice.

'I have been very satisfied this week. If

everything continues to run smoothly I'll be happy to stay for a much longer period.'

'Thank you, Mr Mitchell. If there is anything that displeases you, please let me know.'

When he had disappeared up the staircase, Hester hugged her two children. 'Everybody seems to be very happy,' she said. 'Isn't that nice?'

'Does that mean we're going to stay here for ever and ever?' asked Dorothy.

'Well, for a long time, anyway.' Hester wished the children would truly settle so that their new surroundings would feel like home. Their foremost concern just now was the fact that they could no longer claim her constant attention. She had reminded them more than once that they were lucky to live in the place where she worked; some children had to wait an entire day before they could see their mothers again, added to which they did not live in such nice houses. Dorothy and Susan certainly appreciated the large garden and their spacious rooms. Edith now acknowledged their presence with a brief greeting so they were not so wary of her, and they preferred to eat their evening meal in the kitchen where there was company, rather than upstairs in the apartment. Thank goodness for Kathy. She always made them feel welcome and she chatted with them whenever she had the opportunity.

After eating their dinner that evening the children went upstairs to look for a toy and came back to the kitchen brimming with self-importance.

'We have to give you this,' announced Dorothy, holding out some money.

'He said he was Mr Frost. He said . . . ' Susan paused to remember the exact words. 'He said 'Tell your Mama I'm sorry I was late back today. I never like to be late for my dinner.' And he said it didn't matter about the — er — '

'The receipt?' prompted Hester.

'Yes.' Dorothy nudged her sister. 'Tell Mama what else he did.'

Susan held out a clenched hand and slowly opened it. 'He gave me this. And he gave one to Dorothy, too.'

Hester looked at the penny with a sense of foreboding. 'Oh dear. He shouldn't really give you things.'

'Why not?' asked Susan.

'Well, it's not proper.' Hester was at a loss to explain. No doubt the young man meant well and he could afford it. But it was not a habit that should be allowed to continue. It was surprising that Dorothy had lingered long enough for him to talk to her and give her

115

anything at all. She had always been so shy before.

'Have any of the other gentlemen given you anything?' she asked.

'Only one,' said Dorothy reluctantly.

Hester took a deep breath. 'What did he give you?'

'A sweetie.'

'Only a little one,' protested Susan.

'I see. Who was it?'

'The one who said we were pretty.'

'The fattest one,' added Dorothy.

That must be Mr Best, decided Hester. She would have to speak to him at the earliest opportunity.

'We have to be polite,' said Susan. 'Don't we?'

'Yes, you have to be polite,' agreed Hester. 'But you should say no thank you.'

'We did,' declared Dorothy. 'But he said it would make him very happy. It was only a little sweetie, and we ate all our dinner.'

Kathy broke the tension, bustling in with a tray of dirty plates. 'Did you find that little dolly you were telling me about?' she asked.

'No, we didn't go all the way up,' replied Dorothy. 'We came back to give some money to Mama.'

'I see. That would have been the rent from Mr Frost, I suppose.' Kathy noticed Hester's serious expression and turned away to occupy herself with the tray.

Hester stooped to speak softly to the children. 'You must always be polite to the gentlemen, but try to stay out of their way. And if anybody gives you anything — anything at all — you must be sure to tell me. And you must *never* go into any of the gentlemen's rooms. Do you understand?'

'Why not?' asked Susan.

Hester groped quickly for a satisfactory answer. Her own parents had always insisted that she must never talk to strangers, but the residents could hardly be regarded as strangers.

'Because young ladies must not go into a gentleman's bedroom,' she said. 'And all those rooms are bedrooms.'

They nodded and Dorothy held up her penny again. 'Can I keep it?'

Hester gave each of the girls a quick hug. 'Yes, you can keep the pennies. We'll pop out for a little while tomorrow afternoon and you can spend them.'

Mr Hetherington called the next morning to collect the rent and to give Hester money to pay for purchases and the wages for herself and the other women. He looked around at the hall and glanced up the stairs as if to check that the cleaning had been done properly, then led the way to the office and indicated a chair that stood against the wall.

'Bring that closer and sit down.'

'No thank you, Mr Hetherington. I prefer to stand.'

He opened his mouth as if to repeat the invitation, then changed his mind and merely shrugged. 'Please yourself.' He seated himself behind the table and began to study the account book that had been placed ready for inspection.

'Everything looks to be in order,' he said. 'And you have persuaded both of those clients to change their minds and stay. Congratulations.'

'Thank you, Mr Hetherington.'

'What about the staff? Are they doing everything to your satisfaction?'

'They have been very co-operative and industrious, Mr Hetherington.'

'Have you met with any problems at all that we need to discuss?'

'No problems, Mr Hetherington.'

'Well, in that case I will get on my way again. You seem to have dealt with everything in a satisfactory manner. I must say I am pleased to have my own housekeeper back again. My home feels more like home now.'

Hester smiled and he rose slowly to his feet. 'Well, good-bye then, Mrs Carleton. I hope everything continues to run smoothly. I'll call again at the same time next week.'

Hester saw him out, glad that his visit had been so brief. He had done nothing to cause her to dislike him, had not said or done anything out of place, but she did not feel at ease in his presence. The only explanation for her strange reaction must be that he so strongly resembled her cousin's husband. The men looked alike and both carried themselves with a pompous air. It was years since Cecil had made unwelcome overtures to her, but the incident still rankled.

She counted out four two-shilling pieces, one shilling, three sixpences and six pennies for her wages and put the money into a pocket under the waistband of her skirt. The weight of the coins gave her a sense of prosperity and she hummed a popular tune as she locked the rest of the money away. At last she had money of her own! She could start repaying her debt immediately.

★   ★   ★

Hester allowed the children to take their grandfather for a tour of the house when he and Cora came for afternoon tea on Sunday. By the time he had seen everything the kettle had boiled and the tea was ready to be served.

'Well, I must say you seem to have fallen on your feet,' said Edmund. 'But are you sure it's not too much for you, Hester? It's a big responsibility and you haven't had Cora's experience.'

'I'm managing far better than anyone could have expected,' answered Hester. 'Don't worry, Father. Cora helped me a great deal and everything is going well.'

She had even found time to make a few small cakes for the occasion. They chatted about inconsequential matters until the children had eaten their share, then Hester sent Dorothy and Susan to play in the back garden so that the adults could talk more freely.

'Right then,' said Cora, as forthright as ever. 'How is everything really?'

'Everything is going very well,' replied Hester. 'It really is. Look, I've even sorted all my books and put them on the shelves.'

'There has to be something that's bothering you,' declared Cora. 'You wouldn't be human if you could just walk into a place like this and not find something that you're not quite sure about. Come on, we're good friends. Isn't there any little thing that you'd like to discuss?'

'Well, yes, there is one thing,' admitted Hester. 'Actually, I've been waiting to talk to someone about it.' She described how the two residents had given a sweet and a penny to each child and how she had not known what to do about it.

'Am I being too cautious? I don't want to make them feel afraid, but on the other hand I don't know if . . . ' Not knowing how to finish the sentence she let her voice trail away.

'What do you think?' she asked when there was no immediate response. 'Is it right for residents to do that kind of thing? I don't want the children to have too much. Besides, they might even come to *expect* gifts from everybody.'

'It's natural to want to give little treats to children,' said Cora. 'Especially when they're such well-behaved children like Dorothy and Susan.'

Edmund nodded in agreement. 'Did you say anything to those two men?'

'I was going to, then I decided to wait and see what happened rather than make an issue of it so soon. Besides, I wanted to talk to somebody else about it first.'

Edmund considered for a moment. 'I think you did the right thing. If the children always tell you when someone gives them something you will know what is happening. If it

121

happens too often, tell the men that you don't approve. They are your children, and you are the one who decides what they should or should not have.'

'That's right,' agreed Cora.

During the pause that followed Hester went across to the window to see what the children were doing outside. Dorothy was running along the garden path, bowling her hoop with ease. On the lawn Susan was struggling to master the same skill, her brow furrowed with concentration.

Edmund went to stand beside Hester and he smiled at the sight below. 'They seem to have grown, just in these last few weeks. It's a pity I missed their very early years, Hester. I hope you're going to stay close at hand from now on so that I can see you and the children from time to time.'

'I certainly don't intend to go through another removal just yet,' laughed Hester.

'Good. It's a big garden. Who looks after all that?'

'There's a gardener. He comes twice a week.'

Cora came to join them at the window. 'The girls certainly are growing. What have you done about a school for Dorothy?'

Hester turned to her in consternation. 'School!'

Cora shrugged. 'Well, yes, school. Dorothy must be close to six. You can't leave it much longer. She'll have to start this year.'

'Oh dear. I hadn't even thought about it.' Hester's hands went up to cup her flushed cheeks. 'I can't imagine Dorothy at school,' she said at last. 'She won't want to go. She's so shy amongst strangers. She won't like it.'

'You can't let that bother you,' said Cora. 'It's the law. Most children start when they're only five. When they're six you have to send them whether they like it or not.'

'I shouldn't worry too much about it,' said Edmund calmly. 'You were a shy little thing, Hester, but you managed all right — did quite well in the end. Besides, Dorothy has got used to being with new people now.'

'There must be a school fairly close,' said Cora. 'You'll have to go and see the Headmaster. Do you want me to go with you?'

For an instant Hester was tempted to accept the offer, then she shook her head. They were her children. She would take responsibility for them. Besides, her own husband had been a schoolmaster at Fellmont College. If she could chat to the Principal of an impressive place like that, she could certainly speak to the Headmaster of a small public school without losing her composure.

'No, I'll manage by myself, thank you. It's just that I've had so many other things to think about I just never gave it a thought. I'll do something about it fairly soon.'

'Well, don't leave it too long,' responded Cora. 'You don't want someone from the Truancy Board or somewhere coming round here and asking why Dorothy's not in school. Someone will report you, you know, if you don't do something about it soon. You could take a bet on that.'

Two days later the telephone rang for the first time. Hester took a deep breath and approached it warily. Despite the previous practice her hand trembled as she lifted the instrument.

'Hello. This is Bella Casa.'

'Hello there, Hester,' came a strong male voice. 'I assume the building is still standing and you haven't poisoned any of the customers.'

'Oh, Harold! How nice to hear from you.'

'Well, we hadn't heard from you, so we assumed that you didn't need any help.'

'I'm sorry I didn't contact you. I just seem to have been too busy to think of anything outside this place.'

'That's hardly surprising. Anyway, we

thought we would all visit you this weekend. The children are curious. They want to know where you live.'

'Oh!' Hester blanched at the thought of his four noisy children blundering up the stairs.

'Don't worry. I'll keep my lot outside,' said Harold. 'We thought we'd come to see how you were getting along and take you out somewhere for a change. How about Sunday afternoon?'

The children were excited to learn that they would soon see their relatives again, and Hester found her own enthusiasm mounting during the following days. For one thing, she admitted to herself, it would give her great satisfaction to prove just how well she was coping with her new life. After dinner on Sunday the girls waited by the window, and as soon as they saw the motor car draw up outside they hurried down to greet the family.

Everybody had alighted from the vehicle by the time Hester reached the front garden, and Muriel came up the path to meet her.

'There's no need to ask how you are,' she said gaily, giving Hester a kiss on the cheek. 'You're looking wonderful. Tell me, have the girls got a bathing suit?'

'A bathing suit?' gasped Hester. 'Oh, no!'

'Don't sound so shocked.' Muriel laughed and put an arm around Hester's shoulder.

'Lots of people bathe in the sea here, so you don't need to worry about what anyone will say. Anyway, I guessed that they might not have one, so I brought some extra ones along. They might be a little bit big for Susan, but that's better than being too small, eh?' She laughed again. 'I don't suppose you have one either?'

'Oh, Muriel! No.'

'Well, I'm afraid I don't have one your size.'

'I'm sorry, Muriel, but even if you did have one I couldn't possibly wear it. I'm not even sure that Dorothy and Susan . . . '

'Don't spoil their fun. Look, we're all going to the beach. I hope you don't mind having to sit by yourself while we go into the sea.'

'I won't mind a bit. I used to sit on the sand a lot while the children played at Thorn Bay.'

'Good. And maybe you will come into the water with us next time.'

Muriel turned back towards the motor car, apparently not expecting a response to that remark. Hester made sure the front door was properly closed then went to the gate to receive hugs from her nieces and nephews.

'How are you going to fit everybody into the motor car?' asked Susan when the first excitement was over.

'Fit you in?' replied Harold. 'We're not

going to drive anywhere. We haven't lost the use of our legs yet. No, we're going to leave it here and walk to the beach. Here you are, help us to carry things.'

They soon found themselves amongst a crowd of people who had travelled from Melbourne by train, and when they reached the beach they had to walk quite a distance to find a space that Harold thought was sufficient for their needs. The children immediately started digging in the sand while Harold erected a sunshade and spread a rug for the adults to sit upon. Hester looked askance at the men and women who were sporting in the water. A few were actually walking on the beach in their scanty garments, even holding hands, and one man had his arm around the waist of his female companion. Hester had read in the newspapers that mixed bathing had become a common practice, and she remembered that many Council members and church officials were strongly opposed to the trend.

Muriel chuckled. 'Bathing will soon be an acceptable thing to do,' she said. 'Mark my words, Hester, everybody will be doing it before long.'

'I'm not sure about that. I can't imagine myself disrobing like that.'

'Disrobing!' Harold chortled with amusement. 'You spent too much time with that old-fashioned aunt, Hester. But don't worry, we'll soon bring you up to date. You'll soon be as modern as we are.'

The idea of changing into a bathing suit and going into the water seemed daring and strange to Dorothy and Susan, but they soon became infected by the enthusiasm of the others. Hester watched with mixed feelings as they went to the bathing wagon. They were growing in many ways; their self-confidence had increased almost beyond belief since they had come to live in this new place.

The other children emerged from the wagon first and ran into the sea. Two or three minutes later Dorothy and Susan came hand in hand down the steps, closely followed by their aunt. Dorothy stopped abruptly at the water's edge and backed away quickly before an oncoming wavelet could reach her feet, but Susan continued on without a sign of hesitation. They looked alike, but they were so different, thought Hester. Dorothy was extremely timid, whereas Susan had always been talkative and adventurous.

At last Muriel persuaded Dorothy to wade in. Memories began to crowd into Hester's mind and she smiled as she recalled the day when she had walked on the beach at

Mountcliffe with Neville and Bruce. She had needed some urging before she had taken off her boots and stepped into a rock pool. What a day that had been! Neville and Bruce had been most insistent that she join them in the water and she had stayed in long after her feet had grown too cold for comfort.

Bruce . . . why hadn't he contacted her? He had been so considerate and helpful when little William died. And then there was all the horrible business that followed. It had been a terrible time. How could she have borne it without Bruce's support? Would he answer her letter? She was longing to hear from him again. Having to tell everyone her new address had given her the perfect excuse to write to him. He should receive her letter tomorrow morning.

'My, my! You're having serious thoughts.'

Hester looked up at the sound of Harold's voice. She was relieved to see that he had dressed before joining her again. It would take a long time for her to adapt to this new habit of wearing so little on the beach. Aunt Amelia would be horrified at the scenes around her.

'Hello, Harold.'

'You were looking very serious just now.'

'I was just thinking of all the people I have to write to — to give them my new address.'

'Ah, yes.'

Hester looked around and saw that they would not be disturbed for a little while. 'Harold, I was hoping I would have chance to talk to you alone for a few minutes. I want to start paying off my debt straight away. What would be the best way for me to do it? Should I send you a cheque every week?'

He shook his head. 'No, Hester. I couldn't possibly take your hard-earned money.'

'But I don't want to feel indebted to anybody. I must be independent.'

'That's the very reason why I can't take it.' Harold sat down beside her. 'Look, Hester, you've got to get some savings behind you. You need security. Until you've got a really good nest egg you can't be really independent.'

'But . . . '

'Hester, you've got a good place to live and a wage coming in. But suppose something happened?'

Hester flinched. 'What could happen?'

'You never know. Suppose the owner of that place suddenly decided to sell? It went cheap after the trouble in the Nineties, didn't it? If he suddenly needed money he might have to sell. And what if the new owners wanted to run it themselves — get rid of all the staff and let their own family do the work?

Or convert it into separate flats and not provide any services?'

'Oh dear.'

Harold patted her hand. 'I don't want to frighten you, but you should be prepared for any kind of emergency. Just remember this — a crisis only comes to those who are unprepared. So, you need a nest egg.'

Hester had not allowed herself to think of such a possibility as the business failing or changing hands and the idea cast a shadow over the outing. Her trepidation was soon brushed aside, however. The Carletons were determined to enjoy the afternoon to the full, and it was not long before they set off in search of more excitement. Harold placed their belongings in a depository so that they would be free of encumbrances, then suggested a visit to an ice cream cart.

He was as boisterous and noisy as a child and Hester could not help but compare him with his brother. Gerald had placed so much value on dignity, and he had demanded such quiet behaviour it was no wonder Dorothy had become more and more withdrawn. Gerald had never really played with his children, whereas Harold enjoyed being with his offspring and even encouraged them to be exuberant.

Muriel chuckled when she noticed that

Hester was watching his antics. 'Does Harold embarrass you?'

'Not in the least,' answered Hester quickly. 'I was just thinking how different he is from Gerald. You'd never believe they were brothers.'

'I think Harold is making up for being so poor in the past. He loves spending money, especially on the children.'

'It's not just that he spends money,' said Hester. 'It's the way he behaves. Harold *enjoys* his children.'

'Yes. Well, as he says, they're only young once. You've got to make the most of it.'

When the ice creams were finished and sticky fingers had been wiped clean with handkerchiefs and spit they walked to another stretch of beach where the children rode on Shetland ponies, then they went to an amusement park where Harold bought tickets for the Big Wheel. Dorothy and Susan squealed with excitement as they began the first circuit and Hester gasped with the thrill of gradually rising. Moments later she dared to look down and she gazed in wonder at the scene below. She thought she had never been so high from the ground and she had certainly never seen the world from such a vantage point.

They ended the day with a meal at a café

and all the children were tired but content when they returned to Bella Casa. Towels and other belongings were stowed away in the motor car, then hugs and kisses were exchanged and the Carleton family climbed into the vehicle. Harold was about to start the engine when Adam Frost hurried out of the house, calling to attract his attention.

'You've got a Silver Ghost!' he exclaimed as he came out to the footpath.

Harold paused, always ready to respond to an appreciative audience. 'That's right. Latest model,' he said proudly.

The two women exchanged amused glances and waited patiently while the men discussed technical points. At last Harold started the engine and everybody waved as he drove away towards the main road.

'I saw that motor waiting out here this afternoon and I wondered whose it was,' said Adam.

'It belongs to our aunt and uncle,' said Susan proudly. 'We've been for miles and miles in it.'

'My word, you're lucky. I'd like to have a ride in it.' Adam turned to Hester. 'Your relatives made a good choice. That's a fine motor. The best.'

'Harold always does like to be up to date.'

Adam nodded. 'I'm going to get the best,

too. Father won't agree to me having any motor car at all just yet, but before long he won't have any say in it. As soon as I reach my majority I'll come into my inheritance and the first thing I'll do is buy myself the latest and best model on the market.'

He strode jauntily away towards the house and Hester smiled down at the children. 'Did you enjoy yourselves today?'

They both nodded enthusiastically.

'Can we do it again?' asked Susan.

'Not everything. That was a special day today. But I expect Uncle Harold will bring your cousins to see you again fairly soon.'

'They're lucky,' said Dorothy. 'I wish Uncle Harold was our father.'

Hester ushered them in through the gateway, utterly lost for words. What could she possibly say in response to that?

8

The next day, mindful of Cora's warning, Hester took the children for a walk, heading first to the Council Offices. The clerk at the front desk proved to be a helpful man and he not only told Hester the location of the nearest school, but gave her a list of other addresses she might need, including the library, dentists and the local hospital. She would visit the school tomorrow, she decided, but the next two days seemed exceptionally busy and it was Thursday before she set out alone to make enquiries.

She could hear children shouting and laughing before she reached the corner of the road where the school stood. Obviously it was time for play, for the paved yard was full of children. A shrill voice was shouting in rage as she neared the front gate.

'You bastard. I'll show you. Take that, you little bugger.'

She stopped short, shocked by the language, and looked through the railings in time to see a young boy punch a smaller one in the face. He followed that blow with another that knocked the smaller boy down, then to Hester's horror he kicked him.

'Stop that!' she shouted. 'Stop that at once.'

The youngster turned to look at her, a sneer on his face. 'What's it to do with you?' he demanded. 'Who are you?'

'Never mind who I am. That is no way to behave.'

'Isn't it just. Let's see you bloody stop me,' retorted the boy and kicked the other child again.

Hester hurried into the yard, frightened that he would cause severe injuries. 'Stop it,' she called. 'Stop it at once. That's dangerous.'

A small crowd of children had begun to gather, shouting taunts as they came, and Hester was appalled at some of the words. She had no idea how she should deal with the situation, intent only on preventing the boy from inflicting harm, but before she reached the group a male teacher suddenly appeared. The onlookers drifted quickly away and he grasped the back of the bully's collar.

'That's enough of that,' he said. 'Stand still and cool down.'

He seemed unconcerned about the boy on the ground and it was Hester who helped him to his feet and checked for injuries. His nose was bleeding slightly, but he seemed otherwise uninjured.

The teacher glared at the fighter. 'Go to the classroom and wait for me there,' he ordered.

The boy seemed about to defy him, but he changed his mind and contented himself by poking his tongue out at Hester. He then stalked away and the teacher asked the other boy if he felt all right. The boy nodded at once, eager to get away, and the teacher allowed him to go.

'Sorry about that,' he said to Hester. 'You didn't really need to come in here.'

'He looked as if he was going to cause some real harm,' said Hester. 'I couldn't just walk past.'

'Yes, well, they're not big enough to cause much damage at this age, thank goodness. Thank you for trying, but it wasn't really very sensible. You don't carry any authority.'

'He was using dreadful language.'

The teacher shrugged. 'That's not unusual with some. We don't allow it in the classroom, of course, but there's not a lot we can do about it out here. It's nothing to some of them. They hear it at home all the time.'

Hester left the schoolyard and hurried away along the street. She could not send Dorothy to a school like that! They were ruffians — ill-mannered ruffians. If Dorothy was to go to school she must be educated properly, not turned into a foul-mouthed savage. Her child was too timid to cope in a place like that, but even had she not been, she could not send her there and risk losing all the good work that had produced good manners and good speech.

She was still agitated when she reached the house. Kathy looked up from her job of cleaning the stairs with a small carpet brush, realising at once that something was amiss.

'Oh, Ma'am! Are you all right? Do you need a chair?'

Hester managed a smile. 'No thank you, Kathy. I just saw some boys fighting. It was silly of me to get so upset.'

'Yes, well, I don't suppose you're used to boys. They do tend to fight a lot, you know.'

'It sounds as though you've had plenty of experience.'

'Yes, Ma'am. I've got four brothers.'

Kathy returned to her task and Hester went through the kitchen and out to the back garden. To her relief the two girls were playing quietly and they said there had been no need to call on Kathy for anything. If only things could go on just as they were, thought Hester. What a pity she didn't know anyone in the area who had children of the same age. It would be so good to have some advice.

It was late afternoon before she hit upon the idea of talking to Edith about it.

'Edith, you have lived in this area for a good many years, haven't you?'

'All my life.'

'I wondered if you knew of a school that would be suitable for Dorothy. I went to Ashford Road this morning, but I'm afraid I didn't like it. The children seemed so rough and they were using bad language.'

Edith pursed her lips. 'I went there, years back. I don't suppose it's got any better.'

'Can you suggest any other?'

For a moment Edith seemed unlikely to respond, then she shrugged. 'There's the church school.'

'Which church? Is it Roman Catholic?'

'You don't want that, do you? No, well this one is Anglican. Only a small school, mind you.'

'That would probably suit Dorothy better.'

'You'd have to pay. I expect you know that.'

Hester drew in her breath. She was trying to save money. How much would it cost? But she would not send either of her daughters to the school she had seen that morning. Not only had the pupils been ill-mannered, she had not been impressed by the teacher. He had not seemed the slightest bit concerned about the incident, had not even been embarrassed by the fact that a member of the public had witnessed that deplorable behaviour.

'I'll go and see what it's like,' she said. 'What's the name of it?'

'Saint something or other. Next to the church. You go down towards the tram stop, turn left and it's two, no three streets along. On the right. You'll see the church easy enough.'

'Thank you. I'll go in the morning.' She would find the money, Hester promised herself. A small church school should be just what she wanted. Surely it would not be too expensive. It might take her longer to save the nest egg that Harold had been so insistent about, but at least she would not have to spend her days worrying about what was happening while Dorothy was away from home.

They were in the kitchen preparing the evening meal, everybody engrossed in their own thoughts, when Kathy suddenly shrieked. Hester turned to see the girl drop a large knife onto the chopping board and stare down at her left hand.

'What's happened?' The words slipped out as Hester rushed towards her, but there had been no need to ask. It was plain to see what had happened. Blood had already dripped onto the board from the edge of the girl's palm.

'I've cut myself.' Kathy gripped her left

wrist and held both hands up close to her bosom. 'Oh, I'm sorry, Ma'am.'

'Let me see. Is it bad?'

Kathy kept her hands in the same position, frightened to look at the injury herself and reluctant to show it to anybody else. 'I'll be all right in a minute. Just leave me be.'

Edith brought a chair forward and Hester urged the young girl to sit down.

'Now let me see.'

At last the girl lowered her hand and they were able to see the gash on her palm.

'I'll go and get some linen,' said Edith, and departed quickly to the storeroom.

'I'm sorry, Ma'am,' said Kathy again.

'There's no need to apologise, Kathy. Accidents will happen. Just sit still for the time being.' Hester went to fill a glass with water in case the girl began to feel faint. 'Is it very painful?'

'N-no. I'll be all right.' Kathy decided to take a sip of water, then she gripped her wrist again.

Edith returned with a pair of scissors and several strips of white linen. 'What do you want to put on it?' she asked.

Hester shook her head. 'We won't put anything on. It needs a doctor.'

'Oh, no, Ma'am!' In her consternation Kathy almost leapt to her feet.

Hester put a hand on her shoulder and gently pressed her down again. 'It's too deep for us to take any chances, Kathy. The doctor might have to stitch it.'

'Oh, no! I don't want that! I don't want to go to no doctor.'

'It's the best thing, Kathy. It will heal quicker.'

'I can't afford a doctor,' whispered Kathy.

Hester gave her a comforting pat. 'Don't worry about that. You won't have to pay a thing. But let's cover that cut up first.'

Edith folded one piece of the cloth into a pad then Hester bound the hand firmly and told Kathy to hold it up again while she devised a sling.

'Which doctor do you recommend, Edith?'

'There's one just around the corner. Dr Gibbs. Do you want me to go with her?'

Hester glanced down at the young girl and saw a look of dismay cross her face. 'No, I'd better go — there might be questions about the fee. Can you manage with the cooking if I'm away for a while?'

'Yes, I'll manage.'

'I'll go and get my hat then. I'll tell the children to stay upstairs until I come back.'

Edith came with them to the back gate and pointed out which way they should go. Hester linked arms with Kathy and they walked slowly towards the first corner.

'I'm frightened,' said Kathy in a quivery voice.

'I know it's not pleasant, but there's no need to feel frightened.'

'I'm glad you came with me, Ma'am. I never feel quite right with Edith.'

Hester decided it would be wiser not to respond to that remark. Kathy was obviously wary of the older woman, but Edith had not acted in such a cold manner lately and she had not even quibbled about being left in charge of the cooking today. Before long she might even prove to be quite good-hearted.

A woman opened the door at the doctor's house. 'My goodness,' she said when she saw the sling and a glimpse of bloodstained bandage. 'Come into the waiting-room. It's not time for surgery, but you're in luck, the doctor's here.'

Kathy began to tremble as they waited on the narrow bent wood chairs. 'I don't want him to stitch it,' she said.

'Well, he might decide he doesn't need to,' replied Hester. 'But whatever he does, it will be better than just leaving it.'

A few minutes later the doctor came to an inner door and invited them into the surgery.

'I don't recall having met either of you before,' he said.

'I have only just moved to this district,' answered Hester. 'This is Kathy Thompson. She doesn't live near here, but she works at the Bella Casa Private Hotel, which is nearby.'

Dr Gibbs jotted down some details then went to a corner and washed his hands. 'Right then, let's have a look at the damage.'

Kathy closed her eyes and gritted her teeth while he unwrapped the bandage and inspected the wound.

'Well, I'm glad to see you haven't put any grease or anything on it,' he said to Hester. 'You did the right thing, binding it like that — kept the edges close.'

'I don't want stitches,' said Kathy.

'Don't think they'd help much anyway, not so long as you take care. If you rest this hand, give it a chance to heal, you shouldn't have much trouble.'

He cleaned the cut and bandaged it, then fitted a proper sling. 'Use this for a day or two. It will help to make your hand feel more comfortable. Remember what I said about resting it, and don't let it get wet.' Kathy nodded and he sent her to sit in the waiting-room.

'Could have been worse,' he said to Hester. 'I'm glad you left it alone. People usually want to do something, anything to help, and most of the time they do the wrong thing.'

'I'm glad you were so close, and that you were here.' Hester smiled gratefully. 'Would you like to write the bill now, or would you prefer to send it?'

'Can do it now it you like. And I'll give you a prescription, something to ease the pain. That hand is going to be very sore for a while.' Dr Gibbs quickly scrawled the items and passed them to her. 'Now, while you're here, is there anything I can do for you? Do you have any problems at all?'

Hester shook her head. 'I am very well, thank you. But I am pleased to know there is a doctor so close. I have two young children.'

'Ah, well I hope to meet them some day. Not that I wish them any harm, of course. But if you have any problem don't hesitate to come and see me.'

Hester rose to her feet and he escorted her to the door. 'Don't wait until you have a serious illness on your hands,' he told her. 'The right treatment at an early stage can save you from a lot of grief.'

'Thank you. I'll remember that.' He was the kind of doctor she would like for her children, she decided. He was patient and considerate. He was also much younger than Dr Turnbull, the man who had cared for them in Thorn Bay. Hopefully, that meant he had learned modern methods and could achieve better results. It was hardly likely that Dr Turnbull could have done anything to help little William, she conceded, but he should have been able to recognise his condition. For months he had denied there was any problem, told her she was imagining things. If it hadn't been for Bruce . . . What had happened to Bruce? Had she offended him in some way? It was almost as though he wanted nothing to do with her. Yet he had seemed so . . . so close, so *affectionate* even. But that was before either of them knew she would move so close to Melbourne. Perhaps . . .

'Oh, Ma'am! What did he say? What has the doctor been saying?'

Hester came back to the present with a start and saw that Kathy was staring at her in consternation.

'It's all right, Kathy,' she said quickly. 'The doctor is not a bit worried about your hand.'

'Oh, but . . . '

'I'm sorry if I looked a bit upset when I came out.' Hester took a deep breath and decided she must explain. 'I was thinking about my family. I lost a young child. A little boy.'

'Oh, Ma'am. I'm sorry.'

'It's as well you know. One of the girls might tell you they had a little brother. He was badly crippled.'

'Oh, Ma'am.'

'Yes, well, let's go, shall we? We have to go to the pharmacy first.' Hester raised one hand as she saw the protest forming on the girl's lips. 'It won't cost you anything, so don't worry. It's to take the pain away so that you'll sleep well.'

Edith turned to look at them when they returned to the kitchen, her expression a mixture of sympathy and exasperation.

'Well, you won't be working for a while, will you?'

'Oh, Ma'am!'

Hester hastily laid a hand on Kathy's shoulder. 'Don't get upset. How are you getting on, Edith? Can you manage for a few more minutes?'

'Yes, Ma'am. As I said, we had to make dinners often enough in the past. We'd done most of the vegetables before that happened, anyway.'

'Good. I'll be back shortly. Come on, Kathy, let's make sure you've got everything you need before you go home.'

They went together to the place where the two servants kept their belongings, a tiny room scarcely larger than the linen cupboard. Hester glanced around as Kathy picked up a small wicker basket which had a white cloth neatly folded over the contents.

'There's nothing else of yours here, Kathy?'

'No, Ma'am.'

'Perhaps you'd like to get your tram fare ready now, rather than trying to do it in a hurry when you get on.'

'Yes, Ma'am.' Kathy fumbled under the cloth for a small coin purse and held it with the fingers of her injured hand while she opened it and took out one penny. 'I can put it in my pocket.'

'Yes, it should be safe there. Now then, Kathy, remember what the doctor said. You have to rest that hand. That's why he put it in a sling. So we won't expect to see you back again until Monday at the earliest.'

'Oh, Ma'am, no!' Kathy's eyes filled with tears. 'I have to come to work, Ma'am. I have to keep my job. I can't afford not to come.'

Hester felt the urge to hug her like one of her children, but she confined herself to another friendly pat on the shoulder. 'Don't worry, Kathy. You won't lose your job.'

'But I have to come. Who's going to do everything?'

'We'll manage, Kathy. Don't distress yourself.' Hester gazed at her with compassion. 'You won't lose any money, Kathy.'

She suddenly understood why the servant looked so distraught. When Father had been going through a hard time years ago, she had experienced for herself what it meant to have an empty purse. 'It's pay day on Saturday, isn't it?' she said. 'I'm sure I can find enough to pay you now instead. Wait here.'

She hurried to the office and took Kathy's meagre wage from the cash box intended for household expenses. Kathy received it with fervent thanks, but she still insisted that she ought to come to work.

'I'll be able to do some things, Ma'am.'

'No, Kathy. You have to rest that hand. It will take longer to heal if you try to work with it. You'd be a nuisance rather than a help if that happened. Now you go home, and look after yourself. And don't worry. You'll get your full pay next week.'

She ushered the girl through the kitchen to the back door and with a final despairing backward glance Kathy set off for home.

'She does such silly things,' said Edith. 'She must have been slicing that potato in her hand instead of using the board.'

'Yes. Well, when she comes back we'll have to show her the safe way to do things. I don't suppose she's had any proper training.'

'Not here, that's for sure.'

Hester hurried upstairs to take off her hat and tell the children she had returned, then went back to the kitchen and donned her apron.

'What are we going to do on Saturday then? I can't come in.' Edith's chin jutted in the former arrogant manner.

'I'll manage.' Hester was determined not to plead or argue. 'It's not as though everybody is here at weekends.'

'You mean you'll do the waiting on and all the rooms yourself?'

'I've looked after a house before, Edith.' If she skimped some of the routine tasks there would be nobody there to notice. Provided the men were fed and their beds made they would not complain. Hester pulled the protective shields over her sleeves and moved briskly towards the stove. 'Now then, how far have you got, Edith?'

★   ★   ★

The next morning Hester set her alarm to ring earlier than usual, and even Edith arrived ten minutes before her usual time. She nodded with satisfaction when she saw that preparations were well in hand.

'At a guess I'd say eight for porridge,' she said, and bustled away to whisk the light covers off set tables in the dining-room. The gong was sounded punctually and Edith came back soon afterwards.

'Five porridge now. One egg and bacon for Mr Jamieson, one eggs and meat loaf.' She spooned porridge into the waiting dishes and hastened away with the tray while Hester set out the other items.

Edith clicked her teeth when she came back for the filled plates. 'No, Ma'am. Only one egg and one strip of bacon for Mr Jamieson.'

Hester quickly moved that amount onto a clean plate and Edith filled another bowl with oatmeal. She spoke over her shoulder as she left with the tray. 'Six eggs, bacon and sausage, one with everything for Mr Frost.'

It was hardly more hectic than usual, decided Hester. The men were always in a hurry in the mornings and Edith seemed able to handle the extra work without fluster. How would it have been if Edith had been the one to have an accident and Kathy had to serve everybody by herself? Thank goodness for Edith's experience.

The other woman seemed to have twinges of conscience as the day wore on and Hester did Kathy's share of cleaning rooms.

'I really can't come tomorrow,' she said as she prepared to leave for her midday break. 'Are you going to ask Mrs Wellerby to come in?'

Hester shook her head. 'No, Edith, I can manage for one day. The residents will understand if the service is not quite up to standard and, as you know, some of them go away at weekends. I'll have to call on Mrs Wellerby if Kathy can't come back next week, though.'

She was tired by the end of the afternoon, but she managed to greet each resident with a smile when they came in to pay their rent. Mr Mitchell was the only one not to respond in kind.

'Mrs Carleton, you said I was to let you know if anything displeased me.'

Hester drew in her breath. 'Yes. What exactly is the problem?'

'It's that young fellow, that young Frost. He comes in at all hours.'

'Yes, well he is of an age when he can please himself what time he comes in.'

'He has no consideration for anybody else. He clumps up and down those stairs, doesn't matter what hour of the day or night. And Saturdays! He drinks, you know. He comes stamping in, banging doors, even *singing*! I have the room next to his, you know. He disturbs me every Saturday, and other nights as well sometimes.'

'I'm sorry to hear that. Have you spoken to him about it?'

'Of course I have. Lot of good that's done. He just laughs in my face. I want you to talk to him, tell him he'll have to go if he doesn't mend his ways.'

'Well, I'll speak to him of course. I hope that will solve your problem.'

'It's Saturday tomorrow. I don't want to have to complain to Mr Hetherington.'

Hester watched him go, wondering if any of the other residents felt the same way. She had enough to think about just now without incidents like this cropping up and complicating matters. Young Mr Frost had always seemed pleasant and inoffensive so far. Perhaps it would end with the older man leaving after all, but she must try to make Mr Frost understand that he should be quieter when he moved about the house, especially late at night. Tomorrow would be soon enough to do something about that.

She had decided to let the children help on Saturday, and the two girls felt important when they went downstairs early the next morning. As instructed, Dorothy sounded the gong, then they both went into the dining-room to take orders. Susan was to ask who wanted porridge, while Dorothy stood by to help her keep count and to ask what the others wanted.

The children carried in the first orders of

153

porridge while Hester took a tray with two cooked breakfasts. She had guessed that Mr Jamieson would ask for boiled eggs that morning and they were ready for him almost immediately.

'Oh, dear me,' said Mr Jamieson. 'Not as much as that, Mrs Carleton. I only ever have one egg, and only two slices of toast.'

'Oh, I'm sorry.' Hester was nonplussed. 'You're quite sure you don't want any more than that?'

'Absolutely, Mrs Carleton. Kathy knows. I'd rather you didn't leave all that here.'

'I'm sorry.' Hester quickly took one egg off the plate and two pieces of toast out of the small toast rack.

'Thank you, Mrs Carleton. Tell me, how is poor young Kathy? I understand that she had some kind of accident.'

'She cut her hand. It's not really serious, but the doctor said it would heal quicker if she rested it, so I told her not to come in for a few days.'

Hester turned at the sound of footsteps and saw Adam Frost striding in with his usual jaunty air.

'Good morning, Mrs Carleton.'

'Good morning, Mr Frost.'

'Do you want porridge?' asked Susan at once.

'Yes please, young lady. And then I'll have the full breakfast as usual.'

Hester allowed the girls to carry in his first course, but she carried in the plate of fried food herself.

'I would like to talk to you about something,' she murmured. 'But I don't want to take your time just now. Would you please ring the bell when you return this afternoon?'

'Oh dear. Am I on the carpet for something?' He grinned, not in the least concerned. 'Your wish is my command, dear Mrs Carleton. I will attend as requested this afternoon.'

Hester was washing dishes before she had time to ponder over the strange episode at breakfast. Mr Jamieson had been so emphatic about his requirements. He had claimed that he never had more than one egg and two pieces of toast. But she had always served two eggs for every order, whether boiled or fried. She also ensured that four slices of toast were made for each client, and only rarely had one or two pieces been brought back later. If Mr Jamieson only ate one egg, what happened to the other? Kathy had never said anything about sending in less.

Kathy! She suddenly pictured Kathy's apron with the large greasy stain, and Kathy's horror when it was noticed. The girl must have had a fried egg in her pocket that morning, no doubt with excess slices of toast. Was that what she used to have for her lunch? But she knew now that she could make a proper lunch for herself in the kitchen, so why did she still take extra food every morning? Was it because she was too shy to change the order in case somebody started asking questions?

'What's the matter, Mama? Why are you feeling sad?'

Hester smiled down at Dorothy. 'I'm not really sad, dear. I was just thinking about Kathy.'

'Is she still hurting?'

'She should be feeling much better by now. I expect she's wondering how we're getting along without her.'

'Did Susan and I do well?'

'Very well. I'm proud of you.'

'Do you think Kathy's sisters could have done it better?'

'She has brothers, dear. Four brothers.'

'She has sisters as well. Three sisters.'

Hester stared. 'Are you sure?'

'Of course I'm sure! Kathy told us. She has three sisters and four brothers. She's the oldest one.'

'Goodness. What a large family. That makes eight children.' No wonder Kathy worried so much about money and the need to keep her job. As the eldest child she probably felt obliged to contribute as much as she could to help the family, but her wage would not go far. She only earned one shilling a day, and it cost her a shilling every week just to travel to and from work.

Mr Hetherington called punctually at 10 o'clock and as before he led the way into the office.

'Sit down,' he said. Hester began to say that she would prefer to stand, but he brushed her response aside. 'Sit down. How can I sit if you won't? It makes me feel uncomfortable.'

Hester decided not to make an issue of it. She pulled a chair forward and sat primly upon it as if she were attending a formal At Home at her aunt's house. He looked as if he were about to make some comment, but he changed his mind and began to study the accounts.

'What is this about a doctor's fee?'

'Kathy cut her hand on Thursday. Dr Gibbs attended to it and he said it should heal quickly.'

'What work is she doing in the meantime?'

'I sent her home. The doctor was most emphatic. Resting it will make it heal faster.'

'Well, you will have to dock her wages for the missing days.'

'I can't do that.'

He frowned at her. 'What do you mean, you can't do that? Of course you will.'

Hester steeled herself to face up to him. 'Mr Hetherington, are you going to pay extra wages to those who do Kathy's duties while she is not here?'

'Certainly not. What an idea!'

'Mr Hetherington, Edith and I are quite prepared to perform extra duties while Kathy is unable to be here. But I have to tell you that neither of us would agree to do those extra duties if no payment is to be forthcoming to any of us. If Kathy's pay is to be docked and no recompense is paid to either Edith or myself, then I will employ another person to take Kathy's place.'

'You mean you will sack Kathy.'

'Certainly not!' Hester's cheeks flared. 'I will employ temporary help. And, of course, that person will have to be paid properly.'

He frowned again, then placed his left elbow on the edge of the desk and rested his chin on his fist. He stared at Hester without speaking and she forced herself to meet his gaze squarely.

'You mean that, don't you?' he said at last.

'I most certainly do. If you will not agree, then I shall have to hand in my notice.'

'Supposing I call your bluff?'

'Supposing I do the same?' She needed this job, perhaps even more desperately than Kathy, but she would not back down now.

A tense pause followed, then Mr Hetherington chuckled softly. 'You're only a little thing, a tiny little thing, but you've got courage, I'll say that for you.'

Hester remained silent and at last he gave an exaggerated sigh. 'All right, on this occasion you win. You can pay Kathy her regular wage. But I warn you, I will be looking for excellent service from everybody, and if you cannot provide that excellence, then I shall be the one giving notice to you.'

He left a few minutes later. Few words had passed between them since his ultimatum and when Hester had closed the front door behind him she found that she was shaking. Perhaps she had made an enemy there, unnecessarily so. But it was the principle of it all, she told herself. This was the kind of thing she had heard about when she had attended meetings of the League of New Women in Thorn Bay. One of the main causes of poverty was sickness or accidents. How could workers care properly for their families if they lost their jobs, or their wages were cut, because of mishaps? She had done the right thing standing up to Mr Hetherington, she assured herself, but she had better take care not to ruffle his feelings again.

She made a pot of tea to help settle her nerves and the rest of the day passed quickly as she made all the beds and did some perfunctory cleaning. The children helped by shelling the peas, and she had peeled the potatoes and seasoned the meat dish before Adam Frost rang the bell. He gave a mock salute as she entered the hall.

'Frost here at your command, Madam.'

She fought to restrain a smile. 'Mr Frost, I have had a complaint about noisy behaviour, especially late at night.'

'Ah, that would be the old geezer from number five. His main aim in life is to find a reason to complain. It's his hobby.'

'Mr Frost, would you please take more care. Walk quietly on the stairs.'

'I'll take my shoes off if that will please you, Madam.'

'Please close all doors quietly. That includes cupboard doors as well as all the others.'

He swept an imaginary hat from his head and bowed deeply. 'I hear you, Madam.'

As if that would make a difference, thought Hester. If he drank as much as Mr Mitchell seemed to think, he would come in tonight just as noisily as ever.

She served the soup herself at dinner,

thinking the children might spill it, but she allowed them to carry other plates to the tables and the residents seemed to appreciate their efforts. When Hester went in to serve coffee she found that Adam Frost was urging the girls to accept a penny each.

'Mr Frost, please don't give money to the children,' she said.

'Only a small tip for their good work.'

'I'm sorry, but I don't approve. They must be willing to help people without expecting payment. Besides, they are helping me, so I should decide on any little treat.'

He sighed. 'Very well. As you wish.'

Moments later Hester saw that the girls were at Mr Best's table, one either side of his chair. He was opening a cone of paper and inviting them to look inside. She hurried across the room and saw that the cone was filled with brightly coloured sweets.

'Mr Best, please don't give sweets to the children.'

He looked up and smiled. 'It won't do any harm. Just one little sweetie. It isn't as though I'm going to give them the whole bagful.'

'Those are children's sweets. Did you buy them specially?'

'Yes, I did. I always buy sweeties at the weekend. I see my little nieces on Sundays.'

Hester looked across at Adam, who was

watching the exchange with interest. He spread his hands and gave an expressive shrug. Hester turned back to Mr Best.

'Just one sweetie each, Mr Best. And please make this the last time. I do not want any of the residents to give anything to the children.'

'What a pity. But I will do as you say. Now, Susan, you choose one first, and then Dorothy can choose.'

9

Kathy arrived at her usual time on Monday, looking wary and self-conscious.

'Good morning, Ma'am.'

'Hello, Kathy. How are you feeling today?'

'I'm very well thank you, Ma'am. I can do everything, same as ever.'

She was still wearing a bandage, smaller than before, but was doing her best to keep the injured hand out of sight.

'You mustn't try to do too much at first,' began Hester.

'Oh, Ma'am, I can . . . '

'For a start, I don't want you to wash dishes,' Hester continued. 'Keeping that hand dry for an extra day or two will help, no doubt.'

She kept the rest of her instructions until Edith was also there to hear. 'Kathy, I don't want you to carry heavy trays today. Edith, will you please take the orders and serve all the meals. Kathy will clear the empty dishes and set up the tables again afterwards. And, Kathy, when the dining-room is finished I want you to come to the office. There are one or two small jobs to be seen to before you go upstairs.'

She placed the two chairs close together in the office, and when Kathy came in later she invited her to sit down. The girl obeyed, quivering with fright, and Hester spoke as gently as she could.

'Kathy, you usually serve Mr Jamieson, don't you?'

'Oh, Ma'am. I'm sorry.'

'I gave him too much on Saturday.'

'Oh, Ma'am. I'm sorry, Ma'am. It's not like I wanted to steal. It's just that . . . ' her voice quavered to a halt and two tears slid down her cheeks.

'Who's talking about stealing? Tell me about it, Kathy. Did you eat the egg and the extra toast?'

'Sometimes.' Kathy paused to brush more tears away. 'I took most of them home.'

Hester gazed at her in dismay. She had known hard times, had struggled to make ends meet when Father's money was stolen and he fell into debt, but they had never had to resort to such measures. Imagine taking that stale toast home! Boiled eggs would be palatable enough — but cold fried eggs, hidden in a pocket and then kept in a basket all day!

'I'm sorry, Ma'am. I knew you'd find out. You'd be bound to find out when I wasn't here. I didn't want to steal, really I didn't.'

'We're not talking about stealing, Kathy. Mr Jamieson is entitled to two eggs, even three if he wanted them, and I'm sure he would have given the extra ones to you if you had asked him.'

'Oh, I couldn't do that, Ma'am.'

'Of course not. But we can assume that he would give them to you. I understand that there are eight children in your family, and you are the eldest.'

'Yes. There would have been an older sister, but she died before I was born. And then there was a brother who died when he was little.'

'I'm sorry. It must have been a struggle for your parents.'

Kathy sniffed hard. 'It still is. Dad broke his leg, you see. And he hasn't been able to get a proper job since, just a few hours here and there.' She fumbled for a handkerchief and blew her nose. 'I'm sorry, Ma'am. I won't do it again.'

Hester patted her knee. 'You won't need to do it the same way, but you can still take bread and eggs home.' Kathy stared in disbelief, her mouth open but making no sound, and Hester patted her knee again. 'I'm sure your mother would rather receive plain bread than cold toast, and raw eggs would be more useful, too. They would certainly be healthier than fried ones, no risk of germs. So, we'll put aside some slices of bread and an egg each morning.'

'Oh, Ma'am! Do you really mean it? Oh, but what about Edith? What will she say?'

'There's no need for her to know, is there? You can put them in a tin or a box or something, and place them quietly in your basket.'

'Oh, Ma'am, I don't know what to say. Ma'am, you're so kind. You're just wonderful.' Kathy sprang to her feet, smiling despite the tears. She looked as if she were about to fling her arms around Hester, but she suddenly held herself back, bobbed a curtsey instead and hastened out of the room.

★   ★   ★

'There's a letter for you, Ma'am.' Kathy had gone out to the front gate as usual when she heard the postman. 'Look, Ma'am, here's a letter with your name on it.'

Hester's face lit up with anticipation when she saw the handwriting and Kathy smiled, glad to have been able to do something that was so pleasing.

'I hope it's good news, Ma'am.'

'So do I, Kathy. It's from a friend.'

Bruce had answered! Hester made herself

finish the task she had started before she took the letter away to the seclusion of the office and tore open the envelope. The message inside was brief, taking only one side of a single sheet of paper, but it brought joy to her heart. Bruce apologised for not writing earlier, but he had been extremely busy because of an outbreak of diphtheria in his district. He went on to say that he would like to call on Hester and the children, and gave times when he was most likely to be at home. They could possibly make arrangements more easily by telephone, but she could write if she preferred.

Hester read it several times, wishing she could go to the telephone and call at once, then she folded the page and pushed it back inside the envelope telling herself not to behave like an immature and flighty young girl. It was a formal letter, nothing to get excited about. It would be nice to see Bruce again and show him how well she was coping, but his visit would probably be nothing more than an act of courtesy.

She made her call when duties had been completed for the day and the children were in bed. When it came to the point of actually speaking to Bruce she felt nervous, and as she was still wary of using the telephone her voice sounded strained and unnatural.

'Are you feeling quite well now?' asked Bruce. 'You sound tired.'

'I'm perfectly well, better than I have been for years. But I have to admit that talking on the telephone is still somewhat of a challenge.'

'Ah, I see. Well, is Sunday afternoon a good time for you?'

'It's the best time, Bruce. After midday dinner I am perfectly free.'

'Sunday afternoon it is then. Will three o'clock be a good time?'

'You can come earlier if you like, Bruce.'

'Let's say three o'clock. That will give me plenty of time to find my way. Goodbye, Hester. I'm looking forward to it.'

'And I. Goodbye, Bruce.'

The children were excited to hear that they were to see Bruce again soon. They remembered that he had taken them all for rides in a motor car and he had taken them on a steam train. It was Bruce who had taken them to eat lunch in a restaurant. At the first opportunity they told Kathy about him.

'Uncle Bruce is a doctor,' said Susan. 'He could have looked after your hand for you, Kathy.'

'He's not really our uncle,' added Dorothy. 'We call him that because he's a friend and he didn't want us to call him Doctor.'

'I see.'

'We haven't got any real uncles,' said Susan.

'Yes we have, we've got Uncle Harold. Have you got any uncles, Kathy?'

'Yes. Both my parents come from big families, so I've got lots of relatives — aunts, uncles and cousins.'

'We've got cousins.' Susan was eager to talk about their four cousins and their jolly father, but Edith came down the stairs and Kathy scurried away to busy herself elsewhere.

Hester made a selection of delicacies for afternoon tea on Sunday and considered her wardrobe carefully. Nothing too fancy or formal, she decided, but definitely nothing that would suggest she was in service. No black. Eventually she chose a dark blue, the first time she had worn colour since the death of her little boy, a tragedy which had been followed so soon by the loss of her husband.

When the front doorbell rang she felt unexpectedly shy, wondering what she should say when she opened the door, but then Bruce smiled and her apprehension vanished. He could not be described as handsome, his hair not as fair as Gerald's had been, his eyes not so blue, but he had a pleasant countenance and an aura of reliability and compassion. He was wearing a good suit of navy-blue with a barely detectable stripe.

'Hello, Hester. You are looking extremely well. What a difference since the last time I saw you!'

'Yes, I am very well. How are you?' He was still stocky, but she thought he had lost a little weight over the past months.

'Very well also. Ah, here come Susan and Dorothy. How nice to see you.'

The two girls, unable to hold back any longer, had come into the hall and now they hurried forward, sure of a welcome. They all went together on a tour of the house and garden, the children eager to tell Bruce everything they knew about the establishment, then they settled in the living-room upstairs and Hester brewed tea.

'I will take you for a ride in my motor car before I go if you like,' Bruce promised.

'Yes, please!' the girls chorused.

'Have you got a motor car of your own now?' asked Hester.

'Yes. Not the latest model, of course, and it came to me secondhand, but it's a great boon. I couldn't get through nearly as much work without it.'

'Are you still working with the same doctor?'

'Yes, exactly where I first started before I'd even been to university. I'm a partner now.'

'That must make you feel proud.'

'Yes, ambition achieved. Father is not impressed, of course. His ambition has always been related to profits and increases in personal wealth.'

Some things never changed for the better, thought Hester sadly. The aspirations of his family had been a stumbling block to the start of his career, and that delay had certainly come between the two of them and any thought of their making a life together. She thrust such thoughts aside.

'I hope your accommodation is better than it was in those early days.'

'Not as grand as this house, but certainly comfortable. And I eat well, even if I could often do with a change from chicken or eggs.' He smiled at her puzzled expression. 'People who have space at the back of their houses often keep poultry. If they have no spare cash they pay their bills in kind — part of a chicken, even a whole chicken at times, but more usually with eggs.'

Hester recalled Kathy's conduct and was about to relate the story about serving breakfast when she remembered the children were listening avidly. 'Eggs are obviously valuable,' she said instead.

'They are indeed, especially to growing children. And as I have no children I have become just as adept as some of my neighbours at exchanging eggs for something else that I would prefer — not that I could do that in my home vicinity, of course. It would be offensive to the patients who gave them to me.'

When the children had sampled a small piece of every item on the table they were content to go away to play and the two adults looked at each other in silence for a while.

'You're looking rather tired, Bruce. Are you sure you're quite well?'

'I have to admit to feeling tired, but yes, I am well. As I mentioned in my letter, I have been very busy lately.'

'Diphtheria is a terrible ailment.'

'Yes. I lost five young patients.' Bruce sighed. 'The only positive aspect, the only thing that kept me going, was that some were saved. The Fairfield Hospital does a wonderful job.'

Hester could think of nothing to say in response and they sat in silence again until Bruce stirred and straightened his spine.

'Is everything really as good here as the children have been telling me?'

'Everything is going very well,' she replied. 'Far better than I dared hope. I was lucky. And it was all my stepmother's doing. She found this place and put in a good word for me. If it hadn't been for her I don't know what I would have done.'

'You never thought of going to your aunt, Mrs Bancroft?'

'Oh, no!' Hester could not repress a shudder. 'I couldn't have done that. For one thing, she has very old-fashioned views on raising children. But apart from that, she could not have borne the scandal.'

'I imagine she would find that difficult to handle.'

Hester nodded ruefully. 'She has no wish to be associated with anybody from my side of the family. From her point of view the further apart we are, the better. I'm quite sure she would have preferred us to go to New South Wales, or even Queensland.'

'You did send her your new address, I hope?'

Hester chuckled. 'Oh, yes. She sent a letter almost by return, telling me I had made a dreadful choice. In her mind St Kilda is a den of iniquity. It is a place where the lowest characters from the worst parts of Melbourne come to profit by their evil ways.'

They laughed together and agreed that even if Aunt Amelia were to see some of the mansions for herself she was hardly likely to change her opinion. She fully believed that the whole of St Kilda was a place of sin, fully deserving of a bad reputation, and she had been particularly dismayed to learn that Hester was living unprotected in a house full of men.

'Are all the residents gentlemanly?' asked Bruce, becoming serious again.

'Very much so. They range in age from twenty to about sixty and they all treat me and the staff with respect. They all pay their rent on time as well. One or two of them seemed keen to give presents to the children, but I asked them not to and they abide by my wishes.'

'That's good. The children have grown. Does Dorothy go to school now?'

Hester blushed. 'She should. I intended to visit another school last week, but as it turned out I didn't have time.'

She explained what had happened at the local public school and Bruce nodded.

'I think you're right. A small church one will probably suit her better.'

Hester cleared the table but left the washing-up for later, and soon afterwards they all went for a drive in the motor car. When they turned right at the shore and drove along by the sea, Susan described how they had changed into bathing suits and waded in the water.

Bruce looked at Hester and laughed. 'I can

imagine what your aunt would say about that.'

'It would justify her opinion of St Kilda. Such goings on! That is one of the things I don't need to tell her about.'

When they returned to Bella Casa Bruce helped each of them to dismount then offered Hester his hand.

'I won't come back in the house again. Thank you for an excellent afternoon tea.'

'Thank you for coming. It was lovely to see you again.'

The family stood together on the pavement, waving until the motor car was out of sight, then Hester opened the gate and they filed into the front garden.

'When is he coming again?' asked Susan.

'I don't know, dear. But let's hope he comes again fairly soon.'

During the following days Hester felt restless. The evenings stretched out, quiet and uneventful, and she realised how much she had been missing companionship and adult conversation. She rarely saw the residents, being occupied in the kitchen when they were taking their meals in the dining-room, and when they met at other times they only exchanged a few words. She had nothing in common with Edith outside the subject of work, and Kathy was always careful not to bridge the gulf that lay between an employee and the person in charge. How nice it would be to visit some of her friends at the League of New Women, thought Hester. But they were all far away at Thorn Bay. Even if she knew of a similar group here in St Kilda she would not be able to attend meetings. She was far too busy during the day, and who would look after the children if she went out later?

She sat alone in her living-room one evening, thinking about Bruce's visit, and inevitably she found herself recalling the past and her first meetings with him. The brightest memory was of the day when she paddled in the water for the first time. After that they had visited Barnaby in his old shack on the cliffs.

Barnaby . . . he must be feeling lost and perhaps even unhappy now that his life had changed so completely. He could no longer sit on his shabby verandah watching the waves and the seabirds. He could not come and go as he pleased, eating when he was hungry, sleeping when it suited him. There would be rules to obey at the Home where he was living now, and he would no longer be surrounded by his collection of curios. Hester went to the drawer where she kept her notepaper and settled down at the table. She would write a letter to Barnaby. It would give her something to do and it would probably give the old man a great deal of pleasure. She did not have his correct address, but a letter directed to the Retired Seamen's Mission at Mountcliffe would surely reach him safely.

★   ★   ★

'There's a gentleman to see you, Ma'am. He says his name is Mr Carleton.' Edith obviously doubted his identity.

Hester hastily removed her apron and went out to the hall, to find Harold there, cheerfully talking to a flustered Kathy.

'Hello, Hester.'

'Harold! Fancy seeing you. Good morning.'

'I've been chatting to your assistant here, and it's just as I thought. You need some advice on modern equipment, and it just so happens that I have something that is exactly what you need, and I've got it with me. Wait there.'

The kitchen door closed quietly as Edith decided that her presence was not required. Kathy dithered uncertainly, carpet brush in one hand, dustpan in the other, wondering whether she ought to stay and sweep up the little pile of dust and fluff she had gathered or to hide in the kitchen until this unusual visitor had left.

Before Hester could give her any instructions, Harold was back again, obviously having left his surprise article just outside the front door. He presented it with a flourish.

'There you are, Hester, what do you think about that?'

She looked at the strange contraption, wondering what it was supposed to be. It had a long handle like a broom, but it had a red decorative knob at one end and instead of bristles at the other end there was a red box.

'What does it do?'

'It cleans, that's what it does. Takes all the hard labour out of cleaning.' He turned to Kathy. 'Come on, young lady, show Mrs Carleton. Run this up and down the carpet.'

Kathy looked at Hester for permission, then put her brush and dustpan down beside the little collection of fluff and took hold of the gadget's handle. Harold nodded encouragement and she pushed tentatively.

'It's got wheels,' she exclaimed.

'Right. Now push harder. Pretend you're sweeping the yard.'

Kathy obeyed, pushing the box forward and drawing it back again with mounting enthusiasm.

'Go right over that dirt there, where you

were working before.'

Hester hastily moved the brush and dustpan and Kathy ran the new equipment over the spot.

'Oh, look! It picks it all up!' she cried.

'Come on, Hester, you give it a try,' he urged. 'That's right. Now, what do you think? Don't you think it's just what you need?'

'Well, it's — er — it's certainly impressive.'

'Before you know it, no self-respecting establishment will be without at least one of these. It's called a carpet sweeper and that's exactly what it does. How this place could have gone so long without one I can't imagine.'

Hester smiled, thinking that he must say much the same to every prospective customer. 'How much is it?' she asked.

'For you, Hester, being family, I can make a special price. An even better price for two or more. You'll need more than one, won't you? The staff will be fighting for it if you only have one.'

Hester smiled again. 'I haven't decided to have one yet. Kathy, go and fetch Edith and we'll see what she thinks. She's in the kitchen.'

Edith did not seem overly impressed. She ran the sweeper up and down the hall then handed it back to Harold.

'I've seen one before.'

'So you will know just how useful they can be,' he answered, not deflated in the least. 'Look, Hester, I'll leave this one with you for a few days. You just see how much time it will save you. But I must leave now, I have a lot of appointments this morning. Call me. You've got a telephone, remember.'

Kathy hastened to open the front door for him and he gave her a cheerful salute as he passed. She waited on the doorstep to watch the motor car drive off, then went back indoors.

'Isn't that a marvellous thing?' she said. Edith reluctantly gave a half nod and Kathy chattered on, excitement overcoming her usual reticence. 'We'll be able to do the carpets in half the time with those.'

'Exactly,' said Edith.

Hester was puzzled by her reaction. 'What's the matter, Edith? What is it you don't like about those things?'

'They're machines, aren't they? The curse of the working class.'

'What do you mean, Edith? Surely it's better for workers if they have machines to help them. Machines must save a lot of physical effort.'

'Yes, and cuts down on the number of workers.'

Hester suddenly understood. 'Edith, nobody is going to lose their job if we take any of those sweepers.'

'And what about the next invention? I've heard about electric machines that do even more than that thing.'

'Edith, we can't possibly manage with less staff here. You and Kathy do a lot more than clean carpets. For a start, who would serve the meals?' Hester decided it was better to drop the subject for the time being and get on with the daily routine. 'We can talk about all this later. In the meantime, Kathy, you can use that thing if you want to until you've finished the carpets.'

10

The telephone shrilled on Friday evening and Hester hastened to answer, hoping it was Bruce calling to say he would come again on Sunday. She had to fight down disappointment when Cora's voice came to her instead.

'Hello, Hester. I hope everything is going all right. We're both longing to hear all about it. How would you like to bring the children for afternoon tea on Sunday?'

Hester hesitated. Supposing Bruce rang later? It would be a pity to miss a visit from him.

'You haven't made any other arrangements, have you?'

'Er — no.' Hester's better nature came to the fore. She had promised to see Father more often, and she would not have attained her present good fortune had it not been for Cora's efforts. She must be sociable, if only because she felt so indebted to Cora. 'Thank you. What's the best way to get there from here?'

'I'll tell you how we came to you. Have you got a pencil? It's not difficult, so long as you get on the right trams.'

The children were pleased to take more tram rides and Cora gave them a hearty welcome when she opened the front door of the little house. Hester was wearing her blue dress and Cora nodded approval when she took her coat and hat.

'That's nice. Brings out the colour of your eyes and your hair. Doesn't she look nice, Edmund?'

'Wonderful,' he said, coming forward to kiss Hester's cheek. 'I'm glad to see you're finally out of mourning.'

She let that remark pass, not wanting to trigger any awkward comments. 'How are you, Father?'

'Well, very well. Now, where are my little granddaughters? Aren't you going to come and say hello to me?'

When they had all settled down and there was a suitable pause in the conversation, Hester said, 'Dorothy is going to start school tomorrow.'

'Tomorrow! Are you really?' exclaimed Cora.

'My, you are a big girl,' said Edmund.

Dorothy blushed and hung her head, still not sure that going to school was going to be an enjoyable experience. Hester had taken her to see the building on Friday afternoon and they had waited to see the children coming out. They had all looked happy, but never before had Dorothy seen so many children all at once.

'You will make a lot of new friends there,' said Cora.

She had paper and wax crayons ready to keep the children occupied when they had eaten their tea, and they scribbled away contentedly while the adults chatted. Edmund took them out for ice cream later and Cora leaned expectantly towards Hester.

'Now you can tell me all about it. I expect you're feeling a bit uneasy about Dorothy going out into the wide world, mixing with all sorts of other children.'

'She's not going to the National school. She going to a small one just a few streets away — St Cuthbert's.' Cora raised her eyebrows and Hester quickly explained what had happened in the public school yard. 'I couldn't send her to a place like that. The church school charges a fee, but I can manage it. It's not really very much.'

'I hope you didn't make out that you had an important job.'

Hester laughed and shook her head. 'Not likely. I wouldn't want to take the risk of them charging a larger fee. It's only a few coppers a week, actually, and it seems that most of the families are just ordinary people.

I think it will be a friendly place.'

'Well, as long as you don't expect all the children to behave like little angels just because they go to a church school. Amongst other things, don't be surprised if Dorothy picks up words you don't like. It seems to be a phase that children go through.'

'Have you had any children of your own, Cora?'

'No.' Cora pursed her lips and tossed her head with a nonchalant air. 'I was always too busy to get married until I was a lot older. Don't know that I missed much, though. There always seemed to be plenty of other people's children around.'

'But you understand children. You must do. You seem to get on so well with them.'

'It's easy when they're not yours. You don't have the same worry and responsibility.' Cora settled herself more comfortably in the easy chair and gazed thoughtfully at Hester. 'Would you like me to call in tomorrow? Perhaps keep an eye on Susan while you take Dorothy to school? It might be better for just the two of you to go the first time. And you don't want to feel that you have to rush back.'

'Oh.' Hester hesitated, grateful for the offer, but concerned that she might be taking advantage of Cora's good nature. 'Well . . . '

'I can get there easily enough, and I'd like

to do it. Besides, it will give me a chance to check up on your procedures, make sure you're keeping up the standards I set.' Cora chuckled. 'Seriously, Hester, I'd like to come. I won't interfere with Edith or Kathy.'

Mention of Kathy prompted Hester to tell the story about the toast and eggs. 'The family must be very poor,' she said.

'Yes, and that wouldn't be the only one. But don't let your heart take over from your head, Hester, and don't send too much food home with her.'

'There's usually something left over. Soup, for instance. I told her to bring a bottle every day, just in case.'

Soon afterwards the children bounced in, eager to tell Cora about the new gadgets that Uncle Harold had brought. Hester had finally agreed to purchase two carpet sweepers and the children had enjoyed experimenting with them.

'I hope the owner of that place approved,' said Edmund.

'He said he wanted an up to date establishment,' replied Hester. 'So I took him at his word.' In reality she had doubted that Mr Hetherington would agree to the expense, especially as he had quibbled so much over paying Kathy's wages when she was off work. However, yesterday he seemed to be in a far more generous mood and consented readily to the purchase of two sweepers. His attitude had been so different, so jovial, that no one would have guessed how mean spirited he had been only a short time before.

They left for home well before dark, the girls still enthusiastic about the joys of riding on trams. Hester worried that Dorothy might not settle to sleep that night, but both children were tired after their excursion and needed little persuasion to go to bed. She was the one who was nervous, she thought ruefully. She was still wondering whether she should have kept Dorothy at home a little longer. What was Susan going to do all day alone? Dorothy had often acted like a little mother towards her, especially when their real mother had been so occupied with a helpless crippled child. Hester sighed. Perhaps it was the best thing for Dorothy after all, giving her the chance to spread her wings and enjoy herself without feeling the need to take care of her little sister. She sighed again. Yes, it was time for Dorothy to become part of the wider world. She had adapted to a great change already, and she would surely cope with what came next.

Dorothy awoke early the next morning and soon showed signs of nerves. She snapped irritably at Susan when she began to chatter, and declared that she did not want anything at all for breakfast. Hester tried to concentrate on her work, relieved to see Cora arrive soon after eight o'clock.

'I'm very pleased to see you,' she murmured. 'I think we might have tears before long.'

'Perfectly natural,' replied Cora airily. 'You look after Dorothy while I keep Susan occupied.'

All the male residents had left for their daily jobs before it was time to set out for the school. Hester held Dorothy's hand as they walked along the footpath, trying to think of positive things to say. The little girl nodded from time to time but rarely answered. As they neared the front gate her steps began to slow, and she was reluctant to enter the yard.

'Come on,' urged Hester. 'Miss Jackson will be waiting for us.'

The tears began to flow when they reached the classroom door and the young teacher came to greet them.

'I don't want to go in there,' cried Dorothy. 'I don't want to stay here without you, Mama.'

'I'll come back at lunch-time,' said Hester. 'Shake hands with Miss Jackson, there's a good girl.'

Dorothy went through the ritual she had

been taught, still weeping.

'She'll be all right in a few minutes,' said Miss Jackson. 'We're going to sing first, Dorothy, then there will be a story. You'll like that.' She looked at Hester, indicated the door with a jerk of her head and mouthed, 'You go.'

'Good-bye, Dorothy.' Hester stooped to give her a kiss. 'I'll be back at lunch-time.'

When the morning session ended Dorothy was dry-eyed and apparently composed, but she greeted Hester with a fervent hug.

'Hello, dear. Did you do a lot of new things today?'

'No.'

'Didn't you?'

'Not new. I can draw already. And I can cut. Miss Jackson said I'm very good at cutting out. One of the boys couldn't do it at all.'

Hester hugged her again and smiled with relief. Now that Dorothy knew she could do as well as the other children, and even better than some, her confidence would grow and she would begin to enjoy new experiences.

Miss Jackson came out and gave Dorothy a friendly pat on the shoulder. 'Dorothy has done very well this morning, Mrs Carleton. I was surprised to find that she can already read some words.'

'Yes, well we have a lot of books and we have a story every bedtime.'

'You have given her a very good start. Now, just the morning for today, as we agreed, but she can come for the full day just as soon as you like. You don't have to wait until next week if you don't wish to.'

Hester felt light-hearted as she and Dorothy walked home. Everything was working out so much better than she could have hoped. She had a comfortable place to live and a good wage. Who would have guessed this was the first time in her life that she had ever been employed? She had only worked at home before, looking after Father first and then caring for a family of her own. Life had been hard at times but it had taught her to be efficient and she was handling this new job competently, she knew that well enough. She had some ideas of her own, too. She would not rush, but gradually she would introduce some of those ideas. Bella Casa would really be up to date, perhaps even ahead of the times.

★ ★ ★

Mr Hetherington continued to arrive as punctually as ever each Saturday. He had become more casual in his approach, but

Hester would not lower her guard and she always greeted him in her usual formal manner. One morning he strode into the office, but instead of going straight to the desk where the books lay open, he picked up the chair that she had placed for herself and moved it alongside his.

'It's silly for you to sit right over there,' he said. 'We should look at these books together.'

'I know those columns off by heart.'

'I dare say you do, but I'd prefer you to sit here where we can look at the figures together.'

Hester hesitated, but decided to comply. She moved her chair fractionally, so as to create more of a space between them without making the act too obvious, and when she had seated herself he also sat. They went through the usual routine, he asking and she answering questions, until he declared himself satisfied. He then pushed his chair slightly back from the desk and turned it more towards her.

'We have known each other for long enough now. I think you should call me Roger. And I should call you by your first name.'

Hester tensed. 'That would not be appropriate, Mr Hetherington.'

'Oh, come now. Let's not stand on ceremony.'

'Protocol should be followed at all times.' It

could have been her aunt speaking, thought Hester with a twinge of amusement. She had never expected to find herself using such phrases.

'Oh, come now. It seems a pity not to use your first name, it's so attractive. Hester. I wonder how that came to be chosen.'

She made no response and he sighed. 'Come now, Hester, indulge me in my little whim.'

'Do you call your housekeeper by her first name?'

'Well, no,' he admitted. 'But that's different, of course.'

'There is no difference,' retorted Hester. She rose gracefully to her feet and moved to the doorway as an indication that he should leave. 'Your housekeeper and I hold similar positions. She looks after your private house, while I do the same for your business establishment.'

He looked as if he were about to argue the point, but he shrugged instead and stood up. 'Very well, Mrs Carleton, we will stick to the same old code of conduct. I will be here again at the same time next week.'

If he were to maintain the previous code of conduct, the chairs should be placed in the same manner as before, decided Hester. The next Saturday she opened the account books at the appropriate pages and set one chair only behind the desk. He cast a quick glance around as he entered the office, then without a word he lifted her chair, put it down next to his own and gestured for her to sit there.

Hester did so and he gave a gratified smile. 'Mrs Carleton, I want us to work together as partners. Please don't insist on being so distant.'

She was unsure how to reply so she confined herself to a brief nod and looked pointedly at the books. He sighed softly and turned his attention to business matters.

'Who is this Spirod . . . Spirou . . . '

'Mr Spirodopholous sells vegetables.'

'I can see that. But we have a perfectly good supplier, and an Australian at that. I suppose this foreign chap has offered a lower price. We don't want to buy things just because they're cheap. We have to maintain quality.'

'You couldn't get a better quality. Those vegetables were picked only the day before.' Hester had felt sorry for the vendor, but knew better than to say so. Mr Spirodopholous was a new migrant, barely able to speak English, and she knew how hard it must be for him to make a living. Members of his family had grown the salad vegetables on their own plot. 'Our usual greengrocer doesn't even stock some of the things he had for sale.'

'Don't start using any of that foreign stuff. Our clients like food they're accustomed to.'

Hester hid a smile. The residents had resisted salad dishes at first, but she had continued to send small serves to each table and now most of them were eaten. Nobody had questioned the new green vegetables that had appeared on Thursday evening, but she had never seen them before she met Mr Spirodopholous. He had called them something in Greek, and added, 'In English, zucchini.' That had not sounded like English, but she had agreed to try them and he had explained in sign language mixed with halting words how she should cook them.

'I suppose competition isn't a bad thing,' said Mr Hetherington grudgingly. 'But don't upset our usual supplier. We need regular deliveries when things get short.'

As soon as he had finished with the books he pushed his chair back a little and looked at her appraisingly.

'You are a very attractive lady. Has anyone ever told you that?'

Hester coloured instantly, but managed to keep her dignity. 'As a matter of fact, they have.'

'Ah, yes. Well, of course, you were married.' He leaned slightly towards her. 'You must miss your husband a great deal.'

'Yes.' She would never admit that the later years of marriage had been an ordeal, that the loss of her child had affected her far more deeply than the loss of her husband.

'It is a sad thing when someone so young has no man to care for her, to fulfil her needs.'

'My needs have been fully met, Mr Hetherington.'

He clicked his teeth. 'Don't keep on trying to pretend with me. We both know it's an artificial stance.' He smiled suggestively and gave a slow wink. 'I can give you a good time.'

Hester stared at him with mounting alarm. 'I have no idea what you mean by a good time, Mr Hetherington, but I assure you, I have no intention of even trying to find out.'

He hitched his chair closer and placed his hand on her knee. 'I think you do know.'

'Mr Hetherington!' She stood up abruptly and strode towards the door. 'It is time you left.'

He shook his head sadly and slowly rose to his feet. 'You obviously need time to come to terms with your inner feelings. I have patience. I can wait.'

She would not give him the satisfaction of a reply. She went along the hall to the front door and held it open for him, her expression cold and unrelenting. 'Good-bye, Mr Hetherington.'

He even smiled at her as he went. 'Good-bye, Mrs Carleton.'

Hester closed the door with a sharp slam then went back to the office and sat down quickly. Her hands were quivering now and she was surprised that she had maintained her poise for so long. No wonder she had always felt reminded of Cecil when she was in his presence! He was just like him. He seemed to think that he was attractive to women, that he could make advances whenever he chose. Cecil had always been the same. They were both married, but Cecil had never been faithful to Louisa, and it was evident that Mr Hetherington paid little regard to his marriage vows.

What was she to do now? She did not want to leave here. She was making a success of this business. The children had settled well and she could hardly expect to find another home as comfortable as this. Dorothy had settled at her school, too. It would be unfair to uproot her now. But how could she face that man next week? She would have to do that if she intended to stay. Unless . . . no, she could not give the task to Edith. To begin with she was never here on a Saturday; but apart from that, she would be unable to cope with the books. During the past weeks it had become clear that Edith was barely literate. Kathy could read well and she was intelligent, but a young innocent girl like her must not be left to the mercy of a lecherous man like him.

Less than an hour later Hester felt more resolute and determined to stand her ground. Why should she have to make changes because of a man like him? Why should she feel the need to avoid him? She would face up to him, but she would also find some means of making sure there could be no misunderstanding. It must be plain from the outset that she would never succumb and she would never welcome any advances from him, not even any soft words.

Could she call upon Bruce to help? It would be a good excuse to speak to him, if nothing else. Hester thought of the times they had been together and her mood softened somewhat. Bruce had visited more often of late and, although they had not regained the closeness they had attained after the tragedy in Thorn Bay, they were relaxed in each other's company. Sunday afternoon was always the best time to meet because they could go out walking or driving without having to watch the clock, but she had also enjoyed rare evening visits. They had sat talking while the children slept, and even when lengthy silences had fallen between them such intervals had seemed natural and not in the least uncomfortable. He would surely assist her now. She had even thought of a way to do it.

The telephone was a great boon, she thought thankfully. Bruce was able to contact her whenever he was free, and now that she needed help she could reach him quickly. To her relief, the person who answered the telephone told her that Bruce was on the premises and he came promptly to take her call.

'I know I'm asking a lot,' said Hester, 'but I'm wondering if you could possibly come here on a Saturday morning. Next Saturday, to be precise. Just after ten o'clock.'

'It sounds important. Rather ominous in fact.'

'It is important to me. But I realise that Saturday morning might be a bad time for you.'

'I think I could organise it for once.' Bruce paused and she thought she could hear the rustle of turning pages. 'Yes, I'm sure I'll be able to manage it. I'll come by on Wednesday evening if I may, and you can tell me all about it.'

By Wednesday Hester was beginning to

doubt that her idea had been a good one after all, but Bruce gradually guided her to the reason for her call. She explained that Mr Hetherington seemed to think she would succumb to his flattery and attention, while she wanted to make it perfectly plain that she would not.

'And you want me to appear on the scene at the vital moment,' he guessed.

'Would you, Bruce? Do you think it would have the desired effect?'

'What about your reputation?'

'Never mind my reputation,' she retorted. 'What kind of reputation have I got, anyway, if he thinks he can say and do just what he likes?'

He smiled. 'All right, if that's what you want, I'll come. I'm sure I can give Mr Hetherington the message he needs, and without resorting to fisticuffs.'

'You don't think it could come to that, do you?' she gasped.

'No, of course not. I won't give an inkling that I know anything about him. But you must appear to be surprised by my visit.'

A companionable silence followed and eventually he remarked, 'You have changed a lot, Hester.'

She looked at him doubtfully. 'Is that good, or bad?'

'Oh, good, of course,' he hastened to assure her. 'But you have become so confident and businesslike.'

'I still blush,' she said, knowing that her cheeks were reddening as she spoke.

'Not nearly as much, and not for such piffling reasons.' Bruce grinned. 'You were very timid when I first met you.'

'I never really grew up until I went to live with Aunt Amelia. Well no, it was actually after I left there, I suppose.'

He nodded. 'Your life certainly changed then.'

Hester thought he would pursue the subject, that he was leading up to something important, but silence fell again and the next time he spoke he merely said it was time for him to go. Hester went downstairs to see him out, and she was still in the hall, tinkering with a vase of flowers and wondering if he really had meant to say something about her marriage, when a fumbling and scratching sound came at the lock of the front door. No doubt that was Adam Frost, coming back the worse for drink. No one had complained about him recently, but he was unlikely to have changed his habits, and whoever this was he was having difficulty with the lock.

Hester stepped forward and opened the

door from the inside. A startled expletive followed and a figure stumbled forward and then staggered back two paces.

'Mr Kelly!' she exclaimed.

'Hello, me dear.'

'Mr Kelly, you're drunk!'

'Never. Never get drunk, me dear. Have a little tipple time to time, but never . . . ' He waved the index finger of his right hand from side to side and grasped the framework of the door with his other hand to steady himself. 'Never get drunk.'

Hester motioned for him to come inside and he obeyed. 'Nice of you to stay up, me dear. Didn't have to. I can manage perfec . . . perfec . . . perfectly well.'

'I'm sure you can.' Hester closed the door. 'Be quiet going upstairs, please.'

He put his finger to his lips. 'Not a sound. Not a song.'

'That's right, Mr Kelly. Not a sound. Good night.'

To her relief he went without another word, walking along the hall with deep concentration and then clutching the banister rail to help himself up the stairs. Hester waited for several moments before she followed, wondering whether he was sometimes guilty of the noise for which Adam Frost had been blamed. At least she had faced him with confidence, she thought. Bruce was right, she had changed and she would face Mr Hetherington with that same confidence when he arrived on Saturday morning.

11

Hester ticked the following days off the calendar with emotions that swung from one extreme to another. First she would wish she could avoid Saturday altogether and not have to go through the trauma of meeting Mr Hetherington again. Then she would look forward to the day with a frisson of excitement, anticipating the glee of seeing that awful man discomforted.

She was imagining the scene and smiling to herself as she went upstairs on Friday morning, when she caught sight of Mr Best on the landing and came to a startled halt. She had thought the house was empty, apart from the staff.

'Oh, Mr Best! I didn't know you were here.'

He gave a little bow and a faint smile. 'I'm sorry if I gave you a fright. I'm not usually here, of course.'

'Is everything all right?'

'It is now, I think. I was feeling a little unwell earlier, so I came back again.'

'Can I help at all? Do you need anything?'

'No, I shall be all right, thank you. I'll have

a little nap, and then I might go into the office this afternoon.'

He walked away towards his room and Hester went down again to tell Kathy not to disturb him when she started cleaning her part of the upstairs region. It was to be hoped that Mr Best really was feeling better, she thought. This was a complication that had not occurred to her before. What was she to do if one of the residents had an accident or became seriously ill? Some could go home, as they did each weekend, but what of the others? A few of them had no other home — Mr Kelly for one. So far as she knew, all his relatives were in far off Ireland. But the staff here was small, and they had no facilities or skill for nursing. She gave a mental shrug. Let Mr Hetherington worry about things like that, should it happen. It was his responsibility after all, and it would give him something more important to think about rather than trying to seduce women. That man arrived with his usual air of self-satisfaction the next day, greeting her cheerfully, apparently not in the least perturbed by her firm rejection of him the previous week. He strode into the office and, as before, took the chair that Hester had placed for herself near the window, and put it behind the desk. This time she was ready for him and hastily moved it away again.

'I prefer to sit over here.'

'But I prefer you to sit beside me.'

'I will stand instead, Mr Hetherington.'

'Oh, come now, don't play too hard.' He sat down and looked at her thoughtfully for several moments. 'You don't trust yourself, is that it?' he said at last. 'You don't want to appear too willing too quickly.'

Hester took a deep breath. What would she do if Bruce did not arrive soon? He *had* to come. If not, she would just have to flee.

'I'm right, aren't I? You're just longing to be close to a man again. You're missing the joys of marriage.'

Hester took another deep breath and mustered her courage. 'We have business to attend to. I think we should make a start.'

'I work better with you beside me. Come, forget all this pretence. Admit it. You're ready to make up for lost time, to welcome a close relationship.'

'Mr Hetherington, if you continue to speak in this fashion I shall have no alternative but to leave the room. Any questions about the accounts will have to be dealt with by mail.'

'My goodness.' He tilted his chair back and gazed at her with admiration. 'I knew you had spirit. That is one of your many qualities. But don't protest too hard. I might just take you at your word.'

Hester bit back a hasty retort. She must maintain dignity, on that point she was adamant. Before she could compose a suitable response the front doorbell sounded.

'Oh!' She made no attempt to disguise her relief. 'I must answer the door.'

She left the office door wide open so that any conversation in the hall could be overheard easily. Bruce was waiting on the doorstep, his eyebrows raised in silent query.

'Oh, Bruce!' she exclaimed with genuine delight. 'How lovely to see you.' He entered the hall and she signalled with her head to confirm that Mr Hetherington was in the office. 'What a surprise. Who would have thought you could come by on a Saturday? How long can you stay?'

'Long enough for a cup of tea, certainly. I was nearby, so I couldn't miss the opportunity of seeing you. Have I come at a bad time? Can you stop work for a while, or are you too busy?'

'We are just checking the accounts, but that won't take long. Come and meet the owner of Bella Casa.'

As they entered the office the well-groomed man behind the desk rose to his feet. Hester faced him with complete confidence.

'Mr Hetherington, allow me to introduce a very good friend, Dr Bruce Hutchinson. Bruce, this is Mr Hetherington, the owner of this establishment.'

'How do you do,' said Bruce, stepping forward and extending his hand. The two men shook hands briefly then stood for a moment eying each other up and down, Hester delighted to note that Bruce was wearing his Sunday suit. Nobody spoke again until Bruce moved back to stand close to Hester.

'Good friends,' said Mr Hetherington musingly. 'Have you known each other long?'

'A very long time,' answered Bruce. 'I knew Hester even before I started my medical studies.' He slipped his arm around her waist and smiled down at her with a proprietary air. 'We know each other very well, don't we, Hester?'

'Very well,' she agreed and Mr Hetherington coloured slightly.

'I see,' he muttered.

'I must not interrupt your work,' said Bruce, addressing Hester as if she were the person in charge. 'If you're sure it's not going to take long, Hester, I could wait for you in the hall.'

'Well . . . '

'Don't be concerned about me. There's a

chair there, and I could finish entering some details in my notebook.'

Mr Hetherington came to a sudden decision. 'There's no need for that. I've seen as much as necessary in the accounts.' He closed the book in front of him to emphasise his words. 'I was just about to go.'

'I don't want to feel that I have precipitated your departure,' said Bruce.

'Not at all. Not at all.' Mr Hetherington seemed to be in a hurry to leave. 'Everything is satisfactory as usual, Mrs Carleton. You don't need to come to the door. I'll see myself out.'

They moved aside as he hastened across the room and into the hall. Moments later the front door slammed and they watched from the office window as he walked quickly along the garden path and out by the gate.

Bruce squeezed Hester's waist momentarily, then took his arm away. 'Mission accomplished, I believe.'

'Oh, Bruce, you were wonderful, and just in time.'

'He was being objectionable again, I suppose.'

'Very much so, but I think he might be cured.'

Bruce turned away from the window. 'He might make some very unpleasant comments next time he comes.'

Hester smiled up at him. 'I don't think so. He looked so deflated I'm sure he won't try that approach again.'

'Hm.' Bruce was not convinced. 'It was too easy. I can't imagine him giving up as easily as that. Think of his pride.'

Hester laughed. 'His pride will prove to be his downfall. There he was, sure he was the answer to every woman's romantic dreams, and then you arrive — younger, far more handsome and a man with an important position in the world.'

Bruce gave a little cough to cover his embarrassment. 'Not as important as all that,' he murmured.

Hester wished he would put his arm around her again. She would like to have both his arms around her, she amended. She would even welcome a kiss. Why was it that he always behaved with such decorum, when someone whom she could not bear to have near her was so willing to dispense with social niceties?

'You will stay for a cup of tea, won't you?' she urged.

'Well, I don't know that . . . '

'The water will be hot already. And you could meet Kathy. She'll be proud to make your acquaintance.'

He agreed to stay just long enough for a quick drink of tea and she led the way into the kitchen. Kathy was at the stove, pouring water into a teapot, and she blushed when she saw Bruce.

'Kathy, I want you to meet Dr Hutchinson. Bruce, this is Kathy.'

'Good morning, Kathy.'

'Good morning, Doctor.' Kathy put the kettle down. 'There's nothing wrong with me now. Truly.'

'He's not come here to treat anybody,' laughed Hester. 'Dr Hutchinson is an old friend.'

'Oh, I see. I'll set a tray. Would you like that in the sitting-room, Ma'am, or upstairs?'

'No, Kathy, we haven't got time for that. We'll sit at the table in here. You bring the tea and the biscuit tin. I'll get the cups.'

After some hesitation Kathy plucked up the nerve to join them at the table. Hester told Bruce about Kathy's mishap with the knife and she opened her hand to show him the results.

'It's just fine now,' she said.

'Yes,' he agreed. 'It has healed very neatly.'

He ate three homemade biscuits, but declined a second drink and announced that he must go. Kathy leapt to her feet as he bade her farewell, then sank back onto her chair again. Hester accompanied him to the door, hoping he would give her a kiss or at least a hug before he left, but as usual he only took her hand.

'Goodbye, Hester. I hope your problem has been solved. I don't know when I'll be able to come again, but I will call in advance to let you know.'

'Thank you for coming today, Bruce. I know it must have been difficult for you to get away. Saturday morning must be a busy time.'

He nodded and went out to his motor car without further delay. Hester watched him until he had driven from sight, then closed the door and went slowly up the stairs to tell the children they could now come down to play in the garden. She felt forlorn rather than triumphant. Bruce had slipped his arm around her so naturally when he was facing up to Mr Hetherington. Why, oh why, did he have to be so formal immediately afterwards?

'Mama, Susan is being mean to me. Tell her not to be so mean.'

'Why, whatever is the matter? Surely you can play together without squabbling.' Hester was in no mood to put up with any nonsense from the children.

'She keeps saying she's got a secret, but she won't tell me what it is.'

Hester looked at Susan, who was looking somewhat guilty and obviously expected to be reprimanded. 'Have you got a secret, Susan?'

The little girl nodded and Dorothy gave a squeal of victory. 'There you are, see.'

'But if she tells you what it is, it won't be a secret any longer.'

Dorothy pouted. 'Why does she keep talking about it then?'

Hester sighed and Susan took the opportunity to run out of the room.

'Come here, Dorothy.' Hester held out her arms and the child snuggled into her embrace. 'It will only be a little thing, so don't get upset about it.'

'But she keeps boasting. I don't like it when she keeps showing off.'

'She won't do it for long,' Hester assured her. 'She wants to feel a little bit important, that's all. You go to school now but she doesn't, so you do something special and she feels left out.' She tightened her arms and then gave a gentle push. 'Go and find something to play with. And don't let me hear you two squabbling.'

She stared out of the bedroom window, wondering how they should spend their free afternoon tomorrow. It was clear that Bruce would be unable to come this weekend. She could telephone Harold and Muriel and see if they would like to arrange anything, but it was short notice and the weather did not look promising. Besides, she told herself, she was independent now. She had always managed to look after her children by herself before they left Thorn Bay and she had no need of others to organise activities for her. No, she and the children would go out alone as a family tomorrow. They had not explored far in St Kilda as yet.

Sunday dawned cloudy and chilly. Edith came in complaining about a cold wind, but by midday the sky had cleared and it looked far more pleasant outdoors.

'We'll go out for a walk,' Hester told the children. 'A new way, somewhere where we haven't been yet.'

They all dressed warmly with gloves and scarves, but they had not gone far before they agreed that Edith had been right about the wind. It bit into their cheeks and reddened the tips of their noses, and Hester saw that clouds were beginning to gather again. The children soon lost their enthusiasm for the outing and Hester decided they would all be happier at home.

'It will be better when we turn around and the wind is behind us,' she promised. 'Oh, look, there's an exhibition of photographs. We'll go and have a look at those first.'

The girls enjoyed looking at pictures of household pets, but they grew restless when there was nothing else to see but photographs of the pier at St Kilda and buildings in Melbourne.

'Can we go home now?' asked Susan.

'Yes, we'll go. We'll make a lovely big fire and we'll play a game. We can toast some muffins for tea later.'

The wind propelled them along, reminding Hester of the blustery days when she had walked with the big dog on the cliffs at Mountcliffe. She had never minded cold winds there, she thought, but today she was just as keen as the children to go back indoors.

The girls scuttled in ahead of her when they reached Bella Casa, then stopped short in surprise. Hester was also taken aback at the sight of two figures descending the stairs, one small and young, looking very thin in comparison with her tubby companion. Mr Best paused for a moment, apparently disconcerted by their arrival, then he tugged the sleeve of the little girl beside him and they both came down to the hall. He took the child's hand as they approached the family group.

'Good afternoon, Mrs Carleton.'

'Good afternoon, Mr Best.'

The little girl put her left thumb in her mouth and looked up at Hester with frightened eyes.

'My little niece,' explained Mr Best. 'I do hope you don't mind me bringing her in. But it was so cold outside.'

'Of course not. What's your name, dear?'

The little girl edged away without answering. She was about five years old, Hester judged, far too old to be sucking her thumb.

'I'm afraid she can't answer you,' said Mr Best. 'She can't hear you either. She is completely deaf.'

'Oh dear. The poor little mite.' Hester was instantly filled with sympathy. She went down on one knee and held out her hand. Mr Best urged the child forward and eventually she plucked up the courage to take her thumb out of her mouth and let Hester hold hands. She kept her other hand in Mr Best's firm grip.

'What's her name?' asked Dorothy.

'Rosie.'

'Hello, Rosie.'

The child did not turn her head. She continued to stare at Hester, then suddenly withdrew her hand and tried to hide behind Mr Best's legs.

'Can't she talk at all?' asked Dorothy in bewilderment.

'No. She can't hear, you see. That means she hasn't learned how to talk.'

'But how do you manage to communicate with her?' Hester rose to her feet.

'Well, you can hardly say that we communicate. You can always tell what she likes and doesn't like, but there's not much else you can do. I usually take her out on a Sunday to give her mother a rest.'

'She needs some special help,' said Hester. 'I've heard that there are special schools for children like Rosie. Do you want me to find out more about it? I have a doctor friend who will be able to help.'

'No, actually, she's starting school next week,' replied Mr Best.

'Oh, I see. Well, perhaps we can get to know her better soon.'

'Ah, no. Sadly, she has to go away to school. This is our last visit together before she goes away.'

'What a pity. The poor child won't understand what is happening to her.'

'No, it is a problem. It's upsetting for everybody, but it is all for the best in the end.' Mr Best heaved a sigh. 'But we must hurry away. Her mother will worry if we are late back.'

As they went up the stairs Hester tried to explain how being deaf made such a difference and how difficult it must be for Rosie to understand anything.

'She looked terribly frightened,' said Dorothy.

'Yes. Well, it must be frightening to go to a strange place and meet new people when you can't understand anything that's going on. Imagine how you would have felt if you couldn't hear what Miss Jackson said when you first went to school.'

'Ooh!' Dorothy could remember how frightening it had been without that extra problem. 'She's lucky to have a nice uncle like Mr Best.'

'I like Uncle Harold better,' said Susan. 'When can we see him again, Mama?'

'I don't know, dear. Soon perhaps.'

12

Everything had been going so smoothly and Hester was feeling so confident she decided it was time to try some of her new ideas. The morning tea break, when she and the other two staff members sat down together, had become a far more relaxed routine so that would be the best time to announce her first proposal.

'I think we could cut down on the amount of time spent cleaning,' she began. 'Especially now that we have the carpet sweepers.' She did not look directly at Edith, but she sensed that the older woman had drawn herself up ready to protest. 'If you think you could finish the work a little earlier, you could have some free time during the afternoon.'

'I knew it!' Edith's indignation was so great she almost rose to her feet. 'Start using machines, and the next thing you know, people's jobs are cut. I knew that was why those things were brought in.'

Kathy said nothing, but her eyes widened with alarm and she stared at Hester in dismay.

'Calm down,' said Hester. 'I'm not talking

about cutting jobs. I'm only suggesting that we could do the same amount of work faster.'

'And then get sent home,' retorted Edith. 'What are we supposed to do for money? We can't afford not to work.'

'I'm not talking about cutting your wages. I'm only talking about shorter hours.'

There was a silence while Edith stared in disbelief and Kathy looked from one to the other in confusion.

'We could try it for a week or so and see how it turns out,' said Hester. She had guessed that she would have to explain slowly, but once they understood they were sure to welcome the changes. 'Do you think you could finish all the rooms and the stairs and everything a little faster? Say an hour sooner? That would mean you could have an hour longer for your lunch break.'

Edith's eyes gleamed, but she was still suspicious. 'What about our pay?'

'That would stay the same, of course.'

'You can't mean it. What would Mr Hetherington say?'

'Mr Hetherington pays for the amount of work *done*. How long it takes is not the point.'

'He won't like it.' Edith had begun to consider the possibilities.

'The work will obviously have to be up to

the usual standard. If it begins to slip, then we'll have to go back to the original hours.'

There was another silence while Edith sought for hidden flaws in the suggestion and Kathy gazed down at the table, utterly bewildered. Hester poured herself another cup of tea and waited. She knew perfectly well that the cleaning could be finished sooner. She had watched the servants at her aunt's house filling up time, trying to look busy whenever her aunt came into view, and she had seen the slow and desultory movements here, particularly on the staircase. Both women speeded up the sweeping and polishing when they noticed her coming, and she was quite sure they achieved little when she was out doing errands or taking Dorothy to and from school.

'Tell us again,' said Edith.

'I've been thinking that we could all have a much longer lunch break if we could finish tasks sooner.' Hester had found that she was working faster herself now that she was more accustomed to the kitchen and the quantity of food she had to prepare. Making pies and puddings for such a large number of people had become much easier, and she no longer doubted her judgement on the amount of ingredients she needed.

'Do you really mean it — we'll still get the

same pay if we work less hours?' asked Edith.

'If the work is satisfactory.' It was important to emphasise that point.

Edith was still unsure. 'What made you think of all this?'

'I used to go to meetings in the place where I used to live, and I heard a lot about work conditions. I agreed with some of the speakers. If you can get the job done faster, why shouldn't you benefit? It's silly to spin a job out, just to make up time.'

'Now you're going all political.'

Hester refused to be sidetracked. 'What do you think? Do you need more time to consider it?'

'More time, why? Let's get this straight. If we can get all the cleaning done by lunch time, we get two hours off. And no difference in pay. Is that right?'

'That's right. But the cleaning has to be done properly.'

'I agree,' declared Edith. 'That's fine, isn't it, Kathy?'

Kathy nodded doubtfully, but did not speak.

'When are we going to start?' Now that Edith was sure of the advantages she was eager to begin the experiment as soon as possible.

'Let's try for half an hour today. Do you

think you can do that?'

'Just watch us.' Edith had never been so enthusiastic. 'Come on, Kathy, let's get a bit of a hurry on.'

At twelve o'clock sharp they came to the kitchen together, Edith already untying the strings at the back of her apron.

'Right, we've only got the writing-room and the sitting-room to do now. We'll have those ready in time to do the veggies. So we don't come back till half past one. Is that right?'

'That's right,' agreed Hester, suppressing a chuckle.

Edith went with alacrity, but Kathy dithered near the door looking rather lost. Hester had guessed what might be going through her mind just now so she had made more plans.

'You won't have enough time to go home, will you, Kathy?' She would not be able to afford the extra fare, either, but it was better not to mention that.

'No. Edith's lucky, living so close.'

'I expect you're wondering what to do with your extra time.' Hester looked out at the garden. The weather had deteriorated into a steady drizzle. 'You won't want to go out in that.'

Kathy shook her head dismally. 'No.'

'You can read well, can't you? Do you like books?'

'Oh, yes, Ma'am.'

'You might like to join the public library later, but in the meantime you could borrow one of mine. Come up and see. I've got a lot of books.'

'Oh, Ma'am!'

Kathy had never been into the private quarters and she went in warily behind Hester, scarcely daring to look around.

'Show Kathy where the books are, Susan.'

The little girl was eager to comply. She grasped Kathy's hand and tugged her towards the shelves in the living-room. 'There!'

'Oh, Ma'am! What a lot of books! Are they really all yours?'

'Yes. They belonged to my uncle. When he died all his books were given to me.'

'He must have been a very clever man.'

'Yes, he was. He was also a very nice man. Choose a book that you'd like to read, Kathy. It doesn't matter which one.'

Kathy still felt uncomfortable and out of place, but she went closer to the shelves, torn between the urge to escape and the desire to explore all the wonders before her. Hester watched, remembering the first occasion when her uncle had invited her to choose a book. She had felt almost the same sense of awe.

'Oh, *Silas Marner*! I started that at school, but I had to leave so I never finished it.'

'Well, now's your chance, if you want to.'

'I'll start it again. Oh, you're so nice, Ma'am. I've never met anyone so nice. I'll look after it, really I will.'

'I'm sure you will. You can decide where you want to sit for comfort, Kathy. You might find the sitting-room downstairs a good place.'

'Oh, surely not.'

'There'll be nobody else there. But you make up your own mind. And, Kathy?'

'Yes, Ma'am?' The excited girl had almost reached the door.

'Take your apron off. This is your free time, so you should relax.'

Kathy gulped but made no response. She tucked the book securely under her arm and hurried away as if she feared Hester might change her mind.

Susan clapped her hands with glee. 'Isn't she happy?'

'Yes, that's nice, isn't it? Now we'll have to rush to get ready, otherwise we'll be late meeting Dorothy.'

Within a few days the new system was well established. Edith and Kathy worked with a will, determined to prove they could achieve excellent results, and both were looking more contented. Kathy was turning into a bookworm, spending every moment of her sparc time reading, and Hester decided she must make sure the girl went out sometimes for fresh air.

'Kathy, do you think you could meet Dorothy for me sometimes? She'll be quite happy to come home with you.'

'Yes, Ma'am. Of course, Ma'am.'

They went together the first time, to make sure that Kathy knew the way, and from then on she went to fetch Dorothy while Hester made lunch for them all. She also paid Kathy sixpence. The girl turned pink when she received her wages and Hester explained why there was a little more that week.

'Oh, Ma'am! You don't have to do that. Really!'

'I appreciate your help, Kathy. And I'm sure you will find the extra coppers useful.'

'Oh, Ma'am! Yes, Ma'am.'

'Well then.' Hester always felt that Kathy needed mothering and she was pleased to be able to do something worthwhile for her. The girl was looking healthier these days, her face not so drawn and some colour in her cheeks. She was obviously feeling stronger now that she was eating better. 'Have you finished that book yet? Well, don't forget to tell me when you want another one.'

'There's a note here for you, Ma'am. It's from the school. Miss Jackson said it was important and you must read it immediately.'

'What can they be wanting? Just a moment, Kathy, while I finish buttering these. Did you have a nice time at school this morning, Dorothy?'

'Yes, Mama. Miss Jackson said I'm clever. I can write good letters.'

'Good.' That note could not be anything serious, thought Hester with relief. Nothing had happened to upset Dorothy. She finished arranging a tray, ready for taking upstairs, then picked the note up from the table. Her heart seemed to stop beating when she read the opening words and Kathy cried out in alarm.

'Oh, Ma'am! Whatever is the matter?'

'Diphtheria!' Hester's lips seemed so stiff she could hardly say the word. 'They've got diphtheria!'

'Oh, no, Ma'am!'

Hester read the note again. 'They've closed the school. There's no school this afternoon.'

A silence followed while Hester thought about the dangers of that dreadful disease. She could remember only too well the bleak expression on Bruce's face when he told her about the outbreak in his district. Dorothy had no idea what the fuss was all about, but she knew it was something alarming and she dared not interrupt.

'I thought she'd be safe at that little school,' said Hester at last. 'Oh, I do wish I'd never sent her there.'

'The school is not to blame,' said Kathy bravely. 'You can pick it up anywhere. And Dorothy might not get it.'

'I'm going down there.' Hester looked at the clock and pulled off her apron and sleeve protectors. 'There's sure to be somebody there. I've got to find out more about it. Can you look after the children for me please, Kathy? Dorothy, go and get Susan. You can have your lunch down here in the kitchen today. I'll be back soon.'

Other mothers had reacted in the same way as Hester and she found a little knot of concerned women clustered by the front gate of the school.

'What's happening? What did they say?' she asked.

'Nothing yet. The Head will be coming out any minute now.'

Eventually the principal came out of his office and tried to placate them. Closing the school was only a precautionary action, he assured them. When pressed he admitted that three children were sick. Two had been diagnosed with the disease, while the third was unwell and it was suspected that he also was a victim. The whole school would be thoroughly disinfected and the parents would be notified when it was safe to re-open.

The woman with the loudest voice made herself heard over the questions of the others.

'How are we going to find out what's going on? We want to know who's got it.'

'And how many,' shouted another.

He raised both hands and made soothing gestures. 'We will write to every family as soon as we have information. It's too soon to know any more just yet.'

The group did not disperse until he announced that he had no more to say and went away. Hester returned to Bella Casa, trying to decide what to do next. She would telephone Bruce and leave a message for him to call her as soon as possible, she decided. He would be able to help.

To her surprise, Bruce answered the call himself. 'Hester! You're lucky to catch me. Another few minutes and I would have left.'

'Oh, Bruce!'

'What's the matter?'

Hester told him what she knew, doing her best to speak slowly and not gabble her words. 'I couldn't bear it if anything happened to Dorothy. What can I do, Bruce? Tell me what to do.'

'Well, the first thing is to keep calm. Don't panic. Are those sick children in the same class as Dorothy?'

'No, they're about three years older.'

'Good. So they won't be in the same room and they won't be in the habit of playing together either.'

'But what about all the things they use in school? They share books and skipping ropes, balls and everything. Oh, Bruce, I'm so worried. It seems to spread so quickly. And a lot of your patients died. You told me.'

'Yes, but the circumstances were a lot different. Has Dorothy got any scratches or grazes on her hands, or her elbows or anywhere?'

'I don't think so.'

'So she's quite likely to be safe. She is well nourished and has good basic health. Hester, you must try not to worry. Don't let the children become anxious.'

'I can't just wait and do nothing. What can I do to help?'

He suggested that Dorothy could sleep in a different room from her sister, just in case she had become infected. 'And you've got plenty of hot water there. You could give her a nice bath.'

'Should I burn her clothes?'

'No, just wash them. A good wash should be enough. Keep a watch over both the children, and if you see any signs of sickness, any signs at all, send for a doctor. You've got one very close to you, haven't you?'

'Yes, Dr Gibbs. He seems very nice.'

'Good. So call him if you have any problems.'

All the washing and moving of furniture helped to take Hester's mind off the dangers for a time, but during the following two days she found herself watching the girls almost constantly. They were puzzled by the sudden changes and could not understand why she kept telling them to play apart. Susan tended to follow her sister everywhere, glad that she was at home again and not wanting to miss her company while she was there. Edith pursed her lips when she heard Hester calling to the children yet again.

'If you don't mind me saying so, Ma'am, that won't make no difference one way or the other. If they're going to get it, they'll get it. And that'll be the worse for us and all.'

'Oh dear.' Hester had not thought beyond the fear of Dorothy catching the disease. If she did, would that mean all the residents and the staff and even she herself would be in danger? She had not prayed recently, had not prayed since the terrible last year of her marriage when everything had seemed to go awry, but she prayed now, silently in the kitchen, but aloud later in the sanctuary of her bedroom where Dorothy was sleeping soundly.

★   ★   ★

'Mama! Mama!' Dorothy's shrill voice came down the stairs.

Hester hastened out of the office. 'What's the matter?'

'Susan's gone into a room. You said we mustn't go in the rooms, but she's gone in.'

Hester clicked her teeth and started for the staircase. 'Oh dear. What is she doing?'

'I don't know. I told her not to, but she wouldn't listen.'

As Hester reached the landing Susan appeared at the end of the corridor, her cheeks pink with guilt.

'What have you been doing, Susan?'

'Nothing.'

'Come now, tell me the truth. Which room did you go into?'

Susan half turned as if to point out a door, and Mr Best stepped into the corridor.

'Good morning, Mrs Carleton. Please don't be cross with Susan. I invited her in.'

'Mr Best! Are you feeling unwell again?'

'I'm feeling much better now, thank you. Just a touch of indigestion, I think.'

'Perhaps you ought to see a doctor.' Uncle Jeremy had always talked of his heart trouble as if it were merely indigestion, she remembered.

'No, there's no need for that. He'd only tell me not to eat so much, anyway.'

'I've heard that said before, Mr Best. If it happens again I think you should see a doctor.'

'Don't worry, Mrs Carleton. I'm not really ill.'

'I'm pleased to hear that. But the children have been told not to go into any of the rooms, so please don't invite them in.'

'I'm sorry if I did the wrong thing. But I like children and I miss my little niece, you know.'

'How is Rosie?'

'They say she's getting on very well, but who can tell?' Mr Best sighed heavily and shook his head. 'At least I'll see my other little nieces on Sunday.'

'Do you need anything? Perhaps a cup of tea?'

'No thank you. I feel well enough now. I'll

go to the office soon.'

Hester turned away in time to see Susan poke her tongue out at her sister. She retaliated in the same way, but Hester pretended not to notice. She had enough to worry about just now without having to sort out childish quarrels, and she could only hope that Mr Best would not suddenly collapse from a heart attack.

'Come down at once, both of you,' she instructed. 'And remember, Susan, you do *not* go into any of the rooms.'

'Kathy goes in.' Susan was in a rebellious mood.

'Kathy is working. She has jobs to do. You have no business to be in any of those rooms. If it happens again I shall be very cross, so remember that and do as you are told from now on.'

'I told her not to do it,' said Dorothy in a self-righteous tone.

The girls made faces at each other again, and as the day wore on they seemed to spend more and more time bickering. Kathy came to the rescue several times, finding new ways to divert them and keep them occupied, but Hester began to feel that more was involved than mere boredom and irritability. She welcomed bedtime that evening, but even when the two children were asleep she felt uneasy and she checked them far more often than usual.

The next morning Dorothy's face was flushed and she hardly stirred when Hester spoke to her.

'I don't want any breakfast,' she mumbled. 'I want to stay here.'

'Oh dear, don't you feel well? What's the matter?'

'It hurts,' croaked Dorothy.

'Oh dear! What hurts? What's hurting, Dorothy?'

'My throat.'

'Oh, no!' Hester clutched at her own throat as the implication struck home. It seemed that her worst fears had been realised.

13

Conflicting emotions threatened to send Hester into a frenzy during the next few moments. What was the most important thing to do first? What would happen if she left Dorothy unattended? Was it too early to telephone the doctor? What about the residents? How could she leave ten men to go hungry to work?

She strove to follow Bruce's advice. Stay calm, he had said, don't panic. Dorothy did not seem seriously ill as yet. Her throat was red but she was breathing normally. She obviously had a temperature, but she was only warmer than usual, not raging hot. Hester told herself she had time to organise things efficiently. She would go down and make a start on breakfast. Thank Heaven for gas. It would have been dreadful to have to take time stoking a wood stove. When everything was set out ready she would telephone the doctor. She had kept his number ready to hand ever since news of the disease had come.

Susan seemed as lively and healthy as ever. Hester told her that her sister was ill and she must not disturb her, must not even go into the room, then she hurried downstairs and started getting food out of the larder. To her surprise, Edith arrived less than five minutes later.

'Oh, Edith!' Surely she had not wasted half an hour in panic! Hester looked at the clock and saw that it was only six-thirty. 'You're early this morning!'

'Yes, well.' Edith shrugged. 'The way things were going yesterday, it looked as if there might be a bit of bother today.' She looked at Hester's harassed expression. 'I suppose Dorothy's ill?'

Hester could only nod.

'Yes, well, it looked that way, didn't it?' said Edith. 'Have you sent for the doctor yet? No, well I suppose it's still a bit early in the day.'

'What are we going to do?' Hester needed someone to give her support. She was beginning to feel helpless. She could only see problems — problems that multiplied the more she thought about them. 'What about Kathy? She's got all those brothers and sisters. It would be dreadful if they all got it, too.'

Edith set about stacking dishes on the serving bench. 'There's no point in worrying about things that might not happen.'

'Aren't you frightened, Edith?'

'I was a bit, but I was talking to someone about it last night. As she said, what about all the nurses and the cooks and everybody at the Fairfield Hospital? Most of them go home to their families every night, and they've got all sorts of diseases in that place, not just diphtheria.'

Hester felt a glimmer of hope. 'So you think you and the residents will be safe?'

'Too late to worry about it now, anyway. But as my friend said, it all comes down to something called — er — um — hygiene. We wash our hands often, and I've brought a change of clothes with me today, just in case.'

'Oh, Edith, I don't know what to say.'

'Best not say anything then.' Edith turned away in embarrassment and began to fill the kettle.

'Oh, here's Kathy!' exclaimed Hester. 'You're early today as well, Kathy.'

'Right, now we can really get on,' said Edith. 'You go and look after Dorothy, Ma'am. We'll look after breakfast. We can do it by ourselves, can't we Kathy?'

'Yes, of course. Is Dorothy bad, Ma'am?'

'She's definitely ill. Thank you, both of you. I'll go up and check on her before I telephone Dr Gibbs.'

The doctor promised to come in half an hour and he was as good as his word. Hester met him in the hall, twisting her hands together in agitation.

'Thank you for being so quick,' she began. 'I'm so frightened. I've heard terrible stories about diphtheria.'

He smiled gently. 'You said on the telephone that your little girl has a temperature.'

'Yes. It's gone up since early this morning, I'm sure of it.'

'Ah.' He nodded as though that were significant. 'Now it might be difficult for you to restrain yourself, but if I ask Dorothy any questions, I don't want you to answer for her. Will you remember that please? Right, let's go up and take a look at her, shall we?'

He followed Hester up the stairs and along the corridor to the family's apartment. Susan stood at her bedroom door, staring up at him with curiosity but obeying instructions to stay out of the way.

'Hello,' said Dr Gibbs. 'I've come to see your sister. She's not feeling very well today. Do you feel well?'

'Yes, thank you.'

'Good.'

Hester showed him where Dorothy was lying in the other bedroom, her face now flushed and her eyes somewhat bleary. He introduced himself and asked, 'What's your name?'

She was reluctant to speak, but eventually she answered.

'Hm. You've got a very sore throat, haven't you?' He opened his bag and took out a thermometer. 'Have you ever seen one of these before? Good, so you know what it does. Open your mouth, there's a good girl.'

He made several chatty comments to gain her confidence, then checked the results.

'Yes, you have got a temperature. No wonder you're not feeling very well today. Can you sit up for me please? I want to look at your throat, and then I want to listen to what's going on inside you.'

When he had finished his examination he told her that she would feel better soon and he would come to see her again before long, then he wrote a prescription, packed his bag and went to wash his hands. Hester could barely wait until they reached the hall again before she started questioning him.

'How bad is she, Doctor?'

'You can stop worrying so much,' he said. 'She has tonsillitis. She will be feeling very uncomfortable, but it's not dangerous.'

'But they've got diphtheria at her school!'

'Yes, I know about that. I have several patients who go to that school, but so far none of them have caught it. I think we were very lucky that the first case was diagnosed so soon. And the school Head acted immediately. That was a help.'

'It's three days since then,' Hester fretted. 'Are you sure it's not diphtheria?'

'Certain. That doesn't mean to say it's impossible for her to get it, of course. No one is absolutely sure what the incubation period is. But I think it's unlikely. Keep Dorothy in bed for the time being. She needs rest.' He handed her the prescription. 'This will help to bring her temperature down, and if she gets a headache it will help to ease that. She won't want to eat much, but give her plenty of liquids. She probably likes lemonade. Give her as much as she likes. And she can suck ice.'

Hester was not convinced and she wanted to argue with him, to tell him that he had not spent enough time on the examination.

'What's the matter?' he asked. 'You really should not worry so much.'

Her eyes filled with tears. 'I had a little boy once. The doctor said there was nothing wrong with him. I knew it wasn't imagination, but he wouldn't believe me.'

'I see.' Dr Gibbs took hold of her hand and pressed it gently. 'I can understand your fear. But it's not diphtheria, Mrs Carleton, I assure you. Strangely enough, her temperature would not be so high if it was that. And she doesn't have other symptoms either.'

'I want to believe you. But I'd like a second opinion.'

'You're entitled to that, of course. And I won't feel offended if you do get one. If you have any other concerns, don't hesitate to call me, Mrs Carleton. Just promise me that you'll watch for changes and let me know if there are any.'

'Yes, I'll do that. Thank you for coming.'

She saw him out and watched him drive away, then turned to find Mr Jamieson waiting in the hall.

'I hear that Dorothy is ill, Mrs Carleton. On behalf of all the residents, I wish to express our sympathy and good wishes for a speedy recovery.'

'Thank you, Mr Jamieson. The doctor said it is tonsillitis and it's not dangerous.'

'That's a great relief. I'm so pleased to hear that. Please try not to worry, Mrs Carleton.'

He had no sooner gone upstairs than Mr Best came out from the dining-room.

'They tell me that you had to get the doctor for your little daughter this morning, Mrs Carleton. How is the poor dear?'

'She is feeling ill, but the doctor said she will soon recover.'

'I'm so glad to hear it. Can I bring anything back for her today?'

'No thank you, Mr Best. She just has to rest and drink plenty of fluids.'

'I see. Well, if you need any help in caring for either of your little ones, just let me know. I can sit with them if you need to go out.'

Hester thanked him again, then went upstairs to give Dorothy a drink and tell Susan that she may come down for breakfast. When they entered the kitchen Edith turned at once.

'What did he say?'

'He said it's not diphtheria.'

'Well, thank the Lord for that. You just sit down, Ma'am. We're about finished out there.'

Hester found that her legs were trembling and it was a relief to sit while Edith presented her with a cup of tea and then made toast and boiled an egg for Susan. When Kathy came out with the last tray of dirty dishes, Hester pushed her chair back from the table and rose to her feet.

'I want to thank both of you for being so helpful,' she said. 'It was good of you to come in so early today and do all that extra work. I don't know what I would have done without you.'

Kathy blushed with pleasure and, as usual,

Edith spoke for both.

'You always do the right thing by us, Ma'am, so it's only fitting that we do our best for you.'

'Thank you. Thank you, both. I really do appreciate it. But I have to warn you, the danger's not yet over. Kathy, you must be especially careful. I don't want you to take any risks.'

Kathy began to fill the sink with water, apparently unperturbed. 'This isn't the first time we've gone through this, Ma'am. They had diphtheria at our local school once. And not one of our lot got sick.'

Her words were a comfort, but Hester felt that she would not rest until Bruce had given his verdict. She telephoned at once and was lucky enough to catch him at home.

'Oh, Bruce, will you please come and look at Dorothy,' she pleaded. 'She's ill this morning. She has a terribly sore throat. Doctor Gibbs said it's not diphtheria, but I want to be sure.'

'Don't you trust that doctor?'

'I don't know him well enough to tell. He might never have seen diphtheria. I'm frightened Bruce. It seems as if it's all going to happen again. Dr Turnbull said there was nothing wrong with William. But you knew different. You knew straight away that something was wrong.'

'I can understand what you're going through, Hester. But I won't be able to come until late evening. If things look worse you'll have to call the other doctor back.'

'He says it's only — '

Bruce broke in quickly. 'Don't tell me his diagnosis. I'll make up my own mind when I get there.' He repeated his advice about trying to stay calm and to call Dr Gibbs again if necessary, then ended the conversation.

Hester was relieved to know that he would come, even though it would be a long wait. It was an unusual day. Edith went out promptly at noon and stayed away for two hours as she always did nowadays, but she and Kathy insisted that they could manage by themselves and Hester should spend most of her time looking after the children. Kathy dealt with all the deliverymen, and instead of reading during her break she diced meat and prepared all the vegetables for a large stew. Hester found herself with time on her hands. Dorothy was asleep and Susan was playing quietly so she occupied herself by writing to Cora. Sympathetic and helpful as they were, she could not pour out her innermost feelings to the two downstairs. Writing was not the same as actually talking personally to someone, but it eased the strain a little.

She had almost forgotten it was rent day, but she thought about it in time and went down to the office only minutes before Adam Frost arrived. As soon as the money and the receipt had changed hands he gave her a paper bag.

'It's a game for Dorothy,' he said. 'It will give her something to do if she has to stay in bed a while.'

'Oh, thank you.' Hester found that the game consisted of a set of paper dolls with a collection of hats and dresses. 'Oh! She'll like that. She loves cutting out.'

'I'm glad to hear it.' His eyes twinkled. 'I thought you might object to sweeties.'

Hester chuckled. 'She's not eating much of anything at the moment. But you're right, I think this is much more suitable. Thank you again.'

All the residents enquired after Dorothy and offered wishes for a speedy recovery. Diphtheria had not been mentioned in the dining-room that morning, so nobody had qualms about infection and assumed that the child would soon be well. Hester fervently hoped that her fears would prove to be groundless and that no one would be able to complain later that she had not been truthful about the dangers.

Edith and Kathy had gone home and the

house was quiet when Bruce finally arrived.

'Oh, I'm so glad to see you,' exclaimed Hester.

'Have there been any changes during the day?'

'Not really. Dorothy has been sleeping a lot but she's awake now.'

'That's good. It means I won't have to wake her up. What about Susan?'

'She seems as lively as ever. She's asleep now, though.'

They went up to the bedroom, where Bruce first chatted to Dorothy then examined her. He did everything that the other doctor had done, but he also held up his thumb and asked her to grip it, first with her right hand then with her left. He then asked her to watch his thumb as he moved it slowly from side to side.

'Fine,' he said, then to Hester's surprise he took a comic paper out of his bag.

'This is a story about Billy Bunter,' he said. 'Have you ever heard of him?'

Dorothy shook her head and he smiled. 'He's a greedy boy who always eats too much. But he's funny. I'll leave this paper here for you, so that you can look at it when you feel better. I hope you can remember what his name is. Billy Bunter. Can you say it?'

She said it clearly and he nodded. 'That's

good. I think you'll remember. Tell me his name again.'

When she had done so he said she ought to sleep now and he tucked her in. 'You'll feel better soon. Bye bye, Dorothy.'

'Bye, Uncle Bruce.'

When he had repacked his bag and washed his hands he beckoned to Hester. She lowered the gaslight and followed him to the living-room.

'It's her tonsils,' he said at once. 'They're inflamed, and sore of course, but it's definitely not diphtheria.'

'That's what Dr Gibbs said. You are absolutely sure?'

He nodded and with her relief came an outbreak of tears. He held out his arms and she went into his embrace without hesitation. She clutched at him, finding comfort in his firm chest and sturdy arms, and he let her weep until her emotion was spent. She lingered there with her head resting snugly against him, wishing she could stay there forever feeling safe and cherished, but eventually she withdrew and wiped her eyes with a lace-edged handkerchief.

'Poor Hester, you've had so many crises to deal with in the past few years,' he said. 'Come and sit down. You need to rest.'

That evening it was he who made the tea

and carried in the tray. Hester looked up apologetically. 'I'm sorry about all that fuss.'

'You needed to let it all out. You'll feel better for it.'

'Yes. I'm sorry you had to come all this way after a hard day.' She accepted a cup of tea, but put it down again almost at once, untasted. 'You are sure, aren't you?' she pressed.

'Don't worry, Hester. Dorothy will need care for a few days, but it's not diphtheria. You can watch out for signs of that, just to reassure yourself. Look at her throat in the morning. If she had the disease you'd see a grey membrane at the back of her mouth. That's where the danger lies, it affects the breathing.'

'I'm so glad you came, Bruce. I trust you, and I'll trust Dr Gibbs more now as well.' He nodded and as she finally sipped her tea she thought about the way he had examined Dorothy. He was good with children. She had always known he would make a good doctor, even before he went to university.

'What was all that about Billy Bunter?' she asked.

He chuckled. 'It's one of the tricks they use at the Fairfield Hospital. That disease can paralyse the palate and so on. If children can say that name, it's proof that the palate is not paralysed.'

'I see.' Hester was not sure that she wanted to know all the dangers, but he was clearly not worried about Dorothy and she had full confidence in him.

When Bruce stood up to go he held out his arms again and when she went to him he kissed her on the lips. Hester felt a heady delight in that short moment of ecstasy. He had never kissed her like that before. He had never given her more than a brotherly peck when she was recovering from the disasters of last year, and he had not kissed her at all since they met again this year. It was strange that it had taken the threat of another disaster before they could come together so naturally and with such a meaningful kiss.

* * *

Edith came in the next morning at the same early hour as before and Hester stared in surprise.

'Edith! I didn't expect to see you on a Saturday!'

'Can't stop all day, Ma'am, but I can handle breakfast. Kathy reckons she can manage the rest, seeing as how they don't all come back today.'

'I'm truly grateful Edith. Thank you so much.'

Twelve minutes before ten o'clock the front doorbell sounded and Hester hurried out to the hall. Trust Mr Hetherington to come early today of all days, she thought, but it was a woman who stood on the step.

'Cora! Fancy seeing you!'

Cora bustled in. 'I got your letter this morning. It sounded as though you were going to need help. How's Dorothy?'

'About the same I would say. But I'm not so worried now. Bruce came last night and he said the same as Dr Gibbs.'

'That's a relief. But you're still going to need help, for a few days at least.'

'Edith and Kathy have been marvellous.'

'Yes, but they can't keep that up for long. Is Edith here now?'

'Well, no. She came in early, but she left straight after breakfast.'

'See what I mean? And Kathy should have her time off tomorrow. Let me see what's happening in the kitchen and then I'll go up to see the children.'

Mr Hetherington arrived shortly afterwards and chose to make this a day when he would inspect the kitchen. He stopped short at the sight of Cora, who had not yet removed her hat and coat.

'Mrs Wellerby! This is a surprise.'

'Good morning, Mr Hetherington. I'm just

visiting. I was curious to see how things were going, as you might imagine. The place is running beautifully, isn't it?'

'Yes, I have been well satisfied with the management.'

'I told you, didn't I? I said you couldn't find anyone better than Mrs Carleton, didn't I?'

'Indeed you did.'

He glanced in Hester's direction and confirmed his words with a slight nod. Since that day when Bruce had arrived, giving clear signals that he was a greater rival for Hester's attention, the relationship between them had been cool and formal. Hester always stood in the office, or sat at a distance if they had lengthy discussions to make, and he had given no further cause for offence.

Cora chuckled when Hester came back to say that he had departed.

'He's looking quite subdued. Has he ever tried anything on?'

Hester blushed. 'Do you mean . . . ?'

'He always fancies himself as a ladykiller. Poor man. I didn't say anything in case it made you nervous and looking for trouble. But I was sure you'd be able to handle him all right.' Cora gave a disparaging wave of her hand. 'He's all puff and bluster, but under all that he's got nothing. A pity he thinks so well of himself. Anyway, now that he's gone we can get down to business. You didn't tell him about Dorothy, did you? Good. There's no point in getting him all worked up over nothing.'

Cora stayed until the evening meal was over and brushed aside Hester's concern.

'I'm enjoying the change. I'd never tell Edmund, but I'll confess to you, Hester — I miss my old job. It's boring at home all day with no one to talk to, just cleaning the house and cooking for two. Given the chance, I do believe I'd take on full-time work again. But that wouldn't suit Edmund.'

'No, I can imagine what Father would say.' Hester hesitated for a moment. 'You can come here any time if you want someone to talk to.'

'I'll take you up on that. I've stayed away till now because I didn't want it to look as if I was interfering. But you've got things going with a swing. I'm proud of you.'

'Thank you. I mean it, Cora, come any time. We'll be pleased to see you.'

'I'll be here for the next few days, anyway. I'll look after the children, or do anything else you like. Honestly, Hester, I'll enjoy it.'

Bruce called again that evening and he greeted Hester with an affectionate kiss. After he had examined Dorothy he announced that her condition was as good as could be expected, but they would need patience for a full recovery.

'One day we'll have a cure for infections like this. Something like a magic potion that will get rid of germs almost overnight, but in the meantime we just have to wait and let nature take its course.'

They settled in the living-room with a tray of tea and biscuits and Hester described her day.

'Have you been very busy?' she asked.

'We're always busy. It's just that some times are more hectic than others. We haven't got any particular problems at the moment, thank goodness, but there's always something to deal with.' Bruce smiled contentedly. 'Being here is so restful and pleasant.'

It was comforting and pleasant to have him there with her, thought Hester. How nice it would be if they lived closer, if neither of them had such time consuming duties . . . if they could spend the rest of their days together in such warm companionship.

Bruce broke the spell. 'I must go. I have to be up early in the morning, and so do you. I will look in again fairly soon.'

They went downstairs together and paused near the front door. Bruce took her hand and raised it to his lips, then drew her close and kissed her on the cheek.

'Good night, Hester. Sleep tight.'

'Good night, Bruce. Take care on the way home.'

That kiss had lacked some of the ardour that she had felt with the ecstatic first kiss yesterday, she thought as she watched him walk to the gate. Why was it so? Was it that she had imagined an intensity yesterday, a depth of emotion that had never really been there? She had needed comfort so desperately at the time.

No, that was not it, she assured herself. His kiss yesterday really had been filled with deep feeling. And his farewell kiss tonight had been affectionate. She need not fear that his feelings towards her had changed. Remembering that idyllic moment when he had taken her into his arms last night she could even believe they had reclaimed that dream-like occasion in Thorn Bay — that wonderful time when he had seemed to suggest they could look forward to a brighter future, a future together.

14

'Ma'am! Oh, Ma'am!' Kathy looked and sounded more flustered than she had ever been. 'Oh, Ma'am!'

'Whatever's the matter, Kathy? Who was it?' Hester had heard the front doorbell, but she had let the girl answer it as usual. Callers were rare, except for the customary deliverymen and the occasional hawker who disregarded the notice at the gate.

'They want to see you, Ma'am. It's the police!'

'Police?' Hester felt a quiver of alarm. What could have happened? Both the children were safe at home. Surely nothing had happened to Father or Cora. 'Where are they?'

'Waiting in the hall, Ma'am.'

Hester fought to remain calm as she approached the two uniformed officers. They were large men, both taller than any of her residents, with wide shoulders and bulky chests. One was wearing the three stripes of a sergeant on his sleeve.

'What's happened?' she asked. 'Have you brought bad news?'

'This is nothing to do with accidents or

anything of that sort,' replied the sergeant. 'So you can rest easy on that score. Are you the person in charge?'

'Yes.' Hester's heart was still beating fast and she felt breathless. 'I'm not the owner, but I do manage the establishment.'

'Good. We want to interview a man who is believed to be one of your tenants.'

'There's nobody here just now,' replied Hester. 'They all leave by about eight o'clock, and they won't be back until almost six.'

'This man was seen to come into the building less than fifteen minutes ago. He let himself in with a key. And he was not seen to leave.'

'Oh.' Hester stared at him in bewilderment. 'I wonder who that was? Do you know his name?'

'No. Perhaps you could tell us who it might be, and which room he'd be in. He's quite a short chap, plump, well dressed, dark hair. About forty to fifty years old.'

'Ah, that sounds like Mr Best. He must be feeling ill again if he's come back. Is this important, or can you leave it until he's feeling better?'

'It is extremely important, Madam. And any story about his health is unlikely to be true.' He jerked his head towards the staircase. 'Show us his room please.'

Hester led the way upstairs, still unable to grasp the meaning of this occurrence. What would the police be wanting with an inoffensive man like Mr Best? The sergeant had spoken in a disparaging tone, as if he had no respect for him at all. There must be some mistake, probably a case of mistaken identity. But thank goodness nothing had happened to anybody in her family.

The sergeant knocked loudly on Mr Best's door, then tried the handle.

'Come on, open up,' he shouted. 'It's the police.'

'He must be out,' said Hester.

'Never. Have you got a key?'

'One of the maids will be cleaning rooms up here. She's got one.'

'Get her then. We'll wait here.'

Hester moved away along the corridor and Edith responded quickly to her call, coming out from the bathroom with a cleaning cloth in her hand. She paused and stared at the policemen in astonishment, then hurried towards them.

'Mr Best is lying down,' she said anxiously. 'He doesn't want to be disturbed.'

'I bet he doesn't,' responded the sergeant. 'Open this door for me please.'

It seemed that Mr Best was listening on the other side. Before Edith could insert the key in the lock he suddenly opened the door and gave a resigned shrug.

'I suppose you'd better come in.'

The two officers strode in at once and closed the door behind them. Edith looked at Hester and raised her eyebrows.

'What's it all about, Ma'am?'

'I have no idea. Someone must have made a mistake, I think.'

She did not know what to do next. Should she stay there in case she was needed, or go away and give them privacy?

'Carry on with what you were doing, Edith,' she said at last. 'I'll wait downstairs in the hall, but I don't suppose they will want me to do anything.'

Kathy was hovering near the store room, not knowing how she was supposed to behave.

'Is it all right to go up, Ma'am? I haven't finished at my end.'

'Perhaps you should wait a while. I don't suppose they'll be long.'

Almost immediately they heard footsteps above, then all three men came down the stairs. Mr Best averted his eyes as he passed the women and nobody spoke until he had gone out with the constable.

'Can I have your full name please, Madam?' asked the sergeant. He wrote

Hester's details in his notebook then thanked her. 'Someone will call to see you soon. Will you be here all day?'

'Yes. I don't know that I could be of any help to anyone, though. I don't understand what all this is about.'

'Someone will call, quite soon I hope, and then everything will be explained. Good morning, Madam.'

Edith had been keeping watch from an upstairs window and she hurried down as soon as the men departed.

'They've arrested him!' she exclaimed. 'What's he done?'

Hester made a soothing gesture. 'We don't know that he has done anything. It might all be a mistake.'

'Nothing like this has ever happened here before. This house has always had a good reputation.'

'Yes, well, that won't change,' said Hester firmly. 'It's up to us to make sure that no silly rumours get about. We don't want anybody guessing or jumping to conclusions. When I find out what's happened I'll tell you. Until then, please don't talk about this to any other people.'

She felt distracted and restless as she went about her work and she guessed the other two would be unlikely to keep the news to themselves. How many people could resist the urge to gossip when such an unusual thing had happened? And how would the children have reacted, had they seen the police arrive? They had been playing in the garden, well wrapped up against the chilly breeze, oblivious to the unusual visitors. Would the sight of police uniforms have revived memories of that terrible day when little William had died? Hester had hoped she would never see police in her home again. She would have to make sure that Kathy kept the children busy in the kitchen when the police came back. Or perhaps they wouldn't come at all — perhaps Mr Best would return soon and tell them it was all a misunderstanding.

They ate lunch in the kitchen with Kathy, and the children were helping to clear the table when the doorbell rang. Hester signalled to Kathy to take over her task and went to answer the door herself. A tall man in a fawn shower-proof coat was waiting on the doorstep. He showed her a card and she caught sight of the word Police.

'Mrs Carleton?' he asked. 'I am Detective Inspector Morrison. May I come in and talk to you?'

An Inspector! Hester gulped and nodded, inviting him in with a wave of one hand.

Moments later she had recovered her voice and some of her poise.

'I think we should go to the sitting-room,' she said. 'That would be the most appropriate place, I think. Nobody will disturb us at this time of day.'

'Thank you.' He followed her to the common room, where she chose an upright chair and he did the same. 'Now then, Mrs Carleton, I hope I can depend on your cooperation. We have a serious matter to deal with.'

'Oh. I was hoping there had been some kind of mistake.'

'Unfortunately, no.' He paused for a moment, as if unsure how to continue. 'I believe that you live on the premises, Mrs Carleton, and that you have children.'

Hester gripped her hands tightly together, wondering what would come next. 'Yes. I have two children. Two little girls. What does that have to do with it?'

'All in good time, Mrs Carleton, all in good time. Now I want you to think carefully. Has either child ever been frightened or upset since you came to live here?'

'No, they settled in very quickly.'

'Have they ever said they don't like anybody?'

'No. They don't often see the residents,

actually. I try to make sure they stay out of the way.'

'I see.' He paused again. 'Mrs Carleton, have you ever seen any other children in this house?'

'Only once. Mr Best brought his niece here.'

'Can you tell me about that please?'

Hester thought for a moment then described how they had seen Mr Best descending the stairs one Sunday afternoon, holding a little girl's hand. 'Her name is Rosie. Unfortunately, she is totally deaf and she can't speak.'

The Inspector shook his head. 'I'm sorry, Mrs Carleton, but none of that is true. She is not his niece. Her name is not Rosie, and she is not deaf.'

'But I spoke to her! She couldn't answer.'

'She couldn't answer because she was too frightened, Mrs Carleton.'

The colour slowly drained from Hester's face as she realised the implications. 'Are you telling me that Mr Best has . . . ?' She could not complete the question.

'Yes, I'm sorry. It would appear that he was in the habit of bringing little girls here on Sunday afternoons. I assume there was nobody here usually.'

Hester nodded slowly, thinking about the

day they had seen the child. 'It's usually very quiet after dinner on a Sunday. We go out, my children and I. We came back early that day because it was so cold.'

He asked for more details and wrote down a description of the child. 'I don't like to do this, Mrs Carleton, but I must ask you to let me talk to your children.'

She quailed. 'You don't think . . . ?'

'We have to be sure, Mrs Carleton. Are they both here now?'

'Yes. Dorothy should be at school, but she has been ill.'

He reacted to that, his fingers gripping his pen more fiercely, his whole body seeming to tense, and she hastily explained that it had been a clear case of tonsillitis.

'I see. Now it's going to be difficult for you, Mrs Carleton, but I want you to let me ask the questions, and I don't want you to look shocked or angry, no matter what the children say.' He gave a small smile of sympathy and understanding. 'It's very important that the children tell us everything, so they need to be sure that they won't get into trouble, no matter what they say. Even if they happen to have disobeyed you, you must not look angry. Can you manage that?'

Hester agreed to do her best and he decided to speak to Dorothy first. 'I'll get a clearer picture from her. The other one is too young to tell us much.' Almost as an afterthought he added, 'I should tell you — you could insist on having a woman talk to them instead of me, but that would mean waiting until tomorrow and I would prefer to get this over and done with.'

'Yes, it's all right. You can do it,' said Hester. 'I'll go and fetch Dorothy.'

Dorothy felt privileged to be asked to meet a visitor when her sister had been excluded. She told Inspector Morrison about her school being closed, and then being ill in bed and how two doctors came to look after her.

'A lot of gentlemen live in this house, don't they?' he said lightly. 'Have any of them ever given you anything?'

'Mr Frost gave me a nice game to play with in bed. It has dollies and dresses and hats and everything.'

'That must have been when you were ill, was it? Did he ever give you anything else?'

Dorothy explained about the pennies and he nodded. 'Did anybody else ever give you anything?'

She told him that Mr Best had given them sweeties twice, but Mama had told him not to do it again.

'Did you and Mr Best ever have a secret?'

Hester almost gasped aloud, remembering

how the children had squabbled about a secret — on a day when Mr Best had stayed away from work. The Inspector saw her reaction and raised one hand slightly to remind her not to influence the answer. Dorothy denied having any secrets and he asked her if she had ever gone to see anything in one of the gentlemen's rooms.

She shook her head emphatically. 'No, I never went in anybody's room. But Susan did! I told her not to, but she did. So I called Mama.'

'Whose room was that?'

'Mr Best. He should have been at work, but he wasn't.'

'He didn't go to work today either. Did you see him?'

'No. Is he going to get into trouble for not going?'

'Very much so. He's lost his job, and he'll have to leave here, too.'

Dorothy went back to the kitchen, still unaware of the real reason for the Inspector's visit, and Hester brought Susan in to meet him. She could not help admiring the way he talked to her, eliciting information without frightening her. The only time she looked uneasy was when he mentioned secrets. She turned away from him then and Hester gave her a comforting hug.

'I know someone here who tells children they'll get into trouble if they tell a secret,' said the Inspector. 'But he tells, so it's not a secret any more, is it?'

Susan finally admitted that she had accepted a sweetie from Mr Best and he had told her Mama would be very angry if she knew. The Inspector asked her how many times he had given sweeties to her, and after some rigmarole with thumbs and fingers they decided that he had done it twice since Mama had forbidden him to do so. The second occasion had been on the morning when she had gone into his room.

'Do you like Mr Best?'

Susan shrugged. 'I like Mr Frost better. He makes funny faces. And he sings.'

They sent her back to play with Dorothy, and Inspector Morrison sighed. 'We have been very lucky. If her sister had not been at home that morning, Susan could have been molested. If not then, it would have happened soon afterwards.'

'It's so hard to believe. He always seemed such a nice person.'

'That's why men like that are so successful at finding victims, Mrs Carleton. They seem so friendly and trustworthy that people can't believe they would ever do any harm. Parents even go out for the evening and leave children in their care.'

Hester shuddered. 'He offered to look after Dorothy and Susan for me, but I never left them with him.' She closed her eyes briefly in a silent prayer. 'What will happen now?'

'He'll have to face trial.' The Inspector gave a satisfied nod. 'This time I think we've got sufficient evidence to get him put away where he can't harm another child.'

Hester stared at him in surprise. 'Surely you don't mean . . . ? Are you saying that some people already knew what kind of man he was?'

'This is one of the hardest crimes to prove in court, Mrs Carleton. There are usually no witnesses, and the victims are so young. A child is not considered to be a competent witness.' The Inspector looked searchingly at her. 'I have to ask you this. Are you prepared to come to court and give evidence if required?'

'Oh dear. Will I have to?'

'I hope not. An adult actually caught him with a child this morning, so he should plead guilty. But if he thinks he might get away with it . . . Are you willing to come and give evidence if necessary?'

Hester twisted her fingers together as she thought of her own children's lucky escape.

'Yes. I don't know much, but I'll come and say what I can. We mustn't let him get away with it.'

'Thank you.'

'What happens in the meantime? I mean, court cases take so long . . . '

The Inspector guessed what was in her mind and he assured her that Mr Best would not come back. 'Even if he gets bail he can't be allowed to live here, so someone will have to come and pack all his belongings.'

It did not take long for news of the arrest to filter through to the other residents. Edith and Kathy came back from serving dinner with reports of the threats being tossed to and fro in the dining-room, as to what would happen if 'that blackguard should show his face here'.

Hester sighed. 'I suppose they would have to know sooner or later. It will all be in the newspapers, no doubt. But please don't mention it in front of the children.'

The service bell rang after the meal was over, and Hester went out to the hall to find Adam Frost waiting to see her. His air of jaunty confidence was missing for once and he shuffled his feet uneasily as she approached.

'Can I help you, Mr Frost?'

'Ah. I just wanted to say — er — that is,

look, I didn't mean any harm. Giving things to the girls, you know. Look, I only wanted to give a little present. Nothing else.'

Hester smiled. 'I know, Mr Frost. Please don't worry. Everybody knows that you didn't have an ulterior motive. But I think you understand now that the girls must not get into the habit of accepting gifts from people.'

'Yes. I'm sorry it has to be like that. But I'll be more careful now. With every child, not just here.'

'That would be wise, for your own sake.'

'Yes, well . . . ' He gave a sheepish smile and brought out a brown paper bag from behind his back. 'It just so happened that I brought these for the children. Today of all days!'

'Oh, Mr Frost.'

'Coloured pencils and a couple of little picture books, that's all. I thought Dorothy might be feeling bored, being at home all this time. She can help Susan to colour in.'

'Thank you. They will appreciate that, and so do I. Do you come from a big family, Mr Frost?'

'No. I was the one and only. I have a lot of young relatives on my father's side, but I don't see them very often, unfortunately.'

He was a considerate young man, thought

Hester as she went back to the kitchen. It was a pity he so often gave the impression of being brash and flippant. He would make a wonderful father, and it was to be hoped he would soon meet the right person so that he could settle down and raise a family of his own.

Bruce came that evening, after an absence of more than a week. He checked Dorothy's condition and agreed that she was well enough to go back to school next Monday.

'They opened again last week, but Dr Gibbs said it was better to keep Dorothy away a little longer.' Hester looked quizzically at Bruce. 'You didn't say anything to me about complications.'

He grimaced. 'No, there was no point in making you any more worried than you were. Dorothy was safe enough while she was in bed and being looked after so well. One of these days we won't have to worry about toxins spreading. We'll be able to stop infections dead in their tracks.'

'You said something like that before. Do you really believe it?'

'Yes, it will come. I can only hope it comes in my lifetime.'

He seemed unusually depressed that evening and Hester wondered if he had lost another patient. Eventually she asked what was troubling him.

'The whole world situation troubles me,' he replied. 'Have you seen the newspapers lately?'

'Yes, there are always lots of newspapers left lying about here.'

'So you know what they're saying then. About all the unrest in Europe, about the danger of war.'

'Do you really think it's as bad as they say? Don't they exaggerate a lot to make it sound dramatic?'

'It's bad all right. There's only one thing I'd like to say to some of those politicians; if they're so keen to fight for their policies, they should do the fighting themselves instead of sending innocent young men to do it for them.'

Hester changed the subject by telling him about the events that had taken place in the house that day. He was relieved to know that the children had not been harmed, but he was in no mood to linger and he soon announced that he must go. Hester went downstairs with him as usual and as they paused near the front door he suddenly grasped her and held her tight against his body with an intensity she had not experienced before. However, the expected kiss did not come and when she peered up at

271

his face she saw an expression of anguish.

'Oh, Bruce, what *is* the matter? There is something wrong, I just know it.'

'Oh, Hester, life is so complicated,' he murmured. 'Life can be such a mess.'

He kissed her then with a vigorous, but swift, pressure on the lips, after which he broke away and opened the door himself. There was no farewell, no final comment. Hester watched with puzzlement and dismay as he walked away, hcad down. He hastened to the gate, closed it behind him and climbed into his motor car without a backward glance.

15

Hester went down to begin work the next day with heavy eyes and an aching head after suffering a restless night. She had still not decided what she ought to do. Had she been asking for trouble, bringing two young children to live in a house full of unknown men? There was no one to act as chaperone for herself either.

Darkness had prompted a series of unwelcome images to run through her mind, and eventually she had got out of bed and lighted the gas again. Even then she had been unable to relax. What if Dorothy had not been there to raise the alarm when Susan had been enticed into that room? How could that sly and evil man have seemed so pleasant and friendly? After being so easily fooled, how could she ever trust anyone again? Even after that experience she had hastened to reassure Mr Frost that she trusted him — but could she? What did she know of him, or of any of them? Perhaps she should leave. But where could she go? Where could she go that would be safe? Why was the world so full of evil and corruption?

She had decided it was her duty to tell Mr Hetherington what had happened so she telephoned his house at the earliest opportunity. The housekeeper answered and insisted that Hester leave a message with her because Mr Hetherington could not be disturbed.

'I'll write a letter,' said Hester wearily.

'Wait.' Apparently the woman had decided that Hester had something important to say. 'Mr Hetherington is coming now. Hold the line please.'

Hester pictured his expression as she gave a brief outline of the previous day's events. He received the news with a shocked silence, then predictably he thought first about his own reputation.

'Who knows about this?' he demanded.

'Well, everybody in the house,' replied Hester. 'And it will be in the newspapers before long. You can't keep this kind of thing quiet.'

'Bella Casa has always been a respectable establishment.'

Hester murmured a few consoling remarks then cut him short in the midst of another outburst. 'I have to see to the deliveries.'

'Don't say anything about this to any of those deliverymen.'

'Of course not.' Hester had no patience to deal with his concerns and she hung up before he could launch into a stream of instructions.

When the postman called he brought a collection of mail for residents, a few bills and a letter from Aunt Amelia. Hester put the letter aside to read later. It would contain no important news. The envelope was thin, no doubt holding one of the brief notes that were only written out of a sense of duty. Fat envelopes only came from Aunt Amelia when something had upset her. The longest letter she had ever sent came after the terrible loss of the *Titanic*, when she moaned for page after page about the stress her son Neville placed upon her because he would not give up 'that dangerous job plying the high seas.'

It was almost time for morning tea before Hester opened the letter. She read the small page quickly, then read it again with a sense of disbelief. Aunt Amelia was coming to visit at 2pm on Friday — the day after tomorrow. In typical fashion she did not ask if that were convenient, assuming that Hester would make herself available on the day and at the time she had chosen.

. . . I hope you will ensure that we will be free from interruptions while we chat . . .

In other words she had something on her mind and she did not want the children to be present, decided Hester. They should display good manners by greeting the visitor, and then occupy themselves elsewhere. She sighed and went to join the staff in the kitchen. The conversation there was still mainly concerned with the arrest of Mr Best, Edith pumping Kathy for every detail of what had happened while she was out yesterday. Hester paid little attention. She was still feeling the effects of her sleepless night and the whirling thoughts about the dangers that had threatened her children. Bruce had also added to her anxiety. He had been in such a strange mood all evening. She would have appreciated some move on his part to give her added strength after such a traumatic day, but she had felt obliged to soothe him rather than the other way around.

Now Aunt Amelia had decided to call. What would bring her to Melbourne so unexpectedly? They had not met since the tragedy in Thorn Bay. Aunt Amelia had been so anxious to distance herself from even the slightest hint of scandal it was a wonder she had continued to maintain any contact at all. Friday was likely to be yet another stressful day.

Two men arrived about half an hour later with papers giving them authority to collect all the property belonging to Mr Best. One acted as spokesman for both, saying they had no idea what had happened in court that day; their responsibility was limited to taking charge of the property and returning keys to Bella Casa. Hester was to sign when they had fulfilled their duties. She was relieved to see them depart, and glad to be holding the keys that had been in the possession of that disgusting man. Now she need not fear that he might return. She would have the room thoroughly cleaned at once.

★   ★   ★

Aunt Amelia arrived promptly at 2 o'clock by hired carriage. She was wearing a matching coat and dress, in bottle green and cream, which Hester knew must be the very latest style, and she walked up the garden path with her usual regal deportment. The hair that framed her face beneath the fashionable green hat was still a rich brown with a hint of copper, a colour that could no longer be natural. Hester waited outside on the step watching her approach, while the children hovered nervously in the hall.

'Hester!' she exclaimed, as if she were surprised to see her. 'How are you?

'Very well, thank you, Aunt Amelia. I'm pleased to see that you look well.'

'Yes, my health is comparatively good.' The

older woman frowned slightly. 'I don't know that you can honestly say the same. You look rather peaky to me.'

'I'm very well now, thank you, Aunt Amelia.' In the still of the night the same fears about the dangers of staying in the house had risen to torment her, but she would not mention such matters to her aunt. 'We have had a worrying time recently, with Dorothy being ill, but we are all well now.' Hester accepted a kiss on each cheek, then invited her visitor in and beckoned to the girls.

'And here are the children! How nice to see you, my dears.'

They had changed from play clothes to Sunday clothes in honour of this visit and had been looking forward to it with a mixture of excitement and dread. Dorothy could remember awesome visits to a large house to see her great-aunt, but it was almost two years since they had seen her and Susan did not remember her at all.

At last the ritual greeting was over and Hester gestured to their surroundings. 'As you can see, this is the main entrance. Would you like to look over the house first, or would you prefer to rest and perhaps freshen up?'

'Show me the house, by all means. I must say the exterior looks impressive. The neighbourhood looks quite respectable, too.'

They began with the common rooms on the ground floor, then went to the kitchen. Aunt Amelia looked around with a critical eye then pointed towards a door.

'And what is through there?'

'The scullery and beyond that the laundry and the garden, Aunt Amelia.' Hester led the way out to the laundry, where Kathy was busy at the trough.

'This is Kathy. She has been working at Bella Casa for about two years. This is my aunt, Kathy — Mrs Bancroft.'

Kathy dipped a curtsey and Aunt Amelia inclined her head.

'I thought you said the laundry was sent out, Hester.'

Kathy blushed and cast a frightened glance at Hester, who responded calmly. 'Only the linen is sent out, table linen and so forth. Not our personal clothing.'

'I see.' Aunt Amelia moved on, no longer interested, and Hester smiled reassuringly at Kathy. There was no need to tell her aunt that Kathy occasionally brought some of her own family's clothing to Bella Casa now and used her free time to wash it. A few of the items that had already gone through the mangle obviously belonged to small boys, but Aunt Amelia passed by without noticing.

'A very nice garden, Hester. Do people make much use of it?'

'The girls play out here almost every day. When the weather is a little warmer I expect a few of the residents will sit out here in the evenings instead of in the sitting-room.'

At last the inspection was over and they settled in the family's apartment for refreshments. The girls sat quietly, remembering Hester's instructions to sit up straight and only talk when someone spoke to them. Aunt Amelia smiled benignly.

'I'm pleased to see you have trained the girls properly, Hester. Standards have been slipping over the past few years, and it is up to people like us to maintain good manners and proper decorum.'

As soon as Hester thought it would be acceptable to release the girls she sent them out to play and they hurried away with relief. During the pause that followed Aunt Amelia looked around the room as if searching for some feature worthy of praise.

'Your living quarters are pleasant enough. But I must say how regrettable it is to see my own sister's daughter reduced to this. You should have achieved much more, Hester. You were not destined to end up in service.'

'I am not *in service*.' Hester fought to retain a calm tone. 'I am the manageress, which is a respectable and important position.'

Her aunt merely sniffed, obviously paying little regard to that assertion. 'You have two young girls to assist you in the house, I believe.'

'Well, Edith must be about my age. But yes, there are two.'

'Do they also live in?'

'No. Edith lives very close, but Kathy travels some distance each day.'

Aunt Amelia clicked her teeth. 'I have been concerned about you. Don't you think it might give rise to unpleasant gossip — the fact that you live here, the only female amongst so many men — even bringing little girls to such a place?'

Hester stiffened with alarm. Surely her aunt had not heard about the arrest! No, that was impossible. She must have decided to come here before all that had happened, and the case had not yet been reported in the newspapers. No, that kind of comment was only to be expected from someone with such a staid outlook. Perversely, her aunt's attitude hardened Hester's resolve. She had tossed and turned for two nights, troubled by doubts about the wisdom of continuing to live there, but now she suddenly decided she must stay.

'St Kilda has a bad enough reputation as it

is,' her aunt continued. 'It is full of threepenny tourists. You can read about it in the daily newspapers; mixed bathing on the beach, immoral women on the streets . . . If you will insist on living here you must be very careful, especially in the vicinity of the railway station. And you must never go out after dark by yourself. Prowlers are on the look-out for unaccompanied women.'

Hester shook her head. 'We have found St Kilda to be a pleasant place. That is why so many wealthy people built their mansions here.'

Her aunt sniffed disdainfully. 'And then installed a mistress.'

'Sometimes, yes. But that could happen anywhere.' Hester could not resist the urge to hint at scandal within her aunt's own family. 'Mountcliffe is considered to be respectable, but it is well known that the same kind of behaviour exists there.'

Aunt Amelia changed the subject abruptly, giving brief news of other relatives. She then became silent and stared down at the numerous rings on her fingers, considering what to say next.

'Bruce Hutchinson came to see his parents last week,' she began.

Hester looked at her in surprise. He had said nothing about travelling out of the city.

'Mr and Mrs Hutchinson are very concerned, Hester. It seems that Bruce has taken up a close friendship with you. They do not approve. In fact, they disapprove most strongly.'

Hester drew a deep breath of indignation. So that was why her aunt had deigned to call on her!

'I suppose Mrs Hutchinson asked you to come here.'

'Be sensible, Hester. How could you even consider marriage into the Hutchinson family after what happened? You must do everything you can to discourage Bruce.'

Hester gulped. There had been no talk of marriage. There had been a hint of that once before; but that was a year or more ago, at a time when she was in the depths of despair and Bruce had been sympathetic and rueful, both of them thinking of what might have been.

'You tried to make me do just the opposite once.'

'Things were very different then, Hester. If you had listened to me then the Hutchinsons would have welcomed you with open arms. If only you had listened. Just imagine how much better your life would have been.'

'But would it?' Hester was no longer the timid young woman who complied with instructions and ran errands for her aunt without complaint. Now she was prepared to argue. 'Have you never wondered why they were so eager to marry Bruce off to me? Me, of all people — the poor relation. I didn't come from a suitable background.' She had had more than enough time over the years to ponder this question and she thought her aunt ought to be sensible enough to face the truth. 'Almost anybody would have suited them at the time! Anyone who could sit straight on a chair and use a knife and fork properly. They only wanted to keep Bruce at home, to force him into the family business. He couldn't afford to keep a wife and raise a family of his own while he studied all those years. So he would have had to give up his dreams.'

Aunt Amelia flicked her hand. 'That's nonsense. But if you had done as I said and married Bruce it would have saved you from that other man, and those awful events would never have taken place.'

'And what kind of marriage do you think it would have been?' protested Hester. 'Bruce would not have been happy. He would have been frustrated. It wouldn't take long for the gloss to wear off. I know only too well what frustration can do to a man. If Gerald had not been frustrated at every turn, things would never have happened the way they did.'

Aunt Amelia brushed that argument aside. 'All that is in the past, Hester. You've got to think of the present now.' She paused and softened her tone. 'You must use your influence, Hester. Tell Bruce there can be no question of marriage between you. You should distance yourself from him at once. Make a complete break.'

Hester fought down the urge to abandon the rules of polite society, the restraint that hid true feelings. She wanted to shout at her aunt, to thrust her outside the door, but for the time being she must observe good manners. She took a deep breath and managed to keep her voice low.

'What difference does it make who Bruce marries? He's a grown man. He can make his own choice.'

'Hester, stop and think for a minute. What kind of life would it be for either of you? You would never be welcome in the Hutchinson house. Bruce is very close to his mother. How would it affect him if he could not take his wife to the family home? How could he keep up that special relationship between them if he were to marry against their wishes?'

'The question of marriage has not even arisen!'

Aunt Amelia gave a sigh of relief. 'That's good. It makes the situation so much easier. You can put a stop to all this now, before anybody gets hurt or upset.'

Hester stared at her in exasperation. 'I am not going to do anything at all. I am in control of my own life now. Nobody can tell me what to do or what not to do. I have no obligations to anybody, and I can make my own decisions.'

Aunt Amelia was startled by the heated response. 'If you have any regard for Bruce,' she said at last, 'you will consider his feelings and his future. You would not stand in the way of his happiness.'

'His happiness will come from making his own decisions. Nobody should try to influence him one way or the other. And why make so much fuss about all this, anyway? If his parents really love him, they will accept his decisions in time.'

Aunt Amelia sighed. 'You don't understand. Mr Hutchinson is a Councillor now. He will be running for Mayor at the coming election. He could go in for State politics soon; perhaps run for Federal Parliament.'

'What has that got to do with it?' Hester was losing patience.

'You must see. There can't be even the slightest whiff of scandal. Imagine what his opponents would do with that story. Imagine the newspapers. The son of a leading citizen married to the former wife of that dreadful man!' She could not bring herself to say Gerald's name. 'And what about his off-spring? His offspring brought into such an important family.'

Hester leapt to her feet. 'That is enough! I will not have my children maligned, and I must ask you to leave this house.'

'You have to see, Hester . . . '

'I can see snobbery, bigotry and selfish-ness.' Hester went quickly for her aunt's hat and dropped it onto her lap. 'What happened was tragic. Nobody could have foreseen what would happen. But it was an accident. Always remember that. If anybody ever mentions it — and there's no reason why they should — you ought to point that out. Tell them it was an accident.'

'He was charged, Hester. There's no getting away from that.'

'He was never found guilty.'

'Of course not! Because he never faced trial. He knew he was guilty, and he took the easy way out.'

Hester's face flamed. She hastened to the door and opened it, then gave an imperious waft of her hand. Aunt Amelia took her time over adjusting her hat, as if expecting her niece to relent, then she sighed deeply and went out without speaking. They walked to the staircase and down to the hall in silence and Hester opened the front door.

'Good bye, Aunt Amelia.'

'Hester, dear, we shouldn't part like this. Please don't be angry with me. I mean well. You must believe that.'

Hester struggled to make a civil response. 'I am not part of your immediate family, Aunt Amelia. What I do should have no effect on your life. And you cannot be expected to take responsibility for Bruce. Leave the Hutchinsons to sort out their own affairs.'

'But they are dear friends. And I'm concerned for you, Hester.'

'I don't need your concern. I am managing perfectly well. I'm sorry if you think you have had a wasted journey.'

'Oh, Hester. It's not like you to be vindictive.'

'I'm sorry. But there's nothing more I can say.'

'Think about it. I can't ask more than that.' Aunt Amelia hastened away to her waiting carriage, looking suddenly years older.

Hester held onto her anger as she went back indoors, stoking her rage, fully aware that without it she would break down in tears. She must not give way, she told herself firmly.

She had a meal to prepare. She must collect the rent, face every client with composure and ask if they had any problems. Her own problems would have to wait.

When she was alone that night she covered her head with the bedclothes and pressed her clenched fist against her lips. All the horrors of that fatal night had been revived by her aunt's cruel words. It *had* been an accident, she assured herself. Gerald would never have harmed the baby on purpose. All right, so he had been drinking heavily. He was disappointed that his only son was a helpless cripple. He had no patience with children. But he wouldn't have hurt William. And if he *had* intended to, in his condition he was sure to have missed. No, it was sheer bad luck that his boot had hit the baby like that.

She had probably made an enemy of Aunt Amelia. But what did that matter? She was a very demanding woman, always expecting other people to do what suited her. Wasn't it true that she only contacted people when she wanted something?

16

Saturday dawned bright and sunny, as if to announce that Hester should cast her despondency aside. She went down to the kitchen, feeling heavy eyed and listless but determined to keep her mind off everything that had happened during the past few days. Kathy came in at her usual time looking wary.

'Good morning, Ma'am.'

'Good morning, Kathy. How are you today?'

'Very well, thank you, Ma'am.' Kathy hesitated, then decided to risk saying more. 'Did you have bad news yesterday, Ma'am?'

'Bad news?' Hester stifled a derisive laugh. 'Yes, I did, I'm afraid. I should have been prepared. My aunt very rarely comes, and it always means bad news.'

'I'm sorry, Ma'am.'

'I'm over it now. I'm sorry if I was grumpy yesterday afternoon.'

Kathy smiled. 'Not grumpy, Ma'am, just very quiet and solemn. Do you need anything special done today, with the children or anything?'

'No, thank you. It's beautiful weather. You

go out and enjoy it this afternoon. The next thing we know everybody will be complaining about the heat.'

Mr Hetherington was frowning when he arrived for his usual visit and he sat without reading the accounts, tapping his fingers irritably on the desk. As expected, he began by complaining about the effects of Mr Best's conduct. His room had become vacant without prior notice, which meant it would be lying empty with no rent paid until he had found another client. In addition, harmful publicity might follow. He looked musingly at Hester as if it could be her fault.

'We don't want that kind of reputation here. We never had any trouble of this kind before we had children living on the premises. I should never have let Mrs Wellaby persuade me to allow children in.'

Hester sighed. 'It would have made no difference. It was not my children that were involved. Goodness knows how long it had been going on before he was caught.'

'Yes, well, I suppose you're right. But it is most aggravating.'

Hester tightened her lip, thinking that he himself was more than aggravating, but soon after he had left Harold telephoned and helped to raise her spirits by suggesting an outing the next day.

'A little treat before Dorothy goes back to school. We'll go and take a look at that new amusement park in St Kilda. Can you all be ready by two o'clock?'

'We certainly can. Thank you, Harold.'

The children heard the postman's whistle and went out to the gate with Kathy to collect the mail. They rushed back excitedly with a package.

'Look. It's for you, Mama.'

'It rattles. Listen.'

It was an untidy looking parcel with Hester's name and address written in large uneven block capitals. The brown paper wrapping had obviously been used at least once before and the string was made up of several short pieces knotted together.

'I can't imagine who sent this,' she said. 'I don't recognise the writing.'

'Open it, Mama.'

'Yes I will. Can you find the scissors, Dorothy?'

The children watched with interest as she unwrapped the package to reveal a page from an exercise book, pasted by one corner to the lid of a battered tin box. She gave an exclamation of pleasure as she looked at the message on the paper.

'Oh, it's from Barnaby! Do you remember that nice old man with the big white bird?'

'What did he say, Mama? What's in the box?'

'He says he was very happy to get a letter from me, and he's sent you something to play with.'

'Ooh, how lovely! Let's see, Mama.'

The tin contained a collection of seashells, all varnished to enhance the colours. The girls were thrilled and wanted to tip the shells onto the table at once, but Hester said they must take them outside.

'We'll have to write and say thank you, won't we? You could make him a nice coloured card like you did for Mr Frost.'

She found that she was humming a tune as she weighed out the ingredients for a steamed pudding. There was no point in dwelling on the past, she decided. Life had to go on and there were enough pleasant people in the world to combat the harm that any wrongdoers caused. She would also ignore Aunt Amelia's visit and go on as if she had never heard those hurtful words. Whatever the future held, she would make the best of it.

Almost two weeks passed before Bruce came again. When he stepped into the front hall they stood apart and gazed at each other, feeling an awkwardness that had never affected them before.

'How are you, Hester?' he asked at last.

'Very well, Bruce, thank you. We are all very well. Come on up.'

He sat in his usual chair, but they talked like acquaintances rather than close friends and she made a pot of tea early so as to fill in time.

Bruce looked troubled, but he did not say what was on his mind and eventually Hester decided to force the issue.

'Aunt Amelia came to see me recently,' she said.

He gave a startled jerk. 'Really! Did you know she was coming?'

'She wrote to tell me. You know Aunt Amelia. She wouldn't take the risk of going anywhere without advance warning. She always has to be certain that the person she wants to see will be there when she arrives.'

He smiled slightly. 'She's a very formidable lady.'

'Yes.' Hester plunged on. 'She got the idea from somewhere that I might be feeling ready to marry again.'

Bruce's eyes widened. 'Really?' He hesitated then asked timidly, 'Was she right?'

'I'm not ready for any immediate changes. That's not to say it could never happen, of course. But I don't want to rush into anything.'

'I see.'

'What about you, Bruce? Have you ever considered getting married?'

There was a long pause while Bruce formed an answer. 'More than once,' he said at last. 'But the right opportunity never seemed to come along.'

'I expect your parents would like to see you settle down and have a family.'

'Yes. They're keen to have more grandchildren, of course.' Bruce looked away then back to Hester. 'The problem has always been that our dreams don't match. I don't want to hurt them, but there might come a day when I have to choose — between what they want and what I want.'

Hester felt the urge to scold him, to say that it was his life, he should grow up and do whatever he felt was right, but she held her tongue. She had resolved to stay out of the family dispute and he must find the strength to settle it for himself.

They spoke no more along those lines, but the atmosphere seemed to have eased and they chatted more naturally afterwards. When it was time to leave Bruce gave Hester a light kiss on the cheek.

'I don't think I have been very good company lately, Hester. I do hope you'll forgive me, but life doesn't seem quite so straightforward at present. It might be quite a while before I come again.'

'I hope we can still remain good friends.'

'Good friends, yes. We'll always be that.' He kissed her again, with slightly more pressure than before, then he hurried away as if he did not trust himself to linger.

Hester closed the door and went slowly up the stairs. She was happy as she was, she assured herself. She had a comfortable home and a steady income. Moreover, she had something she had never had in her life before, her independence. She had everything she could possibly need. Why was marriage thought to be so important? She had experienced marriage and it had not always brought joy.

The one thing she did lack, she admitted some time later, was companionship. If only she could have someone beside her in the evenings, someone to keep her company; someone like Bruce. But she had been married for years, she reminded herself. And how often had her husband stayed in to keep her company? No, she should be content with her present lot. She had never been so well off. She had no need of marriage.

★ ★ ★

'There's a letter for you, Ma'am.'

Hester's face lit up with anticipation, but

her eagerness died when she looked at the envelope. It was from the Trustees who looked after Uncle Jeremy's bequest.

'Oh, Ma'am, I hope it's not bad news.'

'It's all right, Kathy. It's just business, that's all, nothing of real interest.'

She took it away to the office for privacy and tore open the envelope. Inside she found a short letter informing her that a representative would call on her the next morning at 10am. If that were not convenient she should telephone to make other arrangements. Why did they need to call on her? Surely they could have written if they had to tell her something. Had all the money gone? She fought down a surge of panic. She could manage, she told herself. Lots of people managed on far less money than she had and she refused to be down-hearted. Despite her intentions she did not sleep well and she felt fidgety with nerves as she waited for her visitor to arrive.

Mr Ferguson was far younger than she had expected, tall and well-groomed. Hester led him to the writing-room, having decided that was more formal than the sitting-room and more suitable than the small office. He accepted a seat with a gracious air and spread some papers on the table before him.

'I have come to explain how the situation

297

rests at present,' he began. 'I will put it into simple terms, but I must emphasise from the outset that you have no need to be concerned.'

His language could hardly be described as simple, but the meaning was clear. Bills for clothing or medical treatment for the family would be paid from the office as before. More importantly, all debts incurred before and connected with the death of her husband, Gerald Carleton, and her child, William Carleton, had been cleared under the terms of the Trust.

'That sad episode is closed,' he ended. 'You have absolutely no debts, Mrs Carleton, unless you have incurred any new ones since leaving Thorn Bay.'

Hester pondered over his remarks for several moments. 'Has my brother-in-law, Mr Harold Carleton, had anything to do with this?'

'I cannot see the relevance of that,' he replied, avoiding the question. 'But it has been noticed that you have not accessed the account this year, except for the payment of one doctor's bill.'

'If I understand Uncle Jeremy's Will properly, the less I spend now, the more will be kept in trust for my children.'

'Ye-e-es.'

'I don't want to spend any more of that money than I need, Mr Ferguson. It's my children's inheritance. They will need that money as they grow up, especially if anything should happen to me before they can make their own way in the world. I don't want that money to run out.'

'It will not run out as easily as that, Mrs Carleton.' He pushed his papers into a briefcase and became less formal. 'The reason I came here to see you personally was to impress upon you the wisdom of using that money, as and when it is needed. It's my job to make you see that you should make use of the money, not leave it sitting in the bank for years.'

'But —'

'The important time is the present, Mrs Carleton. Don't be frightened to use the money. Your children will have a better start in life if you are free from worry.'

She was far from convinced and he gave an encouraging smile. 'Your uncle was a wise man, Mrs Carleton. He could foresee difficulties ahead and made provision for them. He had confidence in you, too. He knew you wouldn't fritter it away. But that does not mean you should be frightened to spend money when necessary. Now I must bid you good morning.'

She would take him at his word and spend some money on Christmas festivities, Hester decided. The last two seasons had passed with little celebration, but her children were now old enough to understand the meaning of the event and to participate in the preparations. They could really enjoy themselves this year.

The girls watched with rising excitement as she unpacked the few decorations that she had gathered over previous seasons. They quickly learned how to make paper chains and Susan clapped her hands with glee when Hester strung the first chain across the living-room.

'More!' she said. 'We want more. Lots more.'

'Are we going to put some downstairs for the gentlemen?' asked Dorothy.

'Perhaps we should,' answered Hester. 'I'll find out who is going to stay here over the holidays.'

Most of the residents planned to go away, but a few still seemed undecided. When Hester asked Mr Jamieson what he planned to do he was more decisive.

'I have my dinner at one of the local hotels.'

'Wouldn't you prefer to have your dinner here?' asked Hester.

'I can't ask the girls to give up their holiday,' he replied. 'No, I will do the same as usual.'

'I will be cooking for my family. One or two more won't make a lot of difference.'

His eyes brightened. 'If there is not a large number, and if you are quite sure it won't be too much of an inconvenience . . . '

'Quite sure. That's settled then, Mr Jamieson. We'll have a family dinner at one o'clock for everybody who is here.'

Hester was writing Christmas greetings to Barnaby when she found herself thinking about Bruce again. What would he be doing at Christmas? Would he be going home to Mountcliffe? It was not possible for all doctors to go away for the holiday. She would invite him to Christmas dinner, she decided. If he were staying in the city he would surely appreciate a meal with friends.

Several days later Bruce replied that he would be pleased to dine with her family and other guests. Hester studied his words with a mixture of amusement and exasperation. He was still not ready to make a stand. Apparently he felt the need for the presence of a group if he were to feel at ease when visiting her.

The children made several paper chains and lanterns to decorate the dining-room, and on Christmas morning they helped to move tables together so as to make one large one in the center of the room. Hester had hesitated over the question of wine, then decided on just two bottles for the men to share. She was busy in the kitchen when Bruce arrived, but she took time to greet him and accept a gift of chocolates and crystallised fruit. He presented each of the children with a stuffed toy, and Dorothy introduced him to Mr Jamieson. Mr Kelly came downstairs next, followed shortly by Mr Pulham.

The last resident to come down was Mr Wright, a newcomer who had just arrived from England when the vacant room was advertised. When he first moved in he seemed timid and ill at ease, but Adam Frost took him under his wing and they both came back the worse for drink on two occasions. Hester made up her mind to reprimand them, but before she did so the problem solved itself. Mr Wright had apparently made other friends and he no longer stayed out so late or came in noisily. He now had enough self-confidence to speak his mind and heated words occasionally came from the sitting-room when he and Mr Kelly happened to be there at the same time. However there was little friction otherwise and no one had complained.

Hester seated Bruce between the two children, much to their delight and his relief. The other men settled themselves and the meal progressed with light conversation and obvious enjoyment. When the pudding had been eaten and nobody had appetite enough for a second helping Mr Jamieson stood to call for a Royal Toast.

'I won't drink to an English king,' Mr Kelly instantly declared.

'And why not?' demanded Mr Wright.

'Because he's no king of mine, that's why. The English stole our land. They've been trampling Irish people into the dirt for hundreds of years.'

'Rubbish.'

'It is no such thing.' Deep colour was rising up the neck of the Irishman. 'Read your history, man. Our land is Ireland and it's meant for the Irish. We don't want an English king, or his army, or his greedy hangers-on. We want our own republic — an Irish Republic for Irish people.'

'So why come to Australia then? Why choose a country with a British system? You want a republic? Why not go to America? Because you know the British system is best, that's why.'

Bruce stared in consternation, while Hester half rose from her chair, wondering if she could help to diffuse the situation. Mr Jamieson hurriedly gestured for her to remain seated.

'Gentlemen, gentlemen,' he said in his quiet and refined tones. 'Don't let's spoil a magnificent Christmas dinner with a political argument. We are far from the British Isles. King George is the King of Australia. I propose a toast to the King of Australia, and also to our wonderful hostess, Mrs Carleton, who has provided this wonderful celebratory meal for us today.'

Mr Kelly was willing to raise his glass to that proposal, perhaps only because he had no desire to snub Hester, and almost immediately afterwards Mr Pulham said he must leave. Hester went to the door of the dining-room with him and he paused there to shake her hand and thank her for the special effort to make the day memorable.

'They have never done that here before,' he said. 'They always made you feel as if you were a nuisance for staying in the house over Christmas.'

'I'm glad you enjoyed it, Mr Pulham.'

'Yes, well, pay no attention to those two arguing in there. They've been at it for weeks. Always the same thing. If they're that keen on politics they should stay over there and sort it out over there, not bring their quarrels here.'

'So long as they only exchange words,' said Hester nervously.

'Ah, yes, they won't descend to fisticuffs, so don't worry your pretty head about that. Thank you again, Mrs Carleton.'

Mr Wright followed him out. He also shook hands and thanked Hester profusely.

'I didn't expect my first Christmas in this country to be so good. I thought I'd be lonely today. Never expected to be with a family.'

'I'm glad you enjoyed it, Mr Wright. Thank you again for the gifts you gave to the children.'

'Only little things. Don't pay any heed to that silly Irishman in there. He knows which side his bread's buttered on. Ask him how many Irish live in England.'

'I won't even mention it, Mr Wright.'

'He will. But don't believe all that hogwash he'll tell you.'

As predicted, Mr Kelly could not leave the table without mentioning the dispute.

'Before you know it the English will be expecting all their colonies to fight for them again. First it was in South Africa, now it's Europe. The English are never satisfied. They're always wanting to increase their power.'

'I'm hoping it won't come to war, Mr Kelly.'

'It will, you mark my words. Too many people aim to make a fortune out of it. What do you think, Doctor?'

Bruce hesitated, unwilling to pursue the subject, and again Mr Jamieson helped to smooth over the situation.

'Today is a holiday, a day when we should be thinking about goodwill to others. Let's leave world problems to another day. Thank you again, Mrs Carleton, for all your hard work, and for making us feel so welcome and contented today. We really do appreciate it.'

'Hear, hear to that,' said Mr Kelly. 'This place'll never be the same if you leave, Mrs Carleton. So I hope you're not in a mind to do that.'

Hester smiled. 'No, I'm not thinking of leaving, Mr Kelly. I'm feeling settled here.'

She looked at Bruce and his face flushed as he lowered his gaze.

'I must add my thanks,' he said moments later. 'Thank you for making our Christmas Day such a pleasant occasion. I'm afraid I must dash away now. Unfortunately sickness never takes a holiday,'

Almost three weeks passed before Bruce contacted her again, and then it was by letter. The words were brief and formal, informing her that he had accepted a temporary post at a remote Aboriginal settlement. He wrote that he believed he could do a great deal of good for the people, but correspondence would be difficult and she should not expect to receive messages from him. He had not included a new address and Hester sighed as she pushed the letter back into the envelope. Bruce was running away, she decided. He could not bring himself to say he would not see her again; but neither would he defy his parents. Would a few months in more primitive surroundings help to stiffen his backbone?

17

The peal of the front doorbell broke into the peace of the afternoon. Hester paused on her way up the stairs then hurried down again. If it were someone selling something she would send him packing in no time.

The well-dressed man on the doorstep looked strangely familiar. He was very much like Mr Hetherington, she thought. He could be his older brother.

'Yes?' she said.

He frowned. 'Oh, come now. Don't pretend you don't know me, Hester.'

She stared for a moment, then recalled that she had often thought Mr Hetherington resembled her cousin's husband.

'Cecil?' she said doubtfully.

'Of course. Aren't you going to invite me in?'

'Oh, yes of course.' Hester stood aside and he strode into the hall. She would take him to the sitting-room, she decided. She had never got on well with him and it did not seem appropriate to take him upstairs to the apartment. Something drastic must have happened. He would not have come here otherwise. She chose the same upright chair as she had on the day when the police inspector had come, waving one hand as an invitation for Cecil to be seated.

'What's happened?' she asked. 'Is it Aunt Amelia?'

He did not answer immediately, but stared at her belligerently. He was not maturing well, thought Hester, taking time to inspect him more closely. For all his money and his self-esteem, he did not present an image of prosperity. Even his expensive hand-tailored suit needed some attention. She had expected him to become corpulent as he grew older and he showed signs of gaining weight, but he seemed to lack the brash strutting deportment that used to irritate her so much.

'Where is Louisa?' he demanded suddenly.

Hester looked blankly at him. 'Louisa?'

'Oh, come now, Hester. This is no time to play games.'

'What's happened? Has something happened to Louisa?'

'You know perfectly well.'

Hester shook her head in confusion. 'You had better begin at the beginning. What has happened?'

'Just tell me where she is. Is she in this house?'

When Hester made no immediate response,

still not comprehending the meaning of his words, he rose to his feet and began to pace about. 'I have to speak to her. If she is here, tell her to come at once.'

At last Hester began to understand what this visit was all about. 'Are you trying to tell me that Louisa has gone away without telling you she was going?'

'Don't play games, Hester. I know you have never liked me, but that's no reason why you should try to deceive me.'

'Deceive you?' Hester glared. 'There is no deceit on my part. What made you think Louisa might be here?'

'Where else could she go? She could hardly go to that poky little cottage where her sister lives. From what I hear there's scarcely room enough for Marian and her husband there. I know you write to each other regularly, and there's nobody else she would confide in.' Cecil sat down again on the edge of his chair and his voice softened. 'Please help me, Hester.'

For a moment Hester felt sympathy for him. He was obviously not in the best of health. His cheeks were pallid, dark circles underlined his eyes and a newly healed scar suggested that a boil had recently erupted on the left side of his forehead.

'I'm sorry, but you're wrong about her

coming here. There's nothing I can do to help.'

Her concern for him vanished with his reaction. He leapt to his feet and waved one arm in a threatening manner.

'Nonsense. I won't stand for any lies. I demand to know where she is. I have the right to know. She is my wife.'

Hester glanced around nervously. The bell pull was hanging on the wall to her right. If Kathy were still in the kitchen she would answer a summons fairly quickly. Feigning composure she rose to her feet, walked towards the bell pull and caught hold of the cord.

'I think it would be better if you left at once. I will call my assistant to see you out.'

'No!' Cecil took a step forward, then thought better of it and retreated. 'No. Look, Hester, I don't mean any harm. Look, don't ring that bell. I need to talk to you.'

'I can't tell you anything, Cecil.' Hester released the cord, but stayed close beside it in case she needed to call for help. 'Louisa has never been to this house. I have not seen her since I left Thorn Bay and I don't know what this is all about.'

'Is that the whole truth?'

'Of course it is. What else can I say?'

Cecil thought for a moment. 'You must

promise to contact me as soon as you hear from Louisa. You will hear from her. I know it.'

'Have you spoken to Aunt Amelia about this?'

'Of course I have!' Cecil's voice rose again. 'Louisa won't go there. She knows her mother would make her do the right thing. She is concerned about this, just as concerned as I am.'

Hester sighed. Her aunt might worry about her daughter's whereabouts, but she would be troubled also by the gossip that was sure to come. If she knew where Louisa was she would do everything in her power to make her return home.

'You must contact me as soon as you receive word from Louisa,' he persisted.

Hester shook her head. 'I am not going to get involved with this.'

'You have to! Whether you like it or not, you're a member of the family. You have to do your duty.'

'It is no business of mine,' said Hester firmly. 'If Louisa has left home, I assume she has good reason.'

'Good reason!' Cecil's face flushed and he waved his fist. Hester hastily reached for a nearby upright chair. She would ring the bell if he made any move towards her, and if necessary she would use the chair as a weapon.

'What's all this talk about reason?' roared Cecil. 'Louisa is my wife. It's her duty to care for me and the house.'

Hester bit back the retort that rose to her lips. He was in no mood to listen to any other point of view and it would be dangerous to argue with him. She pulled the cord several times to make Kathy hurry and spoke as calmly as she could.

'I'm sorry to hear about this trouble, but there's nothing I can do.'

'You could make Louisa see sense.' He struggled to calm himself, aware that his attitude would not achieve the desired results.

'I think Louisa will have to sort this out by herself. Oh, Kathy . . . ' Hester smiled with relief as the girl appeared in the doorway.

'Can I help you, Ma'am?' Kathy looked from one to the other with startled eyes.

'Mr Stroud is just leaving. Would you see him out please.'

Cecil heaved a sigh of exasperation, but decided not to resist. 'You know what you must do,' he said as he stalked out of the room. 'This cannot be the end of the matter.'

Hester released her grip on the back of the chair and sank onto the seat. Thank goodness he had gone. She had always been wary of him, ever since that terrible time when he had pressed unwelcome attention upon her, but she had never felt so threatened before. He really had looked as though he were prepared to inflict a blow. Was that why Louisa had left? Had he become violent towards her?

Kathy hastened back and looked at her with trepidation. 'Oh, Ma'am, are you all right? Oh, Ma'am, what happened?'

Hester raised a smile. 'I'm all right, Kathy. Thank you for coming so quickly. That man is related to me by marriage. He seems to think I know where his wife is.'

'Oh. One of those family fights. So she's walked out on him, has she? Can't say I blame her. Come and have a nice cup of tea, Ma'am. He's got you all upset.'

* * *

Weeks passed before Louisa finally approached Hester by telephone. She began by asking after Hester's health, her voice unusually shaky and hesitant. Scarcely waiting for a response she hurried on.

'Have you heard from Cecil?'

'I certainly have. He came here looking for you. Are you all right, Louisa?' That was a silly question, Hester rebuked herself. It was obvious from the sound of her voice that her

314

cousin was far from all right.

'I knew he'd look for me there. That's why I didn't come, why I didn't tell you anything. You can't tell anybody what you don't know.'

'Where are you now?'

'I can't tell you. Cecil, or Mother or somebody might come bothering you. It will be much easier if you really don't know.'

'Is someone looking after you? How are you managing? To pay for things and so on?'

'It's not money that . . . ' Louisa broke off and a loud sniff sounded down the line. 'Oh, Hester! I need help. You're the only one I can turn to. I have to talk to someone. There's no one else I could possibly . . . ' She sniffed again. 'Can I come and see you?'

Hester thought fleetingly of her intention to keep out of the affair, but gave in at once. Her cousin sounded desperate. How could she refuse to see her?

'Of course you can come. Can you wait until tomorrow afternoon? Dorothy will be at school and I can arrange for someone to look after Susan. That means we can talk in private, just the two of us.'

'Thank you, Hester. Yes, I'll come tomorrow. I knew I could depend on you.'

Hester sighed as she hooked the receiver back into place. It was to be hoped that Louisa were not hoping for too much. What help could she provide? She could listen and sympathise, but there was nothing else she could do. She would absolutely refuse to act as go-between although, judging by her words so far, her cousin had no intention of returning home in the immediate future.

She was shocked by Louisa's wan appearance when she arrived at Bella Casa the next day. The two women stared at each other in silence for a moment, then Hester opened her arms and they clung to each other in an impassioned hug.

'Let's go upstairs,' said Hester, disengaging herself gently from the embrace.

Louisa followed her up to the apartment and stood for a moment looking around at the cosy sitting-room. One wall was almost completely hidden behind rows of books which had once belonged to her own father. The wooden furniture glowed with polish and various surfaces held ornaments of quality as well as the small garish items that attracted children.

'You've got a nice place here, Hester. It really is as nice as you said in your letters. I've been longing to see it.'

'Yes, I have been very lucky. Please sit down.' Hester took Louisa's hat away to the bedroom then went to the kitchen, where everything had been set out ready to supply immediate refreshments.

They barely spoke as they sipped tea from Hester's best china cups. She waited, understanding that, despite her need to talk, Louisa was finding it difficult to begin.

'Nothing has turned out as we expected years ago, has it?' Louisa said at last.

'No. We all have high hopes. But we don't always get what we hope for.'

'Sometimes we close our eyes to things we don't want to see.'

'Yes. But that's human nature, I suppose.'

'The signs were there right from the start.' Louisa's voice rose suddenly. 'I was too concerned with wealth and position. I didn't look at the *man*.'

Hester could think of nothing to say to that, but now she had started Louisa needed no encouragement to continue.

'He always had wandering eyes. He took a fancy to you — don't try to deny it — but I told myself there was no harm in it. I told myself there was no harm in looking — just looking at pretty girls.' She clicked her teeth. 'So we married. He didn't change. He was hardly likely to change, was he? But I still told myself there was no harm in it. Besides, we had to keep up appearances. We had to look as if we had a happy marriage.' Louisa gripped her hands tightly together. 'I soon found out he'd only married me for the sake of his business. He needed good connections. His real love had no such assets. So he married me; and kept her.' She looked defiantly at Hester. 'You knew that, didn't you? It must have been the talk of the town eventually.'

'I heard a rumour,' Hester admitted. Louisa's sister had told her years ago that Cecil not only had a mistress, his behaviour was far from discreet.

'Perhaps I could have gone on closing my eyes to that. We were living separate lives really. But he was not satisfied with one mistress. He still went looking for others!'

'Oh, Louisa.' Hester felt obliged to say something to fill the pause that followed, but her mind seemed blank. She could think of no words likely to offer comfort.

'None of them will have him now.' Louisa's cheeks flushed with rage. 'So now he claims it's my duty to look after him. After the way he's behaved all these years, acting in such a despicable fashion, suddenly *I've* become the one who's responsible for him. But it's his own fault! If he had not behaved in such an outrageous manner, going from woman to woman, he wouldn't be in the state he's in now.'

Another awkward silence followed. Hester

still had no idea what to say and Louisa finally spoke again. 'He's sick, Hester.'

'Oh.' Hester felt that she was beginning to understand. Louisa was feeling the pangs of guilt. She had broken away from an unhappy situation, but she had made vows when she married and now she felt duty bound to go back and care for her husband. 'He didn't look well when he came here.'

Louisa's lips began to tremble. She pressed both hands against her mouth and shrank back into her chair. Hester watched in alarm. Obviously she had not heard the full story yet. There must be something worse to come.

'Cecil was angry when he came here,' she said, trying to aid her cousin in the telling of her story. 'I'd never seen him behaving like that before. Has he been violent towards you?'

Louisa nodded. 'I couldn't go back. I couldn't live in the same house with him again.' After another pause she added, 'At times he hardly seems sane. Throwing things, breaking things . . . there's no telling what he might do.'

Hester leaned towards her. 'So you have definitely made up your mind; you're not going back. But you said you needed help, Louisa. What kind of help do you need? Do you need somewhere to live?'

'No. No, that's not a problem.' Louisa grew more agitated, pressing her clenched fist against her teeth and biting down on the knuckles. Hester watched, not knowing what to do. She felt an urge to rush to her cousin's side, to hug her again and assure her that everything would be resolved in time, but instinct made her sit still and wait.

'I'm frightened,' said Louisa.

'You'll be safe if he doesn't know where you are.'

'It's not that.' Louisa half rose to her feet and then sank back again. 'It's the sickness. That's what frightens me.'

'But . . .'

Louisa took a deep breath, then straightened her spine as if she had reached a great decision and looked Hester full in the face. Someone told me what it is. It's syphilis, Hester. Do you understand what that means?'

Hester drew back, not wanting to hear. She had no real understanding, knowing only that it was a dreaded disease, so bad it was spoken of only in whispers. The subject was never mentioned in decent society. It was a result of immoral conduct.

'You've got to help me, Hester. I'm frightened.'

'How can I help?' Hester gazed at her in consternation. 'What can I do?'

'You can find out more about it. I don't know who else to turn to. I need to know. I might have caught it. But how could I face anybody and ask outright?'

'How am I going to find out about something like that?'

'Ask Bruce. Say you're asking for a friend. Don't let anyone know who it is.' Louisa stretched out her hand in appeal. 'I can't ask anybody else. I daren't let anyone know, not even the merest whisper. People are so scared of it they'd probably turn me out of my lodgings. They think you can catch it just by using the same cutlery or the same cup.'

Hester could not prevent herself from casting a rapid glance at the cup from which Louisa had been drinking only minutes before. She felt immediately contrite and tried to give comfort by taking hold of her cousin's hand.

'Thank you, Hester.' Louisa closed her eyes and sat motionless for a considerable time. 'Ask Bruce,' she repeated at last. 'He would tell you, wouldn't he? You would do that for me, wouldn't you?'

It was not the time to explain that Bruce had gone away and she no longer heard from him. Apart from that, it was not a topic she would want to broach with him. The subject was too embarrassing to contemplate and she would prefer to forget this conversation had ever taken place. Hester wished fervently that she had never agreed to this visit.

'I have to know, Hester. The worry itself is making me feel ill. And I can't leave it any longer.' Louisa withdrew her hand and began to fumble with the buttons on her blouse. 'Look. This is how it started with Cecil.'

Hester stared in dismay, quite unable to speak. The red swelling near her cousin's collar bone was going to turn into a nasty boil.

'You ought to see a doctor,' she said when she finally regained her voice.

'I suppose I will have to if things get worse. But what am I going to say? Oh, the shame of it!' Louisa shuddered at the thought. Her upbringing had been dominated by a mother who persistently emphasised the importance of refined conduct and social standing. 'I can't look a doctor in the face and ask if it's syphilis. It was hard enough to come here and speak about it. You must help me, Hester. Please. Ask Bruce what the symptoms are, and what I ought to do about it.'

The problem nagged incessantly at Hester as she went about her evening duties. She could not ask Dr Gibbs, she decided. Like Louisa, she could not look another man in the face and mention such a delicate subject.

Could she find out as much as she needed to know from a book at the public library? No, a book like that would not be on the public shelves. She would have to speak to a doctor. Perhaps it would be easier if she went to see a stranger, a different doctor in a different area, someone she would never see again. That thought finally led her to the idea of using the telephone. If she did not have to be in the same room as the doctor, neither of them able to see the other, she should be able to cope.

When the children were fast asleep she went downstairs to the office. She had made up her mind to call the surgery where Bruce used to work. There would be no need to ask the operator to search for a number, and that place was distant enough to ensure anonymity.

'Good evening. Dr Hutchinson speaking.'

'Oh, Bruce!' The startled exclamation escaped before Hester could prevent it.

'Who's that? Hester? Is that you, Hester?'

'Oh!' Hester stared unseeingly at the opposite wall, tense with alarm. She could think of nothing to say.

'Hester, what's the matter? What's happened? Are you all right?'

'Yes, I'm very well, thank you,' she answered automatically. She gasped then and bit her lip. Why had she spoken? She should have broken the connection as soon as she heard his voice. Now he would want to know why she had telephoned.

'You obviously didn't expect to hear me answer.'

'No.'

'I only got back here last night. I've written a letter to you, Hester. I've just posted it.'

'Oh.'

'You sound rather upset. Are you going to tell me why you rang this number?'

Hester breathed deeply to compose herself. 'I wanted to talk to a doctor. I thought there was sure to be one there.'

'I thought you had confidence in Dr Gibbs.'

'Ah, yes, but . . . I thought . . . I'd rather not speak to him.'

'You feel embarrassed. That's what your problem is,' he guessed.

He did his best to convince her that doctors looked at all medical matters dispassionately and there was nothing she need hesitate to mention. Hester finally agreed she had better complete her task now that she had begun, and launched into an explanation about a friend who was concerned about catching a dreadful disease. Eventually she made herself name the disease in question and asked for information about it.

'She's terribly frightened, Bruce. There's a boil coming up near her shoulder.'

'There has to be more to it than that. What made her think of syphilis?'

His matter of fact tone gave Hester the confidence to add a few details and she told him that her friend had been living with someone who had the disease.

'I see. Look, Hester, it's impossible to give a diagnosis over the telephone, especially when the patient is not even there. I'll come to see you tomorrow evening and bring a few notes with me, but the only safe thing for your friend to do is to consult a doctor herself.'

'I suppose I already knew that.'

'Yes. I'll come tomorrow. Look, Hester ... ' Now he was the one to sound hesitant and embarrassed. 'Hester, would you do something for me?'

'Of course.'

'I've written a letter to you. Would you ... that is ... would you do me a favour? It will come tomorrow. Please don't open it.'

'You want it back,' she exclaimed.

'No. No, that's not it. I don't regret anything I wrote. But it's very personal. It took me a long time to do it. I'll see you

325

tomorrow, but I don't want you to open the letter until afterwards. And I want you to be alone when you read it.'

'I see.'

'Promise you won't open it.'

Hester paused. This was proving to be a more complicated matter than she could have imagined, but for Louisa's sake she had to go through with it now.

'Very well, I promise I will not open the letter. But you must be sure to come tomorrow evening.'

18

The disturbing events caused another restless night and Hester felt weary the next day. The letter from Bruce arrived in the morning as forecast, and it lay on the desk tantalizing her as she tried to concentrate on orders and accounts. The temptation to open it was almost more than she could bear, but she had made a promise and she was determined to keep her word. Eventually she thrust the letter into the bottom drawer and put a ledger on top. She would look for a more complicated recipe for a pudding, she decided. She must make sure she was physically busy all day and keep her mind fully occupied.

As evening approached the prospect of seeing Bruce again and being in his presence overwhelmed all other thoughts. It was likely to be a highly sensitive occasion, not only because of the topic they were meeting to discuss, but also because of their own relationship. Bruce had obviously decided what he must do in the future, but it seemed that he could not bring himself to state his intentions openly. He could only do so in writing, and only when he felt confident that he would not have to face her afterwards. Hester sighed and told herself she did not care what he did or where he went after today. It was only for her cousin's sake that she had agreed to see him. She would obtain as much information as she could this evening, then cut herself off from him and anyone else who had known her in her previous life. She had made a new start here in St Kilda and she must not allow any of her relatives or former friends to intrude and disturb her peace.

The opening moments of her meeting with Bruce were as difficult as she had imagined, but he maintained a strict formality and she took her cue from him. They exchanged polite remarks about the mild evening weather as if they were comparative strangers, then she led the way up to the apartment and took his hat.

'An awkward situation,' he murmured.

'Yes. Please make yourself at home.'

He was still standing when she returned from the hat-stand.

'You have obviously been out in the sun a lot,' said Hester. 'What was it like, working in such a place so far from the city?'

'It was an education. Dreadful in some aspects, but a truly great experience.'

'Are you going back?'

'No. It was only a temporary position, a case of filling in while the regular doctor went on leave.' Bruce patted his pocket. 'But let's get on with the immediate business. You have a worried friend.'

'Yes.' Hester went to her usual armchair and as soon as she was seated he lowered himself into the neighbouring chair.

'When someone asks for advice for a friend, they usually mean it is for themselves,' he began. 'But I don't think that is the case this time.'

'Oh, no!' exclaimed Hester.

'It wouldn't be Kathy, would it?'

'Oh, no!'

'So all we have to go on is what you have been told. Do you think you know this person well enough? Do you know anything of the background?'

Hester told him that her 'friend' was married, that her husband had been unfaithful for years and he was now suffering from the disease. Bruce composed his next question carefully, trying to avoid embarrassing her.

'Do you know anything about their marital arrangements prior to their being separated? For example, were they sharing a bed?'

'She said they were living separate lives.'

'In that case, she could be safe.'

'But she has a boil coming up and she said that's how it started with him.'

Bruce shook his head. 'That is not quite correct. But no doubt it was the first symptom that she noticed.'

'I've seen him,' Hester blurted. 'He'd just had a boil or something on his forehead.'

'It's quite common for the patient to suffer from lesions and various other skin ailments.' Bruce pulled some sheets of paper out of his pocket and laid them on the occasional table beside his chair. 'You can give these notes to your friend. They explain how the disease progresses, the symptoms and so forth. Only your friend will know whether or not it could have been passed on. I can assure you on one point, though — it cannot be spread by door knobs, eating utensils or anything like that.'

Hester gazed at him dubiously and he smiled slightly. 'I know what people say, but it's not true. You can't catch it from using cups and things. If your friend and her husband have really been living separate lives she might be worrying unnecessarily.'

'If only that were true.'

'She has been suffering stress, probably not sleeping well and not eating properly. That upsets the system. That could be why she has a boil.'

'I do hope so.' Hester dared not place any faith in that outcome. 'Can you do anything for her if she is sick? Can you cure her?'

Bruce sighed. 'No, I'm sorry. However, you must try not to become too involved.' He stood then, as if ready to leave, and looked down at her with real concern. 'You must pay more attention to yourself, Hester. People always seem to push their problems onto you. The trouble is that you are far too considerate for your own good.'

Hester smiled briefly and rose to her feet.

'You've had enough troubles of your own to cope with,' he persisted. 'Please say you'll try not to let people do this kind of thing to you. It's not fair for them to do it.'

'It just seems to happen. I can't turn people away.'

'You'll have to learn to be firmer. You can't take on the woes of the whole world.'

'I'll try.' She smiled again and managed to speak in a light tone. 'Thank you for coming, Bruce. I was dreading this, but talking about it was not as bad as I thought it might be.'

'Thank goodness for that.' Bruce hesitated, not sure what to say next. 'I must go. Try to get a good night's sleep tonight, Hester. And don't bother coming downstairs. I'll see myself out.'

He hurried out of the room without even

offering his hand, leaving Hester standing by the armchair feeling rejected and forlorn. She heard the front door close with a sharp slam downstairs, but she felt no inclination to go to the bedroom window to watch him depart. Even the letter that had tempted her all day no longer seemed important. There was no point in going down to read it, she decided. Tomorrow would be soon enough — if she read it at all. She knew what was in it. Bruce had agreed to abide by his parents' wishes and break off contact with her.

★ ★ ★

'It's going to be one of those days today, I just know it,' muttered Edith as she cleared up a trail of spilt sugar on the workbench. 'Isn't that milkman coming yet, Kathy?'

The younger woman darted away to look at the street again. Almost five minutes passed before she returned, but this time she brought the can of milk with her.

'There's been an accident,' she cried. 'Someone in a motor car hit the side of the milk cart! You should see it. A whole piece broken right off! No wonder the milkman was so late.'

'Well, as long as he didn't get hurt,' Edith responded. 'Put that down, Kathy, and let's get on with things. You should have sounded the gong by now.'

Despite the delay they managed to serve breakfast and clear the dining-room by the usual time. Hester was preparing to take Dorothy to school when the telephone rang.

'Oh, Hester, it's me, Louisa. Did you do it? Have you found out about it for me?'

'Yes.' Hester looked around, worried that someone might overhear. 'I can't tell you now. But yes, Bruce wrote it all down. It's here waiting for you.'

'Oh, thank you, Hester. I'll come straight away.'

'Don't come for a little while. I'm just going out with Dorothy, but I'll be back soon after nine o'clock.'

When the doorbell rang Hester hurried to answer, fully expecting to find Louisa waiting outside, but when she opened the door she found Mr Jamieson and another man. The stranger helped Mr Jamieson into the hall and explained that he was an office colleague. Mr Jamieson had collapsed at work, and he had brought him back to Bella Casa in a motor car.

'I'm sorry to cause all this bother,' said Mr Jamieson. 'There was no real need to disturb you, Mrs Carleton. We could have gone straight up.'

Hester studied his pale face and exchanged glances with his companion. 'I'll call a doctor,' she said. 'Are you listed with a doctor already, Mr Jamieson, or shall I call Dr Gibbs?'

'No, no, please don't make a fuss. I shall be perfectly all right. I'll just have a little rest.'

'We'll let the doctor decide that,' said Hester firmly. 'You go up and get into bed, Mr Jamieson.'

Dr Gibbs prescribed rest for his patient and promised to call again in the early evening.

'I think he's been working too hard lately,' he told Hester. 'He's getting on in years now, but he still wants to do as much as a younger man.'

'It worries me sometimes,' said Hester. 'It would be dreadful if one of the residents had a heart attack or something.'

'You mustn't try to take too much on yourself. If any of them become seriously ill you must send them off to a place where they can be looked after by professionals. We don't want you to be overworked and ending up being ill yourself.'

Louisa arrived only a few minutes after he had departed. Hester had decided it would be more circumspect to put Bruce's notes into an envelope, and both women felt a sense of relief when Louisa tucked the sealed packet quickly away in her black cloth bag.

'Thank you, Hester. I'll read it later.' Louisa hugged her tightly then turned away, wiping tears from her eyes. 'You can't imagine how thankful I am. I'm sorry I had to ask you to do that.'

Hester was close to tears herself. She patted Louisa's shoulder and urged her towards the door.

'I know you can hardly wait to find out what he said. Keep in touch, Louisa. No matter what happens, keep in touch. And try not to worry too much. There is a good chance that you will be safe.'

'Oh, if only if could be so!' Louisa hugged Hester again then hastened away, not looking back as she went along the front path and out by the ornate gate.

Dorothy seemed listless when she came home for lunch and Hester watched in dismay as she pushed her plate away.

'Don't tell me you feel ill as well,' she exclaimed.

'I'm sorry, Mama, but I don't want anything to eat.'

Her forehead felt slightly warmer than it should and she was perfectly agreeable to the idea of taking a nap. Hester tucked her into bed, hoping she was not going to have a recurrence of her previous sickness. By late afternoon the little girl was feeling no better and Hester asked Dr Gibbs to examine her when he called to see Mr Jamieson.

'It's chicken pox,' Dr Gibbs pronounced. 'There's quite a lot of it around at present. I expect her little sister will catch it, too.'

'Chicken pox!' exclaimed Hester. 'She must have caught it at school.'

'It's a common childhood disease. You have probably had it, too.' Hester nodded and he continued breezily, 'It's better to catch it in childhood. Some people put their children in contact with it on purpose, so that they'll get it over and done with. It can be serious for adults, but it's usually mild for children, so try not to worry.'

'I said it was going to be one of those days,' said Edith when she heard the news. 'It started all wrong. I even found a hole in my stocking this morning.'

The flurry of incidents had distracted Hester from her private concerns and the evening work was over, both children asleep, before she remembered Bruce's letter. Perhaps this was not a good time to read it. This had not been a good day. On the other hand, it might be as well to do what some people did about chicken pox — get it over and done with. Hester made up her mind. If she were ever going to read it she would do so this evening.

She went down to retrieve the letter from the drawer in the office and took it upstairs to the apartment. Even then she hesitated to open the envelope. She laid it on the dining table and stared at it for several moments, then suddenly picked it up and made a rapid slice with the letter opener.

She had not expected the first words to say how much Bruce was missing her. Hester gulped and read on. He had started his letter when he was miles away in the remote outback. He described the flat dusty country-side beyond his window and then wrote:

You can't believe how desolate it looks, so dry and barren. It hasn't rained for months. But rain will come eventually and everything will bloom again. If only I could foresee such a prospect for myself. I see only continual desolation for myself, barren and lonely.

The following pages seemed to have been written at different times and to have been composed with considerable effort. Bruce said that he cared for her and he wished with all his heart that she would find true happiness.

You deserve to find a good and loving husband who will care for you and your children for the rest of your life.

He then went on to admonish her, telling her she must not hide herself away, burying herself in work and family responsibilities. She must look beyond her immediate circle of friends and acquaintances and find a new friend to become her husband, someone who truly cared for her. For his part, he could not offer a suitable home; he had insufficient funds and his family would not be supportive. On the contrary, his parents would be distinctly hostile.

They wish me to marry, but only a person of their own choosing. That, I most emphatically refuse to do. So, I am back where I started. As before, I must concentrate on medicine. It has to be the absolute focus of my life.

He ended by stating that he would devote himself to his patients and would never marry.

I hope we can always remain friends, Hester. I could not bear it if I thought I would never see you again. And yet I cannot bear to be with you, knowing I cannot keep you for myself.

Tears welled in Hester's eyes as she folded the letter again and pushed it back into the envelope. Bruce had never revealed his feelings so openly before. He was a reticent man, not the type to express his emotions in romantic phrases, and he must have hesitated to put such thoughts into writing. Despite the fine words, however, the letter only confirmed what she had been telling herself all along. Bruce was still dominated by his parents and he lacked the strong willpower that would be needed to go against their wishes.

As predicted, Susan also succumbed to chicken pox and once again Cora came to Hester's aid, helping to care for the young patients and doing some jobs in the kitchen. She brushed aside any attempts to reward her.

'I've told you, I enjoy coming and doing a few tasks here. Besides, what are friends and relatives for if they don't give a helping hand when needed?'

She went out after lunch one afternoon to buy a few groceries for her own household and came back with sparkling eyes, eager to share some gossip.

'You know how Edith always rushes out of

here, exactly on time — twelve o'clock every day. Have you ever wondered what she does?'

'I expect she goes home,' replied Hester. 'She lives just a few streets away.'

Cora shook her head. 'She doesn't, you know. I saw her today, and you'll never guess what she was doing.'

Hester smiled, knowing that the older woman was fond of reading romantic stories. Perhaps she had seen Edith with a male friend.

'Go on, tell me,' she said. 'I know you're longing to.'

'She was in a shop on Fitzroy Street. Behind the counter! She has another job, Hester.'

Hester stared. 'Are you sure? Was she actually serving a customer, or do you think she might have been there just visiting someone?'

'She wasn't serving. But she was definitely working. Apron on and everything. Making sandwiches and dishing up food. It's one of those places that doesn't know whether it's a shop or a café.'

'I expect they do very well,' said Hester. 'There must be lots of people who want to buy lunch. All our residents have to get something to eat somewhere.'

'No wonder Edith is always in such a hurry

if she's rushing to another job. Are you going to say anything to her?'

Hester shrugged. 'So long as she does her work properly here it doesn't matter what she does in her free time.'

Cora nodded. 'Hardly free time for her, is it? But she must have been delighted when you gave them all that extra time off in the afternoons. Keep your eye on her, though. If she starts to get slack, you'll have to put your foot down.'

Rather than slacking, Edith seemed to have mellowed during the past year and she was more communicative and helpful than she had been in the early days of their association. It was she who remarked that Hester was not looking well.

'Why don't you take a proper rest, Ma'am? We can manage well enough, especially while Mrs Wellerby is here.'

'You're certainly looking a bit peaky,' said Cora. 'Go on, leave everything to us this morning.'

Hester needed little more persuasion. She had felt a pain in her side for two days now, and this morning she had been horrified to perceive a reddening of the skin. For more than an hour she had been hankering for an opportunity to examine the affected area more closely.

'I'll go up for a while,' she said.

In the privacy of her bedroom she started to undress and soon uncovered most of her upper body. She gasped with dismay at the sight of inflamed skin. There was no mistake, she was beginning to develop some kind of rash, but it was nothing like the scattered spots that had erupted on the children. Hester sank onto the edge of the bed, images of Bruce's notes flashing before her eyes. She had been unable to resist the urge to read them before passing them on to Louisa, justifying herself with the excuse that he would have put the paper into an envelope had he not wanted her to see.

Now she could remember some of the words only too well, and they were frightening. The time between catching the bacterium and showing symptoms could be as little as ten days, or as long as three months. One of the symptoms was a rash on one or more areas of skin and another was muscle aches. She had both of those problems. Had she caught that dreadful disease from Louisa? The timing fitted, although Bruce had been so emphatic. He had insisted that it could not be caught so easily. But doctors were not infallible, were they? They could be wrong, make mistakes, just like anybody else. Hester began to dress again, wondering what to do. She could not afford to be ill, and especially with such a terrible condition. Cora was a woman with a great deal of worldly experience and she was not easily shocked. But could she confide in her, bring herself to mention such a sensitive problem? If only she knew how to contact Louisa. She could talk to her; they were both caught up in the same dilemma.

The morning mail did nothing to raise her spirits. An envelope with unfamiliar handwriting contained a letter from the Matron at the Retired Seamen's Home at Mountcliffe. Barnaby had caught a chill which developed into pneumonia and he had died a few days before.

'Poor Barnaby,' she murmured. She hoped his last days had not been too unhappy. He must have missed his old home on the cliffs, but it was a relief to know that he had not been alone at the end.

She tried to hide the state of her own health until she found the courage to share her fears, but whilst preparing breakfast the next morning she almost fainted. Edith continued to organise the meal while Kathy cared for Hester until Cora arrived.

'It's bed for you,' said Cora. 'And I'm going to call the doctor. No arguments.'

Hester could not find the energy to resist,

and she was lying in bed, feeling distinctly unwell, when Dr Gibbs came to the house.

'So now you have joined the list of casualties,' he said. 'Can you sit up for me?'

Cora helped Hester to raise herself and he started by listening to her heart and lungs.

'Hm. Fine. I don't see any spots. Let me see more of you, please.'

'I have got a rash,' Hester admitted.

She dragged up her long nightgown and he stared at the red streak on her side. Clusters of spots had begun to erupt in a line along the site.

'You've got shingles,' he announced.

'What's that?' asked Hester nervously. 'Is there another name for it?'

'It has a long clinical name, of course, but you wouldn't recognize that. No, shingles is common enough, unfortunately. It's related to chicken pox.'

'Chicken pox!' gasped Hester. 'Are you sure? Are you sure it's not something else, something really bad? I was with someone who . . . and I thought I might have caught it. Something terrible. I read about it and it said . . .'

'Reading about serious illness is not always a good idea,' the doctor interposed. 'You can often find symptoms that seem to fit your own case, and that frightens people more than it helps. It seems to have done that to you.'

'Yes. I have been very worried.'

'Well, Mrs Carleton, I can definitely assure you on one point — you have not got bubonic plague, meningitis or any of those other horror diseases. This is shingles.'

'Has she caught it from the children?' asked Cora.

'Perhaps. This comes from the same kind of source. But it often seems to be connected with overwork and worry. It could have hit at any time. It seems to wait in the system until your defenses are low, then attack.'

'It's a relief to know it's nothing worse,' said Hester.

'Ah.' Dr Gibbs took his stethoscope from around his neck and replaced it in his bag. 'We know what it is, and it isn't dangerous. But I have to tell you, Mrs Carleton, it is very unpleasant. You will have pain. Even trying to wear clothes will be a problem. You're also going to get an unbearable itch. On top of all that you will feel very ill at times.' He looked thoughtfully at the two women. 'Someone else will have to care for the children. You won't be able to look after them, Mrs Carleton.'

'I can do it,' said Cora at once. 'I'll stay here with Hester until she is well again.'

'Oh, but . . . ' Hester could see nothing but difficulties ahead.

'No arguments. Thank you, Doctor.' Cora nodded to him and stood up briskly, ready to combat any protests.

'I will leave you to make arrangements,' he said. 'I have to tell you there is nothing I can do to cure this ailment. It's a case of waiting for it to take its course, but I can recommend one or two things to ease the pain and try to help the itch.'

Cora went downstairs to see him out and then returned to the bedroom, already busily forming plans.

'The doctor said this is going to take more than a few days,' she said. 'I'll have to move in here for quite a while.'

'You can't do that,' Hester demurred. 'What about Father? You know he doesn't look after himself properly when he's alone.'

'Then he'll have to come too, won't he?' Cora brightened. 'That is a good idea. It will make a change for him and he could be useful. For one thing he could help to keep the children occupied. They'll soon be ready to enjoy visitors.'

'There isn't enough room for everybody.'

'Of course there is. Have you forgotten the little house you grew up in? All we need is one more bed and a bit of re-arranging. Now who do I know that could lend us a bed?'

Hester closed her eyes and allowed her thoughts to drift. She was too tired to become involved. Absolute peace was all she wanted. Cora could make any arrangements she chose.

19

Hester's father resisted the idea of uprooting himself from his comfortable surroundings and moving into a house where several invalids and numerous paying guests would take precedence over his own demands. However, after concocting an unsatisfactory dinner for himself that evening, spending a lonely night and then partaking of a solitary and unappetising breakfast the next morning, he telephoned Bella Casa. Cora went into the office to speak to him, then hastened upstairs.

'Edmund will be here this evening,' she said triumphantly to Hester. 'What did I tell you? He can carry trays up for Mr Jamieson. That will be a great help, even if he doesn't do anything else.'

'How is Mr Jamieson?' asked Hester.

'He's doing very well. Dr Gibbs says he must not tackle the stairs for a while, but he can get up and sit in the armchair if he wants to.' Cora smiled. 'He's not impatient to do anything more than that just yet, so we won't have to lay the law down. Now all we have to do is make sure that you don't try to do too much.'

'I'm confined just as much as he is,' said Hester ruefully. 'I can't go anywhere without my clothes.'

'The one good thing about this whole business,' declared Cora. 'I don't have to worry about you suddenly coming down and trying to do some work. Now remember, you need rest. You must lie down whenever you feel like it, and don't worry about a thing. We have everything under control, so try to forget all about work and relax.'

She came up frequently to check on the children, reminding them not to pester their mother for attention.

'Mama is ill, too, so she needs to rest.'

'She keeps getting out of bed,' said Dorothy.

'Yes, I know. She can get up if she likes. But she feels very sore so she can't get dressed. Don't forget now, don't hug Mama.'

'We can kiss her,' said Susan.

'Yes, you can kiss her, but be careful not to put your arms round her, 'cause it will hurt.'

A bouquet of flowers came for Hester later that day, with a card signed on behalf of the residents, and she received several notes and greeting cards wishing her a speedy recovery. When Kathy came up in the afternoon to spend some time with the children she stared in surprise at the colourful display.

'Oh, Ma'am, isn't it nice of the gentlemen to send all those!'

'Very nice, Kathy. I don't know that I deserve such a fuss.'

'Of course you do, Ma'am. They all like you very much.'

Edmund arrived a few minutes before the gong was sounded for dinner, carrying a suitcase containing clothes for himself and various items that Cora had instructed him to bring for her. She persuaded him to take Mr Jamieson's meal up on a tray, and gleefully reported to Hester that the two men had found themselves to be compatible — so much so that they had agreed to dine together in the bedroom until Mr Jamieson had recuperated. It seemed that Edmund would settle satisfactorily for the length of their stay.

Louisa telephoned a week later and made an immediate decision to visit when she heard that Hester was ill. Cora met her at the front door, introduced herself and showed her up to the apartment, going away again at once to make tea for them all. Hester had decided she would prefer to receive her cousin in the living-room rather than in the bedroom, but she left her hair down and wore only the loose fitting nightdress and dressing-gown. Louisa gave her a light kiss on the cheek and then gestured towards the extra furniture in the crowded room.

'Oh, Hester! Fancy me coming and bothering you with my problems when you were just about to have all this trouble.'

Hester gave a wry smile. She would never admit to the fear that had struck her when she first felt unwell.

'Cora keeps assuring me it's more convenient to have all of us ill at the same time, but it must be very tiring for them all. We have a patient amongst the residents, too.' She sighed wearily. 'I feel so useless. However, the children are much better now, and I should be improving very soon. How are you?'

'I am very well.' Louisa seated herself in the nearest chair and leaned eagerly towards her. 'I am safe, Hester. That information you got for me was really important. And so reassuring. I began to feel better almost as soon as I read it.'

'Thank goodness for that.' If only she had known sooner, thought Hester with regret. It would have saved her from hours of intense worry.

'Yes. I finally did go to see a doctor. When I was more certain about that other thing. He said I was run down and that's why I had the boil. I only had the one. Since that load was lifted off my mind I've felt like a new woman.'

'What are you going to do now?'

'I have joined a new women's group. The League gave me the address. You remember the League at Thorn Bay?'

Hester nodded. 'I wondered if they had given you any help when you decided to leave home.'

'I couldn't have done it without them,' was the fervent response. 'They gave me an address to go to and an introduction to some people. If they had not helped me I wouldn't have known how to start. Has Cecil bothered you again, or anybody else in the family?'

'No. Aunt Amelia sent a note recently, but she made no mention of either you or Cecil, and I did not tell her I had seen you.'

'Thank you, Hester. I wrote to Mother, telling her not to worry about my welfare. One day I hope we can dispense with all this secrecy.'

'I expect everybody will accept the situation before long,' said Hester hopefully.

Louisa chuckled, filled with a new confidence and sense of freedom. 'It's not as though it's the first time Mother has experienced something like this, is it? Except that Marian ran away to get married and I'm doing just the opposite.'

'Have you written to Marian?'

'Yes, but I didn't tell her where I am. I told

her I had left home, that's all. If she could write back she would probably say I should have done it years ago.'

★ ★ ★

Hester's rash gradually diminished but she felt no better, and as the children's good health returned she found their antics irked her more than they should. Cora and Kathy kept the girls occupied in the kitchen or the garden for much of the day, but she was often disturbed by giggles or petty bickering.

'I feel even worse now than I did before,' she told Dr Gibbs.

'Ah.' He took her hand and felt for her pulse. 'I could have told you that, but I didn't want to discourage you in the early stages.'

'How long is this going to take?'

'Six weeks is quite usual. You will just have to be patient.'

Cora took it upon herself to make other arrangements, and calmly announced that Hester was to spend seven days in different surroundings.

'I can't go away,' she protested. 'What about the children?'

'They will be looked after perfectly well here. Now you know you need to go somewhere quiet, Hester. And everything has been fixed, so there's no point in arguing.'

'But the cost of it! I can't afford to . . . '

'The Trust will pay for it all, Hester. This is a medical matter. Besides, as Harold said, it will save time and money in the long run. You'll get better far sooner.'

'So Harold has had a hand in this.'

'He certainly has. He's going to drive you there.' Cora smiled. 'I agree with you, Harold is a nice man.'

'Has Father met him?'

'Yes. He still can't bring himself to admit that you can't blame Harold for anything that Gerald did, but he was polite to him. And he's pleased that Harold is so keen to help you.'

When the car arrived they found that Muriel had come also to keep Hester company in the back passenger seat. Harold loaded her single suitcase then drove them along the coast to a large two-storied house that had been converted into a convalescent home. It was a joy to be in the fresh air and to see the beauty of the shore after such a long period indoors, but the journey tired Hester and she was content to go straight to bed in her private room.

The next day she was listless and apathetic, feeling too tired even to read for longer than a few minutes, but the pampering and the absolute peace brought results and she soon found she was enjoying the experience. She seemed to have spent all her adult life attending to other people's wants, and had never received such good attention herself. The house was more like a luxury hotel than the hospital she had envisaged when she first heard about the plan, and the informal atmosphere was both friendly and comforting. She began to dress each morning and to move more often to other parts of the building, chatting occasionally with other clients but usually sitting alone, appreciating the comfortable chairs and the view of the sea from the huge window in the front lounge, or the sight of a well-tended garden from the terrace at the rear.

'You are looking much better now,' said Muriel when she and Harold came to collect her at the end of her stay.

'I feel much better, too. I'll be ready for work again tomorrow.'

'That is definitely not on the agenda,' said Harold. 'You will not be going back there for another week at least.'

'We can't allow all this good work to be undone,' added Muriel.

'Oh, but . . . '

'You're coming to our house,' said Harold firmly. 'The children are there already, so you can't refuse. You couldn't disappoint them now, could you?'

Hester gave in, secretly relieved to know that she need not think about taking on any duties for several more days.

'Thank you, both of you. You are very good to us all.'

Dorothy and Susan greeted their mother with great excitement, delighted to know that she was well again. They had fully recovered from their sickness and were thoroughly enjoying the unexpected holiday with their relatives. The noise and bustle would have been a source of great irritation only a week before, but now Hester found that it did not disturb her unduly.

'I'm sorry if you find my lot a bit too loud,' said Muriel one morning when her brood had set off for school. 'I keep reminding them to be quiet, but it doesn't last long.'

'They don't seem to be as boisterous as I remember,' said Hester. 'They seemed to shout a lot and run about more the first time I came here, but I suppose they're all older now.'

'Yes. They should be getting a bit more sense, I suppose.'

Hester had decided she must give a present to Cora, to thank her for all the hard work she had done, but she could not think of anything suitable. She asked Muriel for suggestions and her immediate response was to consult her husband.

'There are lots of new gadgets, things for the kitchen,' said Harold. 'Is that the kind of thing you had in mind?'

'Not really.' Hester thought for a moment. 'I want something that would be useful, yet decorative. Something that Father would like as well. After all, his life has been disrupted, too.'

'Perhaps one of the new fancy lamps. The best thing for you to do is come down to my showroom. You're sure to find something there. We'll do that at the end of the week.'

The next day he surprised the two women by returning to the house soon after he had set off for work.

'There's a letter for you, Hester,' he said. 'Re-directed from Bella Casa.'

Hester flushed with embarrassment. 'You didn't come back specially because of that, did you?' she asked. 'It could have waited.'

'It's from a solicitor's office,' he replied. 'So I thought it might be important. It's not the firm that deals with your uncle's Trust, is it?'

He passed the letter to her and Hester looked at the envelope with a sense of foreboding. 'No, it's not the same name. Oh dear. Why would a solicitor be writing to me?'

'It's probably something to do with the bill for the place where you stayed last week,' said Muriel lightly. 'Nothing for you to worry about.'

Hester opened the envelope and paled at the sight of the first words in the short formal letter.

'They want me to go to the office. What on earth could have gone wrong now?'

'Let me see.' Muriel plucked the letter out of her hand. 'Oh, look, something to your advantage. It can't be bad.'

'They always say things like that to make sure you answer,' said Harold scathingly. 'Here, give it to me.'

He read the letter without comment, then took his watch from his waistcoat pocket. 'It's still quite early, but there might be someone there. I'll telephone right now.'

The two women waited, listening openly to the one-sided conversation. It appeared that Harold was fixing an appointment.

'Right,' he said when the call had ended. 'I can't tell you any more than it says in that letter. There was only a clerk available. When do you want to go, Hester? We can go this morning, unless you think that's too much of a rush. Or tomorrow afternoon if you'd rather.' He regarded her troubled expression with some concern. 'Or we can leave it till much later if you don't feel strong enough. I don't think it's anything urgent.'

Hester hesitated and he passed the letter to her so that she could read it again more carefully.

'They say I should ask a male friend or relative to accompany me. Why would they say that?'

'There's nothing unusual about that,' said Harold. 'Lawyers prefer to deal with men, that's all.'

'They think women can't understand things,' Muriel put in. 'But if they never tell us anything, what can they expect?'

'Never mind all that,' Harold retorted impatiently. 'Now then, Hester, let's look at this calmly. I will come with you, of course. The question is, when? If you feel well enough we could go this morning.'

'What about your business?' fretted Hester. 'You're late already.'

'That doesn't matter. I don't have to be on deck twenty-four hours a day. If you can be ready to leave in half an hour we can go now and get this over with. What do you say?'

Twenty minutes later they were bowling along the road, Harold doing his best to soothe her nerves.

'This is the kind of letter you get when a rich relative dies. You might be the heir to a huge sheep station.'

'I don't have any rich relatives, except for Aunt Amelia, and she has three children to leave her property to.'

She gradually recovered her composure as they drove towards the city. The dreadful events concerning Gerald and little William were over and done with, she reminded herself. This would have nothing to do with that episode, or the debts that were incurred. Perhaps it was something to do with Mr Best. She had not given a thought to him recently. She did not even know if the case had come to trial, although she would have expected Cora to tell her if it had been reported in the newspapers. Perhaps she had to attend court and give evidence. If so, a dreadful experience was awaiting her, but surely that would be the worst news she was likely to hear today.

The solicitor named in the letter proved to be a portly middle-aged man with a kindly expression. He welcomed Hester and Harold into his office, introduced himself and made a few polite remarks, then asked for proof of identification. Harold had anticipated such a request and he produced a handful of papers from his briefcase. The solicitor satisfied himself that everything was in order, then addressed Hester.

'Mrs Carleton, I hope I am not the first to

break bad news, but we are settling the final affairs of one of our clients. Did you know that Mr Barnaby Millhouse had passed away?'

'Oh, Barnaby!' So much had happened since she heard the news of his death that Hester had scarcely remembered the fact. 'Yes, I did know. He was a nice old man.'

'He always spoke very kindly of you and he named you as the main beneficiary in his Will.'

Hester stared in bewilderment. Barnaby had lived a simple life in a decrepit building on the cliffs, surrounded by a clutter of old sailing equipment and objects washed up on the shore. He had given the marine artifacts to a museum, so whatever was left would have no real value. Why had he thought it necessary to call on the services of a solicitor? Surely the staff at the Seamen's Home could have disposed of his few belongings?

'I don't know why he should have mentioned me,' she said at last.

'I met Mr Millhouse and had a long talk with him. He said you were always very kind to him. He was particularly moved when you called to see him on the last occasion.' The solicitor looked down at a paper on his desk. 'He said you had lost both a child and a husband, but you still had enough room in your heart to think of him. You were making a long journey to Melbourne, but you took the time to turn aside and visit him.'

Hester looked down at her clasped hands, guilty tears starting to her eyes. She had not been thinking so much of Barnaby's feelings at that time; she had gone there mainly for the sake of the children. She knew they would like to talk to the cockatoo again.

'Since then you have written several letters. You are the only person who ever did that.' The solicitor pushed his chair back, opened the central drawer of his desk and took out a small blue box, then heaved himself to his feet and went to Hester's side. 'Mr Millhouse left this to you. He said you were the only person worthy of it.'

Hester held the cardboard box in her hand for several moments, remembering how Barnaby used to show off his latest find of a colourful shell or an unusual stone, then she carefully lifted the lid. A wad of tissue paper lay just inside, and when she removed that she found two balls, not quite perfectly round. One was white with an attractive lustre, the other a shiny dark grey, looking rather like a grape. She stared at them, not fully understanding what they might be.

Harold leaned forward to see what was inside the box and drew his breath in sharply.

'Are they genuine?'

'They most certainly are.' The solicitor went back to sit behind his desk, pleased with the effect that he had achieved.

Hester made no move and Harold began to fidget. 'They're pearls, Hester.'

She nodded, too overwhelmed to speak, and Harold turned to the solicitor. 'Have you any idea how much they're worth?'

He inclined his head. 'A fairly good idea. I expect you will want to get them valued as soon as possible.'

'These really are valuable, aren't they?' said Hester at last.

'Yes. At least one thousand pounds.'

'I can't believe it! Barnaby had these? Did he know their value?'

'He most certainly did. He was involved in pearling for some years.' The solicitor leaned forward. 'He told me the story behind those two pearls. It would be too distressing for you to know the details, but those particular pearls meant far more than money to him. He kept them in memory of a friend, a diver who died near Broome, up in the far north-west of Australia. Several people have died because of pearls like that. It was the greed and crime that turned him into a recluse. He said he had never met anyone worthy of receiving those pearls until he met you, Mrs Carleton.

He had faith in you. He trusted you to use them sensibly and with good purpose.'

Hester could think of nothing to say in response. She sat quietly, her thoughts whirling, while Harold and the solicitor completed the legal business. She signed a document, concentrating on keeping her hand steady, then allowed Harold to take her arm and lead her out to the street.

'What a day this has turned out to be,' he exclaimed.

Hester merely nodded mutely and he patted her hand. 'This way. You need to sit down.'

He escorted her around the corner to a nearby hotel, where he settled her in a secluded corner. When the waiter came to their table he ordered tea for her and coffee for himself, but he said nothing more until the drinks had been served.

'You're a wealthy woman now, Hester.'

'A thousand pounds for those,' she murmured. 'I can't believe it.'

'A thousand pounds *each*,' he corrected.

Hester looked up in amazement. 'You can't mean it!'

'I most certainly do. At long last your fortune has taken a real turn for the better.'

Harold soon announced that he was far too excited to concentrate on his own business that day.

'Let's go straight home and tell Muriel,' he said. 'I'll just telephone the office and tell them they'll have to get on without me.'

He left her sitting at the table while he made his call, then guided her out to the street and along to the place where he had parked the motor car. Hester climbed into the front passenger seat, still feeling that she was participating in some kind of dream. Neither spoke as they drove away from the city. She felt incapable of making any sensible remark, while Harold was obviously planning ahead, devising ways to make the best use of the unexpected windfall.

Muriel understood immediately that something highly unusual had taken place. She ushered Hester into the sitting-room then hurried to the back garden and instructed Dorothy and Susan to stay outside and play quietly. When she returned to the sitting-room she took Hester's hat but sat down beside her, too impatient to take the hat away.

'What happened? What did they say?'

'It's just impossible,' murmured Hester, still not believing that it could be true.

Harold could not contain himself any longer so her related what had occurred in the solicitor's office. He took the little box out of an inner pocket in his waistcoat and opened it like a conjuror performing a magic trick.

'And here they are! The most fantastic pearls you're ever likely to rest your eyes on.'

'Oh, Hester!' Muriel gave a shriek of astonishment. 'Oh, they're absolutely amazing. Oh, may I hold one?'

'We'll let Hester do that first,' said Harold. 'Hold your hand out, Hester.'

He took the white pearl from its nest of tissue paper and laid it on her palm. 'It's real, Hester. You're not dreaming. Stroke it. It's real.'

Hester closed her hand protectively over it, then opened her hand again and began to rub the pearl gently with her finger tips.

'It doesn't seem possible,' she said again. 'Barnaby never seemed to be . . . he didn't have much money.'

'He wouldn't spend much if he was a recluse.'

'No, but . . . ' Hester still found it difficult to marshal her thoughts. 'Barnaby was always talking about sailing ships. He often told me about wrecks along the south coast, but he never mentioned diving for pearls.' She thought of pictures she had seen in books and magazines, showing divers encased in cumbersome suits, wearing huge boots and massive helmets. 'I can't imagine Barnaby under the sea, or even letting someone lock him into that awful equipment. He liked open spaces and fresh air.'

'Perhaps he always stayed on the surface, working in the boat,' said Harold. 'But none of that matters. Those pearls are yours now.'

He watched the two women fondling the pearls for several minutes, then went to the wine cabinet and poured two sherries and a whisky.

'This is a time for celebration. Let's put those pearls back in the box and we'll have a toast.'

He handed a glass to each of them and nodded to Hester, clearly ready to suggest it was time they began to consider practical matters.

'You'll have to invest the proceeds carefully. Property would be safe. You could buy a really decent house now, Hester. Or two smaller ones and rent one of them out.' Harold raised his glass. 'To you, Hester. You're a woman of property now.'

1914

20

Hester stared at the soldier standing on the front doorstep. He made an impressive figure with his well-pressed khaki uniform, wide brimmed hat and shiny boots. He was a handsome man, too. She thought she must have met him somewhere before, but for the moment she could not remember where.

'Good afternoon,' she said, waiting for an explanation.

The soldier laughed. 'Don't tell me you don't recognise me, Sis.'

Hester gasped and looked intently at his face. The mischievous grin brought back instant memories of childhood pranks. 'Timothy? Is that really you, Timothy?'

'Tim, these days,' he answered. 'Aren't I allowed in?'

'Oh! Of course. Yes, of course.' Hester opened the door wider and ushered him into the hall, where they stood gazing at each other.

'I can't believe it,' said Hester, still flustered and confused. 'Timothy! You look so different. I would never have known you.'

'Amazing what good training and three

square meals a day will achieve, eh?' He grinned again. 'You haven't changed.'

'Well, I could hardly get taller, could I? And my hair hasn't gone white yet.'

He opened his arms and they came together in a hug as they would have done years ago. Hester felt the tears gathering in her eyes and blinked them away quickly.

'Let's go upstairs,' she said.

'A posh place you've got here,' said Timothy as he followed her up the carpeted stairs. 'Shades of Beach House.'

'I only work here,' she responded. 'And it's not a private residence any longer.'

He reserved any further comment until they reached the family apartment. 'My word, you've done well for yourself, haven't you?' he said, looking around the spacious living-room. 'How did you manage to land in a place like this?'

'Cora put in a good word for me. She knows the owner.' Hester sighed at his mystified expression. 'Father married again. Surely you knew that much. He married Cora.'

'Ah.'

Hester eased the awkward moment by hurrying away to make a pot of tea. Timothy grinned again when she carried in a plate of scones.

'I knew I'd get a tasty bite of something. You always were a good cook, Hester.'

'I hope that's not the only reason you came.' Hester finally settled into a chair and studied him more closely. She had always thought of him as a slender man, not so robust as most others. Now his uniform bulged with the bulk of solid muscles and his complexion was clear and suntanned. Mother had always excused his lackadaisical manner on the grounds of delicate health and a weak chest. Perhaps he would have done better for himself in earlier years had she not spoiled and protected him so much. 'How long have you been in the army?'

'More than a year. Should have done it sooner.'

'Weren't you a bit old to join? I thought the army needs young men.'

'What do you mean, old? I'm scarcely past thirty even now.' Timothy's air lost some of its flippancy and he leaned earnestly towards her. 'They need mature men. There's a war coming, Hester. A big war. I want to be in it, but on my terms. When it starts I'll be in great demand — a soldier who is already fully trained. See, I've got two stripes already. Promotion will come soon enough when the action starts.'

'I don't like to think of you going away to

fight. But there's been talk of a war for so long now. Surely it won't come to anything?'

'It will come sure enough. Until someone stops the Kaiser in his tracks, there'll be no proper peace in Europe.'

'But it's so far away.'

'We've got to help the Old Country, Hester. For our own sakes as well as theirs. If England goes under we'll be stuck for supplies. You have a look at all the things you use and see how many of them come from England.'

Hester shook her head. 'We have enough discussions and arguments about all that in this house. I don't want to think about war. What made you come to see me after all this time?'

'Ah.' Timothy shifted back into his armchair and gazed down at his plate for a moment. 'We're going overseas soon. One of our officers suggested that we should bring our details up to date. Addresses for next of kin and so on.'

'Oh dear. I don't like the sound of that.' Hester sighed deeply. 'Have you been to see Father?'

'Well, no. I — er — I was hoping you'd spy out the ground for me there. Find out if he's willing to see me. I don't want the door slammed in my face.'

'Oh dear.' Hester could not meet his eyes as distasteful thoughts rose to trouble her. Father had never disclosed the reason for the family dispute and did not realise that she knew what had happened. Timothy had stolen their meagre funds. It was only after Timothy had robbed Uncle Jeremy that her uncle revealed how Timothy had done the same thing at home. That theft had caused Father a great deal of stress and woe. Mother had died in extreme poverty. Would Father be willing to forgive now that so much time had passed?

'You will ask him, won't you?' Timothy pressed. 'There's a lot of water gone under the bridge since then. I've changed, Hester. You must see that. Convince him that we ought to meet. We ought to set things straight. It might be the last chance.'

'Oh dear,' said Hester again. It sounded as though Timothy were preparing for death. He was not regarding any forthcoming war like so many of the younger men, who seemed to think it would be some kind of boyish adventure.

'Look, I know I caused Father a lot of grief. If he doesn't want to see me, well, that's that. I'll only try the once. It'll help a lot if you prepare the way, Hester.'

'I'll write to him this evening and arrange

to see him,' said Hester reluctantly. 'He's still in the same house. When can you go — if he's willing?'

'Any day next week. Got a week's leave due.'

'I'll do my best,' promised Hester. A silence developed, during which another thought occurred to her. 'How did you find me?' she asked. 'If you didn't ask Father, who told you where I was? Aunt Amelia?'

'Good Lord, no, I didn't want to see that old bat,' he retorted. 'No, it was Barnaby. He said I ought to seek you out and mend a few fences.'

'Barnaby!' exclaimed Hester. Fury rose in her and she glared at Timothy, half rising from her seat. The last time she had seen her brother had been just after the death of their uncle. He had come to her home then after a long absence, begging, hoping to obtain a share of whatever Uncle Jeremy had left for her. Now, after all those years, he had come again. And he had found her through Barnaby. Had he heard about Barnaby's bequest? Was that the real reason for his visit today? Was he here to scrounge again?

'What's the matter?' asked Timothy. 'What could Barnaby do to upset you so much?'

'When did you last see him?'

'More than a year ago, actually.' Timothy

flushed slightly. 'Before I joined the army. I was still undecided. Anyway, I was talking to Barnaby and he said it was a good idea. And he said I ought to keep in with the family.'

'So it's taken you more than a year,' returned Hester heatedly. 'Why now? Why come now?'

'It seems more important now, I suppose.' Timothy shrugged. 'This is the kind of thing that officer was talking about. We should set things straight before it's too late. Quite a lot of army blokes have unfinished business, apparently.'

'So you went to see Barnaby. Who else?'

'Nobody else I wanted to see. Don't know why I went to Mountcliffe really, except perhaps I wanted to know where you were.'

'But you didn't do anything about it then.'

'No. I just kept putting it off, I suppose. What's the matter, Hester?'

'Do you know what happened to Barnaby?'

'He went in the Seamen's Mission. You don't need to worry about him, Hester. He's got mates there. He's happy enough.'

'So you don't know,' said Hester slowly.

'Know what? Come on, Hester, don't hold out on me. What's up?'

'Barnaby died last year.'

'Ah.' Timothy shrugged. 'Poor old bugger.' He seemed oblivious to the fact that he had used such language in respectable surroundings. 'Well, I suppose he'd had a fair run. He must have been getting on in years. Do you know how old he was?'

Hester shook her head. 'He seemed old the first time I met him. He must have been well over eighty, I think.'

Timothy showed little more interest in that subject and she began to bring him up to date with news of their cousins. He smirked when she told him that Louisa had left home.

'She was mad, marrying a fool like that Cecil,' he remarked. 'Took her long enough to find out how useless he was, didn't it?'

'It's not easy for a woman to leave and set up a new home. A man can just walk out and rent a house anywhere, but a woman can't. She can't even furnish a place unless she can pay cash for the goods. The first thing anybody asks for is a signature from her husband.' Hester paused for a moment, remembering some of the problems she had heard about lately. 'What about your own family?' she asked. 'Where are they?'

He stared in astonishment. 'Family? I never settled anywhere long enough to get a family.'

'Last time you came to see me you said you had a wife and a child. A boy called Edmund, like Father.'

'Ah.' Timothy reddened and gave a guilty

shrug. 'Well, that seemed like a good idea at the time.'

'You thought it might help to persuade me to give you money, I suppose.'

'Aw, don't go on about all that, Hester. I've told you, I've changed.'

To avoid talking about sensitive subjects he began to tell her about his life in the army. Hester was surprised how well he seemed to have adapted to the arduous routines and discipline. He sounded enthusiastic about his career and she began to believe that for once he might have made a wise choice. It had taken a long time for him to settle to anything worthwhile, but perhaps he had found the right direction at last.

After drinking three cups of tea and eating several scones Timothy declared that he must go.

'You won't let me down, will you Hester? You'll make sure Father will agree to a visit.'

'I'll do my best.' Hester glanced at the clock. 'The children will be here soon. Don't you want to meet them, your little nieces?'

'Next week,' he said briefly. 'I'll have to come again to see how you've got on with Father. How long will it take do you think?'

'I've no idea. But I agree that you should get together and put that quarrel behind you.'

'I'll call here next Monday. Thanks, Sis.'

Timothy rose and put on his hat, adjusting it carefully into position. 'Look, I'm sorry I stayed away so long. You had troubles and I didn't do anything to help — not that I could have done much. Still, I suppose a kind word wouldn't have gone far wrong.' He gave an embarrassed shrug. 'Well, as I said, I'm sorry about that. I hope you have good news for me on Monday. Mind you, facing Father is going to take some doing. I suppose that's why I've put this off for so long.'

'Come about five o'clock. You can eat your dinner here, then we'll have all evening to talk and make arrangements.'

Hester watched him walk briskly to the gate. He paused there to give her a jaunty wave then strode away, his military bearing giving him an aura of fitness and competence that was more impressive than the cocky air he used to display. When he had gone from view Hester closed the door but lingered there, her hand still resting on the handle. Surely he had told the truth when he claimed to know nothing about Barnaby's death. If he really did know about the bequest he was a good actor, she decided. Yet how could he have known? She had told nobody except Father and Cora, and had insisted on taking up her usual duties at Bella Casa as if the sudden reversal in her fortune had not taken place.

'I don't want to make any changes, not immediately, anyway.'

'But you could have a much easier life now,' Muriel had urged. 'Don't rush back. You don't need to worry about money any more. Harold has already had some good offers for those pearls.'

'It's our home. The children are happy there and so am I. We have some very nice clients and I feel really strong again now.'

Hester went back upstairs to clear away the tea set, her mind vividly recalling yet again that exciting day when she had returned to Bella Casa and astounded Edmund and Cora with her news. They could talk of nothing else for the next hour, but after the initial excitement Edmund had begun to voice suspicions.

'You shouldn't have left the pearls there with him, Hester. They're yours. You should have control of them.'

'Harold is a businessman, Father. He knows how to sell valuable things like that.'

'He might cheat you.'

'Father, I had no idea of their value. When the solicitor said one thousand pounds I thought he meant for the two together. It was Harold who told me they were worth one thousand each.'

'If you're not there at the sale you won't know how much he really gets. A man like that, he'll keep some back for himself.'

Hester sighed. 'Father, I couldn't possibly sell those pearls myself. And you wouldn't know where to take them either. You don't know any more about pearls than I do. We would have to get an agent, and he would charge a fee. If Harold takes something for his trouble, well then he's welcome to it.'

Edmund nodded. 'You're right, I suppose. Neither of us would stand a chance against traders in that line of business, so you'd have to trust someone.'

'And I trust Harold. He's done a lot for us, Father. Now cheer up. We should all be feeling very happy. None of us need to have any worries about the future from now on.'

'You will have to be careful.' Edmund had been cheated often enough to lose all faith in others. 'Don't let anyone talk you into putting your money into any business that's not safe. And don't let anybody else get control over it, especially a relative.'

Hester still found it hard to believe that those two small glossy balls could provide such riches and come to her from such an unlikely source. Harold had achieved a far greater result than any of them could have imagined.

'I've had a good offer today,' he said during one of his numerous visits. 'The best so far. The main question now is whether to sell them separately or together. Some people like the black, others don't. Hold them in your hand, Hester. They won't belong to you much longer.' He watched her take the pearls carefully out of their box, then leaned forward excitedly. 'They are near round, Hester, just about the best quality you can get. That shape, together with the size . . . fourteen millimetres . . . that's more than half an inch . . . ' Harold clapped his hands together. 'I received a great offer for the pair today. It's going to surprise you.' He paused for effect then announced, 'Four thousand, two hundred pounds.'

Hester gasped. 'You can't mean it! Why would anyone pay so much money for something like this?'

'It's because they're so rare, Hester. People want to possess something that nobody else has.' He smiled at her bemused expression. 'There's no accounting for the price that some folk will pay for things. If it's rare they just have to have it. People used to pay thousands of pounds for one tulip bulb. Idiotic when you come to think of it, but that's life, and that's what a lot of fortunes are built on. A generation from now it will probably be easier to find pearls, and that means the price will drop. A lot of dealers will look around for a different product then.'

The final price, £4,300, had come as a shock, but by the time all the business details had been settled Hester had decided what she was going to do with most of the money. It was Louisa who had given her the idea, when she described how difficult it had been to find decent accommodation. She had become deeply involved with a group called Women's Aid, which had not only helped her to rent two rooms, but had organised employment for her in the office of a local business.

'How did you find this place, Hester?' she asked, looking around the comfortable living-room. 'How did you manage to get such a good place when you had two children?'

Hester explained and Louisa nodded thoughtfully. 'I hope you realise how lucky you were. It was hard enough for me, and I don't have a young family.'

She went on to describe some of the problems that the Women's Aid group tried to overcome.

'A lot of women have to stay with violent men because there's nowhere else for them to go. Our group can look after them for a while, but they tend to go back to their husbands because they can't get anywhere decent to live. Landlords don't want children.'

'Finding someone to look after them while you try to earn some money is difficult, too,' said Hester.

Had it not been for Harold and Muriel she would have been in a real predicament herself. How could she have survived and then paid all those bills if they had not taken her in and looked after her? And without Cora where would she have found work that would provide enough money to care for herself and her family? Hester sighed, suddenly recalling the unsavoury room where she and Gerald had lived when they first married. There was a real need for decent accommodation and kind landlords, she decided. Perhaps she could use her new riches to ease the burden for one or two families.

As she had expected, Harold argued against her idea.

'You don't want to take in children, Hester. There's a good reason why landlords won't have them — they cause damage.'

'But if Women's Aid take responsibility for the rent and for any repairs that are needed, that will solve the problem, won't it?'

'If only it were that easy.'

'I couldn't have managed without help, Harold. From you and Muriel and then Cora. A lot of other women need help, and this is one thing I can do.' Hester tilted her chin, her tone firm and determined. 'Barnaby said he wanted the pearls used for a good purpose. This is something that he would have agreed with.'

Harold spread his hands. 'Well, I can't stop you. I can only advise.' He thought for a moment. 'If you're really set on doing this it will have to be done properly. You can't take charge personally. You're far too soft-hearted.'

'Harold . . . '

'You would fall for every hard luck story they could think of, probably end up giving money to the tenants instead of taking rent.' He shook his head. 'It will have to be done properly. You need contracts, legally binding contracts that will safeguard your rights and your property.' He watched her expression for several moments, then sighed. 'All right then. Give me the address of that Women's Aid mob. I'll get an agent to visit them. If they can give satisfactory guarantees he can make a start on organising things.'

He usually dashed away on some other errand, but he accepted a cup of tea and a slice of cake that day.

'You know, you should get out more than

you do,' he advised. 'You'll end up a recluse like Barnaby if you're not careful.'

'Oh, Harold, of course I won't. I have a family.'

'Yes, well you're a wealthy woman now, so you can afford to get someone to look after the children while you go out. You mustn't let your life slip away.' He took another bite of cake. 'Do you still see that doctor friend?'

Hester blushed. 'Bruce? I haven't seen him for quite a while. He is working in the outback.'

'I would have thought you'd have made a pair by now. He seemed fond of you when we met in Mountcliffe.'

Hester looked down at her hands and he gave a sigh of exasperation. 'You're keen on him, aren't you? Don't you think it's time you started thinking about making a new future?'

'I am quite happy as I am. I have no worries and I have never been so well off.'

'Hm. Well, you want to look beyond the next couple of years. Why is that bloke so slow? He likes you, you like him — why doesn't he make a move?' Harold barely paused. 'He's all right, isn't he? I mean he *is* a *normal* man?'

Hester reddened again. Sometimes Harold

was too straightforward for comfort. 'Yes, of course Bruce is — er — '

'So what's the hold-up? Isn't he free?'

'There are family problems,' murmured Hester.

'You mean he's tied to his mother's apron strings,' snorted Harold. 'Other people cut loose and make their own way. Look at Gerald.'

Hester flinched. 'You wouldn't want Bruce to do the same as Gerald — deny that he had any family.'

'Well, no, that was too extreme. There's no need to go that far. But Bruce needs to stand up to his parents; tell them he'll make his own way in the world.'

'He doesn't want to hurt them.'

'They don't care about hurting him, do they?' Harold spread his arms in an eloquent gesture. 'He's too caring for his own good. If it was one of his patients in the same position, you know what he'd tell him? Knuckle down to it and get on with your own life. Someone needs to tell him, to set him straight.'

Hester decided she must keep herself busy and forget that incident. To begin with she had to compose a short letter to Father. When she settled at the table to write, however, she found she could not make a start. An inexplicable sense of dread seemed to have taken hold of her. She stared at the blank page and finally put the pen down again. She should be glad that Timothy had returned, she told herself. Shouldn't she? Families should be reunited. But Timothy's unheralded arrivals had always seemed to precede some kind of misfortune in the past. Father had settled into a new way of life, peaceful and uneventful. Was it a mistake to disturb that new tranquillity with news of his wayward son?

Her own life had never been so prosperous and satisfying as it was now. Perhaps that was why she was beginning to feel so uneasy. It didn't do to become too happy. When a person was at the peak of happiness, when everything was going even better than could be imagined, wasn't that when disaster was most likely to strike? Hester closed her eyes and willed herself to reject such thoughts. That was sheer superstition. It was perfectly possible for happiness and good fortune to last, and how could Timothy's sudden appearance make any difference? Telling herself she had nothing to fear, Hester picked up the pen and dipped the nib into the ink. She had promised to write, so she must fulfill that promise.

★ ★ ★

The doorbell sounded again the following afternoon, just after Hester had taken Dorothy back to school. Kathy hastened in from the laundry, but Hester forestalled her.

'I'll go. It could be my brother.' Timothy might be feeling too impatient to wait any longer for a response. Or perhaps he had changed his mind. The latter was more probable, she conceded with a sigh. He had never been man enough to face up to his responsibilities, and facing Father after committing such a terrible crime would take a great deal of personal courage. She would not be at all surprised if he wanted to back out, but she would be angry if he did. She opened the door, ready to counter any of Timothy's arguments or excuses, but stopped short in surprise at the sight of the man in the dark grey suit.

'Bruce!' she exclaimed at last.

'I'm sorry if I'm intruding. Were you expecting someone else?'

'Not expecting, just thinking it might be . . . Come in, Bruce. Whatever brought you here today?'

He stepped into the hall without answering the question, and paused to look at her as if he wanted to examine every feature, her hair,

390

her stature, her dress . . .

'This seems to be a week for surprise visits,' said Hester gaily. 'Timothy turned up yesterday. I hadn't seen him for years. Do you remember my brother?'

Bruce nodded absently. 'How nice to see you. Is everybody well?'

'Very well, thank you. Come upstairs and I'll put the kettle on.'

Susan rushed out from the kitchen and greeted him exuberantly, helping to break down Bruce's reticence, and by the time they had partaken of tea and biscuits he had relaxed enough to converse more naturally.

'You're looking very tired,' said Hester. 'And you've lost weight. Have you been ill?'

'No, I've just had a long journey. Travelling in the outback can be very wearing. The last section, in the train, was luxurious by comparison.'

He finally told her that he had quit his job. 'I was feeling too restless to sign on again. The whole world seems to be at sixes and sevens.'

'Timothy has joined the army,' said Hester.

'I expect a lot will rush to do that when the trouble starts. It won't solve anything, of course. Wars never do solve anything. They destroy lives and the property of innocent people, make huge profits for a greedy few and merely put off the original problems to a later date.'

'I'm still hoping it will all be settled peacefully,' said Hester, determined to switch the subject away from war. 'I haven't heard from you for a while, Bruce. What did you really think of the outback?'

He paused before answering and finally gave a slight shrug. 'It was an experience.'

Hester waited to see if he would elaborate, but his thoughts seemed to have gone off at a tangent.

'Did you know my father is in local government now?'

'Aunt Amelia mentioned that he had been elected. That was quite a long time ago.'

'Yes, well, he seems to be making his mark. There's a new hospital and he's put me forward as the doctor in charge.'

'Really!' Hester gripped her hands tightly together. So that was what had brought Bruce back so unexpectedly. This was to be his farewell visit to her before he went back to live in Mountcliffe. 'That will be a very important job, won't it? The crowning touch to your career.'

'Yes.' Bruce's voice sounded weary, as if he needed a long holiday before tackling any new project. 'Father is very proud, of course, and Mother is thrilled.'

'I can imagine how they feel. When will you start?'

'I said I'd contact them next week. Look, Hester, I'd like to see you again before then. Will you be free on Sunday?'

Hester hastily explained that she had made arrangements to visit her father. 'But I will be back by teatime. I have to come back early to look after the children. Would you like to have tea with us and spend the evening?'

Bruce smiled gratefully. 'Thank you. I would like that. Shall we say half past five?'

He confirmed the time of his next visit as he was preparing to leave.

'I'll see you again on Sunday then. But don't rush back on my account. If you have to stay longer than expected at your father's house, don't worry about me. I can wait.'

21

The journey to Father's house took far longer than it should. The tram line was blocked by two other stationary vehicles, and another came up behind while they waited. Passengers began to mill about on the track, trying to find out the cause of the delay, and the inevitable rumours began. A cable had snapped and caused a terrible accident . . . one of those new-fangled motor cars had crashed into a tram . . . lots of people had been killed and injured when a tram actually overturned . . . something had gone wrong with the electricity and every tram in Melbourne had come to a sudden halt . . .

The problem was solved without explanation and eventually the traffic began to move again. There seemed to be another delay when Hester had to change to the second route, but finally she arrived at her destination.

'I'm sorry to be so late,' she said. 'The tram was held up for so long I began to feel it would have been quicker to walk.'

Edmund pecked her lightly on the cheek then wafted one hand in the direction of an armchair and hastened to the bedroom with her hat and coat.

'In your letter it sounded as though you have something important to tell me,' he said as soon as he returned.

'Well, yes, it is important.'

'And you didn't want the children to hear.'

'No, Father, it's not that I didn't want them to hear. I just didn't want any distractions.'

Cora bustled in with a tray bearing the best china tea set. 'Hello, Hester. I had the kettle steaming. How are you, dear? You seem to have had a hard journey today.' They exchanged kisses and she began to pour the tea. 'It seems odd, for you to be here without the children.'

'Well, yes, it seemed a bit odd to come out without them.'

'Where are they this afternoon?'

'Kathy's taken them to see the Pierrot Show.'

'She's a gem that Kathy, isn't she? How's her family getting along these days?'

'They're still struggling, I think. The eldest boy is earning a bit now, but Kathy is always ready to earn as much as she can.'

Cora nodded. 'Still, money's not always the best thing to give her. Take this afternoon, for instance. She's out enjoying herself and that will do her a lot of good.'

Edmund found it hard to contain his impatience as he waited for his wife to hand out the cups and settle down. 'Right,' he said. 'What have you come to tell us, Hester? Is this going to be another wild scheme you're going to put your money into?'

Hester smiled. 'My scheme wasn't wild, Father. Everything is going very smoothly.'

Harold's agent had proved to be a diligent worker who had produced satisfaction on all sides. It had taken time, but Hester now owned two houses, each of which had been divided and altered until it could accommodate two families. Even Harold, keen businessman that he was, could not find fault with the arrangements and agreed that her investment was sound.

'So what have you come to tell me?' Edmund prompted.

Hester licked her lips. Now that she had reached this point she was finding the task more difficult than she had imagined.

'I had an unexpected visitor the other day,' she began. 'I hadn't heard from him for years. I had no idea where he was.'

'So, who was it?'

'Timothy.'

'Timothy! That rogue!' Edmund rose to his feet and began to stalk about in the small space behind his chair. 'What did he want?'

'He was in uniform, Father. He's joined the army.'

'Huh! What brought him to that? He must have been desperate.'

'Actually, it seems to suit him. He's more — er — manly, now, Father. More mature, much fitter. I didn't even recognise him at first.'

'They've done some good then.' Edmund made another small circuit on the carpet. 'So, what did he want?'

'He's trying to put his affairs in order.'

'Ha! Does he know about your affairs? Did he find out about your new riches? Is that what brought him?'

Hester shook her head. 'No, he can't know. Nobody knows except Harold and Muriel, you and Cora.'

'Well, we certainly haven't told anybody,' Cora interposed.

'Of course not.' Edmund shook his head. 'How could he know? You haven't changed much, have you, Hester? Not gone out spending big? So far as I can see you haven't spent much on yourself at all.'

'I have a much easier time now,' Hester assured him. 'But no, I haven't been extravagant.' She smiled contentedly. What a difference it made to have the security of money behind her! She could pay Kathy to do the family laundry and ironing, so she had far more free time, and she could buy treats for the children without worrying about the cost. A few months ago she had even persuaded Father to accept a short holiday at a country resort, where he and Cora had been waited on as if they were highly important visitors.

'Someone must have told him.' Edmund walked to the dining table and put his cup and saucer down then turned to face her. 'What about that cousin of yours — Louisa? The one that left her husband and got you started on that scheme for the houses.'

'She doesn't know anything about all that,' replied Hester. 'I mean she knows about the houses, but she doesn't know who owns them. I never told her about the pearls in the beginning. And after that it just didn't . . . it didn't seem necessary to tell her. It seemed easier to just continue as we were, as if nothing had happened.'

'So he didn't ask you for money.'

'No, Father.' Hester took a deep breath. 'He came to settle his affairs. He's going overseas soon. And he's expecting to be involved in a big war.'

'Mm.' Edmund came to a halt. 'There will be a war. Not much doubt about that. So what did he want you to do? Is he in debt again?'

'I don't think so. He seems to have turned over a new leaf.' Hester took a deep breath. 'He's bringing all his army records up to date. Naming next of kin and so on. And he wants to see you before he goes abroad.'

Nobody moved or spoke for several seconds. At last Edmund inhaled and let the air out again with a rasping groan.

'He wants to see me? After the harm he did?' He turned away and brushed a hand over his eyes, then breathed heavily for a few seconds and faced Hester again. 'Trust him to come to you first. He always could wheedle you into doing things for him. But you don't know what it was he did, what he did to your mother, to me — and to you.'

Hester hesitated, wondering how much she could tell him. 'I didn't know then,' she said finally. 'But I found out later. Timothy stole from you.'

Edmund stared in anger and dismay. 'Jeremy told you!'

'It slipped out one day.' It would do no good to tell Father about the further robbery. 'And Timothy knows that I found out. He is trying to set things right.'

'As if he could!' Edmund pounded the back of the armchair twice with his fist, then suddenly made for the door and strode out to the street, slamming the door behind him. Hester looked uncertainly at Cora.

'It's all right,' said Cora. 'I know about all that business, about the money and your mother being sick and all that.' She sipped her tea thoughtfully, then put the cup and saucer aside. 'Look, men talk to barmaids. After a pint or two Edmund would pour it all out. All his grief, his anger, his worries — everything. He should have been talking to you, but he couldn't bring himself to do that.'

'You were very good to him.' Hester pulled out a small laceedged handkerchief and wiped tears from her eyes.

'I was doing my job. But I wasn't feeling proud of that. I knew he was spending what bit of money he had on beer. All the time I was serving him I knew you were scratching for pennies just to keep food on the table at home.'

'It worried me at the time,' Hester admitted. 'But looking back on it, I've often thought — if it hadn't been for the drink, I don't know how he would have coped. At least it made him sleep.'

'Yes. He wasn't like the usual drunk. You could tell that.'

'And it was you who made him see that life was still worth living.'

Cora blushed, looking discomfited for once. 'I just listened. It came to the point where he could talk without having to down the beer first.'

Hester looked towards the door. 'I do hope he hasn't gone out drinking now.'

'It's Sunday, Hester.'

'Oh. Do you think I did the right thing, bringing all this up again now? I've upset him. Do you think I should have let sleeping dogs lie?'

Cora shook her head emphatically. 'No, I think you had to tell him. If anything happened to Timothy and you hadn't said anything . . . '

They sat in silence for several moments, each busy with her own thoughts, then Hester began to fidget.

'How long do you think he'll be?'

'Long enough.' Cora gave an expressive shrug. 'I don't think there's much point in you staying, Hester. He'll walk the streets till he feels ready to face up to this. And then he won't rush to say anything. It might be better if you're not here.'

'You're right. I'll go now.'

'Edmund or I will telephone tomorrow. I shouldn't worry, Hester. He might not want to do it, but he will.' Cora helped Hester to slip her coat on and gave her a hug. 'Don't lose any sleep over this. It's going to be their last chance to meet man to man, to settle things, and they won't let it slip by. It will be the best thing for both of them, believe me.'

'I do hope you're right.'

'Don't worry. They'll sort it out.' Cora moved towards the door, then checked herself and turned to face Hester again. 'I've heard a lot about this brother of yours. He can charm the birds out of the trees, it seems. Be careful, Hester. Some people never change, so don't put too much trust in him.' She hesitated, as if wary of going too far, then decided to complete her warning. 'Don't let him know you have money behind you now, Hester.'

'I never talk about it.' Hester caught hold of Cora's hand and pressed it gratefully before they came together in their usual farewell hug. 'Thank you for everything. Father was so lucky to meet you.'

The tension of the afternoon almost caused Hester to forget that Bruce was calling to see her. The children jolted her memory as soon as she arrived home.

'We've been helping, Mama. We've got the cakes out and the bread and the butter and everything.'

'Oh, thank you. I hope you didn't do it too early. We wouldn't want the bread to go dry.'

'No, Mama. Kathy said we had to wait.

We've just done it.'

Hester smiled at the young woman. 'Thank you, Kathy. Did you enjoy the show?'

'Yes, it was marvellous. Thank you, Ma'am. We all enjoyed it, didn't we?'

'Yes,' the girls chorused. 'It was good fun, Mama.'

'I'm very pleased to hear it. Now, how would you like to see Kathy out while I have a quick wash? And you can answer the door when Uncle Bruce comes.'

Hester felt rushed and tense when their visitor arrived, but the children welcomed him effusively and she soon began to relax. The adults chatted and joked, encouraging the children to talk about their outing, and the girls went to their room at bed-time with little fuss.

'I seem to have had a hectic day,' said Hester.

'I'm sorry. Perhaps I shouldn't have come,' Bruce responded.

'Oh, no,' she protested. 'It's nothing to do with you. In fact, I'm really glad you're here. You've taken my mind off everything else.'

'I'm glad to hear it.'

A peaceful silence fell between them and after a while Hester went to check on the girls.

'They've had a busy day, too,' she said

when she returned. 'Tell me about the outback, Bruce. Was it very hard, working there?'

Bruce hesitated. 'It was a great experience for the first few weeks. But once the novelty wore off . . . I missed too many things.'

'What kind of things?'

'Things that we take for granted in the city. Fresh milk, fresh vegetables, water. I didn't have my motor car, a telephone, newspapers, a daily postal service . . . ' He seemed to be searching for reasons. 'I missed you, Hester,' he suddenly blurted. 'I missed seeing you and the children, missed being able to sit here talking like this. I think more than anything else I was lonely out there. There was no one I could really *talk* to.'

'I can understand that,' said Hester with genuine feeling. In the quiet of the evenings she also longed for real conversations with someone she knew well. Louisa and Cora made good sounding boards. She could call on either of them if she had a problem, but what she really desired was someone close at hand, someone with whom she could share confidences and niggling irritations, someone who would understand without the need for long explanations. She could talk to Bruce. It was a pity he was about to leave again.

'When will you be going to Mountcliffe?' she asked at last.

'I'm not going.' Bruce drew himself up straighter in his chair. 'I wrote and told Father I don't want his job.'

'You're not going!' Hester was astounded. 'I would have thought that was an ideal opportunity for you.'

'That's what he said. Of course, he thinks I'm ungrateful.' Bruce shook his head regretfully. 'He doesn't understand how I feel.'

'Your mother will be disappointed.'

'Yes.' He sighed heavily. 'But I don't want to work there, always under Father's eye. He'd try to take over, give instructions. He says he wouldn't, of course, but he wouldn't be able to help himself. No matter what the situation, he always wants to be the man in charge.'

Hester watched him, not knowing what to say. Bruce had rarely defied his father and he hated to upset his mother. This must have been an impulsive decision. Perhaps he would change his mind just as quickly. It was to be hoped he did so before it was too late to claim that important post.

'I'm not going,' said Bruce again. 'I wrote that letter before I came back to Melbourne. I was waiting for an answer before I told you

405

anything about it.' He pushed his fingers through his hair with a distracted air then raised his chin. 'I'm a doctor, a medical practitioner, not an administrator. And I couldn't do my work properly in a place where Father had anything to do with it. He'll treat that hospital as a business, not a place of healing.'

'What will you do instead?'

'I don't know yet. I can't go back to the surgery where I was before. Another doctor took over my previous job, and he's obviously planning to stay for the time being at least. But I want to stay within easy reach of here. I want to be able to visit you, Hester.'

Hester could not meet his eyes. He had gone away because his parents objected to his friendship with her. How long would this defiance last, and what effect would it have on their relationship?

'Say something, Hester. If you don't want me to call on you, please say so.'

That remark prompted a brief smile. 'I like to see you, Bruce; we all do. But I can't help you with this. You have to sort out your own problems, both for business and with your family. But whatever you decide, we will always be happy to receive you here.'

★ ★ ★

Cora came to Bella Casa the next morning, having decided she should see Hester in person rather than merely telephone.

'You can tell Timothy to call on us any day,' she said. 'The sooner the better. After working hours, of course. If he comes tomorrow he can eat with us.'

'Thank you, Cora.' Hester hugged her again. 'How is Father?'

'All right, now he's got over the first shock. It came as a bit of a — I don't know — it was like a bolt from the blue, I suppose. Anyway, tell Timothy he's got to come now. If he backs out after all this, I'll come looking for him myself and skin the hide off him.'

Hester chuckled. 'I'll tell him. The children are excited, meeting a new uncle. Actually, Dorothy has seen him once before, but she can't remember.'

Cora brandished her embroidered cloth bag to indicate that she had brought an apron and sleeve protectors with her. 'Well, now that I'm here I might as well make myself useful. Would you like me to shell peas, or slice beans or something?'

Despite Timothy's assertion that he had changed, Hester could not help wondering whether he would arrive on time or whether he would come at all. He had been so irresponsible in the past, quite likely to miss an appointment if he met a pretty girl or started doing something that seemed to be more interesting. She prepared the children for disappointment, telling them a soldier was sometimes called away on duty, but she was feeling depressed herself when they sat down to eat without him.

The doorbell sounded just before they began their dessert. Both girls rushed out to the hall, but at the last moment Dorothy was overcome by shyness and hung back as always. Susan hurried on towards the door, curious to see the newcomer, and when the khaki-clad figure stepped inside she stared up at him in awe.

'This is your Uncle Timothy,' said Hester. 'Timothy, this is Susan.' She took Dorothy's hand and drew her forward. 'And this is Dorothy.'

Timothy greeted them with a natural friendliness and Susan soon began to chatter.

'We've never had a soldier here before,' she said.

'Well, I expect you will see a lot of soldiers soon,' he replied. 'Do you like living here?'

'Yes. We've got a nice big garden. Do you want to see?'

Adam Frost came in while they were still talking in the hall.

'Ah. It looks as if I might be joining you in

uniform before long,' he said to Timothy.

'Better to get in early, I reckon,' was the response.

Hester introduced her brother and the two men seemed to take to each other instantly.

'Are you dining here?' Adam asked. He turned to Hester. 'We have a lot to talk about. Would you ask the girls to set a place for him at my table please?'

'Very well. But, Timothy, you must come and talk to the children until the gong goes.'

The sight of a soldier in uniform raised a great deal of interest amongst the other clients and Hester hoped it would not result in yet another dispute between Mr Kelly and Mr Wright.

'No politics in the dining-room, please,' she said.

'That's right, gentlemen.' As always, Mr Jamieson did his best to uphold a calm and courteous atmosphere. He shook hands with Timothy, and only expressed his surprise quietly to Hester. 'I didn't know you had a brother, Mrs Carleton.'

'None of us had seen him for years,' she replied. 'He appeared out of the blue only last week.'

'Your father must have been pleased to know that he was safe.'

'Yes. Excuse me, Mr Jamieson, I must

attend to the stove.'

Hester escaped to the kitchen, wondering what Mr Jamieson was thinking about her family. He had kept in touch with Father after meeting him at Bella Casa and they had both become ardent supporters of the St Kilda Football Club. Mr Jamieson had visited the little house two or three times. He must surely be wondering why Father had never mentioned the fact that he had a son.

Kathy came in, her cheeks flushed and eyes sparkling. 'Oh, Ma'am, your brother is very nice, isn't he? And isn't he *handsome?*'

'Don't you go getting ideas,' said Edith tartly.

Kathy's cheeks grew redder. 'As if I would!'

Hester chuckled. 'A lot of young women seem to appreciate his looks. But looks aren't everything. I hope you'll remember that when you decide it's time you settled down with someone, Kathy.'

'Oh, Ma'am.' Kathy turned away to hide her face, busying herself with dishes and a tray. She blushed again when Timothy came to the kitchen while they were clearing up after the meal.

'That was a good dinner. Thank you,' he said, pulling out a chair and sitting at the far end of the table from where he could watch everything that went on. 'If you serve a dinner

410

like that every day you'll keep the customers happy.'

'That is our goal,' replied Hester. She smiled at the children, who had been feeling somewhat left out. 'Show Uncle Timothy how to make a pomade. The oranges and cloves are ready in the scullery.'

When the house was quiet again and the children were in bed, Hester and Timothy were able to discuss the purpose for his visit, and she told him he had been invited to eat with Father and Cora the next day.

'Oh, Lord,' he said nervously. The confidence that he had displayed downstairs ebbed away and Hester could see that he was having second thoughts.

'Don't let me down,' she urged. 'Father has keyed himself up to deal with this. Don't back out now.'

'That's easy enough for you to say.'

'Look, Cora won't let this rest. She says she'll come after you if you renege on the meeting now. I'm warning you, Timothy, she's the type who would write to your Commanding Officer.'

'That would really drop me in — er — that would cause me a great deal of trouble.'

'Then do the right thing for once,' said Hester hotly. 'You were the one to start all this, so be a man and follow it through.'

'Yes, all right, all right.' Timothy sat back and gazed around the room. 'You seem to be very well set up here. Is the pay good?'

His words triggered an alarm, reminding Hester of Cora's warning.

'It's sufficient,' she replied cautiously. 'The accommodation is part of the pay, of course, but that's very important. If I had to pay rent somewhere else I couldn't manage on the wages.' That was perfectly true, she assured herself. There was no reason to tell Timothy that she now owned property and was far better off than she had ever been in her life. He should prove that he really had changed for the better before she shared any of her good fortune with him.

Timothy showed unusual diffidence again when it was time for him to leave.

'Will you write to me Hester?' he asked. 'When we're overseas I'd like to think there's someone who cares for me, who cares enough to tell me what's happening back home.'

Hester drew in her breath. Timothy had never asked such a thing before. He had come only when he wanted something, and then gone away again without apology or explanation, never leaving an address.

'I'll give you a business card for Bella Casa,' she told him. 'That has my correct address and the telephone number.' She drew him towards her writing cabinet and took out a card then handed him a pen. 'Now you can write your address and everything in my book. But don't forget, Timothy, you've got to answer. If you want me to keep on sending letters, you have to write back to me.'

22

As July drew to a close, people at home, at work and in the streets seemed to be interested in only one topic of conversation. Bruce, however, still decried the popular obsession with the likelihood of war in Europe, insisting that politicians and press barons were creating false impressions.

'They're building up hostility, influencing public attitudes and endangering the world,' he said more than once.

He was more concerned about lack of facilities in the outback. 'If you get sick or injured out there you're far from help,' he complained. 'People need roads, hospitals. Even telephones would be a great help. I've written articles, but I can't get them published. No one wants to know about problems way out there. Not enough voters, you see. Politicians get publicity when they talk about this war, so money will get wasted on that instead.'

Hester listened and nodded, wishing only that all the crises would go away, but when Bruce was not with her she could not help being caught up in the general air of excitement. Most residents at Bella Casa used to go to their own rooms immediately after dinner, but now several gathered in the sitting-room every evening to discuss the latest news. Their voices often rose with passion and the two housemaids overheard some interesting opinions, which they carried to the kitchen to share with Hester.

'That Mr Kelly and Mr Wright are at each other's throats again,' said Edith one evening. 'A war will start right here in this house if they're not careful.'

'Oh dear, I hope they don't get too wrought up,' said Hester. 'A friend was saying only yesterday that he's worried about some of the immigrants in this country. People have come from all over, Germany, Austria, Turkey . . . What is going to happen to them all?'

'They'll have to go back, I suppose. We don't want Germans here if they're going to make trouble.'

Hester usually waited until evening, or even the next day, to read newspapers that had been discarded by residents, but when the tension rose higher she began to buy a newspaper for herself each morning. She would turn to the inner pages and read the main points of the news aloud during morning tea, ostensibly to save everybody's time, but in reality to let Edith know what was being printed.

She could not hold back a gasp of dismay at the sight of grave news one morning.

'Austria has declared war!' She pointed to the headline and read on: 'What are Germany's intentions? British mediation rejected.'

'No question about it now,' Edith remarked when the main points had been extracted. 'It's a case of when, not if.'

On the last day of July they read about gloom in Europe and the fact that only a miracle could avert the dreaded general war. The enmity between Mr Kelly and Mr Williams came to a head that evening and sounds of a scuffle sent Hester hurrying to the sitting-room. The two men were in the centre of the carpet, pushing and shouting and making ineffectual jabs at each other.

'Gentlemen!' she scolded. 'Gentlemen, stop that at once! Have you forgotten where you are?'

Both men took a step backwards, looking disconcerted, then they glared at each other.

'He called me a traitor,' declared Mr Kelly. 'Nobody does that and gets away with it.'

'I'm speaking the plain truth,' retorted Mr Wright. 'He's against the English. That puts him alongside the enemy.'

'We are not at war,' said Hester. 'Now

please, let's have no more of this.'

Mr Wright opened his mouth as if to make further accusations, then he gave an expressive shrug and stalked away. Mr Kelly shuffled his feet and looked slightly more repentant.

'Sorry, Mrs Carleton. We shouldn't involve you. But I can't stand that pig-headed Englishman.'

He also left the room and Hester turned to find Mr Pulham and Mr Mitchell watching with interest from easy chairs in the corner.

'Well, you're a brave lady,' said Mr Pulham. 'I wasn't game to interfere.'

Hester smiled. 'I can understand that. They would have turned on you, probably.'

'Men like that don't always know how to behave toward ladies,' said Mr Mitchell. 'I'm glad they could see sense. But do be careful, Mrs Carleton. Don't step in if they get too violent.'

'It might be a good idea to evict the two of them before it comes to that,' his companion suggested.

The next day Mr Wright told Kathy that he wanted to talk to Hester before he left for work, and he waited for her in the hall.

'Good morning,' he said as Hester approached.

'Good morning, Mr Wright.'

'I have to hand in my notice.'

'Oh.' Hester wondered briefly whether it was worthwhile trying to dissuade him. It would surely be more peaceful in the house if he left. 'I'm sorry to hear that. I hope — '

'It has nothing to do with the people here,' he said, as if reading her mind. 'Or the service. If circumstances were different I wouldn't think of leaving, but I have to go back to England. I have to fight for my country.'

Before Hester could respond he caught sight of someone over her shoulder and his colour rose slightly.

'Yes, I have to help my country,' he proclaimed in a louder voice. 'England is surrounded by enemies. There are those who'll take advantage of the trouble in Europe. Just watch and see. When England has her back turned, helping those little countries in Europe, those traitorous Irish will step in and stab her in the back.'

Mr Kelly had just left the dining-room and it was impossible for him to ignore such a taunt.

'Ireland is neutral,' he declared hotly. 'And will stay neutral.'

'A fat lot of good that will do you,' retorted Mr Wright. 'Look at Luxembourg and Belgium. You can't kid me. The Huns won't

418

stay out of there.' He looked at Hester again. 'There's going to be bloodshed in those innocent little countries.'

Hester realised there was nothing she could say to diffuse the situation. It was just like the European problem, she thought. Both men had fixed ideas and neither would back down or compromise.

Mr Wright turned away to face the other man. 'Just wait and see. Those Huns will welcome your neutrality — with friends in Ireland they won't have to worry about attack from that direction. They'll even get help to defeat England. But if they did happen to win, what would happen next? They'd take Ireland. Neutral?' He gave a scornful laugh. 'Easy to march in and take it, and they'd do it, believe me. So you Irish had better wake up and make sure we succeed in defeating them.'

He departed before Mr Kelly could think of some witty remark to better him. The Irishman stared after him belligerently, then turned to Hester.

'Look, Mrs Carleton, I'm sorry, but I'll have to give notice.'

'I hope that decision has nothing to do with — '

'With him?' Mr Kelly chuckled with some of his more usual good humour. 'It'd take more than a bloke like him to make me shift. No, Mrs Carleton, it's this mess in the world. There's going to be a war, no point in trying to believe otherwise. So I'm going to do my bit. Just thought I should let you know ahead of time.'

'Well, thank you for telling me, Mr Kelly. But I still hope it won't come to that. Are you planning to go back to Ireland?'

He grinned at that. 'No, Mrs Carleton. I live in Australia now. So I'll fight for Australia. It's a fact that we need the Old Country, so I'll do the necessary. Just don't let on to that fellow, Wright. Let him think what he likes. But between you and me, Mrs Carleton, there'll be lots of Irish who'll fight for Britain in this coming war, neutrality or not.'

On the first day of August Hester took heart from a headline that declared the position was not hopeless, even though Europe stood on the brink of war; but within two days that slight hope faded. She could not understand why so many people gathered to shout slogans and sing patriotic songs, almost as if they were demanding that a war should take place.

'It's mob hysteria,' said Bruce. 'They get carried away by images of glory. They don't think of casualties and what the reality would be.'

When the newspapers reported that the German army had swept into Belgium, Mr Wright took great satisfaction in reminding everybody that he had forecast such action. He gave no details as to how he would manage to travel to England when international shipping was in such chaos, but he left the house as planned, and two days later Adam Frost approached Hester.

'I joined up today,' he announced.

'Oh, Mr Frost!'

'Yes, well they were calling for volunteers and I want to get into this before it's all over.'

'Do you really think it will all be over soon?'

'If you could have seen the huge crowd of volunteers you wouldn't need to ask that. Yes, we'll get them licked pretty soon, Mrs Carleton. Anyway, I don't know yet when I'll actually get into uniform, so I'll pack up now and go home on a visit. I'll pay another week's rent in lieu of notice, so Mr Hetherington can't complain.'

'Oh dear, Mr Frost. You're so close to reaching your majority. You had such plans.'

'Yes, well some of those plans will have to wait,' he said cheerfully. 'I could be back by Christmas. I'll get a more advanced model of that motor car in the New Year.'

He left with far more ceremony than either

of the other men, giving large tips to the two housemaids in sealed envelopes and presenting Hester with a bouquet of flowers. The three women stood on the top step to wave farewell as he went out of the gate.

'I'll miss him,' said Edith. 'He was always one of the more happy-go-lucky ones. Livened the place up a bit.'

'It won't seem the same without him,' agreed Kathy.

Hester gave a last wave to the young man as he climbed into a horse-drawn cab, then went sadly back indoors. It was true that Bella Casa would not be the same without him, but it had not been the same since all this trouble started. Now three of the residents had left, and it was obvious that the others were restless. Only Mr Jamieson seemed to be unaffected by the tumultuous news.

'I'm too old to pay any heed to all this business,' he said quietly when Mr Pulham asked for an opinion. 'There have been wars before, and there'll be more in the future. There's nothing I can do to stop any of it.'

On Saturday Mr Hetherington was incensed to learn that he had lost yet another of his clients.

'How am I supposed to run a decent business?' he fumed.

422

Hester made no attempt to answer. She had guessed he would think only of his own interests, and had been prepared to hear complaints.

'All the reports say that hundreds are rushing to enlist,' he went on. 'They're just dropping their responsibilities and leaving people in the lurch. What about all the important firms? How is business supposed to function?'

He glared at Hester as if she might be to blame. 'Who is going to do all the work that they're leaving undone?'

Hester restrained a smile, remembering Louisa's visit the previous evening and her reaction to events. She had been promoted to fill a position previously held by a man, and she claimed that the more who left to become soldiers, the better it would be for females.

'You watch, Hester,' she had said gleefully. 'The opportunities that women get now will be better than anyone could have imagined. Before this happened I wouldn't have stood a chance of getting a higher place in the office. But I'll have to be sure to make myself indispensable before all the men start coming back again.'

Mr Hetherington clenched his fist and hit of the palm of his left hand several times. 'Well?' he demanded. 'What am I supposed to do? How am I supposed to keep the rooms filled here if everybody keeps running off to play at soldiers?'

His attitude irritated Hester. 'They're not playing,' she snapped. 'It's very serious.'

'Yes, well — by the time they train all those volunteers and get them to England it will all be over, more likely than not. In the meantime, what about all my empty rooms?'

Hester had not given the problem much serious thought, and it was a mischievous urge to annoy him that prompted her response.

'A cousin told me that women are taking over the vacancies in most companies. Perhaps your new residents will be women.'

'Women! Here?' He was outraged by the idea. 'This is a residence for business*men* — *respectable* businessmen.'

'You could have both,' she said reasonably. 'Several hotels have no such rules, and they are highly satisfactory by all accounts. If your businessmen are *gentlemen* — and truly respectable — no problems should arise.'

He turned his eyes away, as if reminded of his own clumsy attempts to embark on a romantic adventure, and quickly changed the subject.

'Food prices are going up already, so I've heard. Keep a sharp eye on our suppliers.

Don't let them make a quick profit at our expense.'

★ ★ ★

Hester tried to protect her children from constant images of war, but that soon proved to be impossible. Propaganda posters were appearing everywhere, bands played martial music and all the pupils at school seemed to be infected with the same war fever as the adults.

'Molly said her Daddy has gone to the war,' said Susan.

'Brendan's Papa has gone too,' said Dorothy. 'And Alice's Papa. Will Uncle Bruce go, Mama?'

Hester smiled and hugged the two girls. 'No, Uncle Bruce won't go. He's too busy here, helping sick people.'

'Miss West said some men are too important. They can't go,' said Susan. 'Is Uncle Bruce important?'

'Very important,' replied Hester firmly. 'He has to stay here. But that is good for us because it means he can keep on coming to see us.'

'Can we go and see the big parade, Mama?'

'Yes, it will be on a Sunday, so we can go.'

'Miss West said there will be lots and lots of people there.'

425

Even Miss West would be surprised by the size of the crowd, thought Hester as they walked towards the Esplanade on Sunday afternoon. The regimental colours were to be presented on behalf of the citizens of St Kilda, but many of the onlookers must have come from miles away.

'What a lot of people!' exclaimed Susan. 'Have you ever seen so many people, Mama?'

'I don't think I have. There must be thousands and thousands here.'

'Can we have a flag, please?' asked Dorothy.

'Yes.' Hester pulled out her purse. She still felt a glow of pleasure at being prosperous enough to buy such things whenever she felt inclined. 'Get one each and come straight back.'

The girls ran back from the vendor waving paper flags, and Hester turned just in time to see some people moving away from a low wall.

'Quick,' she said. 'Get up on there before someone else takes that spot.'

They rushed to the wall and Dorothy gave a little squeal of delight when she saw the view. 'It's marvellous. We can see everything from here.'

'Why did those people go away?' asked Susan.

'I don't know. Perhaps they saw some friends and wanted to be with them.'

After their first excitement the wait became tedious, but at last the crowd quietened and the ceremony began. The children were impressed by the lines of men in uniform, but they were more interested in the fox terrier dog dressed in khaki.

'I didn't know doggies could be soldiers,' said Susan.

An elderly man nearby chuckled and explained that the dog was the battalion mascot. 'See that number on his uniform? Number fourteen. That's the number of the battalion.'

'Were you a soldier?'

'Yes, lassie, a long time ago. Now see, they're going to say a prayer or two, then they'll start marching with the flags.'

When the ceremony was over they walked home by a longer route to look at Christmas decorations in the shops.

'Aren't we going to put paper chains up this time?' asked Susan.

'Yes. We'd better make a start on the decorations,' said Hester. 'Christmas is almost here.'

Mr Jamieson flushed with embarrassment when Hester invited him to join them as usual for Christmas dinner.

'It's very nice of you to ask,' he said. 'But I know I'll be the only one here, and you don't want to make special arrangements just for me.'

'Father will be pleased to have your company. He and Cora will be coming this year, and Bruce, if he can get away. So I'll be cooking a big meal. One more at the table won't make for hard work.'

'Then I am pleased to accept, Mrs Carleton. Thank you very much.'

'We have to try and make things seem as normal as possible,' said Hester.

'Yes, but it will never be the same again, will it?' Mr Jamieson shook his head sorrowfully. 'Only four of us regulars left now. None of these new people seem likely to stay longer than a few weeks.'

On Christmas Day Cora helped Hester in the kitchen while Edmund sat in the garden chatting to Mr Jamieson. Bruce arrived only minutes before the first course was served, bringing soft toys for the children and a box of chocolates for Hester.

'I'm sorry to come so late,' he said. 'Christmas Day is often busy with small accidents. Children tend to swallow things, fall over or get too close to the cooking.'

'Well, I'm glad you managed to get here in time to eat with us,' said Hester. 'I hope you won't be called away.'

'I can stay until four o'clock. Someone else is taking over until I get back.'

'Thank goodness for that. Will you go and ask the others to come in, please? They're in the garden.'

This year the meal seemed to be a real family gathering. No one talked of politics and the only vague reference to war came when Edmund called a toast for absent friends and family members. The sombre moment soon passed and the meal ended in a mood of good humour and contentment.

'Thank you, Mrs Carleton,' said Mr Jamieson. 'I could not have hoped for a better Christmas Day. I have eaten more than my fill, and I shall now retire to my room to take a nap.'

'What shall we do next?' asked Edmund when Mr Jamieson had left.

'The dishes first,' replied Cora. 'Come along, girls, you can help today. Grandfather might have a little snooze in one of the big chairs, and then perhaps we could go down to the Esplanade and see what all the other people are doing today. I expect there will be lots of new clothes on parade, and new toys.'

'Can I bring my new perambulator?' asked Susan eagerly.

'Of course. That's exactly the right thing to

do. And Dorothy should carry her new bag. But first we have to wash the dishes.'

An hour later all the work was done and Bruce and Hester were left alone. They went up to the apartment and settled in their customary chairs.

'It's very peaceful, isn't it?' said Hester after a long pause.

'Yes, very,' he agreed.

Another extended silence followed. Hester would have been content to let the mood linger, but she could see that Bruce was becoming uneasy.

'I don't know that I should keep coming here,' he said at last.

Hester looked at him in surprise. 'What's the matter? Is there somewhere where you'd rather be?'

'You know that's not the case. No, I'm thinking about your welfare.'

'I have no problems.'

He shook his head slowly. 'I think it's time you got out more, made new friends.'

'Actually, I do go out more now that Susan is at school all day. I have joined the St Kilda Patriotic League.'

'They're all women there, aren't they?'

'Mostly,' she conceded. 'Men are usually at work during the day, of course, but some older ones come and do their bit.'

'Exactly.' Bruce raised his eyebrows. 'Don't you think it's time you made one or two friends among younger men?'

'Have you any women friends?' asked Hester bluntly.

'Ah . . . ' He coloured and looked down at his hands. 'I'm much too busy to take part in a social life.'

'Well then. I'm busy too.'

The rest of the family returned in time to bid Bruce farewell. The children walked to the gate with him, chatting about the sights they had seen on their walk, while Edmund went upstairs to rest his feet.

'A nice man, that,' said Cora as Bruce drove away. 'What are you doing about him?'

'What on earth do you mean?' exclaimed Hester.

'Oh, come along, Hester. You know exactly what I mean. You can't hide yourself away from the world for ever.'

'I'm not hiding.'

'You have been a widow long enough. You need to get out more. Where do you go, if not to come and see us, or take the children out?'

'I go to the Patriotic League.' Hester shook her head slightly to rid herself of a strange sensation. She could be dreaming, she thought. It seemed as if the same conversation were about to be repeated.

'I am very happy here,' she said firmly. 'My life has never been so stable and secure. And I have no intention of making any changes, so there is no point in pursuing this topic any further.'

23

Edmund and Cora were noticeably subdued one Sunday afternoon. As if by pre-arrangement, Cora took the children away to play with dough in the kitchen and Edmund explained that their neighbour's son had recently joined the army. Only weeks after enlisting he had been killed in a training accident.

'Some kind of explosion apparently.'

'Oh dear. His parents must be terribly upset,' said Hester. She had not seen the young man for years and remembered him as a mischievous boy only ten years old.

Edmund sighed. 'He couldn't enlist soon enough when the war started. He thought he would see some exotic foreign countries, but he never even left Australia.'

'What a shame. Somehow that seems even worse than hearing that he had been killed in battle.'

'Yes.' Edmund frowned. 'Have you heard from Timothy?'

'I had a letter this week.' Despite her best intentions, Hester could not control a flicker of unease that he was quick to notice.

433

'What's the matter?' he demanded. 'What has he done this time?'

'I worry about him, that's all. The kind of news you have just given me doesn't help.' It would do no good to tell Father that Timothy had begged for money. 'He says he's frustrated,' she went on. 'He also expected to go abroad, to see new places and have adventures, but he is still in this country.'

'Why is that? Is he in trouble?'

Hester smiled faintly at his reaction. 'Apparently he is helping to train all those new recruits. He told me he would be in great demand, and he must have been right because he is a sergeant now. But he's frightened of missing all the action overseas.'

'He'll be safer here.'

'Yes, so long as they don't have any more fatal accidents.'

Hester was not surprised when Edmund admitted he had not yet answered his son's last letter to him. He always had been a poor correspondent and she had known that Timothy would depend on her for news. As she and the children rode home on the tram she pondered over her brother's recent letter. Why did he need money, and why was it so urgent? She had been enraged when she read the few lines, tempted to ignore his request, but filial ties had finally persuaded her to think again. She spent hours helping to raise money for the troops. Was her brother of less value than any other soldier? If she were to give money for comforts, should she not make sure that a member of her own family received what he needed? He said he would be in deep trouble if he could not produce cash. It was not his fault, he claimed. If he were on the battlefield, where he was supposed to be, he would not need any money at all. In the end she had sent £10, with a severe warning that he must not expect any more to follow. Cora had cautioned her, she remembered. Cora had great experience with people and their likely behaviour. Perhaps she was correct and Timothy could not change.

Hester wondered dismally whether his visit and his request that she write had been for the sole purpose of creating a source of money. Had he become a gambler? He had not said how much he needed, only pleaded for as much as she could send. If she had not sent money would he have stolen it? She stifled a sigh. She hated to think of her brother going off to face the dangers of war, but if that would save him from a criminal career she must hope that he would be sent there quickly.

. . . Donald has joined all the others rushing to join up. I pointed out that he wouldn't be expected to go at his age. His response was that Timothy is doing his bit and he is no older than Timothy.

So here am I doing Donald's job. It was either that or lose the cottage, and we have put too much work into this place to let that happen. As you can imagine, the boss was not a bit happy! A woman in charge! Anyway, there's a real shortage of men now, so he didn't have much choice. As a result of all that, I am now writing to you as head cattleman (or woman).

I must finish here. Remind Louisa that she owes me a letter, and I need comfort just as much as those soldiers of hers at the Patriotic League. Tell her she cannot be any busier than I am.

Your loving cousin
Marian

Hester sighed as she folded the letter and pushed it back into the envelope. Donald was an easy-going pleasant person, a gentle man who loved animals and the peace of the countryside. Why would someone like him feel impelled to fight, and to go to the other side of the world to do it? Perhaps she should not have mentioned that Timothy had joined

436

the army last year. But no, what difference would that have made? Donald's decision could hardly have been influenced by a distant relative whom he had never met. It was to be hoped that all this terrible business would be over soon and all the men would come safely home again.

Edith usually returned promptly to her duties at the close of the tea break, but she lingered in the kitchen that morning. Hester watched her hovering near the door and raised her eyebrows enquiringly.

'Did you want to speak to me about something, Edith?'

'Yes, Ma'am.' Edith looked around to make sure they could not be overheard. 'I don't really like to say this, Ma'am, but I — er — I — ' She swallowed and took a breath then finished in a rush: 'I want to put in my notice.'

'Oh,' said Hester.

'It's not that I don't like it here. I like it very much. I like working for you. But I want to better myself.'

'Oh. I see.' Hester had recovered somewhat from her surprise. 'I suppose there must be a lot more opportunities for young women these days. There must be several jobs now where you could get higher pay.'

'It's not the pay, Ma'am. It's the hours.'

Hester nodded. 'I see. Yes, I can understand that.'

'I need the evenings free.' Edith suddenly decided to confide more of her plans. 'I'm going back to school, Ma'am.'

'Oh!' Hester was astonished by that news.

'You know I can't read. You found that out pretty quick, Ma'am, but you never made anything of it and I thank you for that. But it's obvious that I'm never going to get any further in this world unless I can read. And I want to write my own letters. So I'm going to start lessons. But that means I can't work here. We finish too late.'

Hester nodded. 'Well, I'm glad you're going to take the lessons, Edith, and I hope you're very successful. But I shall be sorry to lose you.'

'I'm sorry to leave, Ma'am. I'll never have a better employer, I'm sure of that. Will you give me a character?'

'Of course I will. When do you have to go?'

'Two weeks, Ma'am. Will you manage to get someone?'

'Yes, I'm sure I will,' replied Hester, with more confidence than she felt. Domestic work was no longer so popular now that women were moving more easily into offices and obtaining jobs that were previously held by men.

'Thank you, Ma'am.' Edith gave a self-conscious smile and a slight bob of a curtsey then quickly departed to continue her work upstairs.

The next postal delivery brought a letter from Aunt Amelia. Hester took comfort from the fact that the envelope was so thin. Perhaps this time her aunt would not be complaining and moaning so much about her personal worries and despair. When the *Lusitania* had been sunk by enemy U-boats she had written to Hester pleading that she try to persuade Neville to give up the sea and work on land. She had always feared that her only son would perish on the sea and news of the fighting only served to convince her that her prophecy would come true.

This letter stated that Aunt Amelia would be making a visit two days hence and she hoped for an afternoon free from interruptions. As if I didn't have enough to occupy my mind just now, thought Hester. What would bring Aunt Amelia all the way here at a time like this, when everybody else was concentrating on the drama of world affairs? Perhaps she needed consoling because her daughter had taken on a degrading job working with cattle; but she would know as well as anybody that Marian could not be diverted against her will.

439

Kathy gave a knowing glance when she heard that the aunt was coming, no doubt remembering the disturbing effect of a visit by the same person more than a year ago. She agreed to bring the children back from school and to keep them occupied until the caller had departed. To Hester's astonishment, Aunt Amelia did not come alone. Hester stared briefly at the shorter woman, not sure who she might be, then attended to the obligatory exchange of greetings and kisses with her aunt.

'Hester, dear, you remember Mrs Stroud, don't you?'

Hester turned to welcome the second visitor. Of course, Cecil Stroud's mother! She was a thin woman, showing her age now, her hair white and her shoulders somewhat stooped, but she still maintained an air of dignity and self-esteem. Hester wondered what could have induced those two to travel all the way from Mountcliffe together.

'What a long time it is since we last met,' said Mrs Stroud.

'Yes, a great deal has happened since then,' replied Hester. 'Do come in. I expect Aunt Amelia has told you that I live on the upper floor.'

'We are both still capable of mounting stairs,' said Aunt Amelia briskly, and she led the way up to the apartment.

The fresh smell of lavender-scented polish greeted them in the living-room. Mrs Stroud looked about as she seated herself, as if checking to see whether Hester still kept to the high standard taught by her aunt.

'Quite a pleasant room,' she said, as if mildly surprised.

'Thank you. I'll just put another setting on the tray,' said Hester, and hastened away to the kitchen.

The next twenty-five minutes reminded her of boring afternoons at her aunt's house, when she had to endure the insignificant chit-chat of the regular At Home functions. She handed out teacups and offered tiny sandwiches and cakes, making appropriate inputs to the conversation. They would not broach the reason for their visit until the ritual of taking tea had been completed.

Mrs Stroud opened the subject. 'How often do you see Louisa?' she asked suddenly.

'Louisa?' Hester glanced at her aunt and gripped her hands tightly together in her lap as she paused to consider her words. 'We see each other from time to time, but there is no set pattern. As you must know, I am a working woman so I don't have a lot of free time for visiting.'

'We have come to get her address.'

Hester's eyes widened in dismay. This is what Louisa had feared when she first left home; but they had both believed that danger to be over and the address was no secret between them now. It seemed strange that both mothers should come today, seeking this information so long afterwards. She could only think of one reason why they would do so.

'Does Cecil want to start divorce proceedings?' she asked.

The two older women emitted squeals of shock and Aunt Amelia pressed one hand to her heart.

'Divorce! Oh, whatever made you mention such a thing? We've never had such a scandal in the family.'

Mrs Stroud was the first to recover her poise. She opened her handbag and took out a small notebook and a black propelling pencil decorated with two gold bands.

'I am waiting. Give me the address please.'

'I can't do that,' protested Hester.

'Of course you can. You know perfectly well where Louisa is living.'

Hester looked appealingly at her aunt, but she received no help there.

'Tell us, Hester. Mrs Stroud needs to contact her.'

'Has something happened?' asked Hester

in trepidation. 'Have you got bad news?'

Mrs Stroud pursed her lips with irritation. 'Yes, something has happened. Louisa must come back immediately.'

'Oh dear.' Hester thought quickly. 'I can pass on a message for you. Is it really urgent?'

'Just tell me her address. I can send a telegram.'

'I'm sorry, but I can't do that,' said Hester firmly.

'You mean you *won't*.'

Neither spoke for several moments, each holding the other's gaze and silently willing her opponent to give way.

Mrs Stroud was the one to succumb. 'Your aunt must be very disappointed to see and hear you today,' she said. 'You used to be such a polite young lady.'

'Like a frightened mouse,' retorted Hester. 'I've grown up since then.'

'Really, Hester!' Her aunt's tone brought back vivid memories of times when she had reprimanded her younger daughter. Marian had blithely ignored her then, and Hester decided to do the same now.

'If Louisa won't tell her own mother where she is, obviously she has a good reason,' she declared. 'Whatever made you think you could find out from me?'

Mrs Stroud gave a disdainful sniff. 'Let's

stop playing games, Hester. It is no secret that you act as go-between, passing letters and messages from one to the other. Now I've come all the way from Mountcliffe for this, so please don't waste any more of my time.'

'As I said, I can pass on a message for you and I'm perfectly willing to do that.' Hester leaned forward to add emphasis to her next words. 'It's no use thinking you can bully me into doing anything more. Cecil came here and tried that, but it didn't do him any good. Louisa expected him to make trouble and that's why she wouldn't tell me where she was living.'

Out of the corner of her eye Hester noticed her aunt's startled reaction to that statement, but she focused her attention on Mrs Stroud. She seemed to have shrivelled a little.

'Poor Cecil couldn't come now.' She looked up at Hester, her eyes beseeching. 'You must help me, Hester. Help all of us.'

'Tell me what has happened.'

'Cecil is losing his sight.'

Hester could not hold back a small gasp. Blindness was one of the ailments on the list of symptoms given to her by Bruce. How fortunate that Louisa had managed to escape that dreadful disease.

'You must tell Louisa to come back at once,' said Mrs Stroud. 'It is her duty.'

Hester thought of Louisa's new independence, her pride in her work and her recent involvement in the Patriotic League. The likelihood of her going back to care for a bad-tempered invalid husband was remote. When she made no immediate response the older woman grew more insistent.

'You must persuade her to come. It's not right, her coming to the city — a woman alone. It makes for a poor reputation.'

'It's embarrassing for both sides of the family,' said Aunt Amelia.

Hester felt a tide of rage rising within her. 'Is that what all this is about?' she demanded. 'The family feels embarrassed because people have begun to notice?'

'Hester, dear . . . '

'Don't you realise there are far more important things to be concerned about now?' Hester rose to her feet. 'There's a war on. There are lots of women alone in the city now. They are doing important work, standing in while their menfolk are away.'

'Cecil is not away and he needs her,' Mrs Stroud snapped. 'She is a married woman and her first responsibility is to her husband. You have some influence. Remind her where her duty lies.'

'Why does Louisa suddenly bear all the responsibility?' asked Hester. 'Where are all those other women he was dallying with?'

'Really, Hester!' Mrs Stroud opened her handbag again and pulled out a handkerchief to mop her brow. 'There is no need to be coarse.'

'Apologise at once,' exclaimed Aunt Amelia.

'I am speaking the plain truth.' Hester suddenly felt the urge to dispense with all the restraints her aunt used to impose upon her. What was the point in trying to keep up appearances and skate around delicate subjects when the whole world was in such turmoil? Surely Aunt Amelia knew something of the background to all this. She could close her eyes and ears to some unpleasant details, but she must know the marriage had been an unhappy sham. If not, it was time she learned the truth.

'Cecil was dancing attention on other women instead of caring for his wife,' she said. 'Where are they now?'

Mrs Stroud hung her head. 'A wife's place is in the home. And we all need her. Poor Cecil is a sick man, Hester.'

'And whose fault is that?' Hester was reckless with impatience. 'He's collecting the wages of sin! If he had paid attention to his own duties he wouldn't be in the state he's in now. Syphilis, the pox, or whatever you want to call it, does not come to the faithful man

446

who sticks to his marriage vows.'

'Oh! Oh, I have never been so insulted in my life!'

'Really, Hester! To use such words!'

'There is no point in trying to hide the facts. I'm sorry for Cecil. It's a dreadful fate. But he brought it on himself.'

Both women rose to their feet and Hester made no attempt to persuade them to stay. Aunt Amelia lingered on the porch as the other hastened away towards their waiting carriage.

'Hester, how could you be so unfeeling, and so insulting?' she complained in a low voice. 'The Stroud family has influence in Mountcliffe. This can only add to the embarrassment that I already suffer.'

'Is that all you can think about?' exclaimed Hester. 'That the Stroud family might be upset? Have you never worried about Louisa's welfare? She is your daughter. Do you really want your daughter to live with a man like that — a man who is unkind, who abuses her and throws things at her? And you must know by now what has caused Cecil's illness.'

'Oh dear. Oh dear. I don't know what the world is coming to, I really don't. Nothing is the same as it used to be. Good manners and good behaviour seem to have gone for ever.

Oh, the *shame* of it!'

Aunt Amelia hurried away and neither visitor waved farewell as the carriage started to move. Hester felt unrepentant as she closed the door. She would write to her cousin and tell her what had happened, but she would certainly not try to influence the outcome. She had other matters on her mind. Whatever Louisa decided to do, it was her own affair and she would not interfere.

★   ★   ★

The two housemaids looked glum when they came in for morning tea a few days later.

'What's the matter?' asked Hester.

By way of answer Kathy laid the daily newspaper on the table, folded open at the page devoted to war casualties.

'It's Mr Frost,' she said. 'He's been killed.'

Hester looked with dismay at the photograph of Captain Adam Frost, one of the many killed on the Gallipoli Peninsula.

'So much for being back soon,' murmured Edith. 'How many will come back do you think?'

'Most of them, I hope,' replied Hester. 'But the news isn't good, is it?' She looked down at the photograph again. The military uniform seemed to have changed Adam Frost from a flippant youth to a serious adult and he looked as if he would be a competent officer. She remembered his empathy with children, his cheeky grin and his promises to come in quietly on Saturday nights. He would never own his sparkling new motor car now, nor become a father.

Kathy's eyes watered. 'I liked him,' she said. 'I was hoping and hoping he would be all right.' She gave a loud sniff. 'And now my brother is talking about joining up. He says they're not too fussy about checking your real age.'

Edith seemed about to speak, but she changed her mind suddenly. Leaving her cup of tea untouched she hastily rose to her feet and left the room.

'Oh dear. The news has upset her a great deal,' said Hester.

Kathy wiped her eyes with the backs of her hands. 'It's her man,' she explained. 'They were walking out, and then he went and joined up.' She pointed to the newspaper. 'He's gone to that place.'

They sipped their tea in silence, neither having appetite enough to eat a biscuit. Kathy seemed about to speak more than once, but thought better of it each time.

'You've got something on your mind,' said Hester at last. 'What is it?'

449

'I don't know if this is quite the moment . . . '

'There's no time like the present. What did you want to say?'

'Well, it's — er — ' Kathy squirmed, looking like the timid young girl she had been when Hester first met her. 'Edith told me she's going to leave.'

'Yes, that's right.' Hester hoped fervently that Kathy was not planning to follow suit.

'Have you got anyone yet, Ma'am?'

'A replacement, you mean? No, not yet.' Only two women had answered Mr Hetherington's advertisement, and neither had been likely prospects. Both had complained that the hours of work were not agreeable.

Kathy swallowed nervously. 'My sister needs a job. Would you consider her?'

Hester paused before answering. Would it be a mistake to take two members of the same family on the staff? On the other hand, if Kathy were in charge of a younger sister, wouldn't she keep better control? Kathy deserved to move into a more senior role, but if an older woman came here to work it could lead to complications.

'How old is she?'

'Fourteen, Ma'am. Well, she will be next week. She knows how to clean and to launder, Ma'am. And she's done a bit of cooking. I can teach her everything she needs to know. And she'll be a good worker, Ma'am.'

Hester hid a smile. The younger girl might not have the same enthusiastic zeal as her sister.

'What's her name?'

'Rosie, Ma'am. She'll be a good worker. Really.'

'Perhaps you'd better bring Rosie to meet me tomorrow, and then we'll see.'

★ ★ ★

Louisa came that evening, surprising Hester with her changed appearance. She had always kept up to date with fashion, but now she wore a new outfit that had clearly been designed for wear in business premises rather than a drawing-room. Her different hair style also helped to create the impression of an efficient businesswoman.

'So you had an unpleasant meeting with my mother-in-law,' she said when they were alone and safe from an audience.

Hester gave a more detailed account of the event and Louisa listened without comment.

'Trust that woman to bring Mother with her,' she said at last. 'She always has a lot to say for herself, but she wouldn't come alone.

451

She pretends to be so confident and important, but she always needs her husband or someone to hold her hand.'

'What are you going to do?' asked Hester.

'Do? Absolutely nothing.' Louisa stared at her as if searching for any change of expression. 'You don't really expect me to go running back like a dutiful wife, do you, just because the in-laws have suddenly decided they need me?'

Hester spread her hands, not knowing what to say, and Louisa gave a wry smile. 'You might think I'm heartless, but I have no intention of going back. I have given up on Cecil.'

'I see.'

'I should imagine that he has moved in with his parents, and now they've found they can't cope any better than I did. Not that they'll be doing much for him themselves. They have servants, and they could even afford to pay a full-time nurse.' Louisa nodded thoughtfully. 'I expect their biggest problem is keeping staff. No one wants to work with Cecil, so now they think they'd better try to get their dutiful daughter-in-law back again.'

'I don't think Aunt Amelia understands the situation,' said Hester. 'Perhaps you ought to write and explain it properly.'

'Mother ignored the problems for years. All she was concerned about was keeping up appearances.' Louisa shrugged. 'And his parents would never believe that their precious son could be at fault. Well, they can't blame me for any of this. Cecil must be getting worse very fast. He'll probably end up in an asylum.'

Hester made a pot of tea, and as a means of changing the subject she complimented Louisa on her attire.

'Is that what the successful female boss wears these days?'

'I'm not the boss,' chuckled Louisa. 'But I certainly have a position of authority. I couldn't have hoped to reach such a goal only a year ago.' She sipped her tea and chuckled again. 'Could you imagine a future like this, for either of us, when we used to sit in Mother's drawing-room being polite to all Mother's boring friends?'

'It was good training,' said Hester. 'It gave me self-confidence and Aunt Amelia taught me to keep good accounts. She was very strict about household expenditure.'

'Very stingy you mean,' laughed Louisa. 'But so extravagant over clothing.' She looked critically at Hester's outfit, her head on one side. 'You don't buy many new clothes, do you?'

'High fashion would not go well with my work.'

'No, but — ' Louisa eyed her again. 'Do you still wear a corset?'

Hester reddened. 'I haven't worn a corset since I was ill that time. I couldn't even wear a skirt for a while, and afterwards I just didn't think it was worth bothering with all that lacing. It's much easier to work without all that stiffness.'

Louisa nodded. 'That's what gives you the modern look. You're lucky to be so slender. I have to wear a corset, but at least it's much smaller than those old things we used to have.'

Minutes later Louisa managed to direct their talk towards another matter that interested her.

'What about you and Bruce? I told you years ago that you ought to encourage him. But you wouldn't listen.' She sighed. 'You were made for each other. I told you that at the time.'

'It was impossible, as you very well know.'

'If you had encouraged him, Bruce would have joined the family business and every-thing would have been ideal.'

'I don't think so,' said Hester doubtfully. 'How could Bruce have been happy, when all his plans had been ruined?'

454

'You would have made him happy,' Louisa insisted. 'He would have soon forgotten about all that studying. And imagine how much better off you would have been. You wasted the best part of your life on an awful man.'

'It wasn't wasted,' Hester protested. 'It was good at the start, and I have two little daughters. I wouldn't have them if I hadn't married Gerald.'

Louisa nodded slowly. 'You're right, I suppose. And who am I to be offering advice? I made a worse choice than you did. But you've got an advantage over me, Hester. You're free to marry again.'

That sentiment stayed in her mind and she made another effort to influence Hester before she left.

'Don't let the chance slip you by, Hester. You and Bruce would make a good pair. Forget Mother and all her outdated ideas about social etiquette. Women are a major force in the world now. So don't hold yourself back, waiting for Bruce to make a move. You do it.'

24

Louisa was in a buoyant mood when she called again, far sooner than expected.

'I don't know what you said to Mother,' she exclaimed, 'but you seem to have shaken her out of her old ways of thinking.'

'It couldn't be the result of anything I said,' Hester demurred.

'I think it is.' Louisa gave a smile of satisfaction. 'She's given up admiring the Strouds and all their cronies and now she's out in the real world. She's even joined a local group, Comforts For The Troops, or some such thing, and she says she finds the members extremely interesting.'

'That's good to hear.'

'Yes. She has certainly mellowed. And she seems to understand my position better now. She even apologised for her harsh comments before.' Louisa chuckled softly. 'So I am back in her good books. Now, what about you? Have you done anything about Bruce?'

'Oh, Louisa, you must stop thinking and saying such things. I haven't even seen Bruce lately.'

Despite her protests, Hester's thoughts had

turned to him frequently. More than three weeks had passed without word from him and she had been tempted to telephone, to invite him to dinner or to an outing with the children. On one occasion she went so far as to lift the receiver before stopping herself. How could she even *dream* of doing such a thing? If she contacted Bruce she would only succeed in embarrassing both of them. He was obviously avoiding her. If he wanted to part, had no intention of coming here, it was better to accept that fact and forget him. She should take his advice and find other friends elsewhere.

She saw Louisa out and returned to the quiet apartment, telling herself she had no need of another person in her life. Another idea had been taking hold recently, an intriguing idea that had been growing ever more persistent and more enticing. Quite often now she pictured herself as the owner of Bella Casa. It was entirely possible, she assured herself. As Harold had pointed out, she was a woman of property now and as such she could always raise finance. Mr Hetherington had lost his enthusiasm for the business, unwilling to make changes to suit new circumstances, even as the income dwindled. He would surely decide to sell in the near future and then she would take it

457

over. She would modernise the whole venture and turn decline into success.

Such plans could not dispel all thoughts of Bruce, so she devoted more time to her work in the Patriotic League, knitting socks, writing letters and making little dolls for sale. The tasks helped to distract her when she was alone in the evenings, but she could not rid herself of Bruce's image. Always it stayed in her mind, his face almost as clear as if he were there in the room with her. She loved him, she thought desperately. He was weak, she understood that well enough. He was too weak to stand up to his own parents; but despite that weakness she loved him. He was so good in every other way. He was a gentle, considerate man and she had never felt the same longing before. Years ago she had been entranced by Gerald, had been attracted by his fair good looks and intense blue eyes, swept away by his romantic phrases. But she had never experienced the overwhelming desire she felt now, the longing to be close to Bruce, to cling to him, to be with him always.

Do something, a little inner voice persisted. If you love him you should make some effort. Hester shrugged that impulse aside. A lifetime of training could not be sidestepped so easily. Bruce must make the move, if any were to be made at all.

When he finally came again, early on a Sunday afternoon, he looked tired, even haggard.

'I don't want to intrude if you have made other plans,' he murmured. 'I know this is your only free time with the children. Had you planned on doing anything special?'

Hester fought down her elation at seeing him and managed to answer calmly. 'We are going for a walk on the Esplanade, that's all. You'll come with us, won't you? And then have tea with us.'

They strolled along beside the sea, the children's presence helping them to maintain a formal attitude, appropriate in case of onlookers and enabling Hester to converse more naturally. The girls were pleased to see Bruce again and they had immediately found positions on either side of him. As they walked they filled silences with their chatter, telling Bruce what they had been doing at school, how they had helped to serve scones at the Soldiers' Rest and the fact that Kathy's sister had come to work at Bella Casa.

'Her name is Rosie,' said Susan. 'And she's very nice.'

'She can't do everything yet,' Dorothy confided. 'Kathy comes in on her day off because Rosie can't do things by herself.'

'Well, everybody has to learn,' said Bruce.

459

'I'm sure she'll soon be as good as Kathy.'

After tea they all played Ludo, then finally the two adults were left to their own devices. A lengthy silence developed and Hester regarded Bruce with some concern. He had brightened considerably whilst talking to the children, but now he was showing signs of strain. 'What's the matter Bruce?' she asked. 'Something is worrying you.'

'I don't want to bother you with any of my problems.'

'You know what they say — a problem shared is a problem halved. Even if I can't help to solve it, it might help you if you talked about it.'

Bruce began to knead his forehead with his fingers and she thought he would decline to speak, but he suddenly heaved a sigh and looked searchingly into her eyes.

'Do you think I should join up?' he demanded.

Hester was startled by the unexpected question. 'Join up?' she echoed. 'Why would you do that? You have been against this war since the outset.' Bruce looked unconvinced and she shook her head. 'You said fighting would solve nothing. Even before it all started you said that. You can't have changed your mind.'

Bruce shrugged. 'Father is highly displeased. I'm a great embarrassment to him. He says I'm letting him down and I should enlist at once.'

Hester stared at him in bewilderment and he gave another expressive shrug.

'Father is a politician, you know that. His party is urging young men to volunteer, so of course he is embarrassed. How can he demand that other men join up if his own son won't? It doesn't look good, and it won't help his career.'

'What about *your* career?' asked Hester. 'And what about your mother? What does she say?'

'She's urging me to please Father.' Bruce's second sigh sounded more like a groan. 'That's to be expected, of course. She has to stand by him. She always supports Father in everything he does, always has done, and this is no exception.'

Hester looked down at her hands, not knowing how to respond. She knew that his brothers had already joined the army. Mr Hutchinson should be satisfied that two of his three sons had answered the call.

'Do you think I should enlist?' Bruce asked again.

'It's not for me to say.'

He stared at her with raised eyebrows,

461

silently demanding an opinion, and finally she acquiesced.

'It has to be your decision, Bruce. But, no, I don't think you should. Your heart would not be in it. Doing anything under protest does not produce the best results.'

To her surprise he smiled at that. 'I'm glad we both feel the same way about it,' he said. 'I'd hate to think that you had the same ideas as Father and so many others.'

'Do you mean that other people have tried to persuade you to enlist?'

Bruce gave a wry smile. 'Hester, you live a very sheltered life here. You haven't realised it, but you're protected from the usual hurly-burly of the real world.' He smiled again at her reaction. 'The men that you know here are conservative businessmen, middle-aged or older. You haven't had a young resident for a long time. Do you know what would happen if one came to live here now? He'd be faced by a barrage of questions. Why aren't you in uniform? Why haven't you volunteered? He would not be allowed to feel comfortable.'

'Oh dear. I'd seen the posters, but I had no idea . . . ' Hester allowed the sentence to remain unfinished as another thought occurred to her. 'That means you've had to face the same kind of treatment.'

'Occasionally,' he admitted. 'It's easier for me, though. When people need a doctor badly enough they don't worry so much about patriotic ideals.'

Hester felt encouraged by his revelations. He was not so weak after all, she told herself. When he felt strongly about some purpose he would stand fast and resist pressure. Neither spoke for several moments then she stirred restlessly. 'Why don't you please yourself for once?' she said sharply. 'Forget what everybody else says. What would you really like to do with your life?'

'We can't always do what we want.'

'You often can, if you have the nerve. You have stood up to your father before. You went to university against his wishes, and you refused his job at the hospital.'

'Yes. Well, I'm going to disappoint him again. I won't enlist.'

'He shouldn't expect you to obey his every whim.' Hester's patience was growing thin and her voice rose vehemently. 'How long are you going to continue like this — letting your parents rule your life? You said once that you would marry, except that they were against it. It's impossible to please them, you know that. So why don't you do something for yourself, just once? Make up your own mind. If you want to marry, then go ahead and do it.

Don't ask their permission.'

'Hester, I think you already know there is only one person I would like to marry.'

'Do I know? Do I really know? You have never said.' Hester decided to fling caution to the winds and settle this once and for all. 'Bruce, if you want to marry me, why won't you say so? What is the real problem?'

'Oh, Hester!' He blushed profusely and made as if to stand up, then sank back into his armchair. 'Oh, Hester — Hester. Hester, I — er — I — oh!' He took a deep breath and tried again. 'Hester, I love you. I have always loved you, but I've tried to repress my feelings.' He shook his head dejectedly. 'I can't ask you to marry me. I have no assets. I can't afford to keep you in suitable style.'

'Forget about money,' exclaimed Hester. 'Do you, or do you not want to marry?'

'Hester! Hester we have to be sensible. I couldn't ask anyone to give up the comforts of life and move in with me. Especially you. I couldn't take you to live in a place like Montague. You know what the housing conditions are like there. Just think about that report they published only last year.'

'You don't have to live in the midst of your patients.'

'I have nothing to offer. A lot of my work is *pro bono*. That means without fee,' he explained. 'My paid work is not regular. I'm only a locum. I haven't got a surgery, a set routine or a proper home. I can't offer you any security at all.'

'But I can offer it to you,' returned Hester. 'I've got money now, Bruce.' He stared at her in astonishment and she nodded emphatically. 'I haven't told you before, but I own property now. I have an income apart from the wages here, and we could live quite comfortably even if I give up my work here. So why don't we do it?'

He was silent for a long moment then he swallowed visibly. 'Are you proposing to me?'

Hester smiled. 'I suppose I am. That's not the usual way to proceed, is it? But these are not usual times.'

Seconds later she was enfolded in his arms and he gave her the kiss she had been yearning for throughout the long and lonely evenings. No words were necessary now. They clung to each other in the centre of the floral patterned carpet, aware only of the passion of the moment. The future could wait, all that mattered was the bliss of this magical occasion. Time meant nothing. Hester had no idea how long they lingered there, exchanging kisses, lost in the rhapsody of love.

Eventually she found herself sitting on his lap in the armchair he had occupied earlier.

She was leaning comfortably against his sturdy body, her head resting on his shoulder.

'Hester, we must think of the practicalities,' he said.

She raised her head. 'Are you having second thoughts?'

'Never. But it's true what I said. I can't offer you a home.'

Hester allowed herself to relax again. 'For a start you could work from here, couldn't you? There is a telephone and you have a motor car. And there must be plenty of doctors who need a locum right here in this area. You don't *have* to spend your entire working time in a place like Montague.'

'I can't allow you to go on working when we are married. It's not suitable.'

Hester laughed. 'You sound just like Father. Don't be so old-fashioned. Lots of married women work now. It's considered to be patriotic. The country needs women in the work force.' She would not mention her secret dream. Once Bruce became accustomed to the idea of her continuing to work she could make further plans. If Mr Hetherington showed no signs of giving up soon she would purchase another establishment instead.

It was after midnight before Bruce left, and

he called at the house again during the morning as if to check by daylight that he had not imagined the events that had gone before.

'No change of heart?' he asked softly when Hester admitted him to the hall.

'Of course not. Don't worry, Bruce, everything will be just perfect. I haven't told anybody yet. The children ought to know first, and they'll be delighted.' She squeezed his arm and drew him towards the kitchen. 'Now come for a cup of tea and meet our new housemaid.'

Rosie was excited at being introduced to a doctor, and was surprised to see her sister greeting him with such aplomb. She rushed to the cupboard to get extra crockery and insisted on being the one to pour his tea. He accepted her attentions with grave dignity, but he chuckled when he and Hester went out to the front porch.

'You have a very exuberant young worker there.'

'Yes. We have to restrain her — stop her from trying to carry too much and so on. Fortunately, she has only broken one dish. When she settles down I think she will be as good as Kathy.'

Hester had been so engrossed in her own interests she had not perceived a lack of vitality in Kathy. Lunch-time was drawing close before she noticed the girl's hesitant manner.

'What's the matter, Kathy? Has something happened?'

'No, Ma'am. That is, well . . . ' Kathy took a deep breath and plucked up her courage. 'I'm thinking of putting in my notice, Ma'am.'

'Your notice!' Hester's voice rose with consternation. 'Whatever for? I thought you were happy here. And your pay has increased.'

'It's not that, Ma'am.' Kathy hung her head, not wanting their eyes to meet. 'It's just that I ought to be doing something more important.'

Hester held back an irritable retort and Kathy gained enough confidence to look directly at her.

'Things are bad for the country, Ma'am. Running around cleaning up after old gentlemen is not helping the national emergency.'

The intensive propaganda was having an effect, Hester realised. If Kathy were determined to go there would be no way of stopping her, but she would do her best to persuade her to stay.

'Don't you think that elderly gentlemen deserve a little care and attention?'

'Older people can do my job. Or young ones, like Rosie.'

'What are you planning to do instead?'

'I can train to be a nurse. They're desperately short of nurses.'

Kathy a nurse! Hester remembered the day when the young girl had cut her hand. She had been terrified at the thought of stitches, had been too frightened even to look at the injury. How could she cope with the terrible wounds that some people suffered at work or in street accidents? Even Bruce was appalled at the state of some casualties he had to deal with in his work. This, however, was not the time to make such negative remarks.

'I hope you are not going to rush away without thinking very deeply about this.'

'Oh, no, Ma'am. I wouldn't go till Rosie could do everything here properly.'

'Thank you, I'm pleased to hear that. But do think carefully, Kathy. Find out more about nursing before you do anything.'

★   ★   ★

On his next visit Mr Hetherington had regained some of his old cocksure manner. He had not looked so self-satisfied for months and he made only a cursory inspection of the accounts. He flipped the book closed, leaned back in his chair and linked his fingers across his expanding waistline, watching Hester with a smug air as if he had something important to say. She waited for him to spring whatever surprise he had in mind, guessing that he could not restrain himself for long.

'There are going to be some big changes around here.'

Hester felt a surge of joy which she tried to repress at once. Perhaps her daydreams would be realised sooner than expected. 'Do you mean you are going to sell the house?'

He was amazed at her calm reaction. 'Something like that. It might mean that you have to look for another position.'

Hester entwined her fingers and pressed her hands together, willing herself not to show signs of excitement. He had obviously believed his words would upset her, that she would be frightened of the consequences; but this might be the opportunity for which she had been hoping, a chance to make her ambition come true.

'Can you tell me what has happened so far?'

'It's too early. Negotiations are still going on, but I thought I'd better give you some advanced warning. It's obvious that things can't go on as they are.'

Hester nodded. 'Thank you. I presume you have decided to sell. Would you please keep me informed. This will affect everybody in the house, both the guests and the staff.'

'Yes, I realise that.' He was miffed, disappointed that his news had not had the drastic effect he had anticipated, and he was frowning peevishly when he left the premises.

Hester immediately telephoned to Harold's office and left a message for him to contact her. She was eager to tell him what had been said, hoping he would also be enthusiastic about her ideas, but when she was able to explain the situation to him later he only warned her to be careful.

'I'll make some enquiries, Hester. Did you say anything to that bloke?'

'No. I did not think that would be sensible.'

'Too right. Look, I'll tell you now, Hester, I don't think this would be a good time to buy. But I'll find out what's in the wind. In the meantime, don't commit yourself to anything, and don't say anything to anybody else.'

Three days later a flustered Kathy came to tell Hester that Mr Hetherington had made a surprise visit.

'Sit down,' he said when Hester entered the office. 'And forget the books. I'm not going to look at them today.'

She perched herself primly on her usual upright chair and waited for him to open the conversation.

'Do you still see that doctor friend of yours?' he began.

Hester frowned. 'Do you mean Dr Hutchinson?'

'If that's his name, yes.'

Hester nodded, wondering where this was leading, and he edged his chair forward, resting both forearms on the table.

'When is he going to make an honest woman of you?'

Hester stared in confusion. What could he know of their new circumstances? She had told nobody yet, not even the children. She had been hugging the secret to herself, waiting for the best moment, hoping to make the announcement a memorable occasion for all.

'Well, come on. You were obviously not worried at the thought of having to leave here, so you must have some other plans in mind. Are you going to marry that fellow or not?'

This was not the way she had planned to break the news, and what business was it of his? Hester stared at him with a stony expression and he spread his arms with exasperation.

'It could be important. Look, I told you there were going to be great changes around here.' She nodded and he went on: 'This will be a military establishment.'

That was the end of her dream, thought Hester despondently. She would stand no hope of competing with the army for ownership, so she would have to give up on that idea. She would also have to start looking for a new home.

'Haven't you got any curiosity?' he demanded. 'Don't you want to know what the army is going to use this place for?'

'I don't suppose it will make any difference to me, no matter what they do with it.'

'Ah, now that's where you're wrong.' Mr Hetherington leaned back complacently. 'This is going to become a convalescent home. A place where army officers can recuperate. And you could still be employed here.' He gave a satisfied nod and a wide smile spread slowly across his face. 'Now do you see why your doctor friend is so important? Look what we could offer — a fully experienced manageress, plus a qualified doctor, living on the premises.'

Hester felt a leap of exhilaration. This could be the answer to Bruce's concerns. He had not been comfortable with the idea of moving into Bella Casa, where he would always be conscious that their home depended on the employment of his wife. He would feel more like the master of the household if he were responsible for patients there.

'Well? What can I tell them?'

Hester hesitated. 'We haven't actually made an announcement yet.'

'All right, I won't broadcast it. But if you are going to be married it means proceedings can go ahead.'

'I have to speak to Bruce first. The arrangements might not suit him.'

'All right,' Mr Hetherington grudgingly agreed. 'But be quick. I will call you in two days.'

'I would want to keep the staff we have now,' said Hester. He nodded and she tried to think of all the other points she should raise. 'I suppose this means all the residents will have to leave.'

'Of course. The sooner the better.' He clearly felt no obligation towards his faithful clients.

Hester left a message for Bruce, saying it was important that he call her as soon as possible, and when he did so she impressed upon him the need for him to come that evening.

'I'm not sure that . . .'

'This is one time when your own interests have to come first, Bruce. It concerns our future, your career. Whatever you were going to do tonight, someone else will have to do it for once. Tell them you're not well. Tell them anything, I don't care what, but come here this evening.'

'Is everything all right?'

'I think everything is going to be fine, but we have to make a decision and we must not delay.'

★ ★ ★

From the start Bruce could see advantages for them, but he was far more cautious than Hester.

'We can't agree to accepting a role in all this until we have a definite schedule, setting out exactly what duties everyone is supposed to perform.' He shook his head at her bubbling enthusiasm. 'You are too naive, my dear. When I am married I want to see my wife, to spend time with her. I don't want you to neglect your own family while you run about after other people.'

'I wouldn't . . . '

'I've seen it happen, with some of these women who do so much for charity — the charity becomes more important than anything else. Their own children hardly see them.'

She would have to watch carefully to make sure that Bruce did not fall into the same trap, thought Hester. For years now he had tried to bury his own problems by undertaking arduous working hours.

'I'll find out who's going to be in charge,' Bruce declared. 'Mr Hetherington won't have anything to do with it once the army takes over.' He paused and gave her a light kiss. 'If all goes well we can make arrangements for our wedding.'

'We have to tell the children. We could make a sort of celebration. You must come back here as soon as it has been settled.'

Dorothy and Susan stared in wonder when they heard about the forthcoming marriage.

'Does that mean Uncle Bruce will be our Papa?' asked Susan.

A flicker of dislike crossed Dorothy's face. 'I don't want a Papa.'

Bruce looked at Hester in dismay, but she soothed him with a silent signal. 'Would you like to call him Daddy?'

Dorothy's eyes brightened and she smiled at him. 'Yes. Uncle Bruce will make a nice Daddy.'

'Thank you,' he said. 'Would you both like a new Daddy?'

'Yes,' they chorused. 'Yes.'

'Let's go and tell Kathy,' cried Susan, bouncing about with excitement and clapping her hands.

'Wait a moment. I've made a special cake,' said Hester. 'We'll all go down together.'

They trooped into the kitchen, where Kathy and Rosie were peeling vegetables, and Hester placed an iced sponge cake in the centre of the table.

'Bring the cups and saucers while I make the tea,' she instructed. 'Then you must sit down with us.'

Rosie greeted the announcement with gleeful exuberance, while Kathy responded with a more constrained pleasure.

'I'm so pleased, Ma'am. Congratulations, Ma'am — and Sir.'

'You must both come to the wedding.'

'Ooh! A wedding!' exclaimed Rosie. 'I've never been to a wedding.'

'It will only be a small one, just a few friends. We will let you know when we have a date.'

'Does this mean you will be leaving Bella Casa?' asked Kathy.

'No, it doesn't. And you won't have to leave either.' Hester smiled with satisfaction.

'Wounded soldiers are going to come here, so you will be doing very important work if you stay. You will be helping soldiers to get better. And I expect you can learn about nursing at the same time if you like.'

'I'm glad about that. I didn't really want to go.'

Hester had intended to surprise Father and Cora with her news on Sunday afternoon, but Cora came beforehand on an unexpected visit. Hester looked at her sombre expression and her spirits sank.

'What's the matter? Is Father unwell?'

'No, he's well enough.' Cora looked around as if to make sure they were alone then lowered herself onto the nearest chair. 'But he's worried. He's lost his job, Hester. Trade is bad. Nobody wants new suits. Uniforms are far more important now. It's almost looked upon as a sin to buy a civilian suit at a time like this.' She gripped her hands together and took a deep breath. 'I've come to ask a favour.'

'Yes, of course. Anything. What can I do to help?' Hester thought her stepmother wanted a job for herself, but she had other ideas.

'Would you ask Harold if he can find work for him? He owns a big business himself and he knows lots of people. He could arrange something.'

'Well, yes, I'm sure Harold will be pleased to help if he can.'

'But Edmund mustn't know!' Cora raised one hand emphatically. 'He's a proud man, Hester. He mustn't think he's been offered a special favour. It's got to seem as if he got it on his own merits. And for goodness' sake, never tell him that Harold organised it.'

'Why does he dislike Harold so much?'

'It's nothing personal. It's only because he's Gerald's brother. He can't help that, but Edmund just can't take to him. Besides, Harold is a bit ostentatious, throws his money around.'

'He doesn't really mean to show off.'

'Of course not. It's just that Edmund is so staid.' Cora tossed her head. 'He's too quiet and particular for his own good. If he could act more like Harold he wouldn't have been cheated so often.'

Hester left a note for Mr Jamieson, asking him to ring the service bell when he came in. She thought he might be troubled by the coming changes, but he accepted the news with quiet resignation.

'I'm sorry, Mr Jamieson,' she said. 'This has been your home for a long time now.'

'It's helped me to make a decision,' he replied calmly. 'I have been toying with the idea of retiring. Now I will definitely do it.'

'But where will you go?'

'Don't worry about me, Mrs Carleton. I shall leave the city and go back to the country where I belong.' He smiled at her concern. 'I have friends. No harm will come to me.'

Hester smiled in return. She knew so little about him, she thought. They had lived in the same house, shared Christmas dinners, but still she knew nothing of his personal affairs. She was about to return to her work when he spoke again.

'You know that I see your father quite often? We went to the football last Saturday.'

'Yes. I hope it was a good match.'

'Very good. St Kilda won. But I couldn't help noticing that your father was not his usual self. I hope that . . . your brother, have you had news?'

'Timothy has gone to France now. But so far as we know, he is safe.'

'I'm so glad. I was afraid . . . your father is not usually so quiet.'

Hester decided there was no point in hiding the truth. 'He has to find a new job.'

'Oh dear. It must be a worrying time for him. But perhaps he'll find something less demanding. He writes neatly, doesn't he? Wouldn't he like to work in an office?'

'Father is not good at writing letters.'

'He could copy figures well enough, I'll be

bound.' Mr Jamieson nodded sagely. 'It would be nice if he did not have to keep going out in the winter rain and the summer heat.'

'I don't think he will concern himself with the weather,' Hester responded. 'A steady job is all he needs, but he doesn't have any qualifications so it won't be easy.'

'No. Well, thank you for telling me so promptly about my having to leave here. Do any of the others know yet?'

'Not yet. I'll come into the dining-room and make an announcement when everybody's here.'

25

Hester's second wedding was vastly different from her first. The sun shone with pleasant warmth from an almost cloudless sky, she wore a simple, pale blue dress rather than an ornate white creation, and few guests had been invited. Dorothy and Susan followed their mother up the aisle of the church they attended so often with their school classes, beaming with pride at their role in the current ceremony. Their identical soft pink dresses were decorated with tiny silk rosebuds, and they both carried a small posy of flowers. When the short service was over everybody gathered in the church hall for refreshments and Cora took on the task of marshalling the guests into some kind of order.

'I'm so pleased to be here this time,' murmured Edmund. 'It's a proud day for me.'

'And I'm pleased you could be here, too, Father. I think it's a good omen.'

He pressed her hand and moved on to allow Louisa her turn to congratulate the bridal pair.

'So you've done the right thing at last,' she said bluntly. 'My goodness, I was beginning to wonder what anyone could do to make you act.'

'I have to agree that we did not rush into this,' Bruce responded placidly.

None of his relatives had condescended to attend and, as expected, Aunt Amelia had also declined. Hester regretted that he had no family members there to wish him well, but had to admit that their presence might have dampened the gaiety. The friends who had come were mixing and chatting without inhibition, nobody putting on any airs or trying to impress others. Kathy and Rosie were pink-cheeked with pleasure, almost as excited as the children, and Edith was looking more animated than usual. She expressed great surprise at being invited.

'It's very good of you to include me,' she said. 'But you didn't have to. It's not as though I'm still there at the house.'

'We're pleased to see you,' replied Hester. 'You helped me a lot, especially when I was ill. How are you getting along?'

'Pretty well, Ma'am. I'm working full-time now with my man's family. Actually, I used to put in a few hours there before, while I was at Bella Casa.' Edith glanced around to make sure no one was listening. 'It's good that I went for those lessons. George can send letters to me, and I can answer now. He's gone for a soldier.'

Hester felt a twinge of sadness, knowing that hundreds of couples had been separated by the war, romances often shattered for ever.

'It must be a real comfort to you both, being able to write letters.'

'Yes, Ma'am. It was George who made me take on the lessons. Lucky he did.'

Mr Jamieson waited for a quiet moment to offer his congratulations.

'Thank you for inviting me to such a happy event. So Doctor and Mrs Hutchinson will be managers of the new-style Bella Casa. I'm so pleased this wedding took place before I left.'

Hester glowed with delight at the sound of her new name. The break with the past seemed absolute now.

'Thank you, Mr Jamieson. I hope you will find your new home to your liking and that everything goes well for you.'

'I'm sure it will be perfect, although I am still not accustomed to retirement. I still have the feeling that I have merely taken time for a holiday.'

'I must also thank you for helping Father to get his new job. I understand it was you who recommended him to the management. He couldn't have done it without you.'

'Not at all.' Mr Jamieson brushed that suggestion aside with a waft of his hand. 'Not at all. I happened to know that a vacancy was available and merely suggested that your father should apply. That job was for a copy clerk, actually. It was the company who decided he would be more valuable as a salesman on the shop floor.'

Everybody gathered outside to wave and cheer as the newlyweds drove away in Bruce's motor car. They were to spend a few days at a small hotel at Brighton, while the children were to stay with Edmund and Cora. Kathy and Rosie had also been given a week's holiday. During their absence workmen would be busy at Bella Casa, installing electrical power and making various other alterations.

'You'll find a modern house when you come back,' said Harold jovially. 'You'll wonder how you managed all this time without all the modern equipment.'

'I hope there won't be anything too complicated,' said Hester.

'Electricity is very simple and safe to use,' Muriel declared. 'Now enjoy yourselves, and don't worry about a thing. Harold will keep watch over what's happening at Bella Casa.'

Hester began to worry as sunset approached. The fading light reminded her that soon she and Bruce would have to retire to their room. She remembered only too well the disastrous first night of her marriage to Gerald. Perhaps she should have thought more about that aspect of married life. She had feared and resented Gerald's claims upon her; she had never overcome that feeling of distaste. Perhaps it had been a mistake to enter into another partnership. Life had been pleasant and straightforward while she was a widow. She should have let things drift on exactly as they had for the past year.

'You go up first,' said Bruce eventually. 'I will take a look at the newspaper. And perhaps I will have another cup of tea. Would you like anything else before you settle down for the night?'

'No thank you, Bruce.'

He slipped his arm around her shoulders and gave a comforting hug when he helped her up from her armchair, and she tried not to hurry as she went out to the small foyer and up the stairs. She must not panic, she told herself. She must undress at her usual pace and hang her clothes up properly in the wardrobe. She hesitated when she pulled the first pin from her hair, then took a deep breath and released the long tresses. She would brush her hair and tie it back loosely, she decided, just as she would have done if she were alone at home tonight.

Bruce seemed to spend a long time with the newspaper. She was lying on her back, the covers drawn up close to her chin, when he finally entered the bedroom. Her heart beat faster as he approached the bed and smiled down at her.

'Is that a comfortable mattress?' he asked.

The banal question was so unexpected that Hester chuckled and even relaxed a little.

'It seems so.'

'Good. I'm looking forward to a nice long rest. No calls tonight, or tomorrow, or even the day after.'

He turned away and began to undress, calmly and methodically hanging up his tie, placing the collar stud and the cuff links in the dish on the nightstand then hanging up his shirt and the carefully folded trousers. He cleaned his teeth and had a cursory wash at the washstand, then emptied the water into the waiting bucket. When Hester peeped again he had pulled on the green and white striped pyjamas that had been left ready at the foot of the bed, and was about to put the bucket outside the door.

At last he climbed into the bed. Hester restrained a gasp as his hand lightly touched her side, but she could not prevent the instant

487

stiffening of all her muscles and she knew he must have felt her reaction. Gerald had always complained that she was not a proper wife, that she always rebuffed him, was cold and frigid. She wanted to apologise, but she did not trust herself to speak.

'Hester, we don't need to do anything,' he said softly. 'We can just lie here, perhaps talk a little, just enjoy being here together. It's so nice to know we are together at last. So nice to know that I don't have to leave and go to another place tonight. We have the rest of our lives to look forward to.'

Where Gerald had been impatient, rough and demanding, Bruce was gentle and understanding. He took his time to woo her, gradually overcoming her tendency to shrink from him, until on their fourth night they came together in a way that she had never thought possible. She clung to him, overcome with a sense of joy. As they relaxed into a tender embrace her eyes filled with tears, but this time they were tears of happiness. If only it could have been like that with Gerald, she thought. It would have made so much difference to their life together.

'Bruce, I'm sorry,' she murmured. 'I'm sorry, I — '

'Don't worry your pretty little head about

anything,' he cut in. 'I know you had a hard time before. But that's all in the past. Put it behind you now.'

Two days later they returned to find Bella Casa still resounding to the thuds and clangs of hammers and numerous other tools. A fine white dust hung in the air and lay thickly over every exposed surface.

'Oh, my goodness,' exclaimed Hester as they stood in the hall and looked around.

'Don't get yourself into a state,' said Harold cheerfully as he strode forward to welcome them home. 'Your apartment is all ready for you, all finished and tidied up. Come and see.'

He led the way up the stairs as if he were the person in charge of all the changes, and Hester had no doubt that he had winkled his way into the proceedings. He was always on the look-out for new business opportunities, and somehow he would have achieved a role in all this activity. Harold opened the outer door of the apartment and ushered them inside.

'Look,' he instructed, and flicked a switch on the wall.

Hester gazed in wonderment at the instant flood of light. 'Oh.'

'Electricity.' He was so proud he might have invented the new system himself. 'I told

489

you, didn't I? You're going to be living in a modern house now.'

* * *

Hester was grateful for the days that passed before the building was ready to accommodate its new clients. The delay gave everybody in the family time to adjust to the great changes in their personal lives. Sharing domestic space with an extra person demanded extra thought and consideration, and they had to learn each other's little foibles and expectations. Bruce drove away each day to spend several hours at a hospital caring for sick and wounded military men, and although he said little about his experiences there he often returned with an expression that spoke of despair. Hester longed to urge him to give up that work, to return to general practice, perhaps in a nearby locality, but she held her tongue. Bruce had searched for a post that provided a regular income, determined to look after his new family. Moreover, she guessed that he would find it impossible now to desert the patients he was treating at the hospital.

The children were pleased that Bruce had come to stay permanently, glad that he was no longer a mere visitor but a part of their lives. They greeted him eagerly when he returned home from the hospital but, remembering how cautious they always had to be when Gerald came back from work, they left him in peace and played as quietly as they could. When Bruce had been back long enough to shed any lingering despondency he would call the children to him, and Hester often smiled with relief at the sound of giggles and chatter. Her children finally knew what it was to have a fatherly presence in the home.

Dorothy and Susan had been watching the changes in the rest of the house with a mixture of excitement and anxiety. Hester explained that Bella Casa would soon be full of strangers, who would stay in the house all day instead of going out to business. Some of them would be crippled and some would be feeling very ill. There would be nurses and lots of other new people.

'Will we be able to go in the kitchen and everywhere, like we always did before?' asked Dorothy.

'And what about the garden?' asked Susan. 'Can we still play there?'

'I expect so.' Hester gave the two girls a comforting hug. 'It will be different, but we will soon get used to the new people and the new way of doing things.'

At long last the alterations, repairs and re-decorating had been completed. A party of workers came to clean everything from the new light fittings to the floor coverings and finally came a succession of motor trucks with deliveries of new furniture and supplies. Bruce checked that the medical equipment was in good working order and nodded approval.

'Everything looks fine. We're ready to start now,' he said.

Hester had been too busy to worry about problems that might lie ahead, but when she met the new supervisor for the first time she felt a sense of relief. This time a female was to be in control of the business, a tall, well-built woman with a competent manner, who had many years of experience in a country hospital.

She invited Hester to sit down and gave a friendly smile. 'I'm Dawn Chambers. Between ourselves you can call me Dawn, but in front of others it should be Matron.' She continued before Hester could do more than merely acknowledge that information. 'I'm sure you have been managing here very well in the past. There will be far more people to deal with now, of course, but otherwise your role won't change much. You have seen the preparations. Is there anything that's bothering you, anything at all?'

Hester shook her head. 'I don't think any of us really know what to expect — except for my husband, of course, Dr Hutchinson.'

'It's good to know that a doctor will be so close, but, all being well, we won't have to call on him very often. A visiting medical officer will look after the normal daily routine. You must leave all medical matters to the nurses and concentrate on running the household. We'll be starting with only a few patients, so there won't be a sudden flood. If you see a potential problem, don't hesitate to come and tell me. Don't wait for things to get worse.'

'I have to tell you that Rosie is still very inexperienced,' said Hester. 'She is very willing, always eager to help, but she tends to get flustered.'

'Nobody will be in a rush, no trains to catch or anything. I'm sure Rosie will soon settle down, and we will have three extra maids to help. If we find we need a bigger staff later, then we'll get more.'

Bruce came into the kitchen while Hester was telling Kathy and Rosie about her meeting with the Matron. Rosie hastened to pour him a cup of tea and Kathy plucked up the courage to say what had been on her

493

mind for the past week.

'Dr Hutchinson, do we have to stay out of the way, like — er — can't we help the patients at all?'

Bruce looked mystified but Hester gave a nod of understanding. 'Kathy is interested in learning more about nursing. She actually considered leaving here and becoming a nurse.'

'Then we heard about the wounded soldiers coming,' added Kathy. 'But will the real nurses make us keep out of the way?'

'Ah.' Bruce took a sip of tea. 'The best thing you can do for any of our patients, Kathy, is to forget about nursing and just be yourself.' She stared at him in bewilderment and he leaned forward, anxious to convince her. 'These men have been through a hard time, Kathy, and they'll be tired of hospitals and nurses. What they're looking for is home comfort; something more like a normal home, and some ordinary people. They won't all be confined to bed, you know. They'll be wandering about, looking for someone to talk to, someone who'll help to take their minds off their troubles.'

'Oh,' said Kathy.

'So you will see some of them quite often. You'll be serving them at table, and you'll find them in the lounge, getting in your way when you're trying to clean. They might follow you about. Your problem might be getting your regular work done, but so far as I'm concerned, your best work might be just chatting to a lonely soldier who's looking for a bit of normal company. That's the kind of thing that's going to do these patients more good than anything else.'

The first group of five patients arrived the next morning. Hester drew in her breath as she watched them coming up the front path.

'They look like cadets,' she whispered to Bruce. 'Not old enough to be officers. How could they send such young boys off to war?'

'The majority are young,' he answered tersely. 'You should see some of the privates. Some of them have scarcely left school, but nobody questions their age. They'll recruit just about anyone.'

The five new residents were well on the way to recovery, able to mount the stairs, so they had all been allocated rooms on the upper floor.

'Look at all this,' exclaimed one young man as they entered the hall. 'Carpet. And a chandelier!'

'Now this is what I call a decent billet,' said another. He extended his left hand towards Hester and she noticed with a thrill of horror that his right arm ended just above the point where the elbow should have been. 'Good morning, Ma'am.'

She managed to keep smiling and shake the hand he had offered. 'Good morning. Welcome,' she replied.

Three of the newcomers greeted her but two remained silent, showing no interest in their surroundings, and Bruce sighed as he watched them follow the others up the stairs.

'Those two have a long way to go yet. They're not back in the normal world.'

During the following weeks the house filled with young men, some jolly and active, some struggling against pain and incapacity, a few withdrawn and quivering. Nurses came in each day to care for them, many of whom seemed to be no older than their patients. The numbers of people to be fed kept increasing and the kitchen became a centre of intense activity. Sometimes Hester yearned for the peace and quiet of Bella Casa in earlier times, but reminders that they were doing a great service both for Australia and her fighting men helped to buoy her spirits.

Edith arrived unexpectedly one morning, making her way into the kitchen unannounced.

'Good morning, Ma'am. I'm sorry to intrude.'

Hester turned from the large bowl where she was rubbing lard into flour. 'Edith! How nice to see you. Do sit down. Would you like a cup of tea?'

'No thank you, Ma'am. And I can see you're very busy.' Edith seemed about to turn and flee. 'Perhaps I shouldn't have come like this.'

'Nonsense. Besides, I can continue doing this while we chat. We know each other well enough for that.'

'Yes, Ma'am.' Edith hesitated, then slid a chair out from the table and sat down.

Hester knew from experience that the other woman had something on her mind, but was not yet ready to speak. She would have to keep talking herself before the silence became awkward and difficult to bridge.

'As you can see, we've had a lot of changes here,' she began. 'There are two new kitchen maids. They've gone out for the vegetables, but they'll be back in a minute. The house has never been so full of people. You knew that it had become a convalescent home, I suppose. Some of the patients only come for a short time, but one or two have been with us for weeks. We are just about at full capacity now, so we are very busy.'

'Yes, Ma'am. I heard. That's what made me come.' Edith drew a deep breath. 'Can I come back to work here? Is there any chance?'

Hester looked up sharply and saw the glint of tears before Edith lowered her head. She left her mixing bowl at once, grabbed a nearby cloth to wipe her hands and went around to the other side of the table.

'What's happened, Edith?'

'I'm looking for a new job.'

'I see.' Obviously there was much more to come, but Edith had always been reticent about her personal life, and the reasons for her plight would need to be coaxed gently from her. Hester reheated the kettle and set about making a pot of tea. She was placing the cups and saucers on the table when the two new kitchen maids came in with pails of carrots and potatoes, giggling over some private joke. Hester hurried over to them before they had even noticed the newcomer at the table.

'Look, I'm sorry, but I must ask you to peel the vegetables out there somewhere this morning,' she said in a low voice. She indicated Edith with a small gesture. 'I'm dealing with a problem just now. Make sure you've got everything you need — knives, bowls and so on — so that you don't need to come back. We don't want to be disturbed.'

The girls hastily gathered their equipment

and left the kitchen again, casting a long backward glance at Edith who had given up the effort of trying to look composed and was now drooping despondently. Hester opened the biscuit tin, although it was doubtful that either of them would eat anything, then she pulled out a chair for herself, poured the tea and waited for a suitable moment to speak.

'My father had to find a new job fairly recently,' she said at last. 'It came as a shock after all the years he'd been working for the company. But these are not normal times. Has it closed, that place where you were working?'

Edith shook her head. A short silence followed then she took a sip of tea. 'I couldn't go on working there,' she said finally. 'Not now.'

'What happened?'

'It's a family business. *His* family.' Edith turned to look at Hester and the tears brimmed over. 'It's George's family. My man.'

'Oh, Edith.' Hester suddenly guessed what was coming. 'You mean . . . ?'

'He's dead. My George is dead. We'll never be married now.'

'Oh, Edith.'

Both women rose to their feet and they came together in an embrace, neither feeling the need or the inclination to say anything further. For more than a minute they stayed there, clinging together in silence, then Hester began to stroke the other's back. What could she say? What use would mere words be? This was a scene that must be occurring all over the country. Every day that dreaded message went out to families, telling them their loved ones would never return. This was what Bruce had been talking about, long before it all started. War was not exciting and glorious; it was brutal and tragic.

Edith made the first move to break away. Hester relaxed her hold as she felt the other straightening up and Edith stepped back, fumbling for her handkerchief.

'You've got work to do,' she mumbled.

'Nothing that won't keep for a while.'

'I'll go in a minute.'

'There's no rush, Edith. You need time to grieve. Sit there as long as you like. I'm here if you want to talk.'

Edith merely nodded and sank back onto her chair. Hester went to the sink in the corner and washed her hands then set to work on the pastry again. She mixed the dough and began to roll it out, doing her utmost to avoid looking at the bowed head across the table. From time to time an audible sniff reminded her that Edith was still fighting to control her sobs, and she had to struggle against tears herself. Supposing it were Bruce who had been killed in that terrible business overseas? If she were to lose Bruce, how could she possibly bear it?

26

'There's a visitor for you, Ma'am. He wouldn't give me a name. He said he wants to surprise you. I've taken him to the sitting-room.'

'Thank you, Kathy. Tell him I'll be there in a moment.' Hester looked around quickly to make sure that everything was safe. 'Keep your eye on that pan, please, Edith. It will be boiling soon.'

'Yes, Ma'am.' Edith had joined the staff only days after she had come to the house with her dreadful news. Dawn Chambers had agreed that they needed extra hands, and was glad to know that here was a capable woman who would be able to take charge whenever Hester was absent. Edith was still quietly grieving for her lost fiancé and Hester had no doubt that she shed many a tear in private, but she had not wept again whilst at Bella Casa. In a quiet moment she had confided to Hester that she had left her other job because it upset her too much to be with other members of his family.

In earlier days Hester would have removed her apron before going to the front of the house to speak to a visitor, but now she went just as she was. Aunt Amelia would be appalled if she saw how she was flouting old-fashioned rules, she thought, but such conventions seemed out of place when they were so busy with more important matters. As she entered the sitting-room a handsome man in a navy-blue uniform rose to greet her.

'Hello, Hester! It's a long time since we've seen each other.'

'Neville!' Hester hurried forward to receive a hug from her cousin. 'It certainly is a long time. To what do I owe the honour of this visit?'

'I suppose I was feeling a bit guilty for not coming before. But I also wanted to show off.' Tiny lines were beginning to show around his eyes, but his dark hair showed no trace of grey and his light-hearted bantering tone had not changed. He twitched his shoulders meaningfully and gestured towards his cap on a nearby table. 'Take note of the gold braid.'

'You've been promoted again,' exclaimed Hester. 'But surely, that means . . . ?'

'Yes, I'm a captain at last. I said I would be one day, and I've finally made it.'

'Congratulations, Neville.'

'I have to congratulate you, too, Mrs Hutchinson. It was a pity I couldn't come to the wedding. Alice was sorry, too.'

'Yes, but we couldn't expect her to come all that way, especially with two children. It would have been so nice to see her, though. I'll never forget how much Alice did for me when things were so bad.'

'You were kind to her when she needed it,' Neville responded. 'How is everything going? How is Bruce?'

'Everything is going very well.' Hester gestured towards some nearby chairs and they sat down side by side, looking at each other searchingly for a moment, striving to see beyond surface pleasantries. Neville had always been candid, rejecting his mother's concern for etiquette.

'What about Bruce's family?'

'They are not pleased,' admitted Hester. 'Aunt Amelia must have told you that already. He opposed them on two counts. But marrying me was the greater sin.'

'They'll get over it eventually. Look at my family.'

Hester nodded, but refrained from pointing out that Aunt Amelia had never really accepted Alice as a suitable wife for her beloved son. She tolerated Alice only to ensure that Neville did not break away completely. The one point in Alice's favour was the fact that she had produced offspring.

Neither Louisa nor Marian had children, but Alice had given birth to two boys who would continue the family name.

'Are you on the way home now, or going back to sea?' she asked.

'We'll be sailing at the crack of dawn.' Neville gave a slight shrug. 'I'm likely to be away much longer this time. I'm heading for the Atlantic.'

Hester nodded again. It was not up to her to argue against his decision, and it was better not to tell him about Aunt Amelia's tearful letter. Her aunt had made no mention of the promotion, being concerned only with the perils facing him in his new post. She had pleaded with Hester to write to Neville and persuade him to give up the sea while he was still safe.

. . . he always did pay heed to you. Tell him he has to think about his family, about those two dear little boys. It's too dangerous to go into those European waters. Tell him if he must work with ships he should stay with that Company where he has been up till now. But it's high time he left the sea. Tell him . . .

Neville spoke again, as if reading her mind. 'When this war is over I'll apply for a shore job. I don't see the children as much as I should, and they're growing up. I should spend more time with Alice, too.'

Hester made no response, too full of emotion to speak. *When this war is over . . .* She had even used the same words herself. 'When this war is over I'll stop working, and you must take on a quiet family practice, Bruce.' When would that be, and how many more times would she hear that same refrain? What about Edith and all those other young couples? How many more people would have their hopes dashed?

One of the patients limped into the room, making a welcome diversion.

'My, my,' he said. 'That's not the Royal Navy, is it?'

'Merchant Navy,' answered Neville, extending his hand.

'Glad to see you're not one of that Royal mob. From all accounts they landed us on the wrong beach.'

'It can be difficult to find a small beach on a dark night,' said Neville diplomatically. 'Especially in a rough sea.'

'Yeah, I suppose. You boys do a good job. I wouldn't want to be in your lot, though. I'd rather have a gun in my hand. I always said, if I had to fall I'd make damned sure I took a few down with me. Oops, pardon the language, Ma'am.'

'Granted,' replied Hester placidly. 'Neville, can you stay and have a meal with us? Bruce would like to see you, and the children, too.'

'Yes, do stay,' interposed the officer. 'For one thing you can keep me company for a while. It gets damned boring hanging about.'

The children had fond memories of visits to Neville's house in Thorn Bay and playing with his two sons. They were also proud of his position of ship's captain, and they thoroughly enjoyed his brief stay.

'The girls have certainly grown since I last saw them,' he said to Hester as he took his leave. 'And they have adapted very well to this way of life. I'm glad things have turned out so well for you.'

Dorothy and Susan had adapted surprisingly well to the new situation, thought Hester. They had soon begun to mingle occasionally with the officers, picking up items that had fallen out of reach, fetching newspapers and carrying drinks.

'Relax,' said Bruce, when he noticed Hester hovering anxiously by the sitting-room door one afternoon. 'The men like to see children about.'

'I don't want them to pester anyone, or talk too much.'

'Don't worry,' chuckled Bruce. 'They'll

soon learn to tell when they're not wanted. They'll get snarled at if they overstay their welcome.'

The patients in the first intake had been exceptionally young, but a few older men arrived soon afterwards. Most of them had families of their own and they were pleased to find that two children lived at Bella Casa. One afternoon Hester saw Dorothy leading a blind man out to the garden and she had to clasp a hand over her mouth to control a cry of dismay. There were three steps to negotiate, and Dorothy hardly seemed old enough to take on such a responsibility; yet if she called out she was likely to cause an accident. The man and the child paused on the top step, Dorothy apparently explaining something, and after a moment Hester edged forward to eavesdrop.

'Can you smell them?' asked Dorothy.

'Yes, they're lovely,' the patient answered, lifting his chin and turning his head from side to side.

'There are four red bushes and three yellow ones. The red roses are the biggest.'

'I like red ones.'

'Mr Buxton mowed the lawn yesterday. It's a very big lawn. Do you want to sit in the sun or in the shade?'

'The sun would be nice. It's not too hot.'

'There's a man called Jack over there. Do you want to sit with him or by yourself?'

'I think it would be nice by myself today.'

'All right then. Are you ready to go down the steps?'

Hester felt tempted to rush forward and help, but she willed herself to stand still. The pair went carefully down the three stone steps, turned left on the lawn and apparently had a short discussion about which type of chair the patient should choose. Hester turned away and found that Dawn Chambers was watching her with some amusement.

'Don't worry, Hester. Dorothy won't let him come to any harm. She's a very competent young lady.'

'I can't believe that she's actually doing something like that.' Hester shook her head in bewilderment. 'She used to be so shy. There was a time when she wouldn't even go near people, never mind talk to anybody.'

'Well, Susan is obviously the more talkative of the two, but Dorothy has gained a lot of confidence lately. So it seems that all this warmongering has had one good effect.' The Matron looked around at the garden and took a deep breath, then sighed. 'It's a pity to go back inside on such a nice day, but would you come and look at diet requirements now?'

Several days later Dorothy rushed home

from school several yards ahead of her sister, flushed with excitement.

'Mama, I won a prize! Look, Mama! I won a prize at school.'

'You're a clever girl.' Hester gave her a congratulatory hug. 'How did you win? What did you have to do?'

'We had to write a composition. We had to write about how we can help other people, so I wrote about how we help the soldiers here. And Miss Bennett said mine was the best.'

'Well done.' Hester watched as Dorothy pulled her prize out of a paper bag.

'It's a dress-up game, Mama. Can I start it now? Can I get the scissors and start cutting out now?'

'Yes, so long as you leave room for Susan on the table. She will probably want to get her farm animals out.'

Hester guessed that Bruce would disapprove of the prize. The pattern on the dress of every doll consisted of a flag's design, the main purpose being to display the national flags of all the Allies in the war. She managed to convey a warning signal to him before Dorothy showed him the game and he kept his real thoughts to himsclf.

'Well done, Dorothy. Your writing and spelling must have been very good.'

'Miss Bennett said my composition was the

most interesting one, too.'

When the two girls were safely in bed Bruce shook his head regretfully. 'I don't like the way they keep teaching the children about war. They shouldn't do things like that at school. It's bad enough that our two meet so many soldiers; but at least they're learning here that war brings casualties and it's not a good thing to be involved in.'

He rarely spoke about the casualties he cared for in his daily duties at the hospital, but when he came home his expression often showed all too clearly that he was undergoing stress.

'I'm concerned about you,' said Hester softly. 'If you continue to overwork as you do, you'll end up bed-ridden yourself.'

'It's not the work. It's frustration, I suppose — the knowledge that it's all so unnecessary. All those dreadful wounds. I'd like to get all the politicians of the world into one room and — and — ah, I don't know what I'd do with them. How could you make them see sense?' Bruce rubbed his nose thoughtfully. 'It's a good job I live here. Your clients remind me that some of the patients make a good recovery.'

Hester threaded another length of black wool into her darning needle and inserted the wooden mushroom into yet another stocking.

'Everything seems to be going very smoothly here,' she said. 'I would never have imagined that we could have coped with such a huge number. Yet it doesn't seem overcrowded, and the men seem to like it here.'

'It's like Paradise after what they've been through. How's Kathy coping these days?'

'She definitely could not be a nurse. She can face someone with scars now without giving her feelings away, but she told me yesterday that she could not possibly change a dressing.'

'Hm. There'll be a new patient coming here in a day or two and I think Kathy could do a lot for him.'

Captain Webb arrived by ambulance later in the week and was carried to a room on the ground floor. Bruce went down to visit him that evening, and the following day he intercepted Kathy as she carried dishes back into the kitchen.

'Did you know that one of your rooms has been changed today? We want you to look after number two instead of number five.'

'Yes, Matron just told me. But she didn't say why.'

Bruce gave a faint smile. 'I told her you'd be more suitable for that particular patient. He'll be very quiet for a while, Kathy, but when he settles in I'd like you to encourage him to talk to you.'

'Oh.' Kathy coloured. 'Do you really think that will do a lot of good?'

'A great deal of good. He's lost a leg, Kathy, and until his arm and shoulder improve he can't use crutches or anything, so he's stuck. He's going to get very bored lying there.'

'Oh dear. I'll do my best, Dr Hutchinson.'

'Don't rush into anything. Go in and clean this morning, the same as you always do, and just be yourself.'

Hester looked doubtfully at Bruce as the girl went out again with an empty tray.

'Are you sure Kathy's the one to deal with him?'

'Absolutely.' Bruce kissed her fondly on the forehead. 'Don't worry, Hester. Kathy won't see any wounds, and she'll have just enough sympathy without getting maudlin. She'll be good for him. Now I must rush.' He gave her a hug and another kiss then departed to tend his seriously ill patients at the hospital.

The morning post brought a letter from Marian, but Hester's pleasure quickly turned to dismay. The few words said only that Donald had been killed in action.

Edith looked up from the pie dish she had just covered with pastry. 'Have you had bad news, Ma'am?'

Hester nodded. 'My cousin's husband has been killed.'

'Another one.' Edith heaved a sigh. 'I'm sorry, Ma'am. There just seems to be no end to it, does there?'

'No end at all,' agreed Hester. She looked down at the short note again. Marian had given no indication as to what she would do now, but this would bring about a drastic change in her life. 'My cousin was doing her husband's job while he was away. She's likely to give that up now. But if she does, she'll lose their cottage.'

'That's hard.' Edith's eyes filled with tears and she turned away. 'Still, I envy other people sometimes. Those that were married, especially those that have children. At least they've got something special to remember. George and I shouldn't have waited. Even if we'd only had a week together, at least we'd have been married. As it was, we didn't have any time at all, and it's too late now.'

Hester patted her lightly on the shoulder and moved away to continue her work. There was nothing to be said in response to that bitter speech. Hundreds, even thousands of young women must be having similar thoughts as this war dragged on.

★ ★ ★

When another of Timothy's rare letters arrived, Hester realised that he had never written anything about the actual fighting. She knew that he was somewhere in France, but had no idea whether or not he had been in the trenches she had heard so much about lately. He boasted that he had picked up numerous phrases in French, and claimed to be popular with the young women he met. That claim was typical, for in the past he had always made a play for pretty girls, but he also filled his letters with descriptions of things that would not usually have attracted his attention. He wrote of old mills and ornate village churches, of farm implements, flowers and statues; but he never mentioned damage, mud or noise. As she gathered flowers in the garden, or moved about the house, checking and tidying, Hester sometimes heard snippets of conversation between the officers. Whenever they were talking about their war experiences it seemed that mud, destruction and noise had made the greatest impact on their minds.

The situation must be bad if Timothy could not bring himself to mention such things, she decided. She could only wish again that it would all end soon and that he would come safely home. When she wrote back she answered in a similar vein, giving him only cheerful news. She told him about the children's activities and about patients who made a good recovery, but she did not tell him about serious cases like Captain Webb.

Most of the men who could move about the house and garden seemed intent on exchanging jokes and making light of their problems. A few tended to shun company, while some were reluctant to go home and face their relatives now that they had been disfigured, but Captain Webb was more deeply depressed than any patient they had received so far. With his left leg amputated above the knee, his left arm strapped to his body and all his muscles weak from sickness and lack of use, he felt helpless. He was also conscious of the jagged scar across his left cheek, and tended to turn his head away when anyone approached.

Two days had passed before he responded to Kathy's quiet 'Good morning, Sir.' On the fifth day he actually looked at her when he spoke, and later he agreed to browse through the magazine she took into his room. Kathy reported the daily progress and Bruce smiled with satisfaction when she told him the young officer had said how much he appreciated the little vase of flowers she arranged for him each morning.

'I said you'd be good for him. Let him keep you there talking as long as he likes, Kathy. Don't worry about all the other jobs that are waiting. They'll get done somehow.'

'But — er — '

'Matron knows all about it. In fact, I think we'll have an extra housemaid soon. What you're doing there with Captain Webb is more important.' Bruce rubbed his hands together and nodded to Hester. 'I think we'll be able to get that young man into a more sociable frame of mind quite soon.'

At first Captain Webb resisted all efforts to take him any further than the private verandah outside his own room. Kathy gradually spent more time with him, talking about everyday events, encouraging him to eat and even filing the nails on his one good hand. At last he agreed to venture out to the back garden and allowed himself to be wheeled there in an invalid carriage.

'He's a very proud man,' said Kathy, who was keeping watch from the back window. 'He used to be so strong, always winning trials of strength at the local Show. Now he can't do the slightest thing for himself and he doesn't like people to see him because he feels embarrassed.'

'What kind of work did he do before?' asked Edith.

'His folk have a sheep property. He was a champion shearer.'

'Oh dear,' sighed Hester. 'He won't be able to go back to that, will he?'

'There'll be lots of them that won't be able to take up their old jobs,' said Edith. 'But I wouldn't have cared if George had lost both his legs and a whole arm, if only he'd come back to me.'

Bruce's birthday came at the end of the month and the children took a delight in painting greeting cards for him and making little surprise presents. Dorothy made a pen nib wiper out of some blue material, with the edges stitched to prevent fraying, while Susan coloured a pattern on a slim piece of cardboard and attached a ribbon to make a bookmark. They gave the cards to him in the morning, but kept the presents hidden until he arrived home late in the afternoon.

'Thank you very much,' said Bruce, giving each girl a hug and a kiss. 'I've never had anything like these made for me before. They're wonderful.'

'The postman brought some things for you,' cried Dorothy, scurrying to get the envelopes that were waiting on an occasional table nearby.

'I don't think there will be any birthday cards there,' said Bruce. He was not expecting his parents to relent and send good wishes. 'I dare say there will be nothing but accounts.'

'You've got to open them and see,' Susan insisted.

Bruce glanced at Hester and gave a shrug, then accepted the letter opener and slit the first envelope.

'There you are, you see. It's only an account.' Bruce picked up the next envelope and sliced it with the thin blade. He pulled out a sheet of paper, and as he unfolded it they all stared at the white feather that fell out and floated slowly down to the floor.

'That's a funny present,' said Susan innocently.

For a moment nobody else either spoke or moved. Hester gazed at the fluffy white feather, wondering who could be so cruel as to send such a thing, and today of all days. Surely his own family would not stoop to such depths. When she looked up she saw that Bruce was gazing straight ahead, his expression grim, and she realised it was up to her to smooth over the awkward episode. The children would not understand the implications and she did not want the occasion to be spoiled for them all.

'There won't be any cards in those other envelopes,' she said. 'They're much too thin.

So we'll leave them until after we've had the cake. Would you like to bring it out, Dorothy? Susan, you can carry the lemonade.'

Dorothy followed her when she took the plates and dishes back into the kitchen, and took the opportunity to question her about the feather while Susan was occupied elsewhere.

'That wasn't a present, was it?' she said. 'Daddy wasn't pleased. And you weren't, either. I could tell.'

'No, it wasn't a present,' sighed Hester. 'It was a message.'

'Oh, like the Red Indians used to send messages.' Dorothy had recently read two illustrated books about the American Wild West. 'What did it say, Mama?'

Hester hesitated, then decided it was better to explain the incident before Dorothy heard a different version from someone who might be unkind. 'The person who sent it thinks that Daddy ought to go away to the war.'

'But Daddy is helping the war already. He makes soldiers better.'

'That's right.' Hester slipped her arm around the girl's shoulders and gave her a fond hug. 'His work at the hospital is very important. Always remember that. If anybody ever tells you that Daddy should go away to the war, say that the soldiers need him here.'

Bruce made an effort to look cheerful while the children were about, but later in the evening he sank into a despondent mood.

'I'd heard about that White Feather Campaign,' said Hester, breaking the silence at last. 'I don't suppose you know where that one came from.'

'No, it was just a blank sheet of paper. Those who send the feathers out accuse other people of cowardice; but they're not brave enough to sign their name.'

'That's not the first one to come to you, is it?' said Hester with a sudden flash of understanding.

He shook his head. 'I received one right at the start, and then another just after we got married and came to live here.'

'How could anyone be so outrageous?'

'They don't understand. It's not their fault. Think of all the publicity, the recruiting posters and the flag waving. They think they're helping the cause.'

'But to accuse you of cowardice!' Hester's indignation rose again. 'You ought to be allowed to answer that charge. You're very brave. They couldn't do what you do every day.'

She must not confess that she had peeped into one of the medical books which he studied so arduously whenever he was dealing with a particularly difficult case. A mere glimpse of the pictures had almost made her vomit, and she understood why he kept the books on the top of his wardrobe, out of the children's reach. She could not imagine how anyone could bring himself to deal with the real patients who had suffered such horrific injuries, and a disturbing thought crept into her mind, niggling incessantly throughout the remainder of the evening. How long could Bruce continue to work in such a harrowing place before it affected his own health and well-being?

27

Kathy had become a favourite with all the officers, and they vied for her attention, often claiming help with a task they could easily manage by themselves. Sometimes she complied, just to give them a few moments of companionship, but she was not always persuaded.

'You can do that perfectly well. I'll see you later when I'm not so busy.'

'That girl has certainly blossomed in the past year,' chuckled Cora, as she and Hester watched Kathy weaving her way between the chairs and tables outside, delivering glasses of home-made lemonade. 'You'd never believe she was the same person. She was like a frightened little mouse when we first met her.'

'Yes, she's grown into a very lovely woman,' Hester agreed.

'The next thing you know, she'll find romance and then you'll have to start looking for a replacement.'

'I hope that won't happen too soon.' Hester lingered by the window, waiting to see Kathy serve Captain Webb. 'That poor man has to go back for another operation. Kathy will be upset when he goes.'

'Does he really have to go through something like that again?'

'Yes, unfortunately.' Hester had already asked Bruce the same question and he had explained that the captain was likely to need two more operations to gain full use of his arm and shoulder. If he were to walk again he would need strength and control in his upper body.

'It's a shame to see all these nice young men crippled.' Cora said the same thing nearly every Wednesday, which had become a regular visiting day for her, but she would play cards and board games with the men and chat to them as if they had no disabilities at all. She had not lost the skill which had made her successful as a barmaid, and whenever she saw her in close conversation with a patient, Hester would remember how helpful she had been to Father when he so desperately needed a sympathetic ear.

She came to Bella Casa again on Saturday morning.

'Cora! I didn't expect to see you today.' Hester's cheerful greeting faded away as she noted the expression on her stepmother's face. A feeling of dread washed over her. 'What's happened? Is it Father? Or Timothy?'

Cora took hold of her hand and led her

towards the kitchen table, where she pulled out a chair and turned it into a more convenient position. 'Sit down, Hester. Yes, we've had a message about Timothy.'

'He's dead? You're telling me that Timothy is dead?'

Cora shook her head and Hester instantly pictured her brother in a hospital bed, badly maimed.

'Timothy has been reported missing, Hester.'

'Missing!' For a moment Hester found it difficult to grasp that concept. 'Are you saying they've lost him?'

'They don't know what's happened to him yet.' Cora took Hester's hand again and patted it gently. 'There's still hope, Hester. It's not final. Timothy has been reported missing in action, that's all we know.'

'So he's probably dead, they just don't know for certain. That's what you're saying, isn't it?'

'There's still hope,' Cora repeated. 'He could have been taken prisoner.'

They sat in silence while Hester gathered her thoughts.

'How has Father taken this news?' she asked at last.

'He's worried, of course. I think it would be a good idea if you came to see him tomorrow. You would be a comfort to each other.'

Looking back on it later, Hester decided that those few days made up the worst week she had suffered in years. First came that disturbing news, then the meeting with Father. Cora changed her mind about where they should see each other, and declared that she and Edmund would come to Bella Casa instead. Almost as soon as they arrived she took the children out to play on the beach, giving Hester and her father an uninterrupted period of time together.

'I don't suppose you've heard anything more,' Hester began.

Edmund shook his head sorrowfully. 'I don't suppose we'll hear another word. So far as the army is concerned, Timothy is no longer on their strength.'

'There's still hope,' said Hester softly, clinging to the prospect suggested by Cora. 'He might have been taken prisoner.'

'Or he deserted.'

'Father!' Hester stared at him, aghast at the very suggestion.

'I have been told that is not an uncommon occurrence. There is such chaos out there he could have slipped away unnoticed.'

'Father, you can't believe that Timothy would do a thing like that.'

'Why not?' Edmund shrugged despondently. 'Who knows what anyone might do in similar circumstances? And Timothy could never be relied upon. He would always leave if conditions were not to his liking.'

'No.' Hester shook her head emphatically. 'Timothy would not do that. He had changed, Father. He was proud of his new status, proud to be a soldier. He would not desert.'

'Perhaps not.' Edmund sighed. 'We might never know. Even when this terrible war is over we might not find out what happened to him.'

'We have to be prepared for the worst, I suppose.' Hester gave his hand a light consoling squeeze. 'Timothy did warn us. When he came to see us that last time he did not say it in so many words, but he was warning us that it could be his final visit.'

'Yes.' Edmund sighed again. 'It's as well that I agreed to let him come. Imagine how I would be feeling now if I had let pride get in the way and refused to see him.'

Two days later Captain Webb was carried away to face the surgeon's knife again and Hester had to comfort Kathy.

'It's all for the best, Kathy. He wants to be able to use that arm again.'

'But he's been through so much already.

And he has been feeling so much better lately.'

'That was the reason for his being here. You know that, Kathy. He was sent here to build up his strength, to prepare him for the next operation.'

'It's all so unfair.'

'I know. We all feel the same about so many things just now.' Hester decided that further responsibility might help to distract the younger woman from her morbid thoughts. 'We have another patient coming in today, and by all accounts we're going to need your special charms again to help him.'

Bruce was supportive and understanding about the effect of these events, but Hester slowly came to realise that he also had weighty matters on his mind. He was particularly quiet and solemn the day after Captain Webb had left. When he was sure the children were asleep that evening he asked Hester not to take up any mending or fancy work.

'I have to talk to you, Hester.'

'What's happened? Have you heard more about Timothy? Or is it that someone else has died?'

'No, that's not it. But I have something important to say.' Bruce drew in his breath as if he were gathering courage to continue.

'This is going to come as a shock to you, Hester — but I am going to France.'

'France!' As the startled exclamation burst from her lips, Hester almost sprang up from her chair. 'What do you mean — *France?*'

'I'm going to France to treat the wounded.'

'You always said you wouldn't get involved in this war,' Hester protested.

'I am involved, Hester. I've become more and more involved as time goes by. The only patients I see these days are soldiers or sailors.'

'So what is all this talk about France?' Hester stared at him in consternation.

'They need doctors over there. Treatment needs to start much sooner.' Bruce leaned earnestly towards her. 'Soldiers are dying when they could be saved, Hester. And they lose their limbs unnecessarily. Wounds need prompt attention. Without proper care at the start they get infected. Gangrene and disease have become the greatest enemies.'

'But surely . . . ' Hester could not find the words to say what was in her heart. How could Bruce even think of leaving her now, just when their life together was proving to be so wonderful? They had waited so long for the opportunity to marry; struggled against doubts and objections. They should be allowed to enjoy the happiness of marriage at last.

'I know it's a shock, but I have to do it, Hester. I think I've known for quite a long time now that I would have to do it.'

'You're doing good work here. And you can't leave the patients that you care for at the hospital.'

'They can find older doctors to care for them. Young doctors are needed overseas. That's where the most important work is.'

Hester continued to grope for some means to dissuade him, although that task seemed impossible. Bruce had clearly made up his mind.

'Just think, Hester — think of men like Captain Webb. Supposing he had received treatment much earlier. His leg could have been saved.'

'You can't know that.'

'Of course not. But if my being there saves only one life, or only one limb, it will be worthwhile. I have to go, Hester.'

'You're not asking for an opinion, are you? You're not going to wait a while and think more about this?'

'No, I've enlisted already,' he admitted. 'I was going to tell you last Saturday, but it didn't seem to be a good time, not when you had just received bad news about Timothy.'

They both rose then and Hester rushed into his arms.

'I don't want to lose you, Bruce. I couldn't bear to lose you now. We've had such little time together.'

'You won't lose me, Hester. I'm not a fighting man. I'll be safe behind the lines and I'll come back to you, I promise.'

They clung together in a wordless embrace for a considerable time, then Bruce tilted her face upwards and kissed her gently, first on the forehead and then on each cheek. Their lips met in a long ardent kiss and Hester resolutely pushed all negative thoughts aside. She would enjoy this moment for as long as it lasted; she would not think of the lonely days and nights that lay ahead.

The flood of passion eased and Bruce relaxed his grip, but they remained standing in the same spot, their arms still around each other.

'When is all this going to happen?' Hester's voice was muffled by the threat of tears and the folds of his jacket.

His arms tightened again before he answered. 'Next week. Wednesday.'

'So soon! Oh, Bruce.' Tears overflowed and rolled down her cheeks. 'Can't we have just a little longer together? This is all so sudden.'

'What was it Shakespeare said? 'If t'were to be done, best it be done quickly' — or something like that.'

'Shakespeare always was ready with an appropriate phrase; but I don't find that one very helpful just now.'

'There's a ship leaving for Europe next week and I have to be on it.'

'Will you be wearing uniform?'

'Yes.' Bruce made no attempt to hide the flicker of distaste that crossed his face. 'I didn't want to join the army, of course, but that's the way it has to be. Anyone without uniform would be shot as a spy.'

'Oh, Bruce!'

'Ssh. Don't cry any more, Hester. Let's make the most of the few days we have before I go. Leave everything as it is tonight. Let's just turn off the light and go to bed.'

The following days passed all too quickly, Bruce and Hester doing their best to look cheerful, especially when the children were present. The girls were excited by the news, not comprehending the serious consequences. They had no real understanding of the distance Bruce would travel, nor how long his absence might be. They were eager to see him in his uniform, but he refused to wear it until the day of his departure.

'I'll get used to it on the way over there, but I'm not going to start any sooner than I absolutely have to.'

Matron advised Hester to leave all her

duties in Edith's care and to keep the children home from school.

'It's a time for family. You do not need any distractions.'

When Bruce finally appeared in the living-room, dressed in khaki, the girls cheered.

'You look very smart, Daddy,' cried Dorothy.

'You're the smartest soldier that ever was,' Susan declared.

He gave each of them a fond hug and turned to Hester. 'Behold Captain Hutchinson.'

She had to agree that he looked extremely smart and handsome, but she could not speak as she embraced him, fighting back tears yet again.

'It will all be over soon,' he assured her. 'And in your heart you know I'm doing the right thing.'

He made a final round of the patients at Bella Casa and they all wished him well, apparently pleased that he had become part of the military machine at last.

'Good on you, Doctor,' said one of the mobile patients, giving him a hearty slap on the back. 'You'll get a good reception. Medical men are worth more than gold nuggets out there.'

Bruce had insisted that they must say good-bye at the house, that no member of the family should go down to the docks to see the ship leave. The separation was going to be a hard matter for him to deal with, and he could not bear the thought of the drawn-out agony between the time of boarding and the actual departure of the vessel. To witness the heart-rending scene as all the other families were torn apart was going to be almost too much for him to endure. More importantly, he did not want the children in his family to be caught up in the flag-waving frenzy of mass feeling and propaganda.

'They've got flags and they want to wave them,' Hester reminded him.

'I don't mind their little flags if they're waving them just for me. It's the jingoism I don't agree with.'

When the carriage arrived Hester could no longer hold back her tears and the children began to realise that their new Daddy would not return for a very long time.

'Write to me,' he said softly. 'I want to know what you have been doing. And be good for Mama.'

He gave them all a final kiss, then he slung his kitbag over his shoulder, picked up an extra bag which held personal items and a

few home-cooked sweetmeats, turned resolutely away and walked to the gate. He had
instructed them all to stay on the front porch,
to come no further than the top step, but
when the moment arrived none of them
could obey. Hester joined the two girls in
their rush to the gate, and they went out to
the street as Bruce climbed into the carriage.

'Good-bye. Good-bye,' they called, waving
their flags furiously.

Bruce looked back for just one more
glimpse of his family as the carriage began to
move. He only lifted his hand in one small
gesture, but the others continued to wave
until the vehicle had turned the corner at the
end of the road and was lost to sight.

28

Hester had dreaded being separated from Bruce, but she could scarcely believe the intensity of the loneliness she felt after he left. She scolded herself as her depression deepened. She was not the only wife and mother who had seen her loved one go off to the war. She should cope better than most; after all, she had experience in looking after herself and her family alone. For several years she had coped perfectly well without a marriage partner. Yes, she admitted to herself; living without Gerald had been more of a relief than a penalty. But life without Bruce was like a day without sunshine, dull and dreary. She missed the prospect of seeing him come home at the end of each day, appreciative of the meal she had prepared for him; she missed the sight of him in the armchair, aware of her presence even when he was deep in the study of some medical book; she missed him even more in the dark of the night when the bed seemed excessively large and there was no hope of a comforting cuddle or a gentle word of love.

The children also missed their new father,

and still looked around when they came in, as if they thought he might have returned while they were at school. They knew that many other fathers had gone across the sea to fight in a foreign land, but the distance was beyond their understanding.

'He must be there by now,' Susan insisted. 'Why doesn't he send us a letter?'

'No, the ship will still be on the sea,' replied Hester. 'It's a long, long way to France. We can write letters and post them, but I don't know when Daddy will receive them. And it will be a long time before his letters come back to us.'

She tried to immerse herself in work to keep her mind occupied, filling inactive periods by wandering more often through the house and chatting to the patients. One of the new arrivals proved to be a medical man.

'How did you come to be so badly wounded?' she asked in surprise. 'Did they attack the hospital?'

'Hospital?' he responded with a snort of amusement. 'That's a fancy name for it. A real misnomer, in fact. Our centre was little more than a cave really, and we'd almost run out of supplies.'

'Not many doctors get hurt though, do they?' asked Hester hopefully.

'They sure do. One reason why we run so

short of them, I suppose.' The officer grimaced and gave a nonchalant shrug. 'It's a question of honour, you see.' Hester stared in bewilderment and he decided to explain further. 'Every medical officer tries to get all the wounded under cover before night falls. You don't want them lying out there too long. Besides, it's hard enough to find them even in daylight, what with the mud and all. But daylight makes you an easy target, I suppose.'

'You mean you were in the trenches?' asked Hester with growing alarm. 'I thought all the doctors were away from the fighting, back where it is safe.'

'Whoever told you that?'

'My husband.'

Rosie chipped in unexpectedly, having just entered the room with a jug of water and some clean glasses. 'He's a doctor, too. He's just joined the army and gone to France.'

'Oh, my!' The officer closed his eyes for a moment and then looked at Hester again. 'I'm sorry, Ma'am. I shouldn't have . . . that is . . . ' His voice trailed away and then he tried again to make amends. 'Not every doctor is on the front line, of course.'

'Of course.' Hester forced a smile. 'Don't worry. I won't let your words trouble me. Bruce was obviously trying to make it all sound much easier than it really would be.'

538

'I'm sorry. I should be careful what I say.'

'No, no, not at all. We encourage our clients to talk, you know. It's not good to keep things bottled up.'

Despite her assurances, Hester could not help thinking about the officer's revelations. Over and over again she replayed that conversation in her mind, praying that Bruce would be sent to an area that was far from the destruction and the killing on the front line.

Harold telephoned and brought his whole family to visit for a day, determined to make sure that Hester enjoyed some social activities.

'You've got to get away from this house as often as you can,' he declared. 'You must not go into hibernation just because your husband is not here with you.'

'We thought we might start off with the Pierrot Show,' said Muriel. 'And then the children want to go to Luna Park. Perhaps we can persuade you to go on the switchback this time, Hester.'

She laughed. 'No thank you. The Big Wheel is exciting enough for me. The girls and I can go on that instead.'

During a peaceful interlude when all the children were some distance away, larking about with Harold, Muriel took the opportunity to talk about more serious matters.

'Have any problems cropped up in the past week or two?'

Hester shook her head. 'It's lonely without Bruce, but there's nothing to be done about that. I just have to wait for him to come home.'

'If you ever need any financial advice, or any advice about anything at all, please don't hesitate to ask.'

'Thank you.' Hester smiled gratefully. 'Finance will not be of any concern, thanks to Harold. His agent looks after the houses very well for me. Harold is selling Bruce's motor car for him, too, so just about everything has been dealt with.'

'What about your father? Is he satisfied with that job he got?'

'He has never felt so happy about work. He gets paid on time every second week, and he likes serving the customers. It's a pity he didn't get a job like that a long time ago.' Hester sighed. 'It's not a nice thing to say, but the war did him a favour. He only got that chance because so many younger men have gone away.'

Bruce's first two letters arrived by the same postal delivery and they were welcomed with great joy and excitement. Some paragraphs were personal and not intended to be shared, but Hester read the other sections aloud to the children. Bruce described the ship and some of his fellow passengers, saying he found the voyage tedious after the first few days, but a few minor medical cases had helped to keep boredom at bay. The second letter, written after he had landed in France, told how he had travelled for hours over bumpy roads to a place where everybody worked and lived in large tents. He was about to start on another journey, with a two-wheeled cart which would act as his mobile surgery. A small group of experienced medical orderlies would travel with him, and he said he was pleased to know that at least two of them had been trained to clean equipment and chlorinate water.

'What does that mean?' asked Susan.

'That means they make the water fit to drink,' Dorothy answered quickly, proud of her superior knowledge. 'If water is not pure it makes you sick.'

'That's right,' agreed Hester. 'Well, I'm glad to hear that Daddy has some helpers. We must write back and tell him we received his letters. Shall we start today?'

She always felt a little closer to Bruce when she was writing to him. She looked forward to a quiet evening, expressing her thoughts and telling him about everything they had been doing since she last wrote, but her plan was foiled by an unexpected knock on the door. She hastened to answer, wondering if something had gone wrong downstairs.

'Louisa!'

'Hello,' said Louisa. 'I'm sorry I didn't let you know I was coming, but I was fairly certain I would find you at home. I hope I'm not interrupting anything important.'

'Of course not. Come in. The children have just gone to sleep.' Hester ushered her into the living-room and accepted her hat, then hastened to put the kettle on to boil. Louisa was looking as smart and businesslike as ever, but her mood was far more subdued than it had been of late. Obviously something was preying on her mind.

Louisa waited until the tea had been poured before revealing the reason for her visit. 'Have you heard from Mother?'

'No, not recently. What's happened? Is it Cecil?'

Louisa lowered her gaze and shook her head. 'No. It's Neville. He's gone, Hester. His ship was sunk.'

'Oh, no!'

'Mother is in despair. She even used the telephone to tell me. She couldn't wait for a letter to reach me.'

'Oh, Louisa. I don't know what to say. I'm so sorry.'

'Well, Mother has been proved right again hasn't she? She always said that Neville would meet his death on the sea.' Louisa lifted her cup and took several sips of tea. 'She wants me to go there, to stay with her at Mountcliffe.'

'Will you go?'

Louisa nodded reluctantly. 'Yes, I'll have to go. I can't leave her alone at a time like this.' She frowned and pressed her lips together briefly. 'I won't stay long. I must come back and keep my job. There won't be a proper funeral, of course. But there will be some kind of memorial service.'

'It is quite definite, is it? There's no hope that some of the crew escaped in a lifeboat?'

'No, they were attacked and the ship went down with all hands. It's a terrible thing to do, isn't it, Hester? Sink a ship with everybody on it. And it wasn't even a warship. It's a cowardly thing to do, to shoot at a ship that can't fight back.'

'This whole business is dreadful. Bruce always said it would be like that.' Hester rested her forehead on her hand for moment. 'I'll write to Aunt Amelia tonight. And I must write to Alice. Poor Alice. And those poor young children.'

They were both silent for a moment, Hester thinking of Neville's family in Thorn

Bay. Alice had no other close relatives. Who could she call upon for comfort? And who would provide for her in the future? Aunt Amelia would feel duty bound to offer support, but Alice would not relish the idea of being dependent on her aloof mother-in-law.

'I spoke to Marian by telephone this evening,' said Louisa suddenly. 'It was a bit difficult. I had to get someone to fetch her and that took longer than expected. I had to telephone twice more before she reached the main house. She said she had already decided to leave there and stay at Shafton Farm with Donald's family. She will go there sooner, now that she's heard about this, but I can see arguments ahead.' She smiled faintly at Hester's puzzled glance. 'Mother will expect her to stay in Mountcliffe with her. She will think that Marian owes more to her than she does to Donald's family.'

As expected, Aunt Amelia sent a long letter of woe to Hester, complaining about the way fate had dealt with her family and giving a detailed account of her feelings and suffering. Hester sent a second letter of condolences, and a few days later Louisa came to tell her about her visit to Mountcliffe.

'It is so good to be back here,' she told Hester, heaving a sigh and leaning back in the armchair. 'Being with Mother was such a

544

trial. No one else in the world has suffered such a tragedy, according to her. Oh dear. I was so glad to leave. I could not have borne it for another day.'

'Did you see Alice?'

'Only once. We have never been close. She is upset, of course, but she won't go on and on feeling sorry for herself like Mother. Alice had a hard life as a child, as you know, and she learned to take any bad luck that came her way. She is a very practical person and she will cope with this.'

'And how is Marian?'

Louisa gave a small shrug. 'It's hard to say. She is very unsettled, of course, and she soon lost patience with Mother. I invited her to come and stay with me in Melbourne, so you might see her fairly soon.'

'That would be nice. I haven't seen Marian for years.'

Less than a month later Marian travelled to Melbourne, and soon afterwards the sisters arranged to visit Bella Casa. Marian was thinner than Hester remembered, but she looked strong and robust, her skin tanned by her outdoor farming work.

'Hester, at long last,' she said, holding out her arms.

The two women embraced, knowing there was no need for words to express their feelings and sympathy for each other. Soon they were all seated upstairs in the apartment, catching up on family news.

'I couldn't stay any longer at Shafton Farm,' sighed Marian. 'Donald's parents made me feel so guilty all the time. If it wasn't for me, their son would have stayed on the family farm.'

'He would have joined the army just the same,' Hester pointed out. 'They can't blame you for that.'

'No, but you could tell the way they were thinking. If it wasn't for me, he would have stayed at home till he enlisted. So they would have had him for all those extra years.' Marian made a gesture of despair. 'Besides that, the farm is much too close to Mother. There would never be any peace from her. And I couldn't possibly live with her. Every time I went to see her I would hear nothing but how desolated she was. She only thinks of herself. Donald has been killed. My husband. But she could never spare a moment to consider me or him. It was only Neville that mattered, the terrible tragedy that happened to Neville.'

Hester could think of nothing to say in response to that. She and Louisa exchanged helpless glances and a long silence developed.

'Mother had such hopes for all of us,'

murmured Louisa at last. 'I suppose it's not surprising that she feels disappointed, even cheated.'

'She was always trying to prove we belonged to a superior class, the gentry,' retorted Marian. 'It was all rubbish, of course. Father had money and some good business connections, but what else? Nobody in our family was an aristocrat. Grandfather was only a watchmaker.'

'What about Lord Dearley?' asked Hester mischievously.

'Oh, that silly tale!' Marian pulled a comical face. 'Mother was so proud of that so-called ancestor. But she was never able to prove who he really was. If you ask me — he was nothing more than a side-blow of his father, a bastard child.'

'Marian!' Louisa held both hands to her cheeks and stared at her sister in consternation. 'What a way to talk.'

'Oh, don't start acting like Mother. I thought you had grown up and understood what really goes on in the world.' Marian was unrepentant. 'You, more than anyone, know that so-called high society is filled with disreputable people. And no matter how badly they behave, all the others try to cover it up.'

'That's true,' Louisa admitted. 'Look at

Cecil. Mother always thought he was such a catch. And so did I, fool that I was.'

'Did you hear any news of the Stroud family while you were in Mountcliffe?' Hester ventured.

Louisa nodded gloomily. 'Cecil is in a mental asylum now. The family couldn't cope with his rages. Mother tries to pretend that he has no connection with us, but at least she understands now why I had to leave.'

'He brought it on himself,' said Marian. 'And if the family had insisted that he behave himself, instead of closing their eyes to all that philandering, he wouldn't have got sick in the first place.' She turned to Hester as a means of changing the subject. 'At least you finally married the right man.'

'Yes.' Hester hesitated. She felt impelled to share her fears with someone, and this had been the most open and frank conversation she had experienced for a considerable length of time. Cora would freely give a true opinion, but she did not know enough to understand what lay behind the disturbing images that had begun to trouble her recently.

'What's the matter? Something is bothering you. Come on, you can tell us,' urged Marian. 'We don't keep any secrets from each other, and talking about it might help a lot.'

548

'You're right, I do feel rather worried.' Hester paused to gather her thoughts while the others waited patiently. 'I'm worried about the war, of course; that Bruce will get hurt or even killed. But even if he comes back safely, I'm worried that our happiness won't last.' She looked from one to the other with increasing concern. 'Gerald and I were so happy at the start. It was only when things started to go wrong with his career that our happiness began to fade. After that everything seemed to go wrong. Now things have gone wrong for Bruce. He didn't want to get involved in this war. It has interfered with his career. And we have been married just about the same length of time as when things all went wrong before.'

'You mustn't think the same thing would happen again,' exclaimed Louisa. 'It won't be the same, really it won't.'

'It couldn't possibly be the same,' declared Marian vehemently. 'Listen, Hester, you are talking about two entirely different men. Direct opposites. Gerald was a man who thought only about himself. Nobody else mattered. But Bruce always thinks of everybody else — everybody *except* himself.'

'That's right,' agreed Louisa.

Hester shifted uneasily on her chair. 'Bruce certainly does consider the needs of other people before himself.'

'So he's a very different person. It won't happen the same way again,' said Marian. 'Bruce will continue to make you happy.'

'I'm so glad to hear you say so.' Hester smiled. 'If I ever have doubts I'll remember what you said.'

'Never doubt Bruce,' said Marian stoutly. 'Look forward to the day when he comes back to you. You were meant to be together.'

Their confident assurances helped to bring a brighter turn of conversation and during a light supper they all began to reminisce about pleasant incidents in the past.

'It has been good to see you again after all these years,' said Marian as the two visitors prepared to leave. 'I will telephone in a few days' time. I have been making plans. I'll tell you all about it next time I come.'

Louisa gave an elaborate shrug to indicate that she knew nothing of her sister's future intentions.

'Marian is being deliberately vague about her next move,' she said. 'But I suppose we can take one thing for granted; she will not stay long in the city.'

'You are certainly right about that,' agreed Marian. 'I have no intention of living in Melbourne. And I absolutely refuse to have anything to do with so-called polite society.'

More than a week passed before she and Louisa returned. They arrived earlier than before so that they could spend some time with the children.

'They are lovely girls,' said Marian, when the children had finally settled for the night. 'You are very lucky, Hester. Donald and I were longing to start a family, but it just wasn't to be.' She sighed regretfully then gave a philosophical shrug. 'Still, that's obviously what fate decided for us. If I did have children I couldn't do what I have arranged to do next.'

'Well go on, then,' prompted Louisa. 'Tell Hester what you're going to do.'

'Ah.' Marian looked up with a renewed sparkle in her eyes. 'I'm going to Europe with the Red Cross.'

'You are doing what?' exclaimed Hester in amazement. 'How can you do that? You've never done any nursing. Do you mean you're going to start training to be a nurse?'

'I'm going to be a driver, not a nurse.' Marian laughed with some of her old zest as she watched her cousin's expression. 'I've been working on a farm all these years, Hester. I can drive trucks, motor cars, motor cycles, even a tractor.'

'Good gracious.'

'They welcomed me with open arms. They need drivers desperately, for ambulances and all kinds of things. So now I am going to do my part for my country.'

'What does Aunt Amelia think about that?'

'I don't think she even understood what I was talking about. She doesn't listen to other people these days. Anyway, it wouldn't make any difference no matter what she said. I stopped paying any heed to Mother years ago.'

Hester exchanged another look with Louisa. There was no point in trying to persuade Marian to change her mind. She was determined to go, and Marian had always followed her own inclinations. The only thing left to do was to wish her well and hope that she would not come to any harm.

'You never know, I might see Bruce over there,' said Marian blithely. 'I'll keep a watch for him.'

'Tell him to hurry up and come home if you do see him.'

Hester sighed with regret as she watched her two visitors depart. It was a pity that Marian would be going away again so soon. Her lively spirits came as a welcome tonic when one was feeling low. It was good to know that she was making a new life for herself, refusing to wallow in self pity, but how unfortunate that she had decided to follow such an adventurous path. Who knew what might happen to her in that terrible chaos over there in Europe?

29

Kathy hastened into the kitchen one morning, her cheeks glowing with excitement.

'Captain Webb has come back, Ma'am. You won't believe how well he looks. Come and see.'

Hester chuckled at her enthusiasm. Kathy had never tried to hide the fact that she had a soft spot for the young captain, and she had been delighted when he came back for a second stay. It was surprising to hear that he had come back for a third time.

'Come and say hello,' urged Kathy.

'I will. Tell him I'll come in a minute. I just have to finish something here first.'

Captain Webb certainly did look healthier, and in contrast to his former visits he sounded far more cheerful.

'Good morning, Ma'am,' he said to Hester. 'I'm very glad to see you. I've been looking forward to some more of your fabulous dinners.'

'Thank you.' Hester blushed with pleasure. 'I'm glad to hear that you have a good appetite now.'

'I sure have, Ma'am.' Captain Webb looked

around to make sure they could not be overheard. 'They wanted to send me off to some other place this time, you know, but I refused to go. I insisted on coming here. And the surgeon put in a good word for me; said it was important for my recovery that I come here rather than anywhere else.'

Kathy reported with glee that the captain would come to the dining-room for his meals this time instead of being served in his room. He could cut his own food now and he had grown so strong he could move himself from his bed to the wheeled chair. Kathy found occasion to pass by his chair several times a day, whether he be indoors or outside. Hester smiled to herself, but she also felt a twinge of sadness. This was certain to be his last stay at Bella Casa and Kathy was going to miss him more than ever the next time he left.

When he was finally discharged the captain trundled around the ground floor of the house saying farewell to everybody on the staff. Hester waited on the front porch to wish him well.

'Good-bye, Captain Webb.'

'Good-bye, Ma'am. And thank you.' He gave her a mock salute and held out his hand. 'Next time you see me, Ma'am, I'll be walking. And it won't be on crutches. I'm going to be fitted with a proper leg.'

555

'I'm very pleased to hear it. Dr Hutchinson will be pleased, too. I wrote and told him you were getting on well.'

Kathy accompanied him to the gate and waited until he had been helped into a motor car. As soon as he had left she rushed to the kitchen.

'Isn't it marvellous what the doctors have done for him?' she enthused. 'Won't it be lovely to see him walking?'

'Yes, but we're not likely to see that.' Hester decided there was no sense in building up any wild hopes. 'There will be no reason for him to come back again now. This is a convalescent home, Kathy, not a holiday home.'

Kathy merely nodded to that remark, refusing to be downcast. 'It's amazing how well he looks now. Still, I mustn't stand here talking. I've got lots to do.'

She scurried away to deal with her tasks and Hester turned back to the pastry board. In her mind she was already composing her next letter to Bruce. It was important to send cheerful news to him and he would be pleased to know that the captain had made such good progress. Good news also gave a welcome boost to her own spirits. She did not feel so lonely when she was kept busy, but there were times when she felt exhausted and it seemed there would never be and end to the dreadful war and the stream of broken men coming to the house.

The children sometimes resented the amount of time their mother devoted to patients, and they missed the more casual routine of earlier days, when they could wander about the house and into the kitchen whenever they wished.

'Mama, I do wish you did not have to work all day,' said Susan.

'So do I, dear. But we're very lucky really, you know. We have enough money to buy everything we need and we live in a nice house. Do you remember when we first came here? We couldn't afford to pay for even the poorest house then, and I was ever so happy to get good work.'

'That's what Aunt Cora said.' Susan folded her arms and pouted.

'Things will be different when the war is over.'

'People keep on saying that. But they've been saying it for a long, long time now.'

'Yes, they have.' Hester gave her a hug and a light kiss on the cheek. 'It seems to be going on for ever. But one day it will all be over, really it will.'

She was tidying the children's clothes away one evening, when a tap came on the door to the apartment. A tremor of alarm raced through her and she hurried to answer. What could have happened this time? Was there an emergency downstairs? The last time someone had called upon her without making arrangements in advance, it had been to bring the bad news about Neville.

To her surprise she found Kathy standing in the passage. This had been the young woman's day off from work, and she was obviously wearing her Sunday best. She was fidgety with excitement, but she also looked wary.

'Kathy!'

'Good evening, Ma'am. I hope you don't mind me calling on you like this. I mean, that is . . . '

'Of course I don't mind. Come in.'

'Er — ' Kathy gave a self-conscious lift of one shoulder. 'Actually, I am not alone.'

'Oh?' Hester looked along the passage, but saw nobody. 'Where is your friend?'

'Just — er — ' Kathy turned and called, 'Come on, Victor.'

A tall man in a pin-stripe suit came around the corner from the landing and walked steadily towards them. As he came closer Hester drew in her breath.

'Captain Webb!'

'Good evening, Ma'am.' The officer grinned

and held out his hand. 'I told you I would be walking next time you saw me.'

'So you did. I'm very pleased to see you.'

'I'm sorry to come without warning. But I didn't want to spoil the surprise.'

'You certainly surprised me. Come inside.' Hester watched as he walked carefully to the sitting-room and lowered himself into an armchair.

'Not even a walking stick,' he boasted.

'So I noticed. But fancy coming all the way up those stairs.'

'Actually, I used a stick on the stairs,' he admitted. He looked at Kathy, who was sitting on the edge of the other armchair, her cheeks flushed and her eyes sparkling. 'Well, we're here. Now for the surprise. You can tell Mrs Hutchinson why we really came.'

Kathy's blush deepened. 'We are engaged. We are going to be married,' she said.

'Oh, Kathy!' Hester looked from one to the other. The announcement seemed too soon and too sudden. How could they make such an important decision after such a brief acquaintance? Experience had proved to her that hasty steps into marriage could prove to be unwise. But they were waiting expectantly for congratulations. She must not sound discouraging. 'Well!' she exclaimed. 'Well, you have taken my breath away. This is one big surprise after another. But please accept my best wishes. I hope you will be very happy.'

'I wanted you to be the first to know,' said Kathy. 'Apart from my parents, of course. We have just come from home.'

'Did Rosie know this was likely to happen?'

'Not until now,' chuckled Kathy. 'We kept it hidden from her, because she does prattle, you know. And that's one reason why I didn't ask you if we might come this evening. I thought I might give it away.'

'You must come to the wedding, Mrs Hutchinson,' said the captain. 'Kathy has told me how much you have helped her over the past few years. So you will be a very honoured guest.'

Hester flushed. 'I didn't really do a great deal.'

'You have been very kind and understanding,' he said.

Hester deflected any further embarrassment by declaring she would make a pot of tea.

'This should be a celebration but I can't offer you anything stronger,' she said as she set the tray down on the occasional table.

'Those biscuits will compensate for the lack of champagne,' replied Captain Webb. 'You make lovely biscuits, Mrs Hutchinson.'

As they relaxed into a chattier mode,

Hester learned that Kathy and Captain Webb had kept in touch by letter ever since his first visit to Bella Casa, and she had even been to visit him at the hospital after each operation.

'One good thing about this rotten war,' he declared, 'it led me to Kathy. And now you know why I was so insistent on coming back here for my last period of convalescence. The surgeon gave me a helping hand with the arrangements.'

'Oh, so you knew he was coming back?' asked Hester.

'No, that was a big surprise,' replied Kathy. 'But a lovely one.'

'And we decided then.' Captain Webb gave a satisfied smile. 'We decided that as soon as I could walk up the aisle unaided, we would get married.'

The wedding stood out as a welcome diversion from all the gloom that was beginning to settle on so many people. Matron arranged for temporary staff to take over so that Hester, Edith and Rosie could all attend the ceremony, and the children were delighted to hear that they had been included in the invitation.

'It will only be a simple affair,' said Kathy. 'Only families and very good friends. Nothing elaborate.'

'That's how it should be,' replied Hester.

'We are all looking forward to it.'

With the help of a neighbour, Kathy's mother made a plain white dress with a rounded neckline and long full sleeves. A relative lent a veil, and Kathy carried a small bouquet of pink and yellow roses. To the sound of a piano accordion she walked proudly up the aisle with her father to where Captain Webb was waiting. He was wearing a grey civilian suit, determined to prove that he was no longer governed by army regulations, and he watched his bride approach with an expression that clearly showed the depth of his love. Edith wept during the ceremony, deeply saddened by memories of her own lost love, but she managed to hide her tears and envy when everybody gathered in the church hall for the reception.

Captain Webb's parents looked prosperous and self-confident, but they did not have that air of superiority that Hester had met so often amongst her aunt's acquaintances and they mingled easily with the other guests. They greeted Hester with genuine pleasure, thanking her for all the care and attention that their son had received at Bella Casa.

'It's the nurses who look after the patients,' she protested. 'I don't do that. I only manage the household.'

'It's a happy house because of you. And

562

you do all that wonderful cooking,' said Mr Webb. 'You do a very good job, Mrs Hutchinson.'

Hester was pleased to meet Kathy's parents at last. Mr Thompson was a round-shouldered grey-haired man, who still limped from his old leg injury. His wife was a thin woman, whose lined face showed the rigours of hard times, but she was smiling and proud of her daughter. Hester brushed aside her fervent thanks for all the favours she had shown to Kathy.

'Kathy has always been a very good worker. She deserved any little extras that might have come her way. We are going to miss her when she goes.'

'Yes, well she reckons she'll stay till this war is over,' said Mr Thompson. 'It's all she's been able to do to help the war effort; not much, but she'll see it through.'

'This war will be over soon, you mark my words,' said Captain Webb, who had come up behind them. 'I have it on good authority that the Huns are in retreat.'

★   ★   ★

At long last the joyous news arrived. The Great War was over! Crowds of jubilant people thronged the streets, while flags and streamers appeared quickly in all manner of places, strung across streets, hanging from windows, fastened to lamp posts, to trees and to tram cars. Church bells and school bells rang out the glad tidings, Chinese crackers spluttered and burst, while motor car hooters, bicycle bells, shouts and hand bells added to the cacophony of sound.

Hester took the children out to enjoy the festivities, but brought them home before revellers had time to become intoxicated or too wildly excited. Within Bella Casa the joy was somewhat muted, some patients exhilarated, others regretting that war had cost them so much in health and physical handicaps. Numerous volunteers came, hoping to wheel out those who wanted to share in the street celebrations, but Matron was too cautious to give permission.

'It could be dangerous,' she decided. 'People can be very foolish and they sometimes do the most stupid things when they get swept up into a crowd.'

A few members of staff thought she was much too staid and somewhat of a killjoy, but when they read the newspapers the next day they agreed that she had been wise. Amongst other antics, some foolhardy people had pushed tramcars along the lines, causing them to run away down inclines with passengers still aboard, and some had even man-handled stationary tramcars off the tracks.

'What idiots. Who would have thought they could be so stupid?' demanded Edith. 'Surely they could celebrate without doing things like that.'

Joy and euphoria scarcely lasted for a week in Bella Casa. The fighting was over, but the sick and wounded still needed the same care and after a few days it seemed as if nothing had changed. Everybody on the domestic staff continued with their routine tasks, not giving much thought to the future until Rosie read out parts of a newspaper article during morning tea.

'They're right, you know,' she said. 'All those soldiers and sailors will expect to get their jobs back when they come home. Our Dad will be out again. He's got a good job now, but they told him at the start it was only till the other man came back.'

'What about our jobs?' asked one of the kitchen maids nervously.

'They won't close this place,' said Edith confidently. 'Not yet, anyway. They can't, can they?'

'Our jobs are safe,' said Rosie. 'A soldier wouldn't want to do our work anyway, would he?'

'Victor wants me to stop working now,' said Kathy. 'But how can I, when there are still so many wounded men to look after? Victor is better now, but he could have been a patient still.'

'You have both done your part,' replied Hester. 'You have to think of your own futures now. What is Victor going to do? Are you going to move away to the country?'

'No, Victor can't go back to his old work.' Kathy shook her head regretfully, then looked up with a smile. 'He's going to do something entirely different. Something he would never have thought of before all this happened.'

'Are you going to tell us?'

'I will have to.' Kathy chuckled mischievously. 'None of you would ever guess, not if you tried for days and days.'

'Well, go on then,' said Rosie. 'Tell us. What is he going to do?'

'He's going to be a court artist.'

They all stared in bewilderment and Kathy chuckled again. 'You've seen all the pictures in the newspapers. Whenever there's a big trial there's a drawing of what's happening in the court. Well, that's what Victor is going to do.'

'How is he going to get a job like that?' demanded Edith.

'He's already got it.' Kathy beamed with satisfaction. 'When he was quite young Victor found out that he could draw people well. He only did it for fun before, but he has been taking lessons for the past few months, and now he can draw better and much faster.'

'Oh, just fancy.' Rosie gave a little squeal of excitement. 'There's all those posters and things, too. Next time we see a drawing of a wanted man, perhaps it will be Victor who's drawn it!'

Three weeks later Kathy approached Hester, her diffident manner showing plainly that she had something important to say.

'Oh, Ma'am, I have to tell you, that is, I don't want to really — but I'm going to have to leave.'

Hester smiled. 'Kathy, there is no need to feel guilty. You said you would stay until the war was over, and you have. I was pleased about that, of course, but now you must consider yourself and your husband. We all know Victor wants you to stop working.'

'Yes, well, I would have to, anyway.' Kathy blushed and lowered her eyes. 'I'm with child, Ma'am.'

'Oh, Kathy! Well, I'm very pleased for you. Is Victor pleased?'

'He could jump over the moon. He's even more excited than I am.'

'I'm glad to hear that. It sounds as if you are both very happy in your marriage, Kathy.'

'Oh, we are, Ma'am, we are. I don't believe

there's anybody happier anywhere in the world.'

They held a special afternoon tea in the kitchen to see Kathy off in style, and presented her with a decorated basket full of useful articles for a new baby. Edith did her best to join in the fun, but she was subdued and Hester saw her brush away a tear as her emotion deepened. They all went out to the front porch to wave good-bye, together with four of the mobile patients who were sorry to see such a popular worker leave.

'Well, that's the first of the great changes,' said Edith when she and Hester returned to the kitchen. 'Who do you think will be next?'

'I hope you are not thinking of leaving,' said Hester.

'Me? What hope have I got now?' Edith went to the low cupboard and began pulling out cooking pots so as to hide her face and keep herself occupied. 'These others all have men coming back, else they're young enough to find new ones. My man won't be coming back. And I'm getting too old to attract another one — even if I had it in mind to think about such a thing.'

Hester could find no comforting words to say in response to that and they began to prepare the evening meal in silence. There must be thousands of young women going through the same sad realisation, thought Hester. How lucky she was that Bruce had survived that terrible slaughter. But how much longer was she going to have to wait for him to return? Bruce's last letter had been a mixture of exhilaration, hope and caution. The hostilities had ceased, but his work had not ended. He warned that a great deal of time might pass before everybody could return home. Many young soldiers were expecting to set sail almost at once, not realising how many ships would be needed to accommodate them all.

When the first ships arrived in Australia, bearing troops who were homeward bound, Hester's patience began to fray. When would Bruce come back? Surely he was not planning to stay in France until the very last soldier left? His sense of duty and responsibility was all very well for the men he served, but what about responsibility towards his family? She wrote to tell him about her new hopes for the future. She was looking forward to a new life for them all; a life beyond Bella Casa, a life where she could devote herself to her family and nobody but her family. Any lingering thoughts about setting up a business of her own had long since been abandoned.

Hurry home, Bruce. Please hurry home.

30

Weeks without news seemed to stretch interminably, and irregular letters from Bruce gave no hint as to when Hester could expect to see him again. To hear that other people's friends and relatives were on their way home only served to increase her impatience.

'Marian is not coming back,' announced Louisa during one of her infrequent visits. 'She has gone to England instead.'

'Really?' That news surprised Hester. Whatever could have induced Marian to change her plans? She must have seen some dreadful sights in France, and they had assumed she would want to rush home at the first opportunity.

'That's astonishing,' she said at last. 'I would have thought she could not get back fast enough.' She fumbled for an explanation. 'But, I suppose . . . while she was so close . . . she must want to see London and all those famous places we have heard so much about. At least we know she will be safe there.'

'So long as she doesn't get into trouble,' responded Louisa.

'Why should she? England will be much safer.'

'Yes, except that she has joined the Suffragists. You know what Marian is like. She always has insisted that women should be allowed to vote.'

'Oh dear.'

'Exactly. Oh dear. Marian never was demure and ladylike, and after what she has been doing lately . . . ' Louisa shook her head gloomily. 'The Suffragists stayed quiet while the war was on, supporting the war effort, but they're beginning to rally again. And they will be far stronger now. Women have proved they can do men's work and they won't let things go back to the way they were before.'

'Perhaps they won't need to cause any more trouble. Perhaps their good work will be rewarded.'

Louisa gave a scornful sniff. 'Politicians don't seem to have that much sense. They will have to give in eventually, but I don't believe they will just yet.'

The postman brought no personal letters for Hester the next day and she went to make a routine inspection of the scullery, telling herself she had not expected any news so there was no cause to feel disappointed. She had scarcely left the kitchen before Rosie bustled in, calling out impetuously.

'Mrs Hutchinson! Mrs Hutchinson! Oh, where is she?'

'Don't make such a noise,' scolded Edith. 'Haven't you learned how to behave properly even yet?'

'Well, where is she?'

'She is in the scullery. You will have to wait a minute.'

'I'm here,' said Hester, going back into the kitchen. 'What's the matter, Rosie?'

'It's the telephone. Someone is asking for you.'

'Thank you.' Hester hastened to the office and snatched up the receiver. 'Hello, this is Mrs Hutchinson speaking.'

'Hello, Hester, dear. This is Cora.'

'Oh, Cora. Is something wrong?'

'No, there's nothing wrong. But I think you had better sit down.'

Hester pressed her free hand to her cheek. This sounded ominous. 'What's the matter?'

'Nothing is the matter. I have something to tell you. But I'd like to know that you were sitting down before I begin.'

Hester edged towards a chair and hooked it forward with one foot. 'Very well, I am sitting down. Now tell me what has happened.'

Cora seemed to be short of breath. 'You won't believe this, Hester. We received a letter this morning. I couldn't believe it. I took it down to the store and got Edmund to stop work and open it straight away. It's true, Hester.'

'What's true? Who was it from?'

'From Timothy! He's alive, Hester! He's not dead. He's sent us a letter.'

'Timothy!' Hester felt light-headed. Surely she must be dreaming! But perhaps there had been a terrible mistake. 'When did he write that letter? Where was he?'

'He's in Australia. He's coming down from Sydney, Hester. He wants us to meet the train.'

'I can't believe it.' Hester drew a deep breath. 'What time?'

'Six o'clock tomorrow evening. Can you be there?'

'Of course I can be there! I don't care if everybody has to go without their meals tomorrow, I won't stay here!'

'I know how you feel. We will meet you at the station tomorrow, Hester. What an exciting time that is going to be!'

A large crowd had already gathered at Spencer Street Railway Station when Hester arrived. She had gone early, hoping to find a good position to keep watch for Cora and Edmund, but they were there before her. The two women embraced and Edmund gave Hester a hug and a brief kiss.

'I feel quite nervous about this,' he admitted. 'I don't know how we're supposed to behave. I mean, we don't know whether

Timothy has been in trouble, in a prison camp, or what happened. Where has he been? And why didn't he write to us all that time?'

'What did he say in his letter?'

'Nothing much. Here, read it for yourself.' Edmund handed over a creased envelope and Hester looked at the brief note inside. It had obviously been written in haste and merely stated that Timothy was well. He was pleased to be back in Australia, he wanted them to tell Hester and he hoped they could meet him at the railway station.

'He said he is well,' said Cora, as if to reassure them. 'That's the most important thing, isn't it?'

Everybody in the crowd seemed to be looking up at the huge clock every few minutes as the long wait continued and Edmund sighed several times.

'Time drags so. This waiting seems endless.'

Eventually the signal clanked into position and the train chuffed slowly into the station. Carriage doors began to open before the train came to a stop and a swarm of khaki-clad men quickly filled the platform.

'We'll never see him amongst all those men,' fretted Edmund.

'Let's just wait here and let him find us,' replied Cora calmly.

Hester was searching for her brother's face

amongst the mass of slouch hats surging all around them, and she was taken aback when a lieutenant in a well-fitting uniform and peaked cap hailed them from a few yards away.

'Hello, there! How good to see you.'

'Timothy!' she exclaimed, and they all stared at him in amazement.

Timothy hugged Hester and gave her a resounding kiss, then reached out to his father. All around them families were embracing and exchanging kisses, slapping each other on the back and weeping tears of joy and relief.

'Let's find somewhere quieter,' urged Timothy when all three of them had hugged him more than once. He picked up his bag and they followed him out of the station and into an open space further along the road.

'This is better. Now let's have a proper look at you,' he said.

'I can't believe this. Where have you been all this time?' asked Edmund.

'It's a long story.'

'Why didn't you write?' demanded Hester. 'We thought you were dead.'

'I'm sorry about that.'

'Why didn't you write before now, to tell us you were safe, that you were coming home?' asked Edmund.

'I did.' Timothy watched their faces and

gave an expressive shrug. 'So you didn't get my letters. I must have caught a faster ship. But I did write to tell you I was coming. I was on the way to England then. I couldn't write before. No Post Office.'

'You're an officer!' said Edmund in disbelief, staring at the smart new uniform. 'The army never told us you had been promoted. All they said was you were missing.'

'You've got medals,' said Cora.

Many of the patients at Bella Casa had been awarded medals for gallantry and by now Hester could identify all of them. 'The Military Cross,' she exclaimed, pointing to the white ribbon with its distinctive purple stripe. 'How did you win that?'

'It's a long story,' said Timothy again.

Edmund flushed, obviously remembering his doubts about his son's conduct, and Cora hastily intervened.

'You must come home with us, of course. I've got a meal all ready. And there's a bed. Only a narrow one, but — '

'I can sleep anywhere.'

They did not talk much on the journey to the house. Timothy looked eagerly from side to side, smiling at the sight of familiar landmarks, and clearly relieved to be on home soil again. For the first time Hester noticed a jagged scar running down beside his left ear and disappearing under the hairline at the back of his neck. He had not escaped from the fighting unscathed; but when he was taken to a hospital for treatment, why had the authorities not informed his family? And why hadn't Timothy written to them all that time?

Cora had prepared a hearty stew, followed by a fruit pie and a sponge cake, and Timothy ate large portions of each.

'I've got a week's leave,' he told them. 'I'm going to stay in the army. As you can see, I've been making a success of it.'

He was reluctant to talk about his experiences in France, claiming he could not reveal secrets, but during the following days he gave a sketchy account. A French family cared for him after he was wounded, and when he recovered he worked behind enemy lines, sending information to the Allies.

'How could you do that?' asked Edmund.

'It seems I have an aptitude for languages.' Timothy grinned with some of his old bravado. 'I can speak a bit of German now as well as a fair amount of French. And this scar was useful.' He fingered it thoughtfully. 'If it was dangerous for me to talk I could claim to be deaf — and stupid.'

'The army should have told us what was happening,' complained Cora. 'They told us you were missing, and then nothing at all.'

Timothy shrugged. 'Officially, I did not exist. I was not with a regular unit.'

He declined to say any more and eventually they had to accept that questions would not be answered. Officers at Bella Casa were interested to hear that Hester's brother had made such a dramatic return, but they had a greater understanding of events.

'He's a brave man,' said one, and his companions nodded in agreement.

'All that time in enemy territory,' said a lieutenant. 'Not even a uniform for protection. You must be very proud of him.'

After seven days Timothy left again. His delayed letters arrived the following week, but did not give a full explanation of what had happened to him. He apologised for the long silence, aware that they must have been worried, but said only that he had been unable to write until long after hostilities had ceased. He made light of his wound, but admitted to having lost his senses. When he regained them he found he had been separated from his unit.

The excitement of his re-appearance soon began to diminish and Hester had to remind herself that her work was just as important now as it had been when the war was raging. It was obvious that the aftermath would continue to bring problems. If only Bruce would return, she thought. If Bruce were here she could believe that peace had really come to the world at last.

'Daddy will be here one day soon,' she assured the children yet again. 'He will come as soon as he can.'

At long last they received the joyful news. Bruce was sailing home. Hester and the children jumped about with excitement, but from then on the waiting seemed even harder to bear. On the day of the ship's arrival they made an early start to the docks, but it seemed that hundreds of people had already been there long before, all trying to find the best vantage point.

'This is going to be very tiring and boring,' Hester warned. She looked for a safe place to stand, remembering the huge crowd at the railway station and fearing that people might surge forward in their eagerness. 'We'll stay by that wall over there.'

The ship finally entered the harbour and made its way slowly towards the dock, the rails on every deck lined with cheering, waving men. Everybody on land waved wildly, but then came the long interval waiting for the passengers to disembark.

'This is going to take forever,' complained Dorothy.

'There are a lot of men,' agreed Hester. 'And if Daddy is looking after patients he might be one of the last to leave the ship.'

Sooner than she dared hope, she recognised Bruce at the head of the gangplank. 'There's Daddy,' she shouted. 'Look, he's coming! Can you see him?'

Dorothy and Susan held up the welcoming signs they had made, and Bruce made his way through the crush towards them. For several moments they all clung together, nobody uttering a word, then they moved apart slightly and Bruce hugged and kissed each one. They closed into a bunch again, all speaking at once, oblivious to other family gatherings and those who were still waiting impatiently for their loved ones to come ashore. Bruce unashamedly allowed his tears to fall and time passed unheeded until they felt ready to make a move.

'All we have to do is find a telephone,' said Hester. 'Harold will come for us.'

Harold suggested a good place to wait and promised to arrive there in twenty minutes. The interlude gave them the time and space to look at each other properly and Hester felt a twinge of alarm.

'Bruce, you are so thin! I have never seen you so thin.'

'I have been unwell,' he admitted. 'But that

helped to bring me back sooner than expected. I am so pleased to see you, Hester; to see all of you. You can't imagine how pleased I am to be home.'

'We've been waiting and waiting,' said Susan. 'Mama kept saying you would come soon, but we thought you would never come.'

'I'm home now. And I'll never leave you again.'

He held Hester's hand and kept staring at her as they drove to St Kilda, as if he could not believe they actually were together again, but he also looked avidly at familiar landmarks as Timothy had done. Harold helped Hester down from the vehicle and carried one of Bruce's bags to the front door of Bella Casa, but he declined an invitation to go in.

'You four need to be alone together. We'll meet again soon.'

Bruce wandered around the apartment, admiring the pictures that the children had painted to welcome him, patting pieces of furniture as he passed, picking up and fondling small articles.

'It really is true,' he murmured. 'I'm not dreaming.'

He seemed unable to settle in a chair for more than a few minutes, but Hester felt no deep unease until the daylight faded.

'I've got to make my rounds,' he said, rising suddenly again.

'No, you don't,' protested Hester, hurrying to take his arm. 'Dr Clark is in charge here now. You are on leave.'

'I can't leave them unattended.'

'Everybody is being looked after, Bruce. You don't have to worry about a thing. You are going to have a long rest.'

He sank back into the chair and appeared to be convinced, but Hester soon noticed a slight tremor in his hands. He did not sleep well and when the sun went down the next day the same thing happened again. Hester confided in Dawn, who gave a sombre nod.

'I'm afraid a lot of men have come back with problems. I think you will have to be prepared for your husband to act very strangely from time to time. If you are worried you had better talk to Dr Clark. He served in the Boer War, so he's had more experience than most.'

Bruce had been reluctant to don his uniform when he first enlisted, but now he reached for it automatically. Hester per-suaded him to change into a civilian suit, but he had lost so much weight it no longer fitted properly. The children laughed when they caught sight of him and he played up to their amusement, hunching his shoulders and making the sleeves droop to cover his hands, but Hester decided they must attend to the problem at once.

'That won't do. We'll have to go out today and get you a ready made suit.'

'We don't want to spend money on something like that,' he protested. 'I will soon put weight on again, especially with your cooking.'

'Uncle Jeremy's Will provides clothing for the whole family, so we don't need to worry about the cost. Besides, I have been looking forward to the day when we can go shopping together, so you must come.'

Bruce did his best to relax, but after three days he began to wander about Bella Casa and it was obvious that he was assessing the patients. Two days later he insisted on calling at the hospital where he had worked before joining the forces. He came back looking exhausted and he spent a restless night.

'I can't do anything for him,' he shouted, repeating the same sentence over and over until Hester woke him.

'Bruce, I don't think you should go back to work yet,' she said when he began to dress the next morning.

'I have to, Hester. I can't desert them now.'

When he returned he spoke of his concern

for the men who had been gassed in the trenches.

'We can't cure them, Hester. Some won't survive for long, and the others will never be healthy again.'

Hester was sure he had lost more weight and the tremor in his hands seemed more noticeable. She called on Dr Clark for help and between them they persuaded Bruce to spend a week at home, but on the eighth day he returned to work at the hospital again. A few nights later he was more restless than ever, twisting and turning endlessly and calling out in a voice filled with despair. Hester switched on the light and realised with dread that he was feverish.

'Oh, surely you haven't got influenza!' she gasped. Her mind was instantly flooded with tales of that horror. It seemed that no part of the world had escaped. Thousands of people had died and the epidemic was claiming more victims every day. The newspapers carried daily reports about the terrible disease and several public events had been cancelled so as to prevent the gathering of large crowds.

'Oh, please, God, don't let him have influenza. Bruce, you should have stayed away from sick people.'

She did what she could to reduce his temperature, but when Dr Clark came, soon after sunrise, he confirmed her fears.

'Yes, it's the influenza. You will have to be prepared for him to be very sick; and it could spread right through your family.'

'He mustn't die now,' fretted Hester. 'After all he's been through, he mustn't die now.'

'We'll do our best for him. But as you know, it can be a fatal disease.'

Dawn offered sympathy and immediately told Hester she must let Edith take over all her duties in the house.

'Edith will manage well enough. And perhaps it would be better if you were all isolated from the rest of the household.'

'Do you think it might have spread already?' asked Hester in alarm.

'We'll know that soon enough. But let's hope not. We have always been very careful about hygiene, so perhaps we will be lucky.' Dawn gave a sorrowful sigh. 'All these men have had enough to go through without having to endure that as well.'

Hester went back to care for Bruce, her anxiety deepening as the hours passed. He tried to get out of bed several times, insisting that he must make his rounds.

'We need morphine,' he shouted time after time, and then more frequently: 'I can't do anything for him.' As his temperature rose higher he became incoherent and Hester could not pacify him. The children stayed together in the sitting-room, comforting each other as they listened to the sounds of the delirium, fetching cloths and water whenever Hester called for them.

'Bruce, I am not going to let you die now,' she said as he lay back in a quiet respite. 'We have all been through too much. You must not die now.'

She came to a sudden decision and went to the children. 'Dorothy, will you go down and ask Matron to come up please. Tell her it is not an emergency, but I want to see her as soon as possible.'

Dawn arrived within minutes. 'What can I do to help?'

'I want to employ a private nurse,' said Hester. 'Can you tell me how to do that? And can you recommend somebody?'

'Perhaps we should send him to a hospital.'

'No, we mustn't do that.' Hester shook her head emphatically. 'We've got to keep him away from hospitals. Every time he went to that hospital he came back looking ill. We've got to convince him that the war is over and he's back in his own home.'

'I can certainly help you to find a nurse. But there's — I don't want to pry, but — it will be costly.'

'We can afford it. My uncle left funds for

medical expenses and this is the time to use that money.' Hester managed to smile. 'My uncle was a wonderful man. You could even believe he knew something like this was going to happen.'

Nurse Flynn arrived late the same evening, prepared to watch over Bruce throughout the night so that Hester could rest. The relief of having a professional on hand enabled Hester to sleep for several hours, and she rose the next morning feeling more confident about the outcome. The children still felt well, and now that she had slept she believed she also could withstand the disease.

Bruce's temperature rose to dangerous heights over the next two days, but between bouts of delirium came periods when he recognised Hester and was able to speak lucidly. His strength continued to diminish, however, and Dr Clark made frequent visits.

'I don't believe this is influenza,' he said one morning. 'Was he ill before he came home?'

'He did say he had been unwell,' replied Hester. 'I don't know what was wrong with him, but he did say it brought him home sooner than expected.'

'Ah.' The doctor sighed with satisfaction. 'That probably means we don't have to worry about you or your family. I'll try to get hold of his medical history, just to confirm it, but I believe this might be undulant fever.'

'Is that dangerous?'

'Not like influenza. But we obviously have a weakened patient here, so we have a difficult time ahead. The problem is, this can last for months, with the temperature going up and down. That's where the name comes from, of course. It's also known as Malta fever.'

'Are you sure the children are safe?'

'If this is what I think it is, your husband caught it from contaminated milk. Yes, Mrs Hutchinson, I think your children are safe.'

His diagnosis was deemed to be correct soon afterwards and everybody was relieved to learn that the dreaded influenza epidemic had not invaded Bella Casa.

'Thank goodness for that,' said Dawn. 'That means you can move about the house freely now. But you must not think of coming back to work. Everybody is managing very well in your absence. You must concentrate on looking after your husband.'

Harold and Muriel came to Hester's aid once more, taking the children away to stay at their house while she battled on to save Bruce.

'I have to warn you,' said Dr Clark the same evening. 'Your husband is very weak and I have grave fears for him. Have you notified his family?'

Hester quailed. There had been little contact between Bruce and any member of his family since he had announced that he would marry her.

'No, I haven't. But it sounds as if I must.'

'As quickly as possible. I'm sorry to have to tell you this, but I cannot hold out any false hopes.'

31

Bruce's mother arrived the next afternoon, having taken the first train of the day from Mountcliffe. She had lost her usual confident manner and was wringing her hands in agitation when a housemaid escorted her to the door of the family's apartment.

'Am I in time? Do tell me I'm not too late,' she moaned as Hester opened the door.

'Come in. No, you're not too late. Come and sit down for a moment.'

Mrs Hutchinson followed her to the living-room, but she rejected the offer of an armchair and perched herself on the edge of a straight chair instead, unwilling to remain in that room for long. Hester took her hat and murmured polite phrases about her prompt arrival. She had been dreading a meeting with either of Bruce's parents, but now she found she was the stronger of the two.

'There has been no change in Bruce today. That means he is not any worse, but it also means that he has not improved. I'll take you to see him in a moment, but I have to warn you — he is very weak.'

'Take me now. I must see him at once.'

'He might not recognise you. Don't be upset if that happens. His temperature fluctuates so.'

They went quietly in to the bedroom, where Bruce lay with his eyes closed.

'Bruce, your mother is here. She has come to visit you.'

'Bruce, oh Bruce!' cried Mrs Hutchinson. 'Bruce, tell me you're going to be all right.'

For a moment there was no response, then his eyes flickered open. 'Hester!' he whispered.

'I'm here, Bruce.' Hester went to the other side of the bed and took his hand. 'I'm here. And your mother is here, too. She has come to see you.'

'Bruce, darling, it's your mother. Look at me, dear.' His eyes moved slowly to meet her gaze and he stared at her uncertainly. 'It's Mother, darling. Speak to me, dear.'

He remained silent and his eyes closed again.

'You might like to sit here for a while,' suggested Hester. 'I will leave you two alone.'

'No.' Bruce's eyes opened briefly. 'Don't go, Hester, I need you.' He tightened his grip slightly on her hand and she sat down on the side of the bed.

'I'm not leaving you, Bruce. I will be in the next room.'

591

'No. Here. I need you here.'

She acceded to his plea and the two women sat watching him for several minutes. Mrs Hutchinson made another attempt to make him speak, but he did not respond and eventually he drifted into sleep.

Hester gently withdrew her hand. 'He will sleep for a while now. Come and have a cup of tea.'

Mrs Hutchinson reluctantly left the bedroom, again choosing to sit on an upright chair rather than in a comfortable armchair. She declined to eat anything, but accepted a cup of tea.

'Bruce's father could not come with me today,' she said, obviously feeling a need to explain his absence. 'He is far too busy.'

'His career has always been more important than Bruce,' said Hester bitterly.

'Oh, my dear, I'm sure he . . . ' Mrs Hutchinson broke off, uncertain as to how to counter that accusation. 'We have made mistakes, I have to admit that.'

'The greatest one was urging him to enlist. Well, you can see the result of that. He came back a shattered man.'

Tears welled in Mrs Hutchinson's eyes and she fumbled for a handkerchief. 'I'm sure none of us realised what dreadful events would take place. We could not possibly know.'

An awkward silence followed and finally Mrs Hutchinson gave a sigh of regret. 'We should not have opposed this marriage,' she said. 'It is clear that he truly loves you.'

Hester bit back a resentful remark. They could have enjoyed so much more time together, she thought. If it were not for his parents, she and Bruce could have married long before. Saying so would not improve matters, but she would always have that niggling thought at the back of her mind. If Bruce died now she would always rue those missing years, years when they could have been together.

'Have you made any arrangements for tonight?' she asked as a means to break the silence. 'There is a bed in the children's room . . . '

'A hotel room has been reserved for me. My luggage has been taken there by carriage.'

When Bruce woke he exchanged a few words with his mother and she was more composed when she set off to the hotel. During the following days the barriers between the two women began to crumble and they spoke with less restraint.

'Your aunt has changed a great deal,' said Mrs Hutchinson. 'I scarcely see her these days. She no longer comes to social functions.'

'I suppose you know that Neville was killed in the war.'

'Yes. The war affected a great many of our friends. And it is still affecting Bruce, of course.'

'Did your other sons return safely?'

'Yes, they never actually left these shores. Both of them stayed here, helping to train new officers.'

Their father would have used his influence to make sure they were given safe positions, thought Hester resentfully. Trust him to do a thing like that while he was exhorting others to make sacrifices.

'You lost your brother, didn't you?' said Mrs Hutchinson warily.

'No, Timothy survived! We thought he had been killed. He was wounded; but he came back months after the fighting stopped and now he is fit and healthy.' Timothy was one of the few who had benefited from the war, she mused. Soldiering had made a man of him. He now had a responsible attitude to life and had become an efficient officer. What a pity the experience had had such a devastating effect on men like Bruce.

Bruce's temperature rose once more to alarming heights, but at the end of the week he began to improve and Dr Clark declared he was out of danger.

'We have to build him up now. But I must warn you — we might not have seen the last of the fever. You will have to keep careful watch.'

As he predicted, Bruce suffered a relapse before long and the children went away again to stay with their relatives.

'It's because he was visiting patients,' cried Hester. 'He was doing so well until he started visiting men downstairs.'

'Yes, it's the stress,' Dr Clark agreed. 'He really needs to be somewhere that has nothing to do with military men, especially sick and wounded ones.'

Hester mulled over his words for nearly an hour, then came to a decision. 'Bless you, Barnaby,' she murmured. 'Wherever you are, thank you for your bequest and your kind thoughts.'

She telephoned Harold and he arrived soon after lunch, driving yet another new motor car.

'What can I do for you?' he asked.

'We've got to leave here, Harold. As soon as possible. We've got to get away from soldiers and sailors. You know the best way to go about it. I want to buy or rent a house where Bruce can get better properly.'

Harold raised his eyebrows. 'There was a time when you wanted to buy this place.'

'Yes, but not now. I can't get away from this house fast enough.'

'You don't want to buy,' he said ruminatively. 'Not just yet, anyway. If you start by renting you can make changes more easily later.'

'Will you find somewhere for me? I would like the children to stay at the same school if possible, but we can't be too close to this place.'

Hester went to see Dawn next and she gave a sympathetic nod. 'I must say I have been expecting this would be the outcome. You must not feel guilty, Hester. You did a great job helping the war effort and now you must care for your family. Edith is managing very well and I will recommend that she be promoted. She can take over from you now.'

Harold soon came with news of a house with a garden and four large rooms, any of which could be used as a living-room or a bedroom.

'It has a good kitchen, a water closet and a bathroom. And it is within walking distance of the beach. You must come and see it.'

'I don't need to see it,' replied Hester emphatically. 'If you think it is suitable, that is good enough for me. Tell them we'll take it. We want to move in immediately.'

'I hope you're doing the right thing.'

'I know I am. Dr Clark and Dawn both agree with me.'

'Very well then. I did make a tentative agreement with the owners, so the final settlement won't take long.'

'You're wonderful, Harold. I knew I could depend on you. Thank you.'

He waved one hand disparagingly and looked about to assess the furnishings. 'I'll send my packers in to move all your belongings. You won't have to do a thing. Leave clothes, toys and everything exactly where they are. Now, how soon do you want to go really?'

'I'll have to tell Bruce about it first,' she admitted. 'And the children must have the chance to come back and say good-bye. This has been their home for a long time. We can't just move them to another house without warning.'

'You're right. I'll bring the girls back tomorrow and you can tell me then what day you want to leave.'

Bruce was still frail from his latest bout of fever, but he was clear-headed and he ate most of the broth that Hester had made. She decided the best way to break the news was to remind him of his stance when they were first married.

'Bruce, do you remember saying that you

did not approve of your wife being employed?'

'Of course I do. I realise that it was necessary, but that does not mean my views have changed.'

'I'm glad to hear that because I have resigned. I no longer work at Bella Casa.'

'I see.' He considered that statement for a moment and suddenly realised the implications. 'That means we will have to find other accommodation.'

'I already have. We are moving to a house of our own within a couple of days. There will just be the four of us there, you, me and the children. You will be able to rest and get really well, and we can enjoy being a proper family with nobody else to worry about.'

Bruce smiled faintly. 'Hester, you have changed so much. When I first met you I never suspected that you could be so masterful.'

'I have never needed to be so masterful before. When you are stronger you can take over the role of master, but until then you must let me make the decisions.'

Despite her eagerness to get away and make a fresh start, Hester was surprised to find it was a great wrench to leave Bella Casa. She made a final tour of the house, wishing the patients well and saying farewell to the nurses. The household staff had hurriedly collected enough to buy an ornate vase and a card for her.

'The flowers will be delivered to your new house later today,' explained Edith. 'We didn't want to give you anything that was hard to carry.'

'Thank you. Thank you, everybody. I won't forget you.'

'I, for one, will never forget you,' murmured Edith. 'I would never have got to where I am today without your help.'

Rosie was unable to speak for tears, and Hester decided she must leave the kitchen quickly before she also was overcome by emotion. She nodded her thanks, gave a last look around at the room where she had spent so many working hours and returned to the apartment.

Bruce was astounded to hear that she had engaged an ambulance.

'I can manage, Hester. I know I am not strong yet, but I can walk.'

'I am not taking the chance of you falling down the stairs,' she retorted. 'Besides, the children are thrilled at the idea of riding in an ambulance. You can't deny them that opportunity.'

Susan and Dorothy had been with their uncle to see the new house and they had come back filled with glee at the prospect of living there, but Hester had still not visited. She was pleased by her first glimpse of the exterior, but the disruption of the move and the short journey had tired Bruce and she was concerned for his welfare. How could he rest when all their furniture had been left behind at Bella Casa?

Her fears were dispelled when Harold met them at the front door.

'Welcome to your new home,' he boomed. 'Morning tea will be served in five minutes exactly in the temporary lounge. Please assemble in the front room to your right.'

The front room had been equipped with chairs and a table, and even a couch with a pillow, where Bruce could lie down. Muriel bustled in with a tray and a jug of orange juice.

'The tea will be ready in no time,' she announced. 'And I have taken the liberty of cooking dinner in your kitchen. You will be pleased to know that the gas oven is working perfectly.'

'Thank you, Muriel. And thank you, Harold. I don't know what we would have done without you.'

'No point in having a lot of workers if you don't make use of them,' Harold responded airily. 'Now, as I said, you don't have to worry about a thing. The whole house has been thoroughly cleaned, so the men can carry your belongings straight in.'

The following three weeks were idyllic. For the first time Hester felt confident that their lives had been restored to normal and their problems had been overcome. Most of the businesses that had supplied Bella Casa were pleased to take her much smaller orders, and local shops delivered anything else that she needed. Bruce gradually regained his strength, walking a little further each day until they were able to go as far as the sea front.

'I have ordered some flowers, as a special thank you to Barnaby,' said Hester. 'We would not be here in this house if it were not for him. I am going to put them on the Seamen's Memorial.'

'That is a very nice thought. I will come with you. I can walk as far as that now.'

Hester thought the distance might tax his strength, but refrained from saying so. They could come back in a cab if he grew tired. She had arranged to make the tribute on Saturday so that the girls could take part, and they were delighted to see that the wreath was in the shape of an anchor.

'We must never forget Barnaby,' said Hester. 'His wonderful bequest has been the saving of us.'

They performed a simple, but moving, ceremony at the memorial and Bruce managed to walk back without exhausting himself.

'That was good,' he said. 'It was a fitting mark of respect to a grand old man. And that journey proved I am well enough to start work again.'

'Oh, no, Bruce. Not yet. You haven't given it enough time.'

'I'd go mad just sitting about at home. No, I have to make a start, Hester. I will just go in for an hour or two.'

He came back from his first morning at the hospital looking pale and obviously feeling tired, but he insisted on going again the next day. Two days later the tremor in his hands had returned and then his temperature began to rise. Hester watched in anguish as his condition deteriorated and she finally sent Dorothy to Bella Casa with a message for Dr Clark.

'You were right to send for me,' said the doctor. 'But I'm sorry to say I can't do a lot for him.'

On the following Monday Hester had to inform his parents that Bruce was dangerously ill again. This time Mr Hutchinson accompanied his wife, but he made only one brief visit when Bruce was not aware of their presence. Mr Hutchinson treated Hester with rigid formality, still not ready to accept her as a welcome member of his family, and she was relieved when he left again, supposedly to deal with urgent government matters. Mrs Hutchinson stayed at the same hotel as before, coming each day to be with her sick son.

'I'm so glad Bruce has you to care for him,' she confided one morning. 'If he had come home to us as sick as this he would not have lived. He is only holding onto life because he wants to be with you.'

Hester's remark slipped out before she took time to think. 'It's strange. If Bruce had been allowed to go to university when he first wanted to, we might never have met.'

'That was another mistake. I can see it now. I should have supported Bruce. He should have been allowed to go his own way.'

All that day Mrs Hutchinson looked for ways to help Hester, becoming over-attentive to the children, who were suspicious of the change in her attitude and tried to keep out of sight. She was clearly yearning to make up for the harm caused by her husband's oppressive stance and her meek compliance with his wishes.

'What can I do to put things right, Hester? There must be something I can do for Bruce.

When he looks at me sometimes I just know he's remembering the cruel things that were said.'

It was a bit late for such regrets, thought Hester, but before another hour passed she had an idea.

'I know what you can do for Bruce.' She went to a cupboard and searched for the cardboard box which held his research papers. 'Look,' she said, holding out a folder. 'Bruce spent hours and hours working on this. It's a report about conditions in the outback. Medical facilities are very poor beyond the big cities.'

'What am I supposed to do about that?'

'Get it published. Your husband has influence.' Hester's voice rose. 'Just for once, let him use that influence for Bruce's benefit. I don't care if he has to *buy* space in a journal. This paper should be published. And politicians must be made aware of conditions. That would make Bruce feel a lot better. If he knows that his work has been published he will know that he has achieved something worthwhile and his efforts have not been totally wasted.'

When Bruce woke again she told him that his paper would be published at last. He smiled and gave a little sigh of contentment, but that night his condition seemed to worsen and she feared that he had given up the struggle.

'Don't you dare die now,' she admonished him, not knowing whether or not he could hear. 'You've got a lot more to do yet. Doctors everywhere need more of your reports and your skill.'

In the depths of the night she gave way to silent tears, sitting beside the bed and stroking his hand.

'I'm here, Bruce,' she told him frequently. 'Don't leave me. I won't leave you.'

Shortly before dawn she felt an answering pressure from his fingers. That could have been his last desperate attempt to communicate, she realised, but she must not accept defeat. She continued to talk to him, aware that she was often prattling nonsense, but he did not respond again. Daylight appeared with a soft glow on the curtains and soon afterwards Dorothy crept in with a cup of tea for her.

'I know you haven't been to bed all night,' she whispered. 'I'm not going to school today.'

Hester merely nodded her acceptance of that decision and Dorothy tip-toed out again to start making breakfast. For several more hours they all hovered between hope and anguish, but then came definite signs of improvement.

'Daddy is going to be all right,' Hester assured the children. 'He is still very ill, of course, but he will get better now.'

He will never go near that hospital again, she vowed to herself. That was the cause of his problems. No matter who argued against that idea, she would never be convinced that she was mistaken.

Bruce gradually returned to health and took more interest in their daily activities. Soon, however, he showed signs of becoming restless again and Hester went to consult Dr Clark.

'He must not go back to work at that hospital,' she said. 'But what is he going to do? He is a doctor. He has never wanted to do anything else.'

Dr Clark pursed his lips. 'No, he must not go back there. In fact, he would not be welcomed. That place obviously triggers a bad memory.' He thought for a moment and decided to explain further. 'There are similar cases. There must have been an exceptionally bad incident that he has tried to blot out. But the trigger brings it all back and his body reacts badly. As you have surmised, his condition is not entirely the result of fever.'

'What is he going to do?' asked Hester again. 'He wants to start work.'

'You must prevent him from doing that.'

Dr Clark pushed one hand through his hair with a distracted air, but did his best to sound confident. 'Leave it with me for the moment. I will confer with doctors who deal with these types of cases.'

It took all of Hester's persuasive power and even some mild bullying to ensure that Bruce did not return to the hospital.

'This is a good time to do some more research,' she suggested. 'And you could submit another report while the first one is fresh in people's minds.'

She hoped that a new project would keep him busy enough to distract his thoughts from cases at the hospital, but she feared that frustration might have a bad effect and bring on yet another attack. Would Dr Clark find a solution before it was too late?

32

Bruce took Hester's advice and completed another article about the needs of people in the outback, a task which kept him occupied for more than two weeks. Hester allowed herself to relax a little, but the urge to practise medicine remained as strong as ever and Bruce soon became edgy again. She watched anxiously, dreading another relapse and longing to hear from Dr Clark.

Eventually an errand boy came with a note suggesting that she call at Bella Casa to see the doctor. She put her cleaning utensils away at once and took her shopping basket out of the cupboard.

'I will be back in about one hour,' she told Bruce, and hastened away as if she were going to the shops.

Dr Clark had obviously expected a quick response to his note, for he opened the front door himself and invited her in to his surgery without delay.

'Have you got some good news for me?' she asked, scarcely waiting for them to exchange polite greetings.

'Please sit down. A suggestion has been

made, but I'm not sure it would be the right solution in this case.'

'Would it suit Bruce's condition?'

'It would be good for him, but we have to consider the whole family.'

'If it is good for Bruce it will be good for all of us,' declared Hester. 'We want him to be well. That is all that matters.'

Dr Clark raised one hand. 'Hear me out. We have heard about a small country practice where no patient has been involved in the war overseas.'

'That sounds perfect.'

'You must consider the drawbacks. It would mean leaving the city and moving to a small township in the country. You would have none of the modern facilities you are used to — no gas, no public transport, scarcely any shops and no library. Not even street lighting.'

Hester quailed, but refused to be down-hearted. 'We can manage. Is there a school?'

'A small school, yes.'

'And what about Bruce? If he is taken ill again, how can I get help?'

'The retiring doctor is staying there in the township. He has agreed to keep watch over your husband's health.'

'That is all we need to know. Tell them we will go as soon as possible.'

'Mrs Hutchinson, you really must stop and think about the consequences. For example, there is the question of accommodation. As I said, the previous doctor will be staying there. That means his house will not be available.' A significant pause followed. 'The only vacant house in the area has not been occupied for some time and I understand it is far from luxurious. You have been born and bred in the city. The way of life will be entirely different.'

'Dr Clark, this would not be the first time I have had to adapt to a different way of life.' She smiled at him with a convincing show of confidence. 'The only important thing is to make sure Bruce will get strong and well again. Nothing else matters.'

'In that case we can set the wheels in motion. First of all we have to persuade your husband that he is desperately needed in Humeville. You must not let him suspect that you know anything about these arrangements.' He escorted her to the front porch and gave her a warm handshake as they parted. 'Think deeply about this, Mrs Hutchinson. If you should change your mind, please don't hesitate to say so.'

'I won't change my mind, Dr Clark. That is one thing I am absolutely certain about.'

Hester thought she detected a change for

the better as soon as Bruce heard that he was needed in Humeville. He began to make lists of everything they should do before leaving St Kilda and Hester told the children they would soon be moving away to the country.

'Can we have a dog if we're living in the country?' asked Dorothy hopefully.

'I don't know about that. There will be lots of new things to get used to first.'

'How will we get there?' asked Susan.

'We will go by train first, and then by carriage. Someone will meet us at the station.'

'What an adventure. It will be a real adventure,' exclaimed Dorothy. 'Oh, I'm so glad. I can't wait.'

Harold and Muriel showed no enthusiasm when they heard about the move.

'Are you sure you're doing the right thing?' Harold asked when the rest of the family was beyond earshot. It was the third time he had raised the same question. 'You shouldn't bury yourself in the country like that. You're not penniless, you know. You can afford to make yourself really comfortable in town.'

'Bruce won't get well in town,' Hester explained yet again. 'Yes, I'm positive we're doing the right thing. You must have noticed how much brighter Bruce is already. He has to feel useful and needed, and he knows he is needed there.'

Harold sighed. 'Well, it looks as if you're set on doing it. I can help Bruce to choose a motor car if he'd like me to. He'll certainly need a motor in a place like that.' As always, he began to plan ahead. 'A Model-T Ford would be the best for him, I should think. It's sturdy and it's popular, so he'd be able to get replacements for any parts that go wrong. I know where to get a good used one.'

'And you can help Hester with the removal again, can't you?' Muriel suggested.

'Of course. Leave all that side of the business to me, Hester. We'll get the house cleaned before you go there, and my workers will pack everything for you again.'

'Thank you. It seems dreadful to put you to so much trouble again, and so soon, but I must say I would be very grateful.'

Hester smiled ruefully as she watched them drive away. She was going to miss them and the interesting outings they had made together. Now they would be many miles apart, but she could rely on them for help if she ran into difficulties. Not that she would need any help, she assured herself. She had coped with the move to Bella Casa and all those responsibilities, and she could cope perfectly well with this new venture. Even so, it was a relief to know that other people would be cleaning the house for her. They could chase out all the spiders. If the house had been unoccupied for a long time there were sure to be lots of spiders lurking there. She thrust away all thoughts of other creatures that might trouble her in the country and told herself she could face anything so long as Bruce's health improved.

★   ★   ★

They found there was no station at the place where their railway journey ended. The train merely stopped beside a wooden shed, beginning to move on again as soon as the family had descended to the strip of paving stones that served as a platform for the halt. The conveyance awaiting them proved to be a wagonette with long bench seats. The driver greeted them cordially, but he was almost totally deaf so conversation with him was impossible.

They set off along an undulating road, trailing a cloud of dust. Bruce was looking pensive and after a few minutes Hester decided she must say something positive.

'The scenery is lovely, isn't it? I'm sure we're going to enjoy living in the country.'

'Look at that water, over there past those trees,' exclaimed Susan. 'Is that a big river?'

'It's a lake,' answered Bruce. 'We'll have to

come and visit the lake if we find we're missing the sea.'

'Can we swim in it?' asked Dorothy.

'Perhaps. We will have to wait and find out if it is safe.'

At last they saw the first signs of habitation and soon afterwards they reached a settlement. The driver stopped outside a shabby barred gate and ambled to the rear of the vehicle.

'Your house,' he announced. He helped Hester and the children down to the ground, brushed one hand past the brim of his hat as a farewell salute and drove away without further ado.

Bruce shrugged. 'Obviously he didn't expect a tip.'

They turned to look at the rambling house beyond the gate and for a long moment nobody spoke. The front of the original stone building had been rectangular in shape, with windows equally spaced to either side of the front door, but various extensions had been added since, apparently making use of any materials that came to hand. Bricks, stones and timber had been assembled in a haphazard way, while the corrugated iron lean-to at one side seemed to rely on a heavy beam for support. A tattered cane sunblind dangled crookedly over the front verandah and the rusting corrugated iron roof sagged ominously in one corner.

'Is that it?' exclaimed Susan, askance at the difference between that house and the comfortable one they had just left.

'You didn't say it would look like this,' complained Dorothy. 'You only said there was no gas.'

'We will be like pioneers,' said Hester bravely. She had been warned about the state of the house, but it was more ramshackle than she had imagined. Dismay was creeping over her and she wondered if any more unwelcome surprises lay in wait, but she must remain cheerful and never reveal her doubts. 'Go and explore around the back. I believe there are some fruit trees and a shed. It will be fun living in such an old house.'

Bruce took Hester's arm and drew her close. 'Oh, Hester, how could I bring you here, to a place like this?'

'It's just what we need,' she responded at once.

'I didn't give enough thought to this. We will be back to oil lamps, and a closet in the back yard. You will have to cook on a wood stove again . . . '

'It is all ours, and our time is all our own. No residents to cater for, no noise of traffic, no shouting tradesmen. Listen.' She held up her hand and they listened to the gentle sounds of the countryside. 'It's so quiet and peaceful. It's lovely.'

Bruce must never know how the doctors had conspired to find a practice likely to be suitable for him. Hester told herself that her prayers had been answered and she must be grateful. She could adapt to life in the country, just as others had done before her. Marian had made a cosy home in a cottage that was more primitive than this house, and Bruce had experienced far worse conditions even before he went abroad to the battle-fields. All that was needed here was a little care and effort.

A middle-aged woman came along the road carrying a plate of buttered scones.

'Good morning. I'm Doris Woods. All your stuff arrived safely yesterday. A motor car as well. That's around the back. And I had a nice chat with your relative. He's a nice man. I'm sure you'll find these scones handy. If there's anything else you need, just give me a shout. I live over there.' They could scarcely utter brief thanks before she continued in her breezy fashion: 'Does either of you play the piano?'

Bruce gestured to Hester and the woman beamed at her.

'Oh good. Will you play for us at church?'

'I haven't played for years,' protested Hester.

'Never mind. One hand would do. We won't care if you only play with one finger, so long as you can help the tune along. But I mustn't keep you here talking just now. I'll see you soon. Don't forget, let me know if you need anything.'

Bruce smiled down at Hester as their neighbour sauntered away. 'Well, at least we seem to be welcome here.'

'It will be perfect here, Bruce. I just know it.'

They lingered there by the gate, an arm around each other's waist, listening to the chirps and whistles of the birds, the whisper of the breeze in the trees and the distant bleat of a sheep. Hester's optimism rose and she gave a sigh of contentment. Here Bruce could recuperate, regain his strength and his nerve. They were together, that was all that mattered. They were together and peace had come.

It would take time to overcome all the problems, she knew that well enough. But time was one thing they had in plenty now. They were still young enough to start afresh on a new life. And the new life was going to be like a wonderful journey — a journey they would travel together.

We do hope that you have enjoyed reading this large print book.

Did you know that all of our titles are available for purchase?

We publish a wide range of high quality large print books including:
Romances, Mysteries, Classics
General Fiction
Non Fiction and Westerns

Special interest titles available in large print are:
The Little Oxford Dictionary
Music Book
Song Book
Hymn Book
Service Book

Also available from us courtesy of Oxford University Press:
Young Readers' Dictionary
(large print edition)
Young Readers' Thesaurus
(large print edition)

For further information or a free brochure, please contact us at:
Ulverscroft Large Print Books Ltd.,
The Green, Bradgate Road, Anstey,
Leicester, LE7 7FU, England.
Tel: (00 44) **0116 236 4325**
Fax: (00 44) **0116 234 0205**

HESTER'S CHOICE

Audrey Weigh

Hester Wellerby is sent from an impoverished home in Melbourne to live with wealthy relatives at Beach House. The change in lifestyle is daunting to the shy young woman, but she assures herself that she can cope. Hester has to accept that her only hope of a secure future depends on finding a husband. Aunt Amelia is eager to arrange a marriage that will boost her own social esteem, and she disapproves of Hester's choice. Uncle Jeremy also voices doubts. Can Hester handle the difficulties that lie ahead?

GINNY APPLEYARD

Elizabeth Jeffrey

When Ginny Appleyard's childhood sweet-heart returns after his racing season aboard the yacht *Aurora*, her hopes that he is bringing her an engagement ring are shattered, as Nathan disembarks with Isobel Armitage, the daughter of *Aurora*'s owner. Nathan tells Ginny that he is following Isobel to London to pursue his dreams of becoming an artist. Already distraught at the tragic death of her father, Ginny is further devastated to hear that Nathan and Isobel are to be married. More heartache is in store for Ginny when she realises that she is expecting Nathan's child . . .

THE RICH PART OF LIFE

Jim Kokoris

Teddy Pappas hides the fact his family doesn't own a VCR like a rash. So it comes as quite a shock when they win millions of dollars on the lottery. Now the house is bombarded by a frantic assembly of family, friends and foe, all with a vested interest in the Pappas fortune. Protective Aunt Bess, would-be filmmaker Uncle Frankie, bodyguard Maurice, the vampiral Sylvanius and the predatory Mrs Wilcott gather like flies around Teddy's father. And it soon becomes clear to poor Theo Pappas that being rich is a complication he and his sons could do without.

A SPECIAL INHERITANCE

Margaret James

A story of three very different women, inextricably bound together by their relationship with one man . . . In 1945, country girl Shirley Bell falls passionately in love with Peter, a German prisoner of war, but then he is repatriated. When Shirley finds she is expecting his child, she is glad to accept an offer of marriage from kind, sensible Gareth . . . Delia Shenstone, Shirley's best friend, becomes a brilliant example of what a determined career woman can achieve in a man's world. But privately Delia has her own share of heartache . . . Growing up in a small Midlands town, Shirley's daughter, Jenny, determines to make a success of her life while seeking out her natural father . . .

BEST FOOT FORWARD

Jeanne Ray

Tom and Caroline are having dinner when the 'phone rings. It is their daughter Kay, who is sobbing because she's just been proposed to. The next call is Caroline's sister Taffy, weeping because her husband has just left her. Both of these announcements have immediate repercussions as Taffy moves in and Kay's future in-laws begin frantic and excessive wedding preparations — with Tom and Caroline expected to pick up the tab! To top it all, the foundations of their home are in danger of collapsing and their contractor and his crew have all but moved in . . .

EMMA ELIZA

June Barraclough

Little Emma Eliza Saunders, the eldest child of a poor cottage family in rural south-west Norfolk, grows up in the 1860s with the memory of a boy who befriended her as a toddler but who then vanished from her life. When she is thirteen, Emma goes as a servant to Breckles Hall. Four years later she meets a young man called Jabez Smith, whom she believes is the friend of her earliest days. When the wife of the Hall coachman, George Starling, dies, Emma has to decide whether to accept his proposal of marriage. In the 1920s, Emma recounts some of her life to her granddaughter, Lily, who writes it all down. Lily's daughter then puts together the family history . . .